TALES FROM A ROUNDABOUT: VOLUMES 1-4

JEFF STANGER

www.bluetrolleypress.com

Print ISBN: 978-1-939579-03-4

Publisher's Note: This is a work of fiction. Names, characters, places, and incidents are a product of the author's imagination. Locales and public names are sometimes used for atmospheric purposes. Any resemblance to actual people, living or dead, or to businesses, companies, events, institutions, or locales is completely coincidental.

Cover Design: Mariah Sinclair

Edited by Terry Sowka

❀ Formatted with Vellum

TALES FROM A ROUNDABOUT

VOLUME ONE

1

EPISODE I: PERFORMANCE ART

"Deviant," Sonny Kagan mumbled out loud to no one in particular. "Call me a deviant, I'll show you deviant." He stepped out of his blue Ford pickup truck and watched traffic go by. "Y'all should pull over and watch the show," he said to a family in a silver BMW. The family, not being accustomed to muttering old men in this part of Carmel (or any part of Carmel, Indiana for that matter), ignored him. "It's gonna be a doozy." He laughed as he pulled an old lawn chair from the back of his truck. "Although, not suitable for the kiddies."

Sonny Kagan stepped into the crosswalk just as George Fillmore's shiny white Buick SUV entered the roundabout. Sonny walked slowly, intentionally dragging his tattered lawn chair behind him. He liked the irritating sound it made scraping across the pavement.

George couldn't hear the scraping, but he could see

Sonny, now that he had rounded the west side of the roundabout and had his car pointing east. The old man stopped halfway through the crosswalk, forcing the city councilman to stop his car. Sonny looked taller and more defiant than the last time George had seen him. Then, his six-foot frame had been hunched over like a defeated prize fighter when the Carmel City Council had voted seven to two to prevent him from opening up a strip club in Indiana's perfect city. It would have been his second in Central Indiana.

But now Sonny was standing tall. In the middle of the roundabout crosswalk. And giving George the finger. Where was this crazy old man going, the councilman wondered? Sonny seemed satisfied with the duration of his obscene gesture and continued walking. George took another lap around the roundabout, watched Sonny step inside the center circle, cross the manicured grass, then climb some decorative limestone blocks. He unfolded the tattered lawn chair and sat down.

The councilman stopped again and was about to roll down his window and question Sonny when the sound of horns alerted him that the cars behind him didn't care what the old man was doing. George moved along and vowed to come back this way after he finished lunch and returned to work. As he pulled away, he noticed a bright red ’80s Camaro (fully restored) slide into the street parking next to the cemetery south-east of the roundabout. The license plate said "GLTRGRL."

MATT MOLLER COULDN'T BELIEVE what he saw from the back seat of his mom's three-row Volvo SUV. To his right, a bright red car from when his mom and dad were in college was blasting the kind of rock music ('80s metal) his dad played when his buddies came to stay with them every May for the race. It wasn't rap music, so Matt couldn't come close to telling you who it was or what they were singing. Rap music was all his friends listened to, and that meant it was all he listened to. It didn't matter that rap lyrics were as far as you could get from the life experience of the upper middle class to super wealthy kids in Carmel. They all listened to rap. They all drove Jeeps or luxury hand-me-down SUVs.

So, the red car was a mystery to Matt. So was the Def Leppard. And so was the blonde in the driver's seat. She wore a white tank top which was a size too small and had a tattoo of the *Pyromania* album cover on her left shoulder. Not that Matt had any idea what that was. He did know he could see part way down her tank top from his angle and he could see her tan legs. And for the first time in his adolescent life, he wished beyond all hope a traffic light would break and stay red forever. It didn't.

His mother, completely oblivious to the object of

Matt's desire, accelerated slowly. This let the Camaro get ahead by a full car length and out of Matt's sight. He pleaded with his mother to speed up, but she was talking with a friend on her phone and intermittently telling Matt's twin sisters to stop shouting. Matt usually enjoyed the buffer of his siblings between him and his mother in the front, but today he wished he were in the front passenger seat.

To his surprise and delight, the Camaro's right turn signal came on, indicating that it, too, was getting off on 106th Street. Matt's hopes began to soar. Maybe she was heading towards his neighborhood. His mother was catching up to her on the off-ramp from Keystone Avenue and he stretched to catch even a glimpse of what was stretching out her tank top.

His sisters shouted in unison, "Mommy, look at the old man!" This caused his mother to slow down and Matt watched the Camaro enter the traffic circle behind a Buick. Then it signaled and pulled into a parking space by the cemetery adjacent to the roundabout. Matt was beyond excited. He began texting his friends in the neighborhood, "Get on your bikes and get to my house as fast as you can."

MANDY PEPPERHORNS STOPPED HER CAR, turned off the ignition, and laughed. She'd caught sight of her boss as she entered the roundabout, sitting like a king on his throne on the limestone blocks. This was going to be the easiest money she'd made in a long time. Mandy's real name was Melissa Hewitt, which is fine if you're a realtor or an accountant. It's rather dull if you're a stripper. At least that's what her boss told her when she got her first job dancing. She'd always loved the movie *The Sandlot* and after she went blond, everyone told her she looked like Wendy Peffercorn, the lifeguard in the movie. She decided on a stage name that was a play on the movie character. She even performed in a red swimsuit and sunglasses which more or less matched Wendy's.

But today she didn't have to strip. Well, not all of her clothes anyway. She did have to take off her tank top and her denim shorts and lay out on the grass in the roundabout. But she was planning on laying by the pool anyway. No water here to jump in, but $50 an hour wasn't bad to do nothing.

She opened the trunk of her car and pulled out a large beach towel and the small cooler she had packed with ice and bottled water. Mandy knew the other girls would bring alcohol, but something told her that despite the innocuous nature of the job, she should have her wits about her today.

"Hi, Sonny," she called as she crossed the street into the roundabout.

"Hi, doll." Sonny called all the women at his club, "doll." One of the dancers pointed out it was sexist and demeaning. Mandy responded, "What part of the job isn't?" That particular woman doesn't point things out to Mandy anymore.

Mandy found Sonny endearing. He didn't hit on the women like the other club owners. He didn't go back into the dressing room when they were changing. He kept his hands to himself. Sonny actually had a wife, and he never cheated on her, as far as Mandy could tell. For him, boobs were business. Nothing else.

"Any place in particular you want us to lay out?"

He pointed to a patch of grass and said, "Right there will be fine." The location was strategic. Anyone coming off Keystone from the south would have to look left to see if another car was coming in the roundabout. She would be in their line of sight.

She set her cooler down and spread out the towel on the grass. "Did you bring anything to drink?"

It occurred to Sonny there might be some details he had forgotten when he came up with this idea. "No, doll. Can't say that I did."

Mandy pulled out a bottle of water and walked it over to him. "On the house," she said with a grin. She loved poking at his quirks, and this was one of them. One phrase the rest of the women at the Neon Boudoir had heard Sonny say a thousand times was "Nothing is on the house." Even when the rapper Ice Pudding came in with 20 members of his entourage, Sonny didn't comp them a thing. In Sonny's mind, the VIPs should be paying *more* than the regulars, not getting everything comped for free. This didn't sit well with Ice Pudding.

He took his entourage and his business elsewhere. The way Sonny saw it, his competitor was filled with nonpaying deadbeats. And the people who couldn't get into *that* club came to his place with money to spend.

Sonny laughed at the joke. "Nothing is on the house, doll. Nothing."

"You can pay me a dollar later," she said. She slid off her shorts and tank top, adjusted her swimsuit, and put in her earbuds. Then she laid face up on her towel and got lost in her Def Leppard. She got so into it, she didn't hear her friends arrive. When she finally opened her eyes and sat up to turn over, there were women on either side of her. She also noticed four teenage boys on bikes who had stopped on the sidewalk just across from them on the outside of the roundabout. One boy in particular was staring only at her. Mandy pulled her shades down and gave the boy the same look from the movie that she had given countless customers at the club. The boy nearly dropped his bicycle.

MAYOR THEODORE "TEDDY" Wiggins always took the same route from the City Center to the Carmel Police Department shooting range on the second Thursday of the month. Sonny was counting on this to be the case again. The mayor drove south on Rangeline Road until it intersected with 106th street and then east on 106th. This route allowed him to monitor the progress of a construction project that he had long hoped to be completed. It was years behind schedule, and he was starting to hear from disgruntled constituents. Teddy liked to have his voters gruntled at all times.

And why should they ever be disgruntled, he thought on that sunny day. Urban/Rural Magazine had voted Carmel the best city to live in two years in a row. It had low crime, good schools, a world-class performing arts center, with parks and art around every corner. At least the intersections which still had corners. Carmel leadership had vowed to make Carmel the city with the most roundabouts in the United States. And in only a few years, they had managed to succeed.

I should have the happiest citizens in the country, Teddy thought to himself as he made his way to the shooting range.

Teddy wasn't on his way to shoot, however. The Carmel police had a strict rule about never allowing Mayor Wiggins near firearms. At a political fundraiser in 2003, the mayor had participated in a skeet shooting contest. Teddy shot a mime. Given the general prejudice against mimes by everyday Americans, the incident was largely ignored by the press. It truly was an accident, and Teddy swore he was aiming at the clay pigeon. But the mime's left arm never fully extended again, preventing him from performing his best bit, the trapped-in-a-glass-box routine. He received an undisclosed settlement from the city and now sells replacement windows.

On this day, Mayor Wiggins needed to discuss the upcoming Fourth of July parade with the chief of police. Teddy and the chief liked to hammer things out at the shooting range where there were fewer eyes and ears. There was a lot of pressure on the mayor during parade season. People insisted on staking out their parade spots earlier and earlier each year and local businesses were getting upset. Teddy needed a solution that kept the voters gruntled. Police Chief Baxter would have to come up with something, Teddy thought.

As Teddy approached Keystone Avenue, he could see some sort of commotion. Cars were slowing down and there was a lot of traffic backed up. "It looks like there are people in the middle of the roundabout," the mayor thought. "Those aren't city employees either. They look like. Oh, my word, they are strippers ..."

Mayor Wiggins heard the crunch of his front bumper as it scraped over the curb, then a scream from one of the women in the roundabout. His car didn't hit her, but his dislodged driver's side headlight landed on her towel. (She would later tell the news she was pinned under his car, but it was a lie.) The mayor cursed as he got out of his car. This was his fifth accident in seventeen months. The *Carmel Examiner* would gloss over it, but the *Indianapolis Star* and the local TV stations would make it a big deal. They would imply he was drinking again. He would deny it again. Then he would announce another intersection was becoming a roundabout and everyone would take sides on the issue and forget about the crash.

But this crash was different, he thought. *I wasn't texting this time. I was looking at boobs. Why are there boobs in the roundabout?*

One brunette in a yellow bikini immediately approached him and asked to take a selfie. Before he could think about the electoral impact of such a decision, she had her right arm around his shoulder and her left arm extending the camera. He adjusted his hair and smiled.

The mayor's hair had been a topic for discussion throughout the city for years. He had a dark black mass of hair sitting on top, with gray shooting out the sides and back. Many people thought it was a bad toupee, but nobody had the courage to ask, and none of the stylists in town knew a thing. Mayor Teddy Wiggins took his personal grooming business far outside Hamilton County, Indiana.

After taking the picture, Mayor Wiggins picked up his headlight and asked the woman on the towel if she was okay. "Yeah, I'm good. Mind rubbing some lotion on my back?"

The shock of the crash and the bikini-selfie ambush had caught the mayor off guard. But whereas the proposition to rub lotion on a beautiful woman's back might have caused most men to abandon all reason, Teddy was somehow shocked back into reality. And the reality was all the cleavage made him uncomfortable, even though nobody was actually naked.

Despite the rumors about Mayor Wiggins and his female chief of staff being involved, public displays of flesh brought out the prude in Teddy. Just the previous spring he had agreed to give a little speech to kick off the Carmel High School after-prom party. He was aghast at all the cleavage in the audience and made it a point to let Principal Huff know in no uncertain terms. Huff shared the mayor's thoughts with Associate Vice-Principal Margot Felton-Douglass. She responded with a memo about slut-shaming and sexualizing young girls and demanded to know why the boys weren't held to a higher standard as well. Huff decided he would be better off sitting on the sidelines of this argument and made a note to send the vice principal to speak with the mayor personally.

Mayor Wiggins approached the man in his lawn chair in the center of the roundabout. "Sonny, what is going on?"

"This is a public space. Me and the ladies around you are members of the public. We mean to occupy this space for a while."

"I know what you're trying to do. You're trying to get me back for the council vote last week. It won't work."

Teddy looked around. There were cars everywhere now. Some were honking at the girls. Some were honking at him. He remembered his car was still partially blocking traffic. He jumped back in, put it in reverse, and heard the front bumper crunch some more. Then he put it in drive and made his way to the fire station a block or so to the east. From here he could regroup and call in reinforcements.

MATT HAD PROMISED the rest of the guys there was a really hot blond at the cemetery, and they should all ride their bikes over and see. He said she looked like a Hooters waitress, or what he imagined a Hooters waitress looked like. Carmel didn't have a Hooters or anything like one. There had been rumors a Twin Peaks was coming to town, but it never happened.

But on this day, Matt Moller would become a legend in the eyes of the teenage boys of Lakeshore Estates. For it wasn't one hot woman mourning in the cemetery that Matt had brought them to see. It was twelve strippers in the skimpiest of swimsuits sunbathing in the roundabout.

Of course, the boys were all too scared and awkward to approach the ladies. Instead, they hung back on the sidewalks surrounding the roundabout, giggled and took pictures with their smartphones. A couple of strippers waved, and Mandy Pepperhorns even lowered her sunglasses and gave Matt the same look Wendy gave Squints in the movie. She even offered to let one of them rub lotion on her back. Neither their tongues nor their legs were capable of movement at that point.

William Davis, the youngest and most inexperienced of the boys, suddenly had feelings and questions which had never occurred to him before that day. This made for an enlightening and somewhat awkward conversation later at dinner when Willy shared those feelings with his mother and her new boyfriend, Timothy, who was having dinner with the family for the first time. Timothy, though amused, decided he wasn't ready for raising boys at the onset of puberty. It was his last dinner at the Davis house. And for that, William's mom Marissa vowed to get even with the women of the Neon Boudoir.

THE MAYOR RETURNED with the police chief and the entire fire department who, when they learned there were strippers in the roundabout, decided that on a hot day like this, heat stroke might be imminent. "Public safety must be priority number one," they told the mayor. And they followed him on foot to the scene. They arrived at the same time as Councilman George Fillmore, who was shocked to find the chaos which had unfolded since he had left earlier in the day. He and the mayor pleaded with Sonny to send the strippers home.

The mayor ordered the police chief to remove them all, but Sonny pointed out that he wasn't breaking any laws. Using his iPad, Councilman Fillmore searched frantically in the city codes and regulations for the pertinent language that would end this display. But alas, he was unable to find a single decision by the City Council preventing strippers from sunbathing in the middle of a roundabout. Such contingencies had never been contemplated by anyone in city government. He would draft a resolution this very afternoon, he decided.

THE SCENE STAYED DEADLOCKED until 4 p.m., mostly because the beleaguered police and firemen who arrived didn't want it to end. But as rush hour approached, the officials finally convinced Sonny to move along. The women had had enough sun anyway, and some had shifts starting soon at the Neon Boudoir. Mandy pulled out her last water and opened the bottle. She took a few drinks as she walked on the crosswalk to the outside of the roundabout. After one last sip, she handed it to the boy on the bike who had stayed transfixed on her the entire afternoon. "Here, you look like you could use a drink."

He ducked his head, turned beet red, and said thanks. Mandy chuckled and walked to her car. She rolled down the window, started the Camaro, and cranked up Def Leppard's *Pyromania* album. Matt watched her leave and mentally recorded the album cover he had seen tattooed on her shoulder. He finished the water slowly. He thought about her lips being on the same ring of plastic and, as he finished drinking, imagined what it would be like to kiss her. Then he put the bottle in his backpack and rode home.

When Matt's dad got home, he peeked in on his son. The framed Derek Jeter baseball jersey which normally sat on a shelf above his bed had been replaced by a water bottle. "How was your day?"

"Amazing."

"Really?"

"Can you tell me about it?"

"No, but it was amazing."

Matt's dad paused. Something was off. He couldn't place it at first. But something was out of place. Not a thing. But a sound. What was it? Music. No, he played that station all the time. He listened to the classic rock station so much, it was just background noise to him. He never gave it a thought. But now, it was playing in this room. In Matt's room. And it wasn't the radio. Matt was streaming Def Leppard.

"Def Leppard, huh? Your friend Tony's dad Alex has an entire shed dedicated to them."

"Yeah, I found it on Spotify."

"You hate classic rock."

"Not anymore. Def Leppard is in; don't you know anything, Dad?"

"Since when?"

"Since today."

2

EPISODE II: POLITICAL UNREST

Marissa Davis marched into the lobby of the mayor's office expecting to battle his administrative assistant to set up a meeting. Instead, she had to battle for a place to stand. The office was packed with women in various states of unrest. It seems Marissa wasn't the only mother enraged by the gratuitous flesh displayed at the roundabout of 106th Street and Rangeline Road the previous Friday. Each of these mothers decided that "something must be done" as bathroom time for boys ages fourteen to eighteen in the one-mile radius of the intersection had increased exponentially over the weekend.

As she looked around the room, Marissa noticed several moms from her own neighborhood, including Cheryl Thompson. Cheryl's son Anthony (Tony to Matt, Willy, and the rest) was a regular guest at the Davis home.

"Are you here about the strippers?"

Cheryl responded, "Yes. Can you believe something like that could happen here?"

"My son came home and started asking the most difficult questions. At dinner. With my new boyfriend." Unbeknownst to Willy's mom, he was now her ex-boyfriend.

"Mayor Wiggins better do something. Do you know some people are claiming this is his fault? He pissed off this strip club owner and Friday was about payback."

"Speak of the devil, here he is now."

Teddy Wiggins hated Mondays. There were always people calling or showing up at the office with some grievance from the weekend. Teddy had learned in his first term never to show up at 8 a.m. sharp on Mondays as the true crusaders always showed up when the office opened. Better to wait until 10:30 and let his assistant take the brunt and the messages. That way, he didn't have to see the angry people face-to-face.

Unfortunately for Teddy, on this day, his system didn't take into account the daily routine of angry mothers with children. They had to get kids to school or daycare and thus couldn't make it before 9 o'clock. And since they had relieved themselves of children and were in the company of other mothers, they had all the time in the world to wait for him.

So, it was a complete surprise to open the door to the cacophony of voices and standing room only space. He squeezed his way to the desk of his assistant and glared at her. Ms. Fitzsimmons glared back. She was a tough old bird and not about to take any guff from Teddy this morning. It was up to him to get this unruly mob out of her workspace.

"Mayor Wiggins, calm these women down."

He looked helpless. "How? Why are they here?"

"Something to do with strippers in a roundabout," Ms. Fitzsimmons said, giving Teddy the death stare.

"Well I didn't order them!"

"Nevertheless, do something. I will not have this type of disruption today. It's unsettling."

Teddy was concerned. Ms. Fitzsimmons knew things. Knew things that Teddy certainly didn't want the world to know about him, his backers, and his business partners. And whenever Ms. Fitzsimmons became unsettled, she would let Teddy know she might just have to talk to somebody about being unsettled. It was in Teddy's interest to always keep Ms. Fitzsimmons settled.

"Ladies. Ladies. If I could have your attention, please."

The shouting quieted to more of a murmur and the mayor proceeded. "Is it safe to assume you are all here about the unfortunate display, by non-Carmel residents mind you, this past Friday?"

Not quite in unison, and with a variety of editorializations, they agreed.

"Shameful," shouted one mom.

"Live pornography," shouted another.

"My boys can't unsee what was on full display," added another.

"Okay, okay. I agree wholeheartedly," Teddy said. "And I would be happy to discuss this with you. But I can't fit all of you in my office. Since you are all here for the same reason, could you please select two or three representatives while I get settled in and check my messages?"

The women nodded reluctantly and looked around at each other. None of them were used to *not* having their voices heard by management when they were displeased, so electing a representative would be out of character.

Teddy, of course, knew this and figured it would buy him a good 30 minutes to get coffee, check his messages, and come up with a plan. And he definitely needed a plan. There were many areas of life in which Teddy wasn't the smartest person in the room. But when it came to politics and negotiation, Teddy was a genius.

Just as predicted, it was thirty minutes before Ms. Fitzsimmons called to tell him the ladies had whittled it down to two and they were ready when he was.

Teddy opened the door and welcomed Marissa and Cheryl into his office.

"Ladies, I thank you for coming down to share your concerns. Awful display on Friday. I've got our council working on an ordinance as we speak. I've instructed the police to strictly enforce public decency codes (he hadn't, and he couldn't actually quote what those might be), and I've asked the mayor of Indianapolis to look into any crimes the representatives of the Neon Boudoir might have committed there. However, I am open to any suggestions you might have and welcome your input."

Teddy didn't welcome input as much as he tolerated it. Mostly he hummed the theme of *CSI Miami* in his head while people shared their input.

"I'm grateful for what you're doing—"

Cheryl cut Marissa off. "*We're* grateful. But we believe the Neon Boudoir should be shut down."

"As do I. But I'm powerless to do so. As you know, we would never allow such an establishment to be opened within our fair city. This blight on decency is in Indianapolis. I'm powerless to do anything in that Gomorrah to the south of us. However, I can appeal to the decency of their mayor."

"I just can't let this go. I need to know these women will stay as far from Carmel as possible," said Marissa. "If this isn't met with a sharp rebuttal, they will be back."

Teddy thought for a moment, then offered his advice. "You know there is a loud and powerful army of decency literally right outside these walls. You could command them. You could get them to rise up and protest outside the Neon Boudoir. Shame the men who go into that establishment." Teddy briefly remembered his nephew's bachelor party was coming up and made a mental note to warn him to take the fun to the strip clubs in Speedway, near the Indianapolis 500 track. The Neon Boudoir was in a different part of town.

"I would be happy to contribute," he paused to do some math in his head, "say $500 for paint, signs, and incidentals."

"Oh, mayor, that would be lovely," Cheryl responded.

Marissa added, "Mayor Wiggins, I knew we could count on you."

"I love this city," he said. "And all its citizens. We must preserve our way of life."

"Indeed," said Cheryl.

"Elegantly put," Marissa added.

"Elegant and wise," Cheryl piled on.

"And succinct," Marissa one-upped her.

Teddy had witnessed this at PTA events before. The alpha mom wanted the last word. And realizing there were two alphas competing head to head and knowing his morning had been interrupted enough, Teddy decided to end the competition himself.

"Ladies, I thank you for the kind words and wish you much luck. Ms. Fitzsimmons will work out the donation details with you and I look forward to a full report on your protest soon. To your success." All of this was said as he ushered them with his hands up from their seats and out the door.

He leaned against the closed door and sighed. Then he chuckled and said, "Back at you, Sonny Kagan. Back at you."

THE FOLLOWING FRIDAY, the protests began. Cheryl and Marissa managed to get twenty women from Lakeshore Estates and surrounding neighborhoods to demonstrate at the Neon Boudoir. They made signs, posted on a variety of social media platforms, and contacted all the local news outlets. Most said they would look into it and hung up the phone without any real intention of looking into it. All except Ollie Randall. Ollie "smelled a story here," he told his boss. His producer knew better. Ollie smelled the fragrance of dancer sweat and Jack Daniels.

The Lakeshore Estates women also created a Facebook page and began to upload photos of the men who arrived at the club. Some got right back in their cars and left when they saw the angry mob of housewives. One of the performers, sensing tips were going to be awful if this continued, grabbed the phone of a protester and smashed it on the ground.

Neither Cheryl nor Marissa wanted to enter the establishment to announce their presence. They felt it would be beneath them. So, they knocked on the door and waited for someone to answer. The music was pulsating, so they knocked louder. Someone inside yelled, "It's open."

They knocked again. "It's open."

They knocked with even greater determination. The door swung open and the largest man either woman had ever seen yelled, "It's open."

There was an awkward silence as the ladies sized up the bouncer and the bouncer sized them up. "What do you want?"

"We're here to protest."

"You're here to what?"

"We're here to protest. The strippers and the nudity. All of it."

"The boss isn't going to like that."

"We don't care."

"Why don't you come in and talk to the boss."

"We're not going in there."

"Why not?"

"It's beneath us," Marissa spoke up for the first time.

The bouncer looked at the ground all around him, not fully comprehending her statement. "You want me to bring the boss out here?"

"Yes, that would be best."

"He's not going to like it."

"We don't care what he likes," said Cheryl. She was feeling alive and bold and quite righteous about her mission.

The bouncer returned in just a few minutes. "Sonny says leave."

"We're not leaving."

"Sonny says to leave or else."

"Or else what?"

"Sonny says to leave or else he'll call the cops."

"Call the cops on us? We're not doing anything wrong. He's the one who should be in jail."

"He says you're on private property and you're trespassing."

"Just let him call the cops."

"Sonny isn't going to like this." He disappeared again. After a few minutes, Sonny leaned his head out the door, looked around for the press, then came fully out with a shotgun. The boldness and righteousness Cheryl felt a moment ago diminished in the face of a firearm.

"We are exercising our constitutional right to protest."

"I'm exercising my right to point a gun at you."

"I'm calling the police," said Marissa.

"I'm calling my lawyer and the police," said Sonny.

This tit for tat might have gone on indefinitely if it hadn't been for the arrival of the Channel 7 news van. Sonny realized the PR hazard approaching and had his bouncer take the gun back inside. He smiled warmly as Ollie Randall approached and asked what the disturbance was about.

"These ladies are here to protest my legal and tax-paying business. I figure we both have things to say to the media about this." He paused and glanced at the ladies. Then, slightly bowing to them and Randall, Sonny said, "However, I'm a gentleman and will let you interview these ladies first."

Ollie barked out orders and scouted for the best place to conduct the interviews. He decided to go closer to the road, so the club's animated sign was in the background. When he and the cameraman were ready, the first interview began.

"I'm Ollie Randall with Channel 7 News. We're here at the Neon Boudoir, which is in Indianapolis for you at home, where a protest has been organized by concerned women of Carmel. They say the strippers at this club came to their town and performed in a roundabout and they want the place to be shut down. I'm here with Cheryl Thompson."

"Cheryl, why are you and the rest of the ladies out here today?"

"We're here because we don't want the smut that happens behind those doors over there to encroach upon our city. Just last week these women came into our town, took off their clothes, and disrupted our community."

"When and where did this take place?"

"It happened last Friday at the roundabout at 116th and Rangeline."

"And has it happened before?"

"Not to my knowledge."

"So, these women danced topless in the roundabout?"

"No, they were wearing bikini tops. But there was plenty of cleavage!"

"And did they dance or perform their usual acts?"

"No, they just laid out on towels and talked to the police and firemen."

"So, no actual nudity."

"Not by the legal definition, no. But no mother would send her daughter out in public dressed like that." At the same moment, her daughter was at the Lakeshore Estates pool in a skimpier bikini than what Mandy had been wearing.

"And you say there were police and firemen there?"

"Yes, and we thought they might remove them. Instead, they seemed to be enthralled and even encouraged the ladies. That's the trouble with boobs, you know. They just encourage all the wrong types of behaviors."

"And what is the message you want to deliver here today?"

"That we are here, and we want our voices heard. We want Carmel to remain the kind of city where women aren't objectified in our public spaces."

"Thank you for your time." He turned back towards the camera. "Well, you've heard from the protesters. After the break, we'll hear from the owner of the strip club."

Channel 7 then took a minute to sell Buicks by having a famous movie actor with a southern accent sit behind the wheel of a parked car in the middle of a field of wheat. Why the car was in a field of wheat is anybody's guess, but this particular actor is really popular with women between 35 and 65 who might be likely to buy a Buick and drive it into a wheat field, or so their market research found. Next, the station ran a commercial with a perfectly diverse group of office workers doing office things and high fiving each other in the break room. Viewers remain uncertain if they were selling pants, deodorant, or tooth whitening cream.

Finally, Channel 7 came back to Ollie Randall. "I'm here with Sonny Kagan, owner of the Neon Boudoir. Sonny, what do you have to say to the protesters?"

"To them, I have to say bleep off. I don't need your bleeping judgement and bleeping rules. You can't come to Indianapolis and tell us what to do. Stay the bleep in Carmel where you belong."

Ollie's producer had his hands full keeping the bad words off the air, but he managed to do it.

Ever the promoter, Sonny continued, "and to your audience, I want to say that we're open, despite the circus in our parking lot. Show us a selfie with a protester and your first drink is half off."

"Thank you for speaking with us, Mr. Kagan. That's all from here right now. I'll be back for the 11 o'clock news and will have an exclusive with one of the dancers to get her perspective."

The producer pointed out that the news director didn't want an interview with one of the dancers, but

Ollie mumbled something about thorough reporting and marched towards the door.

As he did, the Concerned Women of Carmel heard the roar of motorcycle engines. The Indiana chapter of the Lawless Exhaust Spreaders rode in for Tata Tuesday at the Neon Boudoir. Sonny had called them and encouraged them to come a little earlier than usual. In exchange for helping to clear the parking lot, he would waive the evening's cover charge.

As the women took in the sights and sounds of the Exhaust Spreaders, they didn't notice a black Cadillac SUV drop off six middle school-aged boys. The boys, too wide-eyed and in awe over the Neon Boudoir sign (an animated woman sliding off a stocking), didn't notice the women carrying protest signs.

EVER SINCE THE staff of the Neon Boudoir had spent an afternoon sunbathing in a Carmel roundabout, the boys of Lakeshore Estates had been obsessed with getting another glimpse of Mandy. They circled the roundabout daily for a week, hoping this miracle of exhibitionism might occur again. It did not.

On an overcast Friday afternoon, they gathered to play video games and discuss the search for the woman in the red bathing suit.

"I don't think they're ever coming back," said Willy with the anguish of a starving refugee.

Matt replied, "Why didn't anyone think to ask their names?"

"If I had been there, I would have gotten names and numbers," said Devon Walsh. He was the only one of the group who missed the event and compensated by claiming he would have not been too shy to walk over and talk with them. Of course, he was the most awkward of all the boys around girls. But like most middle schoolers, he talked a good game around the guys.

"Right. You would have been peeing down your right leg," said Matt.

"We know you were too scared to do anything. Even after she handed you her water bottle," he replied.

"At least I got her water bottle," he answered. "More than the rest of you got."

"She winked at me," said Willy. All the boys turned to him. "I'm going to find her if it's the last thing I do. Does your Mom get the Carmel newspaper?"

"Why?"

"Because there might have been a story about it in the news."

Devon asked, "Why didn't you morons think of that sooner?"

"Well does she?"

"Yes," answered Matt. "She throws the old ones in the garage."

For the first time in the history of Xbox ownership amongst the kids of Lakeshore Estates, a game of Call of

Duty was abandoned mid-mission. The boys scrambled to the garage to find the old newspapers.

Matt handed out issues to Willy and Devon. The rest of the boys checked their phones as young people do. It's important to check your phone at that age. Something may have happened. Something may have happened while the first thing happened. And somebody may have responded to the thing that happened. And then several other people responded to their response and now somebody has added a meme or an emoji and now somebody is offended. In the meantime somebody else is dumping somebody because they didn't text, or chat, or respond when somebody on the text chain mentioned they were offended by global room temperature or the existence of parents who knit, and then an avalanche of snaps, tweets, chats, and texts descends from the sky and each must be reacted to until suddenly you realize Willy is jumping up and down screaming because the newspaper has a picture of Mandy with her name and the name of the club she works at: the Neon Boudoir.

"It's her, it's her, it's her!"

"Willy, calm down."

"How hard is it to sneak into a strip club?"

"Willy, you're not even 5 feet tall. It's going to be really hard," said Devon.

"Maybe we could ride our bikes there and wait by the door for her to show up to work."

Matt replied, "Let me see how far away it is." He checked Google maps. "12 miles. I'm not riding 12 miles."

"I am," said Willy, and he started out the door.

"Wait, wait." Devon grabbed him by the shoulder. "We can Uber to the club. I can charge it to my PayPal account."

"You have a PayPal account?"

"And Venmo and a few others." Devon was the outlier in the group in that his parents made him work. He mowed lawns and did other outdoor work for a local landscaper and that was why he wasn't there for Mandy's original visit to the neighborhood.

"Can you order one now?" Willy was getting excited.

"Sure, I'll take care of it." Devon was feeling a huge ego boost, knowing he was going to provide their transportation. He even ordered a large SUV, so they could feel like rock stars. Nobody bothered to ask their parents' permission. In fact, none of the boys who had stay-at-home moms could actually recall seeing them that afternoon. Little did they know, they would see their moms very soon.

"I WANT YOU TO SUE."

Alex Thompson had spent the day in court challenging the will of a particularly randy insurance company executive. D.H. Higgins had at least nine blood heirs (four from his actual wife) and Alex was representing the Amarista twins (not from Higgins' wife). The twins' mother had been a nanny and house manager for the family for twenty-one years. She felt her loyalty and hard work (and the fact that she adhered to discretion on the part of her twin daughters' bio-daddy's identity) entitled the girls to at least a share in the family fortune.

Mrs. Higgins had other ideas and wasn't particularly in the mood to tolerate another surprise offspring. She had always suspected her husband was shagging his secretaries (he traded up every five years). She could live with it in return for raising her family in Carmel and particularly in the 20,000-square-foot mansion her husband built for her.

What she couldn't tolerate was learning her husband also had been sleeping with two different nannies, Mrs. Higgins' tennis partner of twenty years, and their son's voice coach. All of whom apparently had eschewed birth control.

This made Mrs. Higgins particularly disagreeable and she hired the most disagreeable lawyer in Carmel to carry that sentiment into court. It made for a long day for everyone involved.

So, Alex just wanted a strong drink and to watch SportsCenter when his wife pounced on him with her demand for a lawsuit.

"Sue who, Cheryl?" Alex used her first name when she irritated him. He hadn't called her honey in weeks, maybe months.

"The strip club in Indy. The Neon Boudoir, that's who."

"Why?"

"Why? Haven't you been listening to what I've been saying for the last two weeks?"

He hadn't. "Of course, I have. You protested there, right?"

The women of Lakewood Estates had indeed protested outside the Neon Boudoir recently. It had been a disaster. At first, they thought it might be a success. They were sharing pictures of the men on social media and really driving away business. But then the biker gang arrived, and they didn't mind being photographed.

Next, some of the women whose resolve wasn't so deeply rooted got distracted by the rugged independence of a few of the younger, more handsome bikers, and succumbed to their offer to buy drinks. Those women aren't invited to Lakewood Estates social gatherings anymore.

But the final indignity came when an Uber driver deposited most of their middle school-aged sons in the strip club parking lot. Most of the boys were just coming off being grounded that very day when Cheryl made her demand to her husband to sue the club.

"And why did I protest there?"

"They exploit women?" He answered in the form of a question because he knew he hadn't a clue.

"No," she shouted. "They were stripping in front of children. OUR CHILDREN!"

"You don't need a lawyer, you need police. Really? When did this happen?" He knew he was giving away that he hadn't listened, but he was stunned by this new development and felt his dad outrage growing. Or at least what dad outrage he could fake until he could muster up something genuine.

"The week before the protest. What's wrong with you?" she continued, "In the roundabout at 116th and Keystone."

"You mean the chicks in bikinis? Dave Vernon told me none of them actually got nak ..." He stopped because he recognized her impending rage face.

"Never actually got what?"

"Well, you know." She glared. He gulped. "Naked?"

Her voice dropped to something between a hiss and a whisper. “I want you to find some legal means of stopping those women and that dirty old man they work for from doing ..." She searched for the word she wanted.

Alex tried to help, "from doing?"

"From showing Dave Vernon and all the other boys —teenage or otherwise (she punched his left bicep)— their breasts and anything else!" she shouted.

Tony, their son and the only one who had actually seen the "breasts and anything else" in question ushered his little sister Emma back into her room. They had been watching from the upstairs railing.

"Are mommy and daddy fighting again?"

Tony couldn't lie. "Yes, sorry you had to see that."

"When they get divorced are we going to be separated?"

"No, why would you think that?"

Emma squeezed his hand and Tony marveled at how much the six-year-old understood. "I don't care which one we stay with; I just want to be with you."

Tony gave her a squeeze and watched her bounce into her room. She had already forgotten the arguing.

ALEX DECIDED it might be good to check out Sonny Kagan's past, and the Neon Boudoir in particular, to see if he could find something to go to court with on behalf of his wife. Otherwise, she was going to be impossible to live with.

He had an investigator spend time looking into Sonny, but didn't turn up anything he could use. So, one night after work, he went to the Neon Boudoir. He hadn't been to a gentleman's club in years and he quickly felt out of place.

It was sparsely populated as he arrived, but he noted the steady stream of patrons coming in the door. At this pace, it would be busy soon. These were the guys with nobody to go home to after work, he surmised. As he continued his recon mission, one particular dancer took notice of him. She wasn't performing, so she approached him and asked if he was new. She knew a frightened deer when she saw one. If she came right out and asked him if he wanted a lap dance, he literally would run away. She needed to ply him with booze before she could pry open the wallet.

"Yeah, does it look that obvious?"

"You'll loosen up. How about you buy us some drinks?"

Mandy had already given a subtle look to a server who arrived just as she finished the sentence.

"What can I get you tonight?"

Alex turned to find the server standing behind him. She wasn't fully topless but might as well have been. Alex had spent most of the day confined with other middle-aged male attorneys and a septuagenarian judge. So, his stare could be understood if not completely forgiven.

"Two scotch and sodas coming up," she decided for him. She gave a little chest wiggle to drive home the point and added, "I'll assume you want the scotch from the," more wiggle, "top shelf."

Alex, embarrassed for being caught in a stare, turned red and nodded. As she walked away, Mandy spun him around.

"Hey, I'm getting jealous over here."

"Sorry."

"It's okay, sugar. Let's have a seat."

He joined her on a couch and after he sat nearly a foot away, she slid over next to him.

"I'm Mandy."

"I'm Alex."

"Nice to meet you. What do you do?"

"I'm a lawyer."

"Are you really a lawyer or just trying to impress me?" Mandy felt lying by men was practically a bodily function, so she always assumed the worst. But she didn't care as long as they had cash. She did enjoy toying with them though.

"No, I'm *really* a lawyer."

"And what kind of law do you practice?"

"Estate, probate, wills, and stuff."

"Sounds boring. Is that why you're here?" She looked around and back at him. "To put some fun back into your life?"

Their drinks arrived before he could answer.

"Want to run a tab, honey?" the server asked.

"No, I'll pay cash." He was becoming disoriented but at least had the sense to not leave a paper trail.

Mandy asked, "What shall we drink to?"

Alex raised his glass and that's when he spotted the Def Leppard tattoo on Mandy's shoulder. "Def Leppard," he replied.

She glanced at her arm and then back to him and smiled. "You like?"

"I love. The tattoo and the band. I would say I've seen them forty times."

For the first time in five years of working at the Neon Boudoir, Mandy reflexively put her hand on a customer's shoulder. Not because she wanted to get all the folding currency out of his wallet, but because she wanted to get every moment of every concert out of his head. Twenty minutes later she still hadn't asked him if he wanted a lap dance and he hadn't asked any questions to help his wife's lawsuit aspirations.

"I have a Def Leppard man cave. Well, it's in my work shed out back. My wife didn't want it in the house."

"Sounds like she doesn't have any taste."

"In music, no," he replied.

"Is your wife the kind of woman who would understand a woman like me visiting your shed—purely for rock and roll reasons, of course?"

"I don't think so." The thought of her visiting his Def Leppard shed thrilled and terrified him at the same time.

Mandy frowned.

"But she is going to Ohio in a few weeks," he offered.

"Let me see your phone," she asked. He passed it over without hesitation. She touched the screen and handed it back. "Code?" He punched it in and gave her the phone. She opened his address book and entered her name and number.

Then she handed it back. "Let me know when it's cool to come visit."

She looked around and realized she needed to get back to work. "Say, you want a lap dance before you go?"

"Like you can't even imagine," he said and was

shocked at himself for saying it out loud. He gulped. "But let's start with Def Leppard."

She smiled and pecked him on the cheek, "Anything you say, sugar."

Alex watched her walk away, and of course she turned around multiple times to make sure he was. The investigation into any legal malfeasance by the Neon Boudoir was officially closed. The Def Leppard shed was about to officially reopen.

3

EPISODE III: MODERN BALLET

Every Saturday (weather permitting), Matt Moller rode to Dave's Donuts in Carmel and purchased two chocolate-covered yeast donuts (for himself) and two Boston creams (for his grandpa). Then he rode to the Serenity Senior Living Center and had breakfast with Marshall Moller. His grandpa would then pay him three times what Matt spent on the donuts for the weekly delivery (in cash). Neither his parents nor the nursing home staff were any the wiser.

During these visits, Matt listened to stories about the world which were far more interesting than history class because his grandpa was a skillful storyteller and used way more curse words than his teacher at Falcon Middle School.

On this day, Grandpa was sharing about the time he visited a unique type of massage parlor in the very historically significant city of Hong Kong when it occurred to Matt he could ask him about Mandy.

"Grandpa, there's this girl I sort of like."

"Did you kiss her?"

"No, not yet."

“What are you waiting for? Oh, yeah, you're in middle school.”

“She's a little older than me.”

“How much older?"

"I don't know, hard to tell. Twenty-five maybe?"

"Twenty-five years older? Kid, that's a little weird."

"No, I mean she's about twenty-five."

"Oh, well that's still too old."

"I don't know, she smiled at me and gave me her water. I think she likes me."

"Grandpa would love to have a twenty-five-year-old girlfriend. But that ain’t going to happen. Some of the formerly functional parts of this body are sadly now just decorative if you know what I mean."

Matt just looked at him.

"Of course, you don't know what I mean. Umm, okay think about the donuts. You see lots of donuts behind the glass, but you only get to choose one. They're all great, but only one gets to be yours."

"But we get two donuts apiece each week."

"Right right. Girls aren't like donuts. What are they like?"

"I was kinda hoping you would tell me."

"Right right. It's just that you're going to meet more

than one that you like, but only one is right for you. And I'm guessing the one who is ten or more years older than you isn't the right one."

"But Willy's mom has been married three times. How can she be the only one for three different guys?"

"You want to hear more about the massage parlor?"

"No, I want to know how to get Mandy to like me."

"Mandy. That's a pretty name. What does she do, this Mandy?"

"She's some sort of entertainer for grown-ups. That's what her business card says anyway."

Matt pulled out the card the club owner had passed out at the club the night of the protest. Grandpa looked it over and decided his grandson might wind up being a lot like himself. "Take her to a fancy dinner, buy her some flowers."

"That's it?" Matt said.

"No, but when you've saved up enough money to do those two things, maybe you'll have your license by then."

"I still have a thousand dollars I got for Christmas. That should be enough to take her out."

"What? What fool gave a kid your age so much money for Christmas."

"You did."

"Oh, yeah. I think your mother was pissed about that."

"So, dinner and flowers. Anything else?"

"Start with that, kid, and let me know how it goes."

"Is that how you got Grandma?"

"No, I took her to a Beatles concert."

"And it worked?"

"You're sitting here on a Saturday eating a donut, aren't you?"

Matt smiled and finished his donut. *Dinner and flowers*, he thought. *Is it that easy?*

Sonny Kagan answered his phone in a huff, "Sonny here. What do you want?"

"Mr. Kagan, my name is John Myers. I'm the only member of the Carmel City Council who voted for your club."

"Oh, yeah. Well, what do you want?"

"We both have a beef with the mayor and city council. I think we can help each other."

"You can help me get a club opened in Carmel?"

"Well, no, probably not. It will never get enough votes unless you can manage to unseat three or four members in the next election."

Sonny growled, "Then what good are you? Stop wasting my time."

"Wait, please wait. You're right, I can't help you get your club opened. But I can help you get some measure of revenge."

"Revenge, huh. Revenge don't show up on a balance sheet."

"Maybe not yours, but it will on the city's budget."

"Myers, why would I want to make money for the city that won't let me do business?"

"Hear me out. I'm not talking about making money for the city. And I'm sorry you can't make any money in Carmel at this time. However, together, you and I can help spend some of Carmel's money in ways the mayor doesn't want to and in doing so, embarrass him and the city council."

"Myers, if this is a trick, I will make you pay. There are a lot of loyal customers at the Neon Boudoir who are of the biker gang persuasion if you get my drift."

"No tricks. I promise."

"So, what do you have in mind and what do you want from me?"

"I've got two projects in mind. For the first, I need your connections in the music industry. You know a lot of bands and road managers, right? They're always coming to your club when they're in town."

"That's right."

"I need your help to get the word out about a secret project I'm doing."

"You do realize the type of musicians who come to my place aren't the types that play gigs at the Palladium in Carmel, right?"

"I do. And they are exactly the type of people I'm looking for."

"And the second project?"

"That one is really for you, my gift for helping me

with the first. Carmel has a performing arts grant program with a wide umbrella of artists who apply. Including dance."

"I'm not following you."

"Isn't it about time the Kagan empire or whatever you call your company starts giving back to the community?"

"Myers, what are you talking about?"

"'The grants are open to any club or group; they don't have to be formal 501(c)(3) nonprofits. So, your ladies form a volunteer performing club that dances for senior citizens."

"Senior citizens? Have you lost your mind?"

"Bear with me. Mayor Teddy Wiggins' mother lives in Serenity Senior Living Center. You apply for the grant, and if you win, you have the ladies perform at Mrs. Wiggins' place. The residents, the mayor and the public show up to see some ballet, and instead they get the Neon Boudoir. And Carmel pays you to be there."

"Okay, that's twisted and funny. But how do we win the grant competition?"

"I'll give you the dirt on the program director. You just figure out who to send who can exploit that dirt and get your application into the special pile. Trust me, unless your proposal lands in the special pile, it doesn't even get looked at."

"And you can get us into the special pile."

"No, but I can get you the info you need. You will

have to select the person who can use that info, charm the program chair, and you're in."

"Sounds like my kind of mischief. I'm in. And what is the project you need the rockers for?"

"Let's meet in person for that one. It will make more sense if I show you rather than tell you."

"Is it as good as the senior home idea?"

"Better. And it will spend more of the city's money, and cause Mayor Wiggins even more embarrassment."

"I'm in."

MELISSA HEWITT WALKED into Carmel City Hall and asked reception for the office of Carmel Art Grants. She was wearing a conservative business suit with sensible heels. Everything about her appearance hid from the world that she was, in fact, Mandy Pepperhorns. Sonny had put her up to this and even paid for the suit. It was good money for not having to dance or take her clothes off and she thought the idea was funny.

Inside the small office of Art Grants, an employee asked, "Can I help you?"

"Yes, I'm here to drop off a grant application."

The harried employee responded, "We've been getting those in all day. Everyone who waited until the last minute has been here with a packet." She pointed to a box filled with large envelopes. "Put it with the rest."

"Oh, I didn't just come in person because of the

deadline." Melissa paused and put on her most genuine disingenuous smile. "I wanted to talk to a real person."

The employee looked skeptical. "About what?"

"About this grant competition. What are my chances, really?"

"As good as the rest, I suppose."

"It means a lot to me and I know it would mean a lot to the seniors."

Marjorie Tillman was the only full-time employee managing the grants program. She also had a mother who was in the Blue Magnolia Senior Center. She was intrigued, just like John Myers had said she would be. "What's this about seniors?"

"My grant application is for dance performances to be held at local senior living spaces." Melissa managed a sad frown. "So many of our parents and grandparents love the arts but can't get about. We want to bring dance performances to them. On a small scale, of course, but allow them to experience the thrill of live dancing once again."

From Myers' intel, Sonny and Mandy knew Marjorie's mother was a ballerina when she was young. Her mother reminded Marjorie of that fact all the time. She reached for the application from Melissa. "Let's make sure this goes in a special pile," said Marjorie.

"You're very kind," Melissa said.

Marjorie was clutching the grant packet Melissa delivered as if it was her very own child, "Thank you for bringing dance to these deserving souls."

"Oh, we can't wait to perform for those who deserve it," Melissa answered.

Marjorie hugged her before she left, and Mandy Pepperhorns burst into laughter as soon as she stepped outside the Carmel City Center.

THREE MONTHS LATER, the day of the performance arrived. The Neon Boudoir had received the grant, or more precisely, its volunteer outreach club, Mature Dance & Performance Art, had won the grant. And today the troupe was scheduled to perform for the men and women of Serenity Senior Living Center. It would be a memorable day in the city's history.

Regina Miller knew something was off when the dancers started to arrive. They were bigger than she imagined they would be. Some were tall, some full-figured. Some seemed very full-chested. These weren't the dainty little ballerinas she was expecting.

She reasoned in her mind that since this was a volunteer group of adult women and not younger girls, they must not have aged well. The makeup was a little off as well, she thought. She assumed they would all wear the same costume and makeup, but these ladies clearly weren't on the same page.

"My name is Regina. Welcome to Serenity Senior Living Center."

Mandy stepped forward, "Thank you for having us!

We are so happy to be able to perform for your residents today!"

Still uncertain, Regina looked around at the group of women. "Is this everyone?"

Mandy replied, "Everyone except ..." At that point, Jodi Thompson burst through the door. "... Jodi the Roadie."

Regina looked cross-eyed at her and Mandy recovered, "I mean this is Ms. Jodi Thompson, one of our most breathtaking performers."

Several of the dancers giggled and Regina looked around for clues to the joke she wasn't in on. Her unease was growing, but she pressed on. "Ladies, if you will follow me, I have a conference room prepared for you to be able to change into your ballet costumes."

Jodi snorted and started to speak, but Mandy silenced her with a glare. "That's very gracious of you, Regina. Lead the way."

The ladies followed the nursing home director through a key coded door and down a hallway with administrative offices on either side. At the end of the hall, they came to a board room with a large table with seating for ten people. Regina had instructed the staff to supply several mirrors, bottled water, and a rolling rack where clothing could be hung.

"Is there anything you ladies need?"

"I forgot my glitter," said Jodi.

"Glitter?" What on earth does she need glitter for, Regina thought to herself.

Mandy deflected, "Jodi, these are seniors, not kids." She looked at Regina, "Sometimes when we go to schools, we do arts and crafts with the kids."

Regina was puzzled but decided not to inquire further. "Well, when you're ready, the door across from this conference room opens into the dining hall where everyone will be waiting at 2 p.m. I will make a short announcement and then you ladies can take the stage, as it were. Any questions?"

Jodi mumbled, "Yeah, make sure you roll the guys with cash up to the front."

Regina didn't hear, but Mandy did. "No questions," she said, "and thanks again."

As she closed the door to let the women change, Regina congratulated herself for being so resourceful. I've thought of everything, she whispered to herself. The mayor will be so impressed. She left to check on the other arrangements.

Mandy growled at Jodi, "Are you trying to get us caught before we even start? Behave for five minutes, would you?"

"All right, all right. But we're not making any tip money today and I'm going to be short rent this month."

"We pull this off and Sonny will take care of us. I promise you."

"I don't think Sonny should be getting in a pissing match with the mayor of Carmel. Something bad is going to happen."

"Too late for that," Mandy replied. "We're already here."

"That's what I mean. We're here, Sonny's back at the club. If this gets ugly, we're the ones taking the heat," said Jodi. "We should be getting extra." Several of the other ladies nodded in agreement.

"He's giving you your hourly rate plus an extra $100 for the trouble. That's not enough?"

The ladies thought it over. "Yeah, I guess it's okay, but I still think he's crazy."

"But this is kind of funny," Mandy said.

"What if we kill one of them?"

"Don't think like that."

"No, seriously, what if one of those old dudes has a heart attack?" asked a dancer named Lynda.

"Really? If you were worried about somebody croaking, why did you even agree to come?" Mandy turned to the others, "You're all here on your own. Nobody forced you."

"I did think about it," Lynda said. "But I needed the work. I'm not backing out, Mandy. Promise. I'm just a little worried, that's all."

"If one of them goes, it will be with the biggest smile on his face this place has ever seen," Jodi the Roadie said as she cracked her whip. "Who's got some glitter I can borrow?"

One of the ladies tossed her a bottle. "Thanks. Now, let's do this."

. . .

MANDY WATCHED with the door cracked open as the seniors were wheeled into place. Some walked in of their own accord and sat and chattered expectantly. More than a few friends and family members of the residents were there, too. This was a big deal: the ballet was coming to Serenity Senior Living. And so was Mayor Teddy Wiggins. His mother was a resident and he couldn't resist the opportunity to be photographed with senior voters and culture.

The room quickly filled. And when the mayor arrived and was seated, Regina walked up to the microphone.

"Thank you all for coming today and on behalf of the entire staff and residents of Serenity Senior Living Center, we want to thank the mayor of Carmel, who is with us today." Teddy stood and accepted the modest clapping of the attendees. Regina continued, "We also thank the city council for setting aside funds in the Carmel city budget to support the arts. And without further ado, we welcome the Neon Ballet Troupe."

Mandy signaled to the ladies it was showtime. Then she walked into the room, dressed in a trench coat and high heels. Regina, considering herself somewhat of a connoisseur of the arts, knew enough to recognize ballet dancers don't wear stilettos. Something was definitely off.

Mandy set a boom box on top of the piano and pressed play. The mayor squirmed. Something about this woman seemed familiar.

The music began with the symphonic intro to *Love Will Find a Way* by the band Yes. And this briefly calmed the fears of both the mayor and Regina. But this was a mix created by the club DJ, and when the rest of the ladies came out also dressed in trench coats and stilettos, the mayor knew he had been duped. The music of Yes gave way to Beyonce. The trench coats flew into the crowd. Each dancer wore a tutu to complement her typical club costume.

They commenced with a choreographed number, which for them, was rather tame. For the residents of Serenity Senior Living Center, it was the most scandalous thing that had happened in the history of the facility. Maybe in the history of Carmel, for some of them. However, not all of the residents were turned off by the performance. Quite the opposite, in some cases.

Mayor Teddy had several options, none of which he liked. He could try to break this up. But doing so might put him in close contact with the strippers and since there were phones and members of the media close by, the potential for an untimely photo to be taken out of context was too high.

He could wheel his mother quickly out of the room, but that might slow him down and one of the ladies might try to engage them both and again, turn into an undesirable Instagram photo.

Or he could run. He could head out the door from which the strippers came and never look back. Which of course, is exactly what he did. When it came to the fight or flight question, Teddy was a big proponent of flight.

This left his mother to fend off Jodi the Roadie, who took particular interest in performing in front of the mayor's eighty-seven-year-old mother. The result of their interaction became a very popular Instagram photo of Mother Wiggins playing tug-of-war with Jodi and her whip.

MARSHALL MOLLER HATED THE BALLET. He hated the music, he hated getting dressed up to see the ballet, and he hated the parking battle which came with trying to attend the ballet. All of this he recalled from his life before landing in the nursing home as he walked towards the dining hall for the afternoon show.

He sat towards the back, thinking he could make for the exit when he hit his ballet limit (15 minutes by his estimate). Then he could tell his daughter-in-law he had done something to get involved. He didn't want to get involved, but his family insisted.

Then the music started. And the ladies started dancing. And he decided he liked getting involved and modern ballet was a helluva lot more fun than he had imagined.

He moved up a couple of rows. Then he recognized one of the dancers from the picture his grandson had shown him. It was Matt's would-be girlfriend. He quickly called him.

The call went to voicemail. "Matt get down to the nursing home right away. That dancer you were telling me about is performing right here in the dining hall!"

He knew Matt wouldn't listen to the voicemail for a while, if ever. So, he took a picture and texted it to his grandson.

THE BOYS of Lakeshore Estates were camped out in Willy's basement playing Xbox and watching questionable YouTube videos. All but Willy had worked off their respective punishments for the Strip Club Incident, as it had come to be known.

Willy was still confined to house arrest, as it were. He could have friends over, but he couldn't leave the property. He had two days left until he was free, and he was eyeing another trip to the club. Recidivism had always been a problem for Willy.

The basement at Willy's home looked like a frat house, with empty cups and discarded chip bags everywhere. Unlike a frat house, this didn't smell like cheap stale beer. It smelled like dirty socks and teenage boy funk, with a hint of urine. The light urine scent was because the boys often used the sump pump hole as a toilet.

It was solely used for going number one, but there

was one time when a floater was discovered after a sleepover, and this cost Willy's mom yet another boyfriend.

Matt was just about to visit the sump pump when he felt his phone vibrating. He looked at the phone and saw the call was coming from his grandpa. He shook his head and put it back in his pocket. Then he felt it buzz again. Voicemail. He decided to listen to it later. Then he felt it buzz again. He pulled out his phone one last time and looked at the picture his grandpa sent. He squealed. Then he dropped his phone. Then he squealed again. His friends thought he was losing his mind.

"We have to go. We have to go."

"Where?"

"Nursing home, Carmel Drive."

"Are you crazy, who wants to go to the nursing home?"

"Mandy. Mandy dancing." He could barely form sentences.

"What are you talking about?"

He took a deep breath and said, "The women from the roundabout are at the nursing home."

"Now?

"Now."

No further words were needed. Xbox controllers, bags of chips, and a Red Bull were all dropped in place. The boys ran up the stairs, through the kitchen, past

Willy's mom who was startled out of a nap, and into the garage. Willy opened the overhead door and grabbed his bike. Mom would have to tack on a few weeks to his sentence, he thought. I'm breaking out.

He rolled his bike out of the garage where the rest of the boys were waiting. Without looking back or closing the garage door, Willy escaped his Lakeview Estates prison in broad daylight.

The boys raced through the neighborhood to get to the nursing home. They pedaled long and hard, faster than the time they broke the diving board at the neighborhood clubhouse pool. Faster than the time they blew up one of their teachers' mailboxes. Each of those times they were pedaling away from something. This time they were pedaling towards something. Or better yet, someone. Multiple someones. The most amazing someones their hormone-addled minds could possibly imagine.

REGINA CALLED the police before trying to stop the dancing. This allowed the women to really get into their first routine. They had only rehearsed one as they were quite certain they would be thrown out. They figured if by some miracle they weren't asked to leave, they would all take turns doing versions of their solo routines.

The audience's reactions ranged from appalled (the senior center's coherent women) to thrilled (the coherent men) to drooling (those who were drooling in the first place). A few women stood and shook their fists or canes at the women. Some got up to leave. A few started dancing where they were.

To their credit, the women of the Neon Boudoir didn't actually take off their clothes. They may have thrown a few articles into the crowd, but no forbidden body parts were visible when the police arrived (something Sonny had stipulated in advance). This made it difficult for the officers to charge the women with anything. They had an invitation and a grant from the city. The only person who was naked when police arrived was one of the residents. And he was regularly naked, according to the staff.

In the end, the police cited Mandy and the dancers with public indecency, knowing full well it wouldn't hold up in court. But the mayor's chief of staff and Regina insisted they charge the women with something, and nobody wanted to cross Teddy Wiggins when his mother had been violated, as the chief of staff put it.

However, later that evening, when a Serenity staff member was tucking the mayor's mother in, she said, "What a lovely day. Can we do it again?"

When Mandy and the rest of the dancers reported back to Sonny, he was ecstatic. He shared the tale with John Myers over the phone. John Myers was pleased and set up a time to meet with Sonny so he could get his help with phase two.

"I can't imagine how you're going to top this," said Sonny.

"Today was just the opening act," John replied. "You're going to help me deliver the headliner."

When the boys of Lakeview Estates got to the nursing home, several police cars were parked at the entrance. Officer Nick Bell tried to stop the boys from entering but they ran past him. "Dammit, come back here," he yelled.

He instantly regretted it because Marjorie Hill-Blewit, a former schoolteacher, was facing him with a disapproving look. She raised her cane and said, "Potty mouth," striking the officer on the shoulder. She shuffled back inside, leaving Nick to ponder how much he hated being the new guy. The new guy gets hit by old ladies with canes. The other guys get to interview strippers. There was no justice in the criminal justice system.

Inside, the boys found Matt's grandpa. He had flecks of glitter on his forehead and a smile as wide as Montana. "Some busybody broke up the show." He pointed to three of the women being interviewed by three times as many cops. "But they're still here."

The boys became frustrated by their lack of a clear view, what with all the policemen. So, they fanned out, ignoring the staff who implored them to leave the dining hall. Marshall pointed to Mandy, "She kissed me."

Matt was jealous, and curious at the same time. "How was it?"

"Not bad for a kiss on the forehead. I could see down her shirt." Matt's eyes became as big as basketballs. "I suppose I shouldn't tell you that. Your mother won't let you come see me again."

"I won't tell, her. Promise."

"Hey, your buddy's trying to make time with my girl."

Matt turned back to see Willy following Mandy like a puppy. She had extracted herself from the police questioning and was making for the exit. Marshall got her attention.

"Oh miss, you forgot something."

Mandy stopped and looked at the old man. He slowly rose from his chair and reached into his back pocket. She knew what was coming. And though she felt bad taking the old man's money, this had been a big hassle and a buck is a buck. She just hoped he had more than a buck.

With a sultry gait, she crossed the room, making eye contact with Matt, who stood mouth agape. She stopped just a foot shy of Marshall, and Willy nearly ran into her behind. Though he didn't touch her, she felt his presence and looked back. Willy turned red and retreated a few steps.

She turned back to Marshall. "You still hanging

around, sugar?"

"I wanted to say thank you and offer you a little tip." He brandished a twenty-dollar bill.

She took the money, "You're so sweet." Mandy hugged him. Marshall felt a stirring that hadn't been active in a decade or so. Maybe everything wasn't just decorative these days. He felt dizzy but had the presence of mind to whisper something in her ear.

Mandy stepped back and turned to Matt. "I know you. You're the kid who tried to get into the club."

Willy interrupted, "I was there, too."

She looked at him and back at Matt. "Were you trying to get in to see me?"

Matt nodded.

"That's so sweet." She stepped in close, gave him a peck on the cheek, and said, "See you around, handsome." Mandy looked back at Marshall and winked. Matt was so flustered, he forgot to ask her to dinner. Or if she liked flowers.

She patted Willy on the head as she walked by, and he was instantly filled with glee for the touch and jealousy for not getting a kiss like Matt got.

Mandy crossed the room like a model on the runway and just before she exited, glanced back to make sure the old man and the two boys had their eyes on her. They did. She blew a kiss back and disappeared.

In unison, Matt and Willy said, "I'm getting a Def Leppard tattoo."

Marshall said, "I'm no deafer than your mother."

Matt said, "We can't both get one. She kissed me."

"I touched her butt."

"Because you were following her like a dork. She wasn't impressed."

"She was too."

"No, she wasn't. She thinks you're a goon."

"She only kissed you because your grandpa paid her to."

"That's not true."

“Yes, it is.”

“Grandpa, did you pay her for the kiss?”

He replied, “I tipped her for being delightful. That's all I have to say.”

Willy persisted, "I would have gotten a kiss too if my grandpa had been here with cash."

“Well he wasn’t, and you didn't. So, I'm getting a Def Leppard tattoo. You can get something else.”

“Good luck trying to find someone to do it. You're underage and your mom will never allow it.”

“You've got the same problem. How do you think you're going to get one?”

They both pondered this roadblock for a few minutes. Grandpa got up and started walking back to his room. He was too lost in the memory of Mandy to say goodbye. They were too focused on how to get a tattoo to care.

"Ronnie West," shouted Willy.

"Who's Ronnie West?"

"He's the guy Chad Duncan's sister is dating."

"Chad Duncan? You mean the kid who collects beetles? We haven't played with him in years."

Chad lived in the same neighborhood as the boys. But like most neighborhoods, there are a few kids whose personal likes and obsessions cause them to fall out of favor from the rest of the crowd. Chad was one of those kids. At an early age, he found insects of all kinds to be much more interesting than people.

Chad's sister Tyler found other ways to disgust her parents. She dated a tattoo artist who was five years older than her. The Duncans were appalled when she came home with a scorpion tattooed on her ankle. She argued that one on her body was better than the hundreds of live creatures her brother had living in his bedroom. Mr. and Mrs. Duncan had nothing to come back with.

"I bet if we offered him enough money, he would do the tattoos without having a note or permission from our parents."

Matt thought it was a good idea. But he didn't want Willy getting to the boyfriend first. "Maybe we should talk to Chad tomorrow. Find out the boyfriend's phone number."

Instantly suspicious, Willy asked, "What are you doing the rest of the afternoon?"

"I'm just going to go home. I think I have chores." He knew Willy didn't believe him.

"Yeah, I think I have chores too. I'll see you later." They both started walking towards the double door exit from the dining hall. Then the walk became a trot. The trot became a run. And by the time they passed Officer Bell outside on the way to their bikes, he swore they looked like the Roadrunner and Wile E Coyote.

4

EPISODE IV: SHE SHEDS, MAN CAVES, AND BOY BASEMENTS

The neighborhood boys of Lakeshore Estates shoved the open bags of stale chips off the coffee table in the basement of Willy's house. It was time to compare tattoos. Matt had bribed Tyler Duncan's boyfriend, Ronnie West, to do it for him since he had ridden to Ronnie's house fastest from the Serenity Senior Living Center. Willy had arrived shortly afterward. Ronnie wouldn't tattoo both boys because he feared the wrath of multiple parents should word get out who did it.

Willy appealed to his cousin's boyfriend, Fernando, who had recently gotten out of jail. He had both received and given jailhouse tattoos and was eager to try it on the outside. Unfortunately, Willy didn't ask to see pictures of the jailhouse tattoos Fernando had done and was unaware of their poor quality.

Instead, he saw the dragon on Fernando's arm and

assumed it was an accurate representation of his artistic ability. It wasn't. Willy didn't make the connection in his head that the recently released felon had not tattooed himself.

Fernando had paid for the dragon on his twenty-first birthday and it was glorious and intimidating. He celebrated its gloriousness by robbing a Dollar Hut to pay to have the dragon colored in. This led to his incarceration and experimental tattoo artistry.

Both boys agreed not to look when their tattoos were done, but to reveal them to the group at the same time. Hence the grand reveal party in Willy's basement. It was grand, in the sense that it would be a defining moment in the history of the boys of Lakeshore Estates. And a party, in the sense that Willy's mom made cookies.

The rest of the boys had been waiting all day for this. They were bragging about what tattoo they would be getting, knowing full well they didn't have the guts to endure their parents' ire should they somehow manage to get one.

"I'm going to count to three and then you both reveal your Mandys," Tony said. Each boy had an image of Mandy in his mind and was eager to see if the respective artists had captured that vision. "One, two, three! All right, roll up those sleeves," ordered Tony.

. . .

Willy and Matt rolled up their sleeves. Half the boys had their eyes trained on Matt, the others on Willy. The boys looking at Matt were in awe. Arched above and below the image were the words Mandy (on top) and Neon Boudoir (below). In the middle was a full body representation of Mandy in her Wendy Peffercorn red one-piece swimsuit. The cleavage displayed was enough to elicit the kinds of feelings middle school boys like to feel, yet not so much she looked freakish. The artist did an admirable job of capturing Mandy's facial features and the boys would eventually discover as much once they were done ogling her legs and chest.

Across the coffee table, the reaction was much different. The boys looking at Willy were horrified. The woman on Willy's arm looked like an extra in the TV series *The Walking Dead*. She was captured from the waist up (Fernando said he wasn't quite ready to draw legs). He had tried to make her hair flow, but instead, it looked like she touched one of those static electricity globes. Her breasts were nearly busting out of her shirt, but the effect looked more like a scene from *Alien* than anything sexy. He tried to capture her smile, but it came off more like a frightening scowl. All in all, she looked like a zombie.

The boys looking at Matt oohed and aahed. The boys looking at Willy laughed and pointed. Then the two groups switched to the other respective tattoo. It was clear who won. Matt laughed at Willy's tattoo and that's all it took. Willy leaped onto the table and then onto Matt. It took a minute to separate them. As the boys continued to ridicule Willy's tattoo, he just wanted to fight more of them.

"Get out of my house," Willy shouted. "All of you!"

Willy slumped on the couch and the boys quietly left. He was angry at them. Angry at himself, and angry at his mom for the grounding and the lecture he was going to get when she found out what he had done. Matt would be getting the same punishment and lecture from his parents, but at least he had a tattoo worth getting grounded for. Willy didn't and he knew it. Most of all, he was mad Matt had gotten to Ronnie West before he did.

ALEX THOMPSON TOOK a big risk by not waiting for his wife to go out of town before inviting Mandy to the man cave. Cheryl hadn't been home in the evening for nearly two weeks. Every night, the women of Lakewood Estates had gathered at Marissa Davis' she-shed to discuss the fight to bring down the Neon Boudoir.

Alex noted that this was even longer than the number of consecutive nights they had met to oppose the blues bar which tried to open near the Carmel Arts District & Design District, which itself was longer than the number of nights they met to oppose letting *actual* artists have a commune *in the Arts District.*

The kids were at a school play or a soccer match, he

couldn't remember. He just knew one of the neighbor moms was going to drop them off at 9 p.m.

So, he had invited Mandy from 7 to 8:45 p.m. and he made sure there wasn't a speck of dust in the man cave. The driveway at the Thompson house wrapped around back, so it was easy to hide her car from the view of nosy neighbors.

Mandy arrived wearing denim shorts and a Def Leppard T-shirt. She had on a lot less makeup than she usually wore to perform, but Alex was still tripping over his words and steps as he ushered her to the cave. He opened the door and let her take it all in.

"I can't believe it. Is this one of their guitars?" She moved towards the wall opposite the door. A guitar was mounted and signed by the entire band. Next to it were cymbals, signed by the drummer. She spun to her left and saw a wall of ticket stubs, bordered by at least fifty concert t-shirts. The Union Jack flag was painted on the floor, with the Def Leppard logo in the center. There was a working Def Leppard pinball game on the wall opposite the ticket stubs. And next to it was a stereo system. Alex picked up a remote control and pressed play. The *Pyromania* album began to play.

Two red leather chairs sat in front of the stereo system along with a table in between. Alex pointed to the chairs and they both sat down. Neither spoke until the album ended forty-six minutes later.

"I could live in this room," said Mandy. "I bet you spend every night here."

"Not as often as I would like."

"That's a shame. Why not?"

He looked her in the eyes, "Nobody to share it with I guess."

"Right, your wife's not a fan. None of the guys you hang out with like Def Leppard?"

"Some do, but they've all got lives, I suppose."

"Shame, if I lived close, I'd be here all the time."

"Want to see my concert photo album?"

"Sure!"

Alex got up and pulled a few old-fashioned photo albums from a drawer. He had a smile a mile wide and Mandy couldn't help but point it out. "You look as happy as anyone I've seen in a long time."

"You're the first person I could ask the question 'do you want to see my concert album' and not feel totally lame saying it."

She put her hand on his arm without thinking again, "Ah sugar, that's sweet. And there's nothing lame about Def Leppard."

At twenty to nine, Mandy left. Nothing had happened physically between the two. In his head, Alex hadn't cheated. He had just spent an evening with a fellow fan. Same as if one of the guys had come over. But in his heart, he was deeply smitten. And he knew he was in trouble.

~

Marissa Davis called the meeting of the Lakewood Estates Association Moms to order. There were twelve of them squeezed tightly in Marissa's she-shed. Janine Walsh had baked gluten-free cookies and brownies and at least three of the moms were actually eating them. The rest held them on elegant napkins and waited for the dog they were sure they remembered from the last meeting to wander inside.

This group also ran the Falcon Creek PTA, although non-Lakewood Estates moms held perfunctory positions of ceremonial status but no real power. The ladies in this shed ran the neighborhood, the school, and the movement to ban ladies who worked in the physical arts and entertainment industry from crossing the 96th Street border between Carmel and Indianapolis.

"Thank you all for coming tonight. I would like to start the meeting with an update from Cheryl regarding any legal action we might be able to take."

Cheryl stood up and said, "I'm afraid I don't have any news. My husband was unable to uncover any dirt or evidence of malfeasance we could use to have them shut down."

Janine started in, "How hard did he look?"

"Now what's that supposed to mean?"

"I just mean if he wanted to find something," Janine responded, "he would have found something."

Cheryl had said the same thing to her husband the night before. She wasn't pleased with his lack of results and told him so in no uncertain terms. But to have one of the other moms point it out was tantamount to an attack on the authority and status Cheryl enjoyed in the Lakewood Estates hierarchy. She couldn't let such an attack go without a response.

"My husband is an excellent attorney and very thorough in all that he does. If he's turned up nothing so far, it's because the degenerate who runs the strip club has hidden his malfeasance very well."

"Or maybe they're just not doing anything illegal," said Jen McDougal. Everyone turned to her and glared as if she had broken wind. Dissent was not permitted in this group, Jen quickly remembered. Jen often spoke her mind without thinking, which was why she never was put in charge of any committees or held a position of power. But she loved brownies and would even tolerate a gluten-free one to get out of the house, away from her three elementary school-aged kids, and around adult women.

"Of course, they're doing illegal things," answered Marissa. She looked at Cheryl sympathetically, "And I'm sure Cheryl's husband will turn something up eventually."

Cheryl gulped, "Actually, he's not going to be able to continue. What with the D.H. Higgins case and all." She waited for the nods of envy and approval. Everyone knew about the Higgins case, and any status lost from her husband coming up empty would be offset by the status of handling a high-profile case. "He simply won't have the time."

There were nods and condolences all around as they all agreed Cheryl would be left to do everything around the house and he really didn't appreciate all that she did. Having transitioned smoothly from scape-goat to victim, she sat back down and decided to not push her luck.

"We need to find another way to take them down," Cheryl said.

"Another protest?"

"No, it didn't work out so well the first time," Cheryl continued. "At least we were there to prevent some of the boys in this neighborhood from getting inside that awful establishment." Several mothers looked at the ground and said nothing. The sting of having their own sons roll up in an Uber on the same night as their protest hadn't worn off.

"Maybe we could set up a sting operation? Go undercover and catch them in the act of doing illegal activities." Everyone again turned to regard Jen and she realized her best move was to get another brownie and not speak the rest of the meeting.

Another twenty minutes of lousy ideas forced Marissa to table the discussion and move on to other agenda items, including the Fourth of July parade and fireworks, a fall bonfire, and the sighting of a coyote near the lake. When the meeting was over, Cheryl hung around after everyone left.

"Can I confide in you, Marissa?"

"Sure, anytime."

"I mean right now."

Marissa sat down and gestured for Cheryl to do the same. "What's on your mind?"

"I'm leaving Alex."

"Why? Is he abusing you?"

"If that includes my ears, then yes."

"Your ears?"

"He started listening to heavy metal music again."

"I thought you moved all that to his man cave."

"Yeah, but he's started listening in the car and while he takes a shower."

"Oh, you poor thing."

Cheryl wasn't sure if it was sincere or sarcasm. "I'm done. Done with his know-it-all arrogance. His dismissive attitude towards my friends ..."

"Your friends?"

"Yeah, he doesn't like you at all." Marissa was aghast. Cheryl looked around the shed as if all the ladies were still there. "I don't think he likes any of the women in this neighborhood."

"That phony! He's always so nice to me when the two of you come over," said a voice from outside. In walked Janine Walsh, Devon's mother. Janine was the neighborhood gossip and had a clairvoyant ability to know when people were about to discuss something really juicy. So, after going to her car, she had doubled back to the shed instead of leaving.

Cheryl shot back, "That's because he wants to represent you in *your* divorce. And how long have you been listening to us?"

"My divorce? My husband and I are doing just fine," Janine replied. "And I've only been there for a few minutes." She patted Cheryl's shoulder. "You poor lamb."

Cheryl continued, "Alex thinks he can size up a couple and tell who will 'win' the divorce. Then he sucks up to that person and waits out the marriage."

"What a cynical bastard," said Janine.

"Yeah, but he's usually right." Janine's mouth dropped and Cheryl backpedaled, "But not about you. He's way off there."

Janine sat down and considered the implications of what she just heard. She realized if Alex was right, he also thought she would win, whatever that meant. Her face brightened, "So, he thinks I would come out on top, huh?"

Cheryl grew frustrated. "Can we get through my divorce first?"

"Sorry," Janine answered.

Marissa continued, "Are you a little bit afraid to divorce a divorce attorney?"

"Yes, but there's an all-female divorce firm in town and they're anxious to take him down a peg or two," Cheryl replied.

"Wow, you've already hired someone."

"Yes, they're serving him papers tomorrow."

Janine asked, "How am I just hearing about this?" Cheryl and Marissa glared at her.

"Well, I had to put the protest first. There just hasn't been time."

Marissa asked, "Do you think he will be upset?"

"Probably, losing half his crap. But I don't care. I can't listen to 'Pour Some Sugar on Me' one more time. If I do, I might pour boiling water on him."

"So, he's a know-it-all with a bad taste in music. How is he with the kids?"

"They think he's Superman—when he's around. Which is never."

"I'm really sorry to hear that. Will you make him move out right away? As far as I'm concerned, he can start sleeping in Dave Vernon's man cave tomorrow."

Janine couldn't resist. "Why Dave Vernon's?"

"There have been five divorces in this neighborhood in the last decade. They all wind up in Dave V's man cave until they can get back on their feet."

"I didn't know that."

"The guys think he has the best booze. Or at least the largest supply of booze."

"Do you think Alex will start dating right away? Will you?"

"Me, I'll be on LetsDate.com by Friday. Him? He'll be alone for a long time. Nobody's *that* into Def Leppard."

~

The following weekend, the boys biked all the way to the public library, locked up their bikes, and walked to the Carmel Arts & Design District. All the boys in the neighborhood whose parents didn't monitor their social media had been following the events calendar of the Neon Boudoir. And one event each boy had made a note of was the Carmel International Art Festival.

The Neon Boudoir's newly formed charitable organization had secured a booth at the event before the incident at the senior living center. Someone on the steering committee had the idea of allowing a small number of nonprofits to raise money at the art festival by selling bottles of water. The booth opportunities (six in total) were open to the first nonprofits to claim them —minus four booths taken by the daughter of the steering committee member who had suggested it. She was raising money for the Carmel pom-pom squad.) The other two were taken by Mature Dance & Performance Art. Though the event organizers couldn't take back the booths from them, when the mayor found out he imposed a strict dress code. No bikinis. No miniskirts. No cleavage. They also put the two water booths operated by the ladies at the far ends of the exhibits.

The art fair was held in the Carmel Arts & Design District, where Rangeline Road meets Main Street. Art vendors set up booths lining both sides of the streets and stretching two blocks in all four directions. The ladies of the Neon Boudoir were relegated to booths at the end of the north and south blocks.

The members of the Mature Dance & Performance Art club stuck to the dress code while sporting matching pink and black activewear. And though the clothes certainly showed off their assets, they were no less dressed than most of the teens and twenty-somethings in their Athleta and Lululemon apparel. Despite being in a less desirable part of the festival, they had no shortage of customers for bottled water.

After a rush of customers around noon, Mandy took a break. That's when she noticed the boys from the roundabout standing off to the side of her booth. She recognized Matt from the senior center and lowered her sunglasses.

Matt slowly approached Mandy. It was time for the big reveal. She smiled as he came near. "Haven't seen you in a while, sugar. Have you been staying out of trouble?"

"I got something for you," he said.

"Aww, that's sweet." She couldn't see anything in his hands. "What is it?"

He rolled up his sleeve and revealed the tattoo. She was blown away by the artistry but a feeling of dread came over her. She was going to have to give Matt the letdown talk. Mandy had experienced plenty of regulars at the club who fell head over heels for her. They would buy her gifts, pledge their undying devotion, write her poetry, and generally make fools of themselves. As long as they kept the cash coming, she knew how to string them along. But she could always spot the fragile ones and typically cut them off as soon as possible.

Matt was a fragile one. And despite living in Carmel, she didn't think he would have the ready supply of cash which would make stringing him along pay off. Also, he was in middle school.

"Sugar, this is some fine ink you got here. I'm really flattered."

"Thanks. I listened to Def Leppard the whole time I was getting it."

This kid was deeply smitten. Mandy would have to tread lightly. "I hope you don't mind my asking, but did your mom actually okay this? You're too young to get one without a parent."

Matt bristled at the mention of his age. "I'm more mature than you think. And I can make my own decisions."

"I'm sure you can," she backtracked.

"I got this on my own. I don't care what my parents think. I'm even moving out as soon as I graduate." He paused and smiled at her, "I'll have a place of my own."

"Sounds like you got it all figured out."

"And when I do, we can hang out," he smiled at her again.

He was persistent, she had to give him that. "Sounds like fun, sugar. But I don't know if I'll still be living in Indy by then."

Matt's heart sank. "What do you mean?"

"As soon as I get enough money saved, I'm moving to Santa Fe."

"Where is that?"

"New Mexico."

"How long is it going to take you to save enough money?"

"Ten, maybe 12 more months." She looked at him and knew he was doing the math in his head. She continued, "you will only be in the ninth or tenth grade by then, am I right?"

He nodded. "You're going to meet lots of girls and break lots of hearts right here in Indiana. I'll be long gone in Santa Fe.

"I could come with you."

She tried not to laugh. "Honey, Carmel parents don't let their underage kids move in with exotic dancers. Check that. No parents do."

"I could get emancipated."

She looked over his shoulder at the city scene behind them. Then she looked in every direction. "Emancipated? From this?" Mandy became agitated, "There's no crime here kid. There's no poverty. There aren't any homeless people. No graffiti. You never wake up in the morning wondering if your car is still outside. And you want to get emancipated from all that?" She leaned in and gave him a little kiss on the cheek, then leaned back holding both his shoulders. "You seriously don't know how good you got it, kid." She released his shoulders and put her sunglasses back on. "I gotta go. See you around."

On Sunday afternoon, the day after Mandy had broken the news to Matt, the boys overheard the moms talking on the porch at the Thompson house. Tony's dad was on his way to pick up the last of his belongings and Cheryl wanted moral support. She didn't like that all the boys were there, and she was about to send them to another kid's house. They went out into the garage before she could come in and disperse them.

"Wow, Tony, too bad about your parents," said Devon. "Are you going to be okay?"

"Yeah, I'm fine. I figured this was going to happen eventually."

Matt asked, "Does your dad have a new girlfriend?"

"My mom says he does," he replied. "Well she didn't tell me. But yesterday I heard her on the phone with Matt's mom and she was saying she knows something's up. I think the reason she doesn't want us here is because she's worried he's going to show up with her."

"Where are you going to live?"

"Mostly with my mom? She says my dad may move out of state in a year or so."

Willy replied. "I think that's a bad idea."

"My dad moving?"

"No, staying mostly with your mom," said Willy.

"Why?

"I'm telling you right now, you're going to live with your dad." Willy was getting excited. "And we're going to move in with you."

"What are you talking about?

Willy was the only one looking outside the garage. Tony's dad had pulled up to the curb instead of the driveway. In the passenger seat was a blond-haired woman with sunglasses. She pulled them down and winked at Willy, just like she did the first time they saw her in the roundabout. Mandy was Alex Thompson's new girlfriend.

5

EPISODE V: THE TOMB OF THE UNKNOWN ROADIE

John Myers was the least outspoken of the nine members of Carmel City Council. He tended to go along with the majority and shied away from controversy. He owned an independent commercial real estate company that did well enough to keep him on billboards throughout the county—a distinct advantage when it came time to run for office. He didn't really enjoy politics, but being on the council helped him keep watch over policies which impacted his business and if it meant he had to vote a particular way to ensure a zoning issue went in his favor later on, he had no qualms with it.

This made him the last person anyone would expect to cross Mayor Teddy Wiggins—which is exactly what John intended to do for his second act of revenge on the mayor. It started with a seemingly harmless motion. The councilman suggested the roundabout at 126th

Street and Keystone Avenue have some monument to music. Many of the city's roundabouts had been upgraded with art, plants, and other features in recent years. John encouraged the members of the council to consider a tribute to the art of musical performance.

"I'm making a motion to consider the plan being distributed to you now," he said as papers were passed to each member of the council. "The motion is to use the $250,000 left in the roundabout beautification budget the fiscal year ending June 30, to put a sculpture celebrating Franklin and his contributions to musical performance. And of course, Taylor will do the sculpture of his head with accompanying symbols of his craft."

"I think it's a fine idea," George Fillmore responded. "And of course, Mayor Wiggins is a big fan of Morty Franklin and will be behind this all the way." This was met with nodding heads of approval.

John Myers chuckled to himself. His motion did not actually say "Morty" Franklin. It just said Franklin. Just like the sculptor's name was not "Monique" Taylor, the woman who had done the other sculptures and art around town. No, Councilman Myers used last names on purpose. He was vague on purpose. He wanted this passed without discussion, approved before it could be taken back.

"Will the council need a sketch of the work, or can we just move on with it?"

"We need some idea of what you have in mind," George responded.

"It's just that I would like it to be a surprise for the mayor, unless you have any objections," John responded. "Of course, that last statement would have to be stricken from the minutes in order to do so."

"This is a fabulous idea," shouted Martha Bickmore-Welsh. "It will be all I can do to keep the secret when I go backstage to greet the performers at the Palladium this weekend." Martha greeted anyone she wanted at the Palladium, whether they wished to be greeted or not. She was on the Palladium board and the Bickmores (of the Bickmore-Welsh family) had once owned the land on which it sat. She was a philanthropist, patron of the arts, and delighted to claim she had "performed opera in New York, don't you know."

"Do try to contain your enthusiasm, Martha," John warned.

"I performed opera in New York, don't you know," she answered.

"I seem to recall that," George responded. Heads nodded all around again.

Martha raised her left arm, pointing in the general direction of New York. The rest of the council feared she would break out in song. "But the Great American Songbook still holds a dear place in my heart." She put her other hand over her heart. "It is fitting that such a monument be put in *our* fair city." She looked at Clair

Bee, the stenographer. "Strike the last statement of Mr. Myers from the record. We're keeping this a secret."

Clair Bee struck the last statement and took a sip of vodka and La Croix from an Under Armour water bottle she kept next to her chair. It had become a drinking game among the city's staff to do a shot whenever Martha referenced the opera. As a result, read the last item on the agenda from any council meeting and you're bound to find a typo or two.

George Fillmore objected. "Martha, I'm the chair. It's my job to tell Clair to strike the last statement."

She gave him a dismissive wave. "Go on then."

"Clair, let's just state that we've empowered Mr. Myers to take care of the monument in the roundabout of 126th and Keystone Avenue." He looked around the room. "Everyone agreed?"

Martha responded, "John's work on the beautiful tree in the 96th Street roundabout was exemplary. And the other two he supervised were featured in national magazines. I think we can trust him to deliver something we will all be proud to view."

Most of the members shook their heads in agreement. None raised an objection.

George continued, "Let's vote. All in favor?" Eight ayes. "All opposed?" One nay. "Let the record show Sy Kinsler voted no. Motion carries."

Sy Kinsler, the only Libertarian on the council, always voted "no" to any government spending out of principle. He was elected as an at-large member before someone discovered over fifty percent of the ballots for the election were printed without his opponent's name. As the election was close in the mayoral race (within twenty votes), the possibility of a recount was terrifying for the mayor and the party in power. So, Mayor Wiggins and his backers convinced Sy Kinsler's opponent (Janet Jefferies LeClure) not to challenge the results. She promptly found her place of business (LeClure Luxury Linens) in a property tax-free zone for a decade.

John smiled and quietly participated in the rest of the meeting. Part one of his plan was complete. The ruse of a surprise for the mayor meant he now had nobody overseeing as he spent $250,000 on a tribute to Franklin—Franklin *Myers,* that is.

John Myers had lost his brother Franklin to pancreatic cancer the previous year. Franklin had moved back to Carmel after forty-five years on the road as a guitar tech, road crew manager, and eventually production manager to some of the most famous (and infamous) rock bands in history. In the world of music, he was known as "Filthy Frank."

In the 1970s, Frank gained a reputation as a reliable roadie and the nickname "Filthy Frank" as a degenerate partier. When Noah Bleekman of the Rusty Spoons turned thirty, it was Filthy Frank who organized the notorious Noah's Ark party—complete with two dozen sets of female twins dressed in matching but scanty animal costumes. The Feminist Music Critics of

America organized a protest at the Rusty Spoons' next concert.

It was Filthy Frank who filled the J.C. Nichols Memorial Fountain in Kansas City with K-Y Jelly, although Mötley Crüe, Kiss, and Sinead O'Connor have been blamed for the incident over the years. But probably his biggest act of depravity happened during a summer music festival in Europe. Singer, dancer, and actress Sophia Chavez (SoCha) was on the bill and her roadies (along with her contract rider demands) were making life miserable for the other roadies at the three-day event.

She had a dressing room decorated in all white, twice the size of all the other performers. Her contract stated nobody but she was allowed to use the backstage restroom for the entire day of the show. The rest of the crew and other bands had to share two Porta Potties outside or make a quarter-mile trek back to the lot where the tour buses were parked. Five other acts performed before her and they couldn't use the backstage restroom. It was diva behavior at its worst. And Franklin Myers wasn't having any more of it.

So, Filthy Frank tampered with her bottled water supply (flown in from Fiji) and added a clear laxative. Exactly 32 minutes into the show, the singer quickly left the stage while her band and dancers performed a lengthy improvised jam session. Meanwhile, SoCha was forced to use the outside Porta Potty because the roadies had chained the backstage bathroom right when she took the stage. The delicate princess had to take a lengthy dump in the Porta Potty filled with the aroma of three days' worth of roadie fudge marinated in 95-degree summer heat and humidity. By the time she was done, she began vomiting.

When she returned to the stage, she was paler than her all-white backstage palace. To mock her after the show, all the non-SoCha roadies hummed Procol Harum's *Whiter Shade of Pale* as her roadies took down her stage setup. Some laughed at the joke. Some were embarrassed to be on her crew and vowed to leave at the next opportunity, even if it meant finishing the summer touring with Billy Joel.

Filthy Frank wasn't just filthy. He came up with some innovations which helped make stage setup and teardown more efficient. He became a wise and experienced production manager. And he was always working to help other roadies who were down on their luck.

When he retired, he wanted to open a small museum to honor the work and lives of the unknown roadies who make all the big shows for which you and I pay hundreds of dollars possible. So, he returned to the town in which he grew up and came up with a plan to pay tribute to the men and women of the profession he loved.

He took his idea before the Carmel City Council to ask for its support, both financially and otherwise. The council turned him down. He wasn't as polished as the usual presenter in these meetings, what with the roadie clothes and the black cowboy hat with the silver skull on its band. He looked like Lemmy from Motörhead. Some of the council members even mocked Filthy Frank, even though his councilman brother was sitting in the room with them.

When Mayor Teddy was asked about the proposal by the Carmel Bugle, he was as dismissive of the concept as he was of the people it sought to honor, "A roadie museum in Carmel? There would be people in Metallica tank tops as far as the eye could see. Of course, I'm not in favor of that. I'm glad the council had the sense to pass on it."

Franklin Myers died one year later, his dream never realized. At the funeral, all John could see were the smirks on the faces of his fellow council members when Frank had presented his idea. John was bitter and angry at the council and the mayor. And now he had set in motion his revenge. Next, he had to enlist the help of someone who also had a grudge against the people who ran the city. John Myers went to meet Sonny Kagan.

Five months later, Teddy Wiggins drove to the unveiling and ribbon cutting bursting with excitement. He loved the Great American Songbook. He worshipped at the feet of Morty Franklin, and he adored the art of Monique Taylor. This was going to be a pivotal day for Carmel. A major thoroughfare of the city would become a monument to the music he loved. Thousands of cars every day would pass by it and admire the art, the artist, and the mayor who makes it all possible, he thought.

At least those were the words he was going to use once the curtain was drawn and he made his closing comments. He hadn't yet seen even a rendering of the sculpture, as it was supposed to be a surprise. But word had leaked out about its connection to music and today was the day.

Teddy parked his car and proceeded to the roundabout, which was closed for the afternoon's ceremony. "How is it looking? Can I peek behind the curtain?" he asked John Myers.

"No, this is supposed to be a surprise."

"But you know Martha let it slip. I know what the surprise is, so just a little peek." He reached for the curtain and John lightly slapped his hand, much to the mayor's surprise.

"No," John said. "I want your reaction to be captured authentically along with everyone else's. This is going to be a singular moment for the city."

Mayor Teddy squeezed John's arm, "I can't wait." Then he winced when he saw some rock and roll types dressed in black. "Who are they?" he asked.

"They're just part of the setup crew for today's musical accompaniment," John replied.

The mayor frowned. "Will they be gone before the cameras get here?"

"I'm certain they will be right where we want them by then," John replied. "Oh, and by the way, the council gave your assistant a new script for today."

"What? You know I don't like last-minute changes."

"Just a few thank-yous and whatnot. Nothing a seasoned politician like yourself couldn't handle."

Teddy reached for the curtain again and John reached to slap his hand. Teddy slowly pulled his hand back and felt around his hair to make certain everything was in place. He eyed John with suspicion, then left to shake hands and schmooze with the public. Well, not the public per se, but the segment of the public that wrote large campaign checks.

The only person who was not happy that day was Martha Bickmore-Welsh. She was still upset about not being invited to sing. "How could you honor the Great American Songbook and not have me sing?" she asked John. She had been at him for months and took the lack of her inclusion as a personal affront.

"Martha, not again. We're going on in two minutes."

"I should be singing *If My Friends Could See Me Now*. I know Morty would have been so pleased to hear me perform." She looked around for the performer. "Speaking of which, where is he?"

"He's not coming."

"Not coming? Is he ill?"

"Not as far as I know."

"Was his plane delayed?"

"No, that's not it either."

"But this is his big day! How can you honor the man and he not be here? We need to cancel this right now." She made for the podium, but John cut her off.

"He's not here because we didn't invite him."

"Didn't invite him? I don't understand."

"You will in a moment," he responded.

Mayor Teddy interrupted. "It's time to get this started. Where are Monique and Morty?"

"They aren't here," Martha replied.

"How could they not be here?" Teddy was getting red in the face. "Are they stuck in traffic? We can stall for a while."

"Teddy, who on earth are those people?" Martha gestured to a group of musicians dressed in black.

"I don't know. John, who the hell are those people?"

He responded, "They are the musical performers for today."

"They look like a heavy metal group," said Teddy.

"They are."

"How can you have a heavy metal group sing *If My Friends Could See Me Now*?"

"Exactly what I've been saying for weeks," Martha interjected.

"They aren't," John replied.

"Wait, what is this?" At that moment, the mayor's aide handed him the new script. "Where the hell have you been? I've had no time to review this." John's accomplices made sure the assistant had a flat on the way to the event.

John interrupted before the beleaguered assistant had a chance to speak. "Too late, it's 2 p.m."

Mayor Teddy nervously walked up to the podium, clutching his script. "Good afternoon and welcome to this monumental occasion. We are here to pay tribute to the music and performances which have made our country great." His voice wavered, gripped by uncertainty. "And to the artist who has captured that in the creation we are about to unveil. Now I would like to introduce John Myers of the city council, who spearheaded this project."

As Teddy walked off the stage, he whispered in John's ear, "What have you done?"

"You will see soon enough."

John began, "Ladies and gentlemen. Not long ago, our city and the world of music lost one of its vital citizens. Behind every great performance is a crew that sets up the stage, manages the lights, monitors the sound, and tears it down at the end. Their names are unknown because they operate out of the limelight. Of course, I'm talking about the roadies. And Carmel, Indiana, is proud to honor one of our own and the profession of rock and roll roadie with the Tomb of the Unknown Roadie."

The band immediately began playing *The Load Out* by Jackson Browne. As they did, the curtain came down, revealing John's tribute to his brother and all the roadies who ever lived.

Throughout the roundabout were bronze roadie

statues, posed in a variety of roadie activities. Some were pushing crates of equipment, while others tuned instruments. A lighting rig stretched across the roundabout and roadies were dismantling it. In the middle of the sculpted stage were Marshall amplifiers. On top of the stacks was a casket draped with microphone cords. Under the casket was an inscription which read, "Tomb of the Unknown Roadie." To the left of the stage was a singular statue. A roadie, wearing a black cowboy hat with a silver skull pinned to the front, pointed instructions to the rigging guys. He wore a vest with no shirt underneath. On his right bicep was a tattoo of a Gibson Flying V guitar.

Teddy was aghast but willed himself to remain composed as all eyes were darting from him to the sculpture and back again. This seemed out of line for Mayor Teddy Wiggins. This seemed out of line for Carmel. How did this get approved, the crowd wondered? He started to read the new script that had been handed to him right before the start of this debacle.

Martha Bickmore-Welsh was not as skilled at stoicism. After clocking both Teddy and John with her purse, she marched to the podium to take charge. The soundboard operator cut the mic. Those in the front row heard her vow to have the display removed. Which is exactly what Teddy said to John.

"I will have this ripped out of here by tomorrow afternoon," he swore.

"You can't," John replied. "You signed an agreement to keep it here for ten years."

"You little weasel! You're finished. Don't you dare try to run for city council again."

"I don't plan to," he responded. "And mayor, keep it down. The press is waiting."

The song finished and Teddy looked out over the puzzled crowd. Both the Indianapolis and Carmel media were present, and they had lots of questions. Frankly, so did Teddy.

"Mayor Wiggins, you seemed surprised by this monument. Were you aware of this tribute to roadies?"

He thought for a moment, collected his thoughts, and answered, "What a unique vision John Myers has brought to the city of Carmel. I can say none of us expected this," his voice trailed off, his attention now focused on the spectacle behind the crowd and cameras, "nor did we expect to see Metallica tank tops as far as the eye could see."

Walking up the ramp from Keystone Avenue was a long procession of musicians, roadies, and their families. They had parked their cars on the shoulder and blocked the ramp with a tour bus. Every band touring near the Midwest had detoured to Carmel. Mixed among the rockers were Alex and Mandy, who had been tipped off by members of the Def Leppard fan club. Trailing them were a pack of boys on bicycles.

Looking south on Keystone Avenue, it was like the

closing scene in the movie *Field of Dreams*, an unending stream of rockers come to pay tribute to Filthy Frank.

It was glorious, even if Marsha Bickmore-Welsh didn't get to sing *If My Friends Could See Me Now.* Hours later, long after the mayor had sworn revenge on John, and Martha Bickmore-Welsh had informed everyone not in black that she had sung opera in New York, the roundabout had turned into a party. And as the sun went down, the roadies and rockers who crowded the roundabout convinced the band to play *The Load Out/Stay* one more time as they all sang along. And everyone stayed, just a little bit longer.

NEVER MISS A BLOG POST

Sign up for my newsletter and get *72 Hours in Savannah* for FREE.

START READING

TALES FROM A ROUNDABOUT

VOLUME TWO

1

EPISODE VI: HEAVY IS THE HEAD

Cooper Langley brushed the debris off his shoulder and surveyed the damage he had caused. His red Audi S5 convertible had come to rest on a sidewalk leading away from the roundabout he had driven through. "Through" being the operative word, as Cooper didn't drive around the roundabout as the traffic gods intended. He drove through the middle of the roundabout as it seemed a more direct route to the other side. Despite being drunk, he could see he had made a mess of things.

It was 3 a.m. on a Tuesday morning, so there were no other cars in sight. It was cold, however, and the Carmel High School junior could see his breath. In this moment, he realized he should have put the top on his Audi before leaving his girlfriend's house. It had been unseasonably warm when he went to the party at 2 p.m. on Monday. But this is Indiana and regardless of your views on climate change, Indiana weather is unpredictable. The reason there was an all-night party at Payton Wellstone's home on a Monday was this was the first week in January and school hadn't started yet after the holiday break. Payton's parents were in Aspen or Tahoe (she couldn't remember) and the young lady was bored.

So, twenty-two promising young men and women came together for some old-fashioned high school debauchery and Cooper could debauch with the best of them.

But now his reckoning had come. He drove drunk. He drove through a roundabout drunk. He drove through the mayor's *favorite* roundabout drunk. Cooper stepped out of the car and took in the debris around him.

Teddy Wiggins, mayor of Carmel, Indiana, loved this roundabout best because it was named after him. Of course, he was able to convince everyone at the dedication of the statue and official grand re-opening of the intersection that he was "humbled and surprised that the statue was of him." In fact, he had commissioned the original statue (him sitting at his desk), a second statue (him shaking the hands of a voter), and a third (him waving to the crowd from the Grand marshal's vehicle at the 4th of July parade) and finally the one they actually placed at the roundabout (him staring off into the distance).

The one they chose was titled "Teddy Wiggins'

Vision of a Future Carmel" and it was now in three pieces. The torso was in the street. The base was under the car. And the head was resting partly on the door frame and partly in the lap of the girl sitting in Cooper's back seat, which he discovered when she called for help.

Up until that moment, Cooper had forgotten he had a passenger and this development confused him greatly.

"Are you okay? he asked.

"I don't think I can move."

"Oh, god. Is your spine broken?"

"I can't feel my legs, but I don't think it's because of a spinal injury. In case you can't tell, the head of the mayor is in my lap. And he weighs a ton, so I'm kind of pinned in here."

"I'll call for help. No, I can't call for help. I'll get arrested. I'll call my bros."

"If your bros are the same guys from the party, none of them are in any condition to come help us."

"I don't know what to do."

She growled at him, "How about you get in the back next to me and push this damn head off me."

"Don't yell at me! Why are you in my car, anyway?"

"I'm Selina Roberts."

Cooper was blank.

"I'm in your chemistry class."

Still nothing.

"You were flirting with me after your girlfriend passed out."

The young man was still at a loss.

"You told me you would give me a ride home and I thought you were the most sober kid at the party. Obviously, I was wrong."

"So, where do you live?"

She jerked her thumb over her shoulder in the opposite direction from where the Audi was pointed. "That way. I was trying to get you to turn around when you crashed."

He tried to piece it together in his mind. "Oh, yeah. It's starting to come back to me. Why were you in the back seat?"

“Because you put your hand on my thigh. I climbed in back just before we got to the roundabout.”

Cooper remembered trying to look up her skirt as she climbed back. He also remembered that is why he forgot about the roundabout.

"So, are you going to help me out here or am I going to have to call the fire department?"

"Oh, sure. Sorry the mayor's head is in your lap," he replied.

"The real mayor used to date my mom. I've seen his head in worse places."

Cooper tried to ponder that, but he was still buzzed, and the mental images weren't forming properly. He refocused as best he could on rescuing the girl.

He leaned into the car and pushed on the head of

Teddy Wiggins, which was about the size of a large exercise ball. Teddy didn't move. "You're going to have to get in the back seat in order to get enough leverage," Selena insisted.

Cooper complied and was able to get under the head and push upwards. It moved enough that Selina could slide away towards Cooper and out from under Mayor Wiggins. She remained in the back seat, waiting for feeling to come back into her legs. Cooper was still holding the head, trying to decide if he should let it go or try to push it off the top of the Audi.

As he waited for the light bulb of inspiration, the headlights of justice appeared. Cooper gave the head a shove and it rolled out of the car and into the roundabout. The drunk student was mesmerized as he watched it roll towards the lights.

THE POLICE CAR came to a stop and a single officer remained in the driver's seat looking at Cooper. The sixteen-year-old caught in his headlights appeared to be five foot ten with an athletic build and sandy brown hair. Like most high school boys in the Midwest, he was wearing shorts and a hoodie, despite the cold. David Lupinski had been a Carmel police officer for all of ten months after working fifteen years as a cop in Detroit. And although he was annoyed about the young man in front of him and the paperwork that was about to ensue, this frightened kid wasn't likely to shoot at him because 1) he was in Carmel, and 2) he was currently pissing himself. Officer Lupinski rubbed his greying beard, observed the puddle forming at Cooper's shoe, and made a mental note of it. Best to let it freeze on the kid's shorts before putting him in the back of the squad car.

I better throw a puke bag back there too, he thought. *This kid's gotta be a puker.* In twenty years of law enforcement, he had come to realize that the cleaner he kept the back seat of his squad car, the better his work environment and his overall mental health would be. So, he always assessed perpetrators for their likelihood to leave a mess and he had a kit in the trunk to deal with a comprehensive variety of scenarios and bodily fluids.

Cooper didn't put up a fight. In fact, he kneeled in his own pee with his hands on his head before Officer Lupinski had said a word. The teenager could see his own breath, but his legs were warm.

"Are you drunk, son?"

"Yes."

"You don't have to answer that," came a female voice from the back of the convertible.

"He already did," Lupinski replied.

"He doesn't have to take a breathalyzer either."

"Are you his attorney?"

"No, I'm his ... I was just catching a ride."

"Yeah, well, Uber might have been a better choice. Step out of the car, please."

Selina wobbled as she got out. Not because of the

booze so much, but because her legs were still tingling. Lupinski noticed her tights were ripped across both thighs where the head had been resting. She was scraped but not bleeding.

"Have you been drinking?"

"My legs are numb," she replied.

"What were you two doing just before the crash?"

"He was driving. I was in the back seat."

"And what were you doing in the back seat?"

"Shouting 'Don't hit that statue.' Can I call my mom?

"From the station. You're riding back with me and the demolition driver."

"I just want to go home," she said, stomping her feet. "Gawd! What's your deal?"

"Look, miss. I have three daughters. There is literally no tantrum you could throw right now that I can't withstand."

"My mother used to date the mayor. You're going to be sorry."

"I'm pretty much going to be sorry the rest of the night. But you're still coming to the station with me and piss boy."

Cooper was sobbing. "What's going to happen to my Audi?"

"It's going to be towed and impounded."

He sobbed some more. Selina was disgusted, by the smell and his lack of composure. Lupinski noticed her reaction to Cooper and asked, "He belong to you?"

"Oh, gawd no." She took out her phone and

captured the sobbing teen in his most embarrassing state. "Once this goes up nobody else will want him either."

Lupinski asked, "Don't you think that's cruel?"

"I'm about to be grounded for the next week or so," she replied. "Might as well have some fun."

"Being a cop and a dad was so much easier before social media."

Selina rolled her eyes. "I would kill myself if I had to grow up primitive like your generation."

Officer Lupinski walked her to the car in silence. After he guided her to the back seat, he retrieved the pee-and-puke kit from his trunk, spread a plastic sheet on the seat next to Selina, and retrieved the sobbing Cooper (who was still kneeling in his nearly frozen pee). The smell told him that Selina was not going to enjoy the ride.

By this time, other officers were arriving. Some of the old timers shook their heads. Sergeant Al Sherman said, "Ooh, this is going to be bad."

"Why is that? asked Lupinski.

"That's the mayor's favorite roundabout sculpture."

"Why is that?"

"Because it's him. He's the statue!"

Lupinski tilted his head and got another look at the face on the pavement. "Huh, I didn't even realize it. I was too focused on the teenagers who cut him down."

"You know, I always figured this would happen," said

Sherman. "But I always thought it would be the mayor himself who drove through this one."

The additional officers got a big laugh at the mayor's expense as they directed an approaching car around the debris. "I'm going to take these two in and call their parents. I'm sure they are in for a tough time."

"Not as tough as you are," Sherman replied.

"What do you mean?"

"This is Carmel. The parents are more likely to blame us for the roundabout being in their son's way than they are him for being drunk."

"You're kidding?"

"No, I'm not."

"And I thought Detroit gangbangers were bad."

"I've got twenty bucks says you wish you had a seasoned criminal over the parents who bought that kid a 2019 Audi S5."

Officer Lupinski took another look at the convertible and said, "I should probably just give you that twenty now."

SELINA ROBERTS WAS the daughter of former NBA star Dave "Shooter" Roberts and Lindsey Malone. Lindsey kept the house and kids in Carmel after their messy divorce in 2018. Dave, who was a college basketball analyst, was caught on video at an Atlantic City hotel with a young sideline reporter from the same network.

Now Dave calls Division II basketball games for a Texas cable access channel and the young sideline reporter has a book deal. Lindsey is an interior decorator who doesn't particularly have a good eye but can mimic just about any style she DVRs on HGTV, so she's never out of work. People used to say that Lindsey and Selina could pass as sisters —both with long flowing chestnut hair and striking green eyes. But the divorce had been rough on her mother and people didn't say that anymore.

Selina didn't call her mom at first. When she got to the station, she called her friend Marci Emerald, but Marci didn't respond or answer her texts. So, Selina called her mother.

"Mom, I'm at the police station, I need you to come get me."

"No, you're not. You're having a bad dream. Now go back to sleep."

"Mom, I'm not dreaming. Get down here."

"Then I'm dreaming. Good night, dear." She hung up.

Selina called her back. "Mom!"

"Why are you shouting?"

"Come to the Carmel police station. Now!"

"Honey, I told you, you're asleep."

"Mom, did you check on me before you went to bed?"

"Seriously, baby. It's like a hundred steps to that side of the house. I don't think I've been over there since

Thursday." It actually was Monday. "Besides, I respect your privacy."

"Mom, I'm really in jail."

"And I'm really in need of a good night's sleep. Do you know how hard I work since your father left us?"

"*You* kicked him out mom."

"He was all over the internet with that sideline Barbie. What was I supposed to do?"

"Give him another chance?"

"You have no idea what I put up with."

"Gawd, Mom. Can we focus on my problem? I'm in jail, can you pick me up?"

"What did you do?"

"Nothing. I was getting a ride home and the boy who was driving crashed."

"Are you hurt?"

"No, but he was drunk, and I've had a few so they brought us both in."

"All right. I'm coming."

"Mom have you been drinking?"

"No, I've been sleeping."

"I meant before you went to bed."

"You're going to lecture *me*? I'm not sitting in jail."

Selina replied, "I just don't want us to spend the night together here."

~

Cooper's call went a lot worse. His father was ex-military, which meant Cooper was going to catch hell when he got home. His dad was also an ambulance-chasing attorney. So, the police were going to catch hell when he got to the station.

Paul Langley burst into the lobby of the Carmel police station and started giving orders immediately. "Tell me where my son is now."

From behind the front desk, a middle-aged woman with dark brown hair asked in a slight southern accent, "Who's your son?"

"You know damn well who he is. You're doing this because he's *my* son and you all want to stick it to me. Well, I'm not having it."

"Sir, my name is Linda. I just started the night shift two weeks ago and I just moved here from Raleigh, North Carolina. I don't have the faintest idea who you are or who your son is, so why don't we start with some names?"

The fact that she had no idea who he was only enraged him more. A former marine, Paul Langley ran a small law practice in Indianapolis. He'd had a partner or two over the years, but they usually left within a short amount of time. To say he was abrasive was an understatement.

He was six feet tall with thinning blonde hair. Muscular from an obsession with weightlifting and an addiction to steroids. He often looked like he was about to rip out of his suits like the Incredible Hulk. His neck was so muscled, it barely swiveled anymore. If you spoke to his right or left, he had to turn his body to face you.

Cooper was his oldest child and only son. He had four daughters ranging from five to fourteen years old. His son and oldest two daughters were with his first wife. His next youngest daughter's mother was an IUPUI law student who clerked for him one summer, and the youngest's mother was his current live-in girlfriend.

Officer Lupinski came out to meet him. "I understand you are Cooper's father."

"I am and his attorney. Are you the arresting officer?"

"I am."

"Why wasn't my son taken to a hospital first?"

"He was looked at by an EMT. They cleared him."

"I want their names. I'll be suing them too."

"Suing them for what?"

"Negligence."

"You haven't even seen your son."

"I spoke to him. I know what you and the others at the scene failed to do."

"And what did we fail to do?"

"Protect my son."

"And what about the rest of the public?"

"What about them?"

"He was driving drunk."

"Allegedly."

"He was twice the legal limit."

"I'll be challenging those results."

"Of course you will." Lupinski shook his head. "He hit a statue. It could have been a pedestrian or another moving vehicle."

"My son was in a crash, and your only thought was to bring him to jail and not get him the critical care he needs. Sounds like negligence to me."

Lupinski released Cooper into his father's care and watched them leave. Then he slipped out a side door, got in his car, and followed the Langleys. This wasn't Lupinski's first rodeo, and he figured his dashboard camera recording would come in handy down the road. As he expected, the Langleys did not go to the hospital to get the "critical care Cooper needed." They drove to the Langley home and went inside.

The officer waited about 40 minutes and then all the house lights went out. Apparently, the "critical" care would come in the morning. The Langleys went to bed and Lupinski went back to the station to finish filing his report.

As THE NIGHT SHIFT ENDED, a heavy winter storm came through central Indiana, dumping six inches of snow and canceling school. This left the boys of Lakeshore Estates to their own devices in more ways than one. Matt Moller, Tony Thompson, and Devon Walsh gathered at Willy Davis' house to play Xbox. Though they were each in seventh grade, Devon was tall enough to pass for a high school student. Willy was barely five feet tall, and the shortest kid in his grade. Matt and Tony were average. Average height. Average students. Average at sports. If they didn't have different color hair, blond and dark brown respectively, you couldn't tell them apart. After a couple of hours of shooting each other (on screen), they all got restless.

Matt asked the group, "Did you hear Cooper Langley got decapitated last night?"

Willy responded, "Decapitated? Is that when you get your nuts chopped off?"

"No, that's castrated," said Matt. "He got decapitated."

"Nuh uh, no way," Tony chimed in.

"It would have been all over the news," Willy said. "And that's all my mom watches in the morning."

"They probably didn't want people to find out and go looking for his head," said Matt.

"Why, is it gone?"

Devon returned from the restroom, "You should light a match. It's about to get putrid in three, two, one …"

The tallest of the four middle school boys, Devon had pinpoint accuracy regarding the timing of his stench. The rest of the boys yelled and threw chips, pillows, and whatever was in reach at him.

After they calmed down, Matt continued, "My

sister's best friend got a ride home with him last night, and she said that they were in a wreck and his head landed in her lap."

"Sick!!" cried Tony.

"Are you sure?" asked Devon.

"That's what I heard," said Matt.

Willy said, "Where was the wreck?"

"In the roundabout at 126th and Gray Road," Matt replied.

"What are we waiting for? Even if they found the head, there's got to be blood everywhere," said Willy.

"But it snowed 6 inches this morning," Tony answered. "It's all gone."

"No, way," said Devon. "If he got his head cut off, there's no way you won't be able to see all that blood through the snow."

Willy was ready to leave the stench of the basement. "Let's go!"

"Hey, that's a pretty long bike ride," Tony said. "Think your mom could take us?"

"Doubt it, but I'll ask," said Willy.

He ran upstairs to ask his mother if she would take him and his friends to see the blood from Cooper Langley's early morning decapitation. Willy's mom vomited. She did that a lot lately in the mornings. Willy hadn't put it together yet.

"We're on our own," he announced upon his return.

Matt replied, "Okay, let's get to it."

The boys filed out of the basement and got their

bikes. Luckily for them, the city had plowed the roads between their homes and the roundabout in question. The only challenge they faced were the few cars that were out and about. The plows had left the roads somewhat narrow, and the drivers were irritated to find a pack of boys out on the icy roads.

When they arrived at the roundabout, Tony immediately had doubts about the veracity of the story. "Matt, are you sure your sister's friend said *Cooper* got decapitated?

"Yeah, why?" he replied.

Tony pointed to the pile of mayor in the middle of the roundabout. "Because the mayor doesn't have a head." Sure enough, the statue of Mayor Teddy Wiggins was headless.

They all yelled at Matt. "You moron. You made us ride all the way here!"

"Come on guys, look around," Matt said, trying to recover from the embarrassment. "There must be some blood around here."

They searched for thirty minutes, an eternity in boy time, and found no large concentrations of blood. The plowed road had revealed what looked like some frozen Mountain Dew (or urine) and what may or may not have been frozen vomit.

Inside the roundabout, they looked over the broken statue and noticed the head, initially hidden by drifting snow, had been placed next to the other pieces.

A small hill that came down from the golf course

and tapered into the sidewalk next to the roundabout had several unmanned sleds at the base. As Tony took this in, he had an idea.

"Hey, guys. Let's take the mayor's head," he said.

"Why?" asked Devon.

Tony replied, "Why not?"

Matt asked, "What would we do with it?”

"We would have it. That's what.” Tony continued, “While the whole town's looking for it, we would have it in Willy's backyard.”

"Why my yard? You know my mom would find it.”

“No she wouldn't,” Matt chimed in. Stealing the head would make everyone forget that he failed them on the decapitation story. “In all the years we've played back there, has she ever come out any farther than the back deck?”

Willy thought for a moment, “I guess not.”

“No, not once,” said Tony. “Even when she lays out in her bikini, she does it in the front yard so Mr. Boyken can have a look.”

"My mom doesn't lay out for Mr. Boyken,” yelled Willy. “Take that back."

"It's true, Willy,” said Devon. He and the rest of the boys had caught Mr. Boyken looking at Willy’s mom more than once last summer. Nobody brought it up in front of Willy until now.

The other boys nodded their agreement.

"We all know the sun's better in the back yard,” said Matt. “It's for Boyken.”

"It is not," he protested. "She does it so we can have the yard to ourselves."

"Haven't you ever noticed he's always working in the front yard when she lays out?

"Screw you guys," Willy said. "That thing isn't coming to my house."

"It has to, it's the only place we can hide it," said Matt.

"Come on, Willy," pleaded Tony.

"Not another word about Mr. Boyken," Willy insisted.

Matt replied, "Okay, but how are we going to get it home?

Tony pointed, "Those sleds. Matt and Willy still have the ropes on their bikes from when they pulled us on our skateboards. We tie the sleds to the bikes and put the head on the sleds."

"How do we keep the sleds together?"

"I'll use my belt," Tony replied.

Willy's eyes grew big, "You're going to steal the sleds and the head?"

"Yeah, why not?"

"I don't know," Willy replied. "That's a lot of stealing."

"It's the mayor's head. He's a celebrity," Tony reasoned. "If LeBron James' head was in the snow in this roundabout, would you steal it?"

"Are you saying he's as big as LeBron James?"

Tony replied, "No, but I've seen how adults act

around the mayor. He's a star. Not TikTok level star, but he's a star."

"He's right," Matt said. "Let's do it."

The boys looked to see that no one was coming back for the sleds and snatched them. Tony tied them together with his belt, and all the boys pushed, pulled, and maneuvered the bronze head of Teddy Wiggins on top.

Next, they tied the sleds to the bikes and took turns riding them, so Matt and Willy didn't have to do all the work of pulling the load. The boys also took turns covering up the head with their winter coats, each riding a mile without one, jumping off, and taking their coat back. This kept any suspicious drivers passing them along the way from knowing they had absconded with Carmel city property.

When they got home, they debated for a good ten minutes on returning the sleds to the hill, so the owners could have them back, but then they started playing Xbox and forgot.

They not only forgot the sleds, but they forgot the head of Mayor Teddy Wiggins. It sat through the winter, tucked away behind the small barn in Willy's backyard. It sat through the spring, as grass and weeds grew all around it. It wasn't until June that the boys remembered their stolen treasure.

~

Mayor Teddy Wiggins didn't take the news well the day after Cooper Langley's accident. "I want a driver to pick me up in five minutes. Take me to the roundabout."

Twenty minutes later, Teddy was at the scene. The director of public works met the mayor, the police chief, and Wiggins' chief of staff there. A crew was already trying to tidy things up.

"Most of the damage was to the statue itself," said the director of public works. "The boxwoods and the small evergreen we can replace."

Mayor Teddy asked, "Where's my head?"

The rest of the men looked around the roundabout. "It was here last night," the director responded.

Teddy was furious. "So where is it now?"

"My men assured me they put all the pieces back inside the roundabout."

The mayor took charge. "Fan out, all of you. I want that head."

The men spread out and searched the inside and outside of the roundabout. They looked for the head for thirty minutes, which is an eternity when you're dressed in a suit and tromping through snow.

They failed to find a head. "Sir, I know we've been looking all around, but there is a huge indentation next to the other pieces of the statue, lots of small footprints, and sled trails heading south out of the roundabout."

"What are you getting at?"

"I think some kids stole your head."

"Those little bastards. They have no right." Mayor Teddy pointed to his leather cap and shouted, "That's *my* head!"

He looked at the police chief. "Well, don't just stand there! Go get my head!" To his chief of staff, he said, "If they don't find my head, heads are going to roll!"

"It already has," whispered a member of the cleanup crew, which elicited laughs from his co-workers. Mayor Teddy stormed after the police chief.

The trail went dead as soon as it hit the pavement. The salt trucks had done their job, and the sun had come out after the storm. Despite the cold temperature, the snow and ice were melting fast on the road. But to indulge the mayor, the chief drove south out of the roundabout for a few miles, looking for any clues. None presented themselves, so he drove back to his office and ignored the mayor's calls the rest of the day.

2

EPISODE VII: STATUES

Teddy Wiggins hadn't had a serious challenger for the office of mayor in years. Despite complaints of cronyism and rampant government spending, the mayor remained popular enough to win every election. Nothing seemed to stick. Even in the early 2000s when he accidentally shot a mime, his popularity only grew.

This election year was no different. But even the seemingly invincible mayor of Carmel could have bouts of insecurity. *The public can be fickle*, Teddy thought. *What if they've grown tired of me*, he wondered? *Maybe I need to shoot another mime*? Luckily for the mimes of central Indiana, Teddy's opponent wasn't going to pose a serious electoral threat.

Stanley Widemon was an idealist from Chicago. Or more accurately, from Crown Point, Indiana. He told everyone he was from Chicago, because like most people from northwestern Indiana, they either tell people they're from Chicago or "the Region." It's a way for Hoosiers to glom onto America's Second City while pretending they're not actually Hoosiers.

When Stanley moved his financial planning business to Carmel, Indiana, in the late '90s, it wasn't his choice. He would have been quite content to live in the Region for the rest of his life. But Cynthia Glasser-Widemon was a force of nature and Stanley's wife. Cynthia insisted they move to Carmel, where she had grown up, to raise their children there.

Stanley reluctantly agreed and then set about trying to find a purpose beyond his chosen profession. He thought of starting a nonprofit which focused on financial literacy. But Cynthia pointed out that the Glassers (and by extension the Widemons) don't run charities, they serve on their boards.

Stanley looked for a homeless shelter whose board he could join but couldn't find one in Carmel. For that matter, in his first year living there, he had yet to see an actual homeless person.

Over time, he got involved with a variety of nonprofits, but none of the experiences was fulfilling. Finally, he stumbled onto his unlikely mission: politics. Stanley discovered that there were very few Democrats in office in the city of Carmel. Democrats in Hamilton County were so insignificant that nobody he knew could recall meeting one in person.

So, Stanley decided to run for city council as a Democrat. He lost. Then Stanley ran for school board, a nonpartisan race, but voters knew his background. He lost. Next, he ran for clerk. And shockingly, he won.

Three weeks before the election, Stanley's opponent, Larry Simmons, was arrested by Indianapolis police at a city park known to be frequented by prostitutes, both male and female. Stanley's opponent was found with one of each, a kilo of coke, and an empty White Castle Crave Case.

The prostitutes claimed they weren't paid for sex. They were paid to eat the White Castles off Larry's naked body. Larry claimed they were lying and that they had "drugged him and forced him to the park and were about to do God knows what to him and thank heavens the police came when they did!"

Everyone got minor slaps on the wrist, but even the Carmel political machine couldn't sweep this one under the rug. Too many memes were circulating on Twitter.

And this is how a Democrat became the city clerk of Carmel for the first time in thirty years. Stanley kept his idealism to enough of a low boil that he managed to get elected to a second term. But he wasn't content with the limited amount of change that he was making. Being a clerk meant he did mostly filing and record keeping. He needed to see Carmel move in what he felt was a progressive new direction.

Stanley believed the only way he could do this was

run for mayor. The jump from city clerk to mayor is a big one, though. Luckily Stanley caught another break. Claude Lestage, long time board member was struck by an out-of-town motorist who entered a roundabout in the wrong direction. Unable to perform his duties, an interim appointment to Claude's seat was necessary. The job was offered to Stanley Widemon. It was a chess move by Teddy. He thought Stanley would lose in the next election and it would allow him to appoint a Republican as city clerk in the meantime. All it really did was embolden Stanley.

Cynthia Glasser-Widemon wasn't keen on the idea of Stanley running for mayor at first. She felt this might put them at an awkward position with the people she routinely socialized with around town. Her social standing had already taken a hit when he ran all those times as a Democrat. But his seemingly cooperative tenure as clerk had returned her to the good graces of her social circle.

However, the more she thought about the power and prestige that came with being Mrs. Mayor, the more the idea became appealing. She had her own visions regarding roundabout art. Ideas that were far beyond what had been done to date by Mayor Teddy Wiggins and friends. She wanted something grand and iconic. Something that would be as well-known as the Statue of Liberty. And with Stanley as mayor, she could make it happen.

After weeks of secret deliberation, she approached

her husband as he ate his breakfast. The day before, she had had her hair cut and colored (auburn) in what her stylist described as the new power haircut (the blunt bob). She was already showered, dressed (navy power suit), and wearing five-inch heels. The heels themselves were a power move, despite the pain they caused. It gave her extra height as she stood over him.

This was a tactic she had perfected over the twenty years they had been married. Whenever she wanted to win an argument, she wore extra high heels and stood while he sat. She had an inch in height on him without the shoes. Additionally, he was marathon runner thin, while she (although fit) outweighed him by twenty pounds. The fact is, Cynthia intimidated her husband both physically and mentally.

Cynthia waited to begin until he had a large spoonful of grapefruit in his mouth. It's hard to say "no" right away with a mouthful of citrus pulp. He read the newspaper as he ate, so she stared through the bald spot on his thinning brown and grey hair.

"Stanley, I've been thinking about my roundabout statue idea."

He mumbled and chewed. Juice ran down to his chin.

She continued, "I've decided that you should allocate money for a statue in the roundabout at Carmel Drive and Third Avenue."

Stanley swallowed and replied, "There isn't a roundabout at that intersection."

"Of course not. I want you to put one there, then put up my statue."

"Why there?"

"Because, if you make it tall enough, you will be able to see it all the way down most of the Monon Trail and from the Palladium."

The Monon Trail is a walking/biking trail that was created over a decommissioned rail line. The Palladium is an opulent concert hall at Carmel's Center for the Performing Arts.

"Something that tall is going to cost a lot of money. I have plans to re-allocate roundabout art funds to financial literacy programs."

She leaned over the table, getting within a foot of his face. "In your second term, dear. In your second term. We agreed you would focus on one of my ideas in your first term. Never forget who your largest campaign contributor is likely to be."

He couldn't forget. She reminded him every day that her father, Basil Glasser III, would be making a significant contribution.

She stood back up so she could tower over him. He gulped. "I suppose we could find a way to accomplish that."

"That's better."

"But aren't we getting ahead of ourselves? We haven't even won the election. Let's focus on the campaign first."

"Right, right," she said without conviction. Cynthia

had plans that she couldn't get out of her mind. The election was a road bump. The statue was a calling.

In the weeks since she had the idea, she had sketched out different statues with different subjects. She didn't immediately land on her masterpiece. Some of the concepts in the running were Hillary Clinton, Madeline Albright, and Madam C.J. Walker.

Finally, she decided on the Greek goddess Diana. She created a Pinterest board of Greek statues. Unbeknownst to her husband, she even commissioned an artist to create an eighteen-inch-tall scale model. Little did she know that the two hundred dollars she spent on the statuette would become the downfall of her husband's campaign.

CHERYL THOMPSON and Marissa Davis were discussing politics over LaCroix and celery sticks. Both were craving the ice cream the boys were eating on Cheryl's enclosed back porch. Tony, Willy, Matt, and Devon devoured bowls of mint chocolate chip while they plotted their next move for the afternoon. For the most part they ignored the conversation in the other room. Until the subject of heathens came up.

"His wife is a heathen. I heard they do animal sacrifices and have orgies in their back yard," said Cheryl.

"I don't know about the animals," Marissa

responded, "but I did hear things got pretty R-rated in their back yard."

Since Stanley Widemon had dared to announce he would run for mayor, a wave of disinformation had washed over the city of Carmel. All sorts of wild rumors were being spread amongst the PTAs, HOAs, and CYOs. If the organization had at least three letters in its acronym, somebody was spreading dirt on either Stanley or his wife. None of it was actually true.

This claim, however unrealistic and unfounded, sparked the curiosity of the boys on the porch. It had been quiet for weeks in the Lakeshore Estates neighborhood and the boys were bored out of their minds. But things were looking up. They all knew where the Widemons lived. They even knew Hannah Widemon, daughter of Stanley and Cynthia. She often hung out with Tony's older sister. And up till now, had not given the slightest hint that her homelife included some of the things that were being said about her parents over LaCroix and celery.

The boys all filed off the back porch and sat down at an outdoor dining table under a blue and green umbrella. They were deeply curious and planned to keep an eye on the Widemon house for any sign of debauchery they could observe firsthand.

Willy scrolled social media for something they could use and discovered a campaign event was going to happen at the Widemon home. "Guys, they're going to have a fundraiser this Saturday night!"

"You heard what Mrs. Thompson said—orgies and animal sacrifice," Matt replied.

Tony asked, "Hey, doesn't Kevin Willis live right behind her house?"

"Yeah, I'm pretty sure he still lives there," said Willy.

Matt asked, "And didn't he used to have a tree house?"

"Let's go see if it's still there!"

The boys rode to Kevin's house. Kevin wasn't exactly in the inner circle, but not so far out that he was caught off guard when they all rode up. They managed to play it cool.

"Hey, Kevin, we're going riding around the lake today," Matt said. "Want to come with us?

"I don't know," he replied. "I was about to go play Xbox."

Willy said, "Tommy Hardin parks at the back of the Korean Methodist Church to make out with Cindy Fults every Wednesday afternoon at 4:15. If we hurry, we can get there before she takes her shirt off."

Kevin's eyes got wide. Matt sealed the deal by pointing out, "There aren't any boobs in Call of Duty."

"I'll get my bike."

Kevin was given a front row seat for the Tommy & Cindy matinee. The boys had discovered a short dirt path leading away from the main bike trail around the lake. This side path went behind a row of bushes that bordered the church parking lot. From there they could watch, but the young lovers couldn't see them.

The view only provided a top up scene. And usually, Cindy laid down on top of Tommy before she had her bra undone. But this was as close as any of the boys had been to the real thing and it became a standing appointment. Letting Kevin in on it took off weeks of work they would have needed to get him in a place to ask for a sleepover on the night of the Widemon's party.

After the young lovers sank too far down into the car to be seen, the boys went to work on Kevin.

"So, I bet you've seen wilder things than this from your next-door neighbors," Tony said.

"What do you mean?"

"The Widemons," said Matt. "Don't they have orgy parties in the backyard?"

"They have parties, but I've never seen anything going on."

Willy didn't buy it. "Come on, you've never watched from the tree house?"

"I didn't know there was anything to watch," Kevin replied.

Matt asked, "What about Hannah?"

"What about her?"

Matt continued, "Ever see her doing anything wild?"

"I saw her take off her sundress once."

Devon giggled. "Did you see anything?"

"Nah, she had on a swimsuit underneath."

"Cool," said Willy.

"So, how about you invite us over Saturday night,

and we all watch the party from the tree house," said Tony.

Kevin hesitated, but then agreed. "I guess."

Willy asked, "You got internet in the tree house?"

"Of course. Have a TV up there too."

"Awesome," said Willy. "We can play Xbox until the orgy starts."

Kevin asked, "What is an orgy exactly?"

They all looked around, not wanting to speak because none of them knew.

“Didn’t any of you Google it?” Kevin started to pull out his phone.

“No, ever since we all showed up at a strip club the same day our moms were protesting in the parking lot, our parents have been checking our search history,” said Tony.

Kevin slid his phone back in his pocket.

Matt took the lead, "It's when a bunch of people have sex."

Devon asked, "At the same time?"

"No, they go in order," Matt replied. "That's what the 'or' part of the word is."

Tony was skeptical. "Are you sure?"

Kevin was incredulous, "With each other? Like with everybody watching?"

"Of course not," Willy replied. "Who would do that?"

Matt answered, "I think they have a tent and people take turns going in."

"And then what happens?" Tony and Kevin said in unison.

Matt was shooting from the hip now. "You eat bacon-covered shrimp and celery until it's your turn."

Willy realized, "Hey, if they're in a tent, we're not going to see anything!"

'They don't do it in a tent," Matt answered. "I think they do it on a table."

Devon said, "I wouldn't want people watching me do it."

Willy responded, "But you're going to go into the tree house and watch *them*."

"That's different," said Devon. "They don't know I'm watching."

"People don't watch," said Matt. "While they're doing it on the table, everyone else has to play volleyball or look at the bonfire."

"Are you sure?" Tony and Kevin asked in unison again.

"Of course," Matt said. "Nobody is going to watch other people have sex."

Willy asked, "What are you talking about? Have you never heard of porn? What about that stripper we went to see?"

"This is different," Matt said. "People don't want to see the people who live next door having sex. They don't go to parties in their own neighborhood and watch the weird fat guy who lives in the cul-de-sac have sex with his wife."

In unison they all said, "Mr. Steiner."

"I guess you're right," Devon said.

"Orgy just means outside," Matt said. "People having sex outside and nobody watching."

"Except us up in the tree house," Tony and Kevin said, once again in unison.

"Right!"

THE BIG NIGHT FINALLY ARRIVED. The Widemons had invited fifty guests to the campaign cookout. Invitees included a virtual Who's Who of the Who's Not in Carmel—given that the usual A-list names found in the *Carmel Bugle* were all supporting Teddy Wiggins. No, these were the small business owners and corporals of industry who didn't get a notice from the in-crowd of city politics and power. With an outsider like Widemon running, maybe it was their turn.

The Widemons had an open bar, catered barbecue, and a DJ. The backyard was nearly a half-acre with a pool and covered patio. A covered tent held tables and a portable dance floor. Around the pool, high top tables and chairs were placed.

Most of the ladies wore sundresses and most of the men wore Tommy Bahama shirts. It was tasteful, well behaved, and anything but what the five boys in the tree house in the neighboring backyard expected.

The deluxe structure existed before Kevin's family

moved in, but he had convinced his parents to make major upgrades. This included electricity, a TV, an Xbox and a futon couch. The tree house spanned the distance between two large oaks and had a ten-by-twenty-foot interior. The walls were covered with posters of rap and punk artists, the actress Margot Robbie, and Spiderman. The plywood floors were littered with chip bags and cheese stick wrappers.

Willy asked, “Why hasn’t anyone had sex yet?”

Matt replied, “They aren’t drunk enough yet. It will happen, be patient. Have another taco.”

The boys had ordered Taco Bell via DoorDash. One of the upgrades Kevin had insisted on was a path from the front yard to the spot in the back where a rope ladder led up to the tree house. He then put a DoorDash sign in the yard with painted red arrows on the stone pavers that made up the path.

Earlier, Matt had noticed a second rope ladder on the other side that, if let out, would let someone from the Widemons' yard climb up.

He asked Kevin, “Why is this ladder here?”

“Don’t know,” he replied. “This tree house was here when we moved in. I’m guessing the kids who lived here before were friends with Hannah Widemon.”

Devon and Willy chewed on tacos and surveyed the collection of outsiders eating and drinking down below. They were scouts, just waiting to report the first sign of debauchery to the rest of the boys.

One particular outsider was Paul Langley. Things

had taken a turn for the worse since Paul's son Cooper had been arrested for DUI. Paul tried to sue the city for negligence. The arresting officer had submitted a dashcam video of Paul *not* taking his son to the hospital and a judge threw the case out before it even got started. A movement had been under way to get Langley disbarred for a variety of offenses against the profession. This latest one may have been the final nail in the coffin.

So, Paul was here to support anyone who could take down Mayor Teddy Wiggins. With an eye to his second career, he was looking for a political appointment once the new regime took office. Unfortunately for the attorney, he had two weaknesses: young women and alcohol. Both had sabotaged his aspirations in the past. It was about to happen again. With a bacon-wrapped shrimp in one hand and a bottle of Aztec Hillbilly IPA in the other, he set about annoying the Widemons' daughter.

Hannah Widemon was wearing a brand-new sundress, the only consolation she took from being forced to attend her parents' party. The dress was white with a crimson red floral pattern. If it had stopped there, the high school sophomore would have been fine. But her mother made her buy wedge shoes with straps in the same pattern and a wide brimmed sun hat with matching ribbon. Hannah felt she looked ridiculous. Her mom felt she looked like the perfect vision of a mayor's daughter.

Hannah was unaccustomed to wearing that high of

a heel, making it difficult for her to evade Paul Langley. "Have you ever considered a career in law," he asked.

"No sir, I haven't."

"You should," he said. "I think you're legal material."

Hannah picked up on the smarmy vibe he was sending. "I've always wanted to be a vet, but now that you mentioned it, workplace harassment law seems like an avenue I might explore."

The reference, like most things, went right over his head. "You can explore any avenue of the law you want." He put a hand on her shoulder. "Just another year and you'll be old enough. You should think about it."

She stepped back out of range and was about to deliver a snarky blow for women everywhere when a loud crash caused everyone to turn towards the fence. An eight-foot section had fallen inward, and black-clad protesters streamed in. Blacktifa had arrived.

Blacktifa was Carmel's answer to Black Lives Matter and Antifa. It was comprised of young people (all of whom were white) who were rebelling against their establishment parents. And since neither group could find enough recruits in Carmel, they decided to combine forces and save on bulk-ordered logo wear.

Their business savvy was far greater than their grasp of complex social issues, however. So, mostly they repeated whatever social commentary was trending on Instagram or Twitter, without any real depth of understanding what they were talking about.

They had even less understanding of which party cared about which issues. Which is how twenty of them came to be protesting in the Widemons' backyard against the very outsiders they purported to want to see elected. Cynthia Glasser-Widemon had unwittingly hired a member of Blacktifa to create the scale model of her proposed Diana statue. That member reported back to the group that the Widemons were going to erect a marble monument to income inequality as soon as Stanley Widemon was elected.

The Blacktifa members carried signs, shouted slogans, and grabbed ribs from the catering table. A vegan member of the group slapped the ribs out of the hands of the carnivorous members. They consoled themselves with mac and cheese.

Other members demanded that politicians stop raping the environment. One shouted that this party was too white. A dozen or so Black Widemon supporters shook their heads and ducked inside the house for cover. Several of Stanley's Hispanic supporters grabbed tiki torches out of the ground and began beating protesters like human piñatas.

Cynthia dialed 911 and demanded this riot be stopped. Stanley tried to negotiate. "Please, please," he said. "We will listen to your demands. Just leave us alone." They shouted over him.

Several guests within earshot thought Widemon sounded very un-mayoral and decided not to write checks at the end of the evening, should that part even happen. This was the beginning of the end for the Widemon for Mayor campaign.

One member of the Blacktifa group stood and surveyed the situation, unimpressed with either the party or the other activists. Noticing a tree house in the neighbor's yard overlooking the party, the protester started walking in that direction.

One large Blacktifa protester came charging towards Hannah. Paul tried to wrap his arms around her in an act of chivalry (his claim) or lechery (her interpretation). She responded with an elbow to Paul's ribs and a push into the pool. As quickly as she could in the annoying wedges, she made her way to the fence just below the tree house.

"Drop the ladder," she yelled.

The boys scrambled back against the wall of the tree house.

"Dammit, I know you're up there. Drop the ladder so I can get out of here."

Matt dropped the ladder over the side, and Hannah climbed up. Once inside she quickly pulled up the rope. Paul Langley was out of the pool now and wandering in their direction.

Hannah sat down and started undoing the straps on her shoes.

Matt asked, "What are you doing?"

"Taking off my shoes. What are you guys doing?"

Willy replied, "Waiting for the orgy?"

"The what?"

"The orgy! Isn't that what's going to happen next?" He looked back down. "After whatever this is?"

Kevin looked into Hannah's eyes for reassurance, "Is this how the orgy starts?"

Hannah regarded the middle-school boys assembled in the tree house. It smelled of sweaty boy funk. But even that was an upgrade over Paul Langley's cologne. "There's no orgy. They're just going to ask all these people to write checks to support my dad's campaign for mayor."

Willy was not convinced, "Then does the orgy start?"

"Who the hell told you guys there was going to be an orgy?"

The boys looked at each other but didn't say a word.

Then they heard a shout from outside.

"Hannah, why did you push me?" No response. "Hannah, can I come up there and dry off?"

She leaned out the tree house window and threw a shoe, hitting Langley in the face. "Guess not," he muttered and wandered off.

A few minutes later, another voice came from the Widemons' backyard. "Hey, let me up?"

Hannah and the boys looked down from the tree house. A bald androgynous person dressed in black with desperation in their eyes glared back at them. Hannah spoke first, "Who are you?"

"I'm Bulb."

"You're one of them. You ruined my parents' party."

Hannah didn't know whether to be angry or grateful. "Why should we let you up?"

"Because I'm *not* one of them."

Matt replied, "Yes you are, you're wearing the Blacktifa shirt."

"Okay, I came with them, but they're all morons. They're protesting the wrong candidate. I'm renouncing them."

Willy looked at Matt, "What does renouncing mean?"

Matt responded, "Means they're quitting that team."

"Huh," Willy replied.

They looked back down. Bulb pleaded, "Come on, please let me up. I just want to get out of here before the police arrive. Can't you hear the sirens?"

Hannah started to lower the ladder.

"No," the boys protested. Matt tried to grab her arm, but she shrugged it off.

"I think I owe it to Blacktifa, despite the destruction," she said. "You guys were watching. That pervy lawyer was hitting on me."

"Okay," Kevin said, "but not all of them. Just this one. The rest can find another way out."

Hannah agreed. It was his tree house after all. "Right. Just this one." She dropped the ladder and Bulb scurried up. They pulled up the ladder behind the ex-Blactifa member and tried not to call any more attention to themselves.

Bulb didn't leave immediately, choosing to watch

the police break up the protest. The boys didn't seem to mind. A few Blacktifa members bolted when they heard the sirens. The rest wanted to get arrested as an act of rebellion. The police paid no attention to the tree house until Paul wandered back to that part of the yard again.

"Hannah, you still up there?"

Hannah answered with another shoe to the face. Officer Lupinski took note of the response and walked over to the attorney. Paul slurred as he spoke, "Oh it's you." He pointed to the tree house, "She hit me."

"I didn't see anything," Lupinski lied. "Why don't you head back over to where the rest of the guests are giving their statements?"

He stood there for a moment and watched the drunk attorney stumble to where his fellow officers were interviewing the party guests. Without looking up the officer said, "I would guess it's going to take us a good hour before we check that tree house for anyone connected to this protest. I sure hope we don't find anybody up there."

He walked away and the kids sighed with relief. Hannah realized she was still wearing the stupid hat and tossed it out the window of the tree house. Another cop saw it and pointed over Officer Lupinski's shoulder, "Behind you in the tree house. There's more of them!"

Bulb, Hannah, and the boys of Lakeshore Estates scrambled out the other side of the tree house. Waiting at the base of the rope ladder was another DoorDash driver. This one had five jumbo cups from Smoothie

King. Each of the boys grabbed a cup and ran out of the Kevin's back yard. They didn't stop until they got to Willy's place. Instead of going inside, they hid behind the shed. Bulb and Hannah followed.

Bulb asked, "Why did you all run? You didn't do anything wrong."

"I didn't either," Hannah said. "But I've had enough from adults for one night.

Bulb sat down on a large mound. "So, you won't turn me in?"

Willy sipped on his Pineapple Surf Smoothie, "No, that was pretty awesome."

"Could you come break up a party my parents are throwing next week?" asked Devon.

By now it was getting dark, and it didn't appear that anyone had followed them to Willy's house. This unusual mix of young people sat and talked while the boys drank their smoothies and even shared with Hannah and the odd protester. As the night wore on, Bulb became uncomfortable and kept shifting. Finally, the ex-Blacktifa member took out a cell phone and turned on the flashlight app. The mound Bulb had been sitting on was the head of Teddy Wiggins. Bulb studied it and said, "Hey, how much do you want for this thing?"

~

City Council Member George Fillmore had been dreading this day for weeks. Fiona Pendersnipe had successfully managed to get a controversial item on the agenda for that evening's council meeting. Fiona was one of two rogue members on the board, the other being the sole Democrat, Stanley Widemon. Although Fiona ran as a Republican, Mayor Teddy Wiggins didn't trust her. She always wore sandals (even in the winter), dressed in flowery long dresses, and styled her hair in long grey pigtails. In short, she looked more like a professor of medieval poetry than a city councilperson in a conservative town like Carmel. (She in fact taught soldering at Ivy Tech Community College and owned a vegan bakery.)

Three weeks before, George had visited Fiona's bakery in search of scones for his daughter. He overheard the owner of the women's fashion store located next door talking with Fiona. He discovered that Katrina Moss had filed a complaint with the city about the lack of diversity among the statues that were scattered around the arts district. Between 2005 and 2012, Carmel spent $1.4 million on fifteen statues placed around the area known as the Arts & Design District.

The subjects were painted bronze by Seward Johnson, an artist from New Jersey who had never set foot in the state of Indiana. The statues were a source of pride (or ridicule) depending upon who you asked for comment. They included a woman walking her dog, a man reading the newspaper, a man holding a child on his shoulder and a policeman directing traffic. The statues could be found in the Arts District to this day.

But Katrina Moss wasn't satisfied. She felt they didn't represent a diverse community. In reality, they more accurately portrayed the city than most people were comfortable admitting. Carmel was 85 percent white as of the most recent census.

Demographics aside, Moss was determined to push the city into adding statues of people of color, members of the LGBTQ community (although many argued that one statue, a man reading the paper, if not gay, was certainly bi-curious), and the differently abled.

George left the shop without ordering, a mistake he suffered for dearly later when he came home to his wife and daughter empty-handed. He forgot the scones because he knew that the statue complaint would enrage the mayor, especially if Katrina gathered more support and Fiona agreed to champion her cause.

Indeed, after two weeks of hoping it would go away, Mayor Teddy called George to his office the night before the meeting. The mayor was still fuming that former council member John Myers had duped the city into putting up a monument to roadies at the 116th Street roundabout, and he wanted to obscure it with lots of shrubs and trees.

The agreement that the mayor had unwittingly signed stated that the city couldn't take down the Tomb of the Unknown Roadie, as it was named, for 10 years. However, there was nothing in the terms of the agreement that prevented the city from planting things around the statues. So, Mayor Wiggins got the bright idea to hide it with trees and other assorted nature. But nature costs money and that portion of the city's budget already had been allocated. The only wiggle room left for this fiscal year was a small discretionary line item in jeopardy of being reallocated to inclusive statues.

When George arrived at the mayor's office, Ms. Fitzsimmons informed him that his honor was on a call and to have a seat. Ms. Fitzsimmons looked like a schoolteacher from the fifties: grey hair in a bun, always in a dress, and sporting horn-rimmed glasses. She was in her late sixties but continued to work. Teddy thought it was simply to spite him. He was afraid of her. She knew too many of his secrets. George was afraid of her, too.

As George waited, he looked at himself in the reflection of the glass on a portrait of Teddy. The mayor had insisted it be hung opposite the waiting room couches and chairs, so people had to look at Teddy while they waited for Teddy.

George pushed around some thinning black hair that was out of place and checked his mustache for crumbs. His suit looked a little wrinkled; he hadn't managed to get it to the dry cleaners in a couple of weeks. He looked tired. He considered his reflection, then looked at the image of Mayor Teddy. He had been doing this man's bidding for twelve years, and it had worn him out. But he didn't know how to get off the treadmill.

"He'll see you now," announced the mayor's administrative assistant.

George entered Teddy's office and Teddy threw a copy of the *Carmel Bugle* across the room at him. George failed to catch it and the paper hit the door he had just closed. "Have you read the paper today?"

The weary man had a little spunk. He looked at the paper on the floor and then back at the mayor, "No, I'm not a speed reader." He picked the paper up, handed it back, and sat in a leather chair facing the mayor's desk.

Teddy Wiggins walked to the front of his desk and leaned against it. "Sorry about that," he said, temporarily calmed. "Have you heard what Fiona and this Moss lady are up to?

"Yes, and I've seen it's on the agenda for tomorrow."

"What the hell is an inclusive statue?

George replied, "You know, people of color, LGBT, etc. They want a trans person."

"Why the hell does she bring this up now? Those statues haven't been diverse for fifteen years."

"You know, BLM and all," George replied. "I think they call it being woke."

Teddy replied, "Woke?

"It means enlightened to social justice ..."

Teddy hit him again. "I know what woke means. I just don't like the word. You know I'm an open-minded

Republican, but the word 'woke" sounds about as retarded as ..."

George cut him off, "Mayor, we don't use that word anymore."

Mayor Wiggins looked around to see if anyone heard, even though they were alone in his office. "Let's just forget that last comment, okay George?" George nodded in agreement. "The point is the statues are fine the way they are. I need to publicly be *for* these inclusive statues, but I need you to torpedo this Moss woman when she brings it up at City Council."

"How did this get in the newspaper to begin with?"

Mayor Teddy fumed, "I wondered the same thing. Seems *the Carmel Bugle* isn't running a tight ship anymore. Hired some idealistic reporter fresh out of IU journalism school and she up and interviews Katrina Moss about the statues. I called the publisher and lit into him like you wouldn't believe. We can't have idealists here." By this point, Teddy was almost shouting. "Idealists are like cockroaches! I've got a town to run."

"City, sir. It's a city, not a town," George replied.

Teddy glared at George and raised the newspaper.

"Town, city. Whatever. I understand," George replied.

"Do you? I really hope so, because I want that money spent on trees, not trannies. Say, that's a good slogan. Maybe we can leak this to some Bible thumpers and get them stirred up to protest this Moss lady." He paused and looked at George, whose face looked like the mayor had just farted. "Of course, if you come through, we won't need that will we?"

George shook his head, "Sir, that's another word you can't say. You simply can't say the 't' word anymore. It's considered hate speech."

"Thumpers?"

"No, the other 't' word."

"Tranny?"

"That's the one," said George. "It's offensive and insensitive."

Teddy looked around again to ensure nobody had heard him. "Any chance you can type up a list of these words in a memo? There's a new banned word every week. I can't afford to get canceled, George. Like I said before, I've got a town to run."

"Certainly, sir." George considered his next statement carefully. "Back to the vote. You know it's not just up to me? Have you expressed your concern to other members of the council?"

"No, just you. Like I said, I can't be seen publicly to be *against* the statues, so I need you to whip the rest of them into shape. Lord knows if I say anything to Martha Bickmore-Welsh, she'll slip up and say I asked her to vote against it. Remember the Gas & Go vote?"

He did remember. Mayor Teddy leaned on all the council members to vote against a Gas & Go station. He wanted a Brickyard Mart three blocks away because it was on his route to the nursing home where his mother lived, and Brickyard had better donuts. After the vote, a reporter asked Martha Bickmore-Welsh why she voted against it and she (having been drinking red wine from a coffee thermos the entire meeting) told the press Teddy told her to. From that point on, Teddy always used George as his surrogate to get his wishes across to the board.

The next morning, George called Stanley Widemon to confirm his vote. Since Stanley was running for mayor against Teddy in the upcoming election, George was certain that he would support Fiona. Instead, Stanley threw a curveball at the bewildered councilman.

"I'm going to vote against."

"What?"

"Yeah, I've got a proposition for you. It can make you look good and keep that discretionary line item discretionary."

"I'm sorry, I meant to call Stanley Widemon."

"You are speaking to Stanley and I'm not putting you on."

"Okay, I'm listening."

"Instead of using that line item on inclusive statues this year, tell them that you're going to include triple that amount for a variety of inclusive statues *next year*. Say you're rejecting this little pittance this year because diversity is too important. Declare that we're going to make it the cornerstone of next year's budget. Then, everybody wins. The council looks woke. The mayor keeps his tree money."

"How did you know about the tree money?"

"Never mind. Do we have a deal?"

George was highly suspicious, but this sounded like a win-win. "Okay, but don't you try to double-cross me."

"Wouldn't think of it."

"Now, that I've done you a favor, I need one from you," said Stanley.

"Oh, here it comes."

"Hear me out. This is going to make both you and the mayor happy."

"Okay, what is it?"

"There's an intersection on the northwest side of the city scheduled to undergo transformation to a roundabout."

"So. That's literally all we do in this city."

"I know. I want you to get the mayor on board to postpone that one to next year and instead do the one at Carmel Drive and Third Street."

"Why?"

"I have my reasons. Look, the budget that has been allocated to the first one will more than cover the one I'm proposing, plus the artwork inside."

"But these things take planning, permits, studies and whatnot."

"It's already been done. This one is on the schedule; I just want you to bump it up a year. And for you to put the art in the roundabout that I choose."

"Why on earth would I do that? You must have something pretty solid to bargain with."

"I do. If the mayor agrees, I'll drop out of the race."

"Big deal. He's polling way ahead of you."

"But if I drop out a week before Election Day, nobody else has time to challenge him. I drop out now, who knows who might come out of the woodwork."

George thought about it. Bringing this deal on Stanley's behalf to the mayor would bring him a lot of favor down the road. And Stanley was right. Dropping out the week before would be a guaranteed win.

"Okay. I'll run it by the mayor. What do you have in mind for the center of that roundabout?"

3

EPISODE VII: THE RISE OF THE LEDERHOSEN MAFIA

Marci Emerald checked herself for ketchup stains on her Trippy Red T-shirt, then ordered her friend Bethany to take the picture. She gave a wry grin, held up the middle finger on both hands, and waited for Bethany to complete the task.

Bethany returned the iPhone to Marci and the social media influencer marveled at how good she looked. The sun was setting, and it cast the perfect glow on the back porch of her home in the Village of West Clay. In fact, the lighting was so good that the nineteen-year-old decided the picture didn't need any Instagram filters or manipulation. The picture was perfect. She was perfect. And her life would get back to being perfect soon, she was convinced.

"Screw them. Screw them all," she said. "I'm tagging CNN, HuffPost, and all the rest."

This was to be her last image on Instagram before going dark, she had decided. Her family attorney had urged that her previous post should be her last. It was a picture of her looking solemn in a $2,800 suit, navy with pinstripes, and an Oxford blouse. It was accessorized with pearl earrings and a pearl necklace. The shoes were $1,500 pumps from Nordstrom that Marci Emerald felt were boring, but the strappy heels she wanted to wear didn't convey the level of contrition her attorney felt was necessary given the circumstances. The picture was taken entering the prestigious law firm of Dunham and Thorn and was her family's idea of a final statement on the matter at hand.

But Marci Emerald was accustomed to getting the last word. If she had to sign off from social media for a while, then she was going out with a bang.

The reason for her lawyer-imposed social media silence was the legal scandal in which her mother and father had recently found themselves. Marci Emerald was the daughter of Shelly Sanders-Russo. Shelly, when she was Shelly Sanders, was the star of the 1980s hit show *Our Happy Family*. In the '90s, she married Mario Russo, the Italian race car driver. Eventually, when she stopped acting and he stopped racing, they settled in Carmel, so he could manage an Indy Car racing team. Shelly still did made-for-TV movies, but mostly she managed her daughter Marci Emerald's burgeoning career as an influencer.

Marci Emerald had four million Instagram followers, all of whom lived vicariously through the "virtual perfect life" she posted online. And upscale brands lined up to shower her with clothes, cosmetics, and accessories so that four million sheep with less than perfect lives could buy a piece of perfection. However, perfection has a shelf life. And it seems that Marci Emerald's expiration date was nearing sooner than it should for a nineteen-year-old.

It all started when a *Teen Vogue* reporter went to do an article on Marci Emerald and discovered that she was listed on the Stutz University website as a volleyball player. Unfortunately for Marci Emerald, the reporter actually played volleyball for crosstown rival University of Indianapolis and knew all the players on the Stutz team. When she asked the influencer questions a volleyball player should know, Marci was stumped.

It appeared that Marci Emerald, along with the help of her mother and father, faked a sports history to get her into Stutz University, the most prestigious private school in Indiana next to Notre Dame. The volleyball coach was implicated along with a company that arranges these sorts of things, and a national scandal was created.

Shelly Sanders-Russo vehemently denied all wrongdoing. Her attorney had instructed her and her husband to continue to deny wrongdoing from their yacht in the Mediterranean. Shelly Sanders-Russo felt this was a good plan as denial is bad for the complexion and should be warded off by sunshine and sea air.

Their attorney agreed to guide Marci Emerald in making a statement and wrapping things up in Indiana, while preparing her for the inevitable "gap year" that she would need to take from her studies. The companies that supplied Marci Emerald with all her freebies decided that other rich young girls with unattainable lives would be better vehicles to sell their wares and wished her the best.

So, Marci Emerald was mad at the world. Mad at her parents. Mad at her sponsors. And mad at the attorney. And this was her statement—to send a final Instagram post to the world—giving it the bird. The world, it seemed, was about to return the favor.

CYRIL MONROE MADE the front page of the *Indianapolis News*, the *Carmel Bugle*, and *USA Today*. He also has more than four million (as of this writing) views of "The Octoberfest Incident" on YouTube. He can't wait to watch it himself when he gets out of jail. The video also was picked up by CNN, Fox News, *The Daily Show* and both the Jimmys. MSNBC's *Politics Nation* planned to show it, but their expert panel got into such a shouting match over whose fault the incident was—Trump supporters, Bernie supporters, or the effects of climate change—that they ran out of time and were forced to go to commercial.

What Cyril did to attract such attention will live in

infamy in the hearts and minds of Carmel residents forever. He approached Mayor Teddy Wiggins at Octoberfest (or what passes for it in an Indiana suburb) and doused him with sewage water. Mayor Teddy's supporters were naturally appalled while his detractors secretly wished they had the gumption to do something so bold.

The mayor was enjoying a pretzel and talking with friends on that particular evening. Before him were three cups, whose emptiness he communicated repeatedly by irritated glances to his assistant, Jonathan. The assistant was uncomfortable with retrieving a fourth beer as it might lead to a fifth. The fifth beer is where several ill-considered policy proclamations had been made in the past, and the mayor's more influential donors had instructed Jonathan not to let the mayor get to the fifth beer again in public.

The mayor once agreed to consider a low-income housing project on the city's north side after a fifth, sixth, seventh and eighth beer one night at a local restaurant. He was dining with local nonprofit leaders and Jonathan wasn't there to monitor the proceedings. His other handlers weren't there to monitor the proceedings, either. So, after one too many proceedings, the mayor suddenly began to have a heart for the poor and downtrodden.

However, his handlers and city council stepped in to save the day. It seems there was a loophole in the Indiana law that addressed low-income housing for people with special needs. The loophole gave builders the right to choose any specific illness or disability and dedicate a percentage of a project towards that group. The project was completed by a local builder who bought the property for $10 from the city (which paid $2 million for it). In exchange, Cadby Construction LLC agreed to rent units to anyone with progeria at 75% below market rate. After twenty-four months, any units that didn't get claimed by sufferers of the disorder would revert to full price. This was all legal because of the loophole.

Carmel voters never bothered to investigate the disorder, or they would have known it only affects one in four million births and sufferers don't usually live past the age of thirteen. This gave the builders a good five-year cushion between the mortality rate and the actual age anyone could legally sign a lease. The developers got the land for next to nothing, had the state pay a substantial portion of the building costs in order to house people with special needs, and were in no danger of actually having to rent to anyone with that specific health issue.

Cadby Construction LLC made a pile of cash, some of which was earmarked for keeping the mayor and certain city councilpersons in office. Meanwhile, the mayor's handlers breathed a sigh of relief and vowed to keep a lid on their puppet's drinking in public. And the public carried on, secure in the knowledge that their community was generous and willing to step up to help the poor and disadvantaged.

But the handlers didn't have the power to fire Jonathan, at least not directly, while the mayor most certainly could and would if the next beer didn't arrive soon. So, with Teddy Wiggins being distracted with the compliments of the Tompkin family on how lovely the new abstract art was in the 136th Street roundabout, Jonathan snagged the mayor's keys and made his way to the beer vendor.

Unfortunately, this left no one to keep an eye out for Cyril. Seeing his opportunity, Monroe sauntered up in full lederhosen carrying a large stein in each hand. The mayor misread the man's intentions, thinking one of the beers was for him. As he reached for the stein in Cyril's left hand, the angry voter poured the one in his right on the mayor's head. The second stein followed, and Cyril began his protest speech:

"The residents of Orchard View didn't want to be annexed. Yet you annexed us anyway. We didn't want your water, but you forced us onto the city's water system. And now this is the water we must drink. There is sewage in our drinking water because your people hooked everything up incorrectly. So, you drink it Mr. Mayor. *You* drink it."

A delayed shriek came from the mouth of Ada Tompkin. She jumped up and distanced herself from Teddy as the smell explained the brown matter in the water that had just covered the mayor. She glared at Cyril, and said, "Well, I never!"

This was no exaggeration, as it was indeed the first time she had witnessed a poo-water baptism, and the whole thing made her sick. Then she turned her disgust on Teddy. "I told you not to bring those Orchard View degenerates to Carmel. Now look at what you've got. Poo all around you."

Jonathan returned in time to hear Mrs. Tompkin calling out for the police. Mr. Tompkin was too terrified to speak. He nervously watched everyone dressed in lederhosen, worried someone might approach him with beer steins. There might be more of these poo terrorists, and he wasn't taking any chances. Assessing the situation, Jonathan used his walkie-talkie to call for security.

The police arrested Cyril without incident, although he did continue to shout poo-related expletives at the mayor and repeat the phrase, "Death to tyrants!"

Not surprisingly, several people caught the incident on video, but most were after the fact. The two best versions went viral, one shot by Cyril's Libertarian nephew Nathan Bean and the other by the Tompkins' granddaughter. Mrs. Tompkin demanded her granddaughter delete the video, but Zoe Tompkin posted it on Snapchat immediately and lied to her grandmother that it was gone. Zoe Tompkin also drank her grandparents' beer in all the commotion and posted about that on Snapchat, too. Zoe was held in high regard for the rest of the semester at Carmel Middle School.

Nathan's version went on Reddit, YouTube, and Twitter. The video was viewed by a million people in less than twenty-four hours. He also set up a GoFundMe to help with his uncle's legal bills, raising over $100,000 for bail. But it was all for naught as the mayor convinced the judge to deny bail for the "death to tyrants" comment.

The following Monday, the deputy director of Carmel Utilities was fired, but not before he got a twenty-minute earful from the mayor about how poorly his team had messed up installing the new sewer and water system in Orchard View.

Then he turned his wrath upon the remaining utilities staff. Mayor Teddy insisted top priority be given to correcting the mistakes that had caused toilet water to come through kitchen faucets of various Orchard View residents.

"Today it was your boss. Next, I'll fire all of you if one more person pours poo on me, city council members, or anybody in city government," he shouted on his way out the door. Teddy was angry. Teddy was humiliated. But he understood that the voting public probably would sympathize with the people whose plumbing was askew.

Some days, Mayor Teddy Wiggins regretted annexing Orchard View, although he would never admit it. Orchard View is a small sliver of land between

Carmel and Indianapolis. The previously unincorporated neighborhood became a target of annexation in 2004 but fought back against the city for twelve years. Residents lost their final appeal in 2016 and within two years, the takeover was complete. However, lingering hostility remained and the recent move to force all the residents to pay $8,500 for the privilege of Carmel city water hadn't helped. And of course, the comedy of errors in executing the project made things worse. You can't keep poking people who just want to be left alone. Eventually, they are going to act out.

The second and most important result of the Octoberfest Incident (as the *Carmel Bugle* named it) was the formation of the Lederhosen Mafia. This fringe group of pranksters and ne'er-do-wells arose out of the frustration that they shared with Cyril. They, too, had been wronged by Carmel city government. They, too, had fought to be heard to no avail. And they, too, wanted to have a video go viral and be seen on late night talk shows. So, an initial group of six men, three women, and a gender-fluid person found each other on some backwater internet message board. Soon they were meeting regularly and planning and plotting all sorts of mischief. The most serious offense was the kidnapping of a socialite/social media influencer.

The person who refused to be gendered went by the singular name of Bulb. Bulb is bald and androgynous in appearance, usually dressed in all-black attire. Despite Bulb's eccentricities, Bulb had the apartment best suited for meetings and so the Lederhosen Mafia began plotting their shenanigans there.

The first order of business was to produce an equally viral-worthy stunt to pull at the upcoming Christkindlmarkt that took place from mid-November until Christmas Eve. It didn't give them much time to plan, but it was the only German-themed event on the calendar until the next October and given the name of their newly formed criminal enterprise, they thought they should take advantage of it.

THE FIRST MEETING at Bulb's apartment got off to a shaky start. Dave, a recent dropout of the University of Chicago, didn't like the idea of Bulb leading the group. He was still finding himself, having gone through an emo phase, a K-pop phase, and a two-week fascination with surf guitar. He was hoping the Lederhosen Mafia might be the place where his life made sense. It was also the place (at five-foot-ten and 230 pounds) he hoped to finally throw his weight around.

"Why are you named Bulb, anyway?" he asked. "Is that a reference to light bulb? You think you're brighter than all the rest of us?"

"I *am* smarter than all of you," Bulb replied. "But no, it's not a reference to illumination. It is acknowledging that like a tulip bulb, I"—Bulb looked all around the room for dramatic effect"—am buried in this place. But soon I will spring forth. Bulb is my transition name. I'm becoming."

Zoe Tompkin, the middle school girl who had a front-row seat at the Octoberfest incident (and who lied about her age to join the group) said, "Becoming what?"

"You're not prepared for that answer," Bulb replied. "But when I do, I won't dress in all black. I will be complete. And I will be glorious."

Dave smirked, "Well in the meantime, you've joined the Lederhosen Mafia."

"I lead the Lederhosen Mafia," Bulb replied.

"Then lead by conforming to the dress code."

"I'm a nonconformist."

Natasha, a twenty-three-year-old personal assistant, replied, "But you offered to host."

"I got caught up in the moment. Now I'm having second thoughts."

"Look, we're all nonconformists," said Raymond. He was tall with curly red hair, and despite his desire to wreak havoc in Carmel, was the peacemaker of the group. "But if we're going to be a *gang* of nonconformists, we sorta have to agree to some rules."

Bulb sighed. "Don't you see the irony here?"

Zoe looked around for cues from the others, not wanting to say something stupid that gave away her age. Not picking up on anything, she chose silence.

Dave replied, "Not so much."

"If nonconformists become an organized group,

they are conforming. How can we self-actualize if we are betraying our core values?"

Dave interjected, "Values? I thought we were about sticking it to the one-percenters with some wicked pranks. I didn't sign up for values."

Raymond offered, "Can't you just *self-actualize* with the whole androgyny thing you've got going on and *group* actualize with the costume?"

"Group actualize? That's not a thing," said Bulb. Looking up at the ceiling, "Why did I do this?"

Dave said, "You know I thought this club was going to be more Octoberfest German, not avant-garde German. This guy looks like that Mike Myers character on *Saturday Night Live*."

Zoe saw her chance. "Bulb has NO pronouns. You misgender Bulb when you refer to Bulb as a guy." Bulb nodded to Zoe for the support.

Raymond asked, "Sprockets?"

"No, I don't think his name was Sprockets," said Natasha.

Dave became irritated, "No, the sketch was called "Sprockets.' The character was named Dieter." He turned to Bulb, "I apologize for the ..." he stammered, "gender thing."

Bulb was suddenly excited. "You think I remind you of the Dieter character?"

"Yes," he replied, choosing his words carefully. "But in a good way."

"I've always admired nihilists. Almost became one,

but despite my commitment to atheism, I really like Christmas and so I couldn't commit to being an extreme pessimist twelve months out of the year."

Natasha was intrigued, "I wouldn't take you for a fan of Christmas."

"I find commercialism tedious but dressing up as Santa and ordering around elves gives me pleasure."

The entire room was staring at Bulb and a long uncomfortable pause fell over the room. Finally, Bulb said, "Was I conversing out loud just now?"

Dave shook his head yes.

"I will wear the lederhosen and we won't speak of these things again." Bulb glared at everyone in turn. "Understood?"

Dave nodded his head yes, again. The rest of the room mumbled their agreement and Bulb laid out the agenda for the rest of the meeting. It was agreed that when the Christkindlmarkt opened, they would burn down the Glühwein Pyramid. This was a traditional German wooden pyramid that Carmel made the centerpiece of the Christkindlmarkt.

That is until the second meeting of the Lederhosen Mafia, which also took place at Bulb's apartment. When the meeting came to order, Bulb announced, "There's going to be a change in plans."

Dave was irritated, "A what?"

"A change. We're not going to burn down the Glühwein Pyramid."

Zoe was disappointed. "Why not?"

Bulb replied, “We're going to kidnap Marci Emerald instead.”

Several members replied, “What?”

Raymond said, “I didn't sign up for kidnapping.”

“They won't know it's us.”

Dave replied, “They can see our faces! In case none of you have considered this, because believe me it's kept me up at night, these uniforms don't exactly hide our identity. I mean Antifa, they wear masks. We wear silly shorts. In the cold, mind you!"

Natasha stood next to Bulb, “Chill, it's going to be okay.”

Zoe asked, “What's going to be okay?”

“The kidnapping,” said Bulb. “She will be drugged, so she will never know it's us.”

Dave asked, “Shit! What is the matter with you? We could do hard time for a kidnapping.”

“Not Marci Emerald,” said Natasha. “People hate her now. She's an entitled bitch."

"A rich entitled bitch,” Raymond said. “The world doesn't miss kidnapped girls from the inner city. An influencer, people are going to look for.”

"Not this influencer,” said Bulb. “Are you kidding, after the college entrance scandal? Nobody is going to cry over this. We're going to be heroes. Besides, we have an inside person to help us pull it off.”

“Who?” Zoe asked.

“Me,” replied Natasha. “I told you all last week I was

a personal assistant. I just never told you who I worked for. I'm Marci Emerald's P.A."

Dave said, "I'm starting to warm up to this. Hear him out. Sorry, hear Bulb out."

"We spike her drink at Christkindlmarkt and then grab her in the parking garage. Her daddy has a parking spot reserved for her. Then we take her to our warehouse lair, make her use her phone to send all kinds of messages via Instagram. Then we drug her again, drop her off in a Starbucks somewhere and boom, we're in the clear."

Raymond shook his head and replied, "This is crazy." He did a double take, "Wait, we have a lair?"

Bulb replied, "Temporarily. I've got a space that was condemned by the city."

Raymond had questions but was too afraid to ask.

Zoe was feeling like one of the adults. "No, this could actually work."

"Don't tell me you're on board with this?" asked Raymond. "What about all the planning that went into the burning of the Glühwein Pyramid?"

Zoe was instrumental in coming up with the plan for burning down icon of the Christkindlmarkt. But it was more important to her to fit in and fool the grown-ups than to champion her own agenda. "I'm on board. We can always burn it down next year."

Dave added, "And, since the Christkindlmarkt lasts a month, that can be our backup plan if Marci falls through. I think we gotta go with Bulb on this one."

Bulb relished in winning over the person perceived to be the most difficult. The others would fall in line now. "I know we had a solid plan and that you were all working hard to put it in motion, but this will make us famous. This will make us global; the Glühwein Pyramid wouldn't have gone much farther than the local news."

"But doesn't she have an entourage? There are usually people all around her," said Raymond.

"Not as many as there used to be," said Natasha. "And I can help misdirect them."

Bulb said, "Are you all in?"

MARCI EMERALD ARRIVED at the Christkindlmarkt with only two members of her entourage in tow. Natasha was joined by Shayne, a semi-pro snowboarder who hung out with Marci Emerald when he was in town rather than his parents, who lived only two houses down from the influencer's family.

In a small purse, she carried her Cairn terrier, Hermes. Hermes was wearing a mini ugly Christmas sweater that matched the one Marci Emerald was wearing herself.

This is going to be easier than I imagined, Bulb thought. Natasha brought Marci the spiked Glühwein and within ten minutes, Marci was compliant and vulnerable to suggestion. Her personal assistant suggested that she send Shayne out on the ice rink to clear the view for her inevitable selfie. As soon as the picture was taken, the Lederhosen Mafia clipped Shayne on the way back to the ice rink exit. While he was down, Natasha distracted Marci with shiny lights, but she didn't forget all about her friend.

"Where's Shayne?"

Natasha replied, "He ditched us for some girls."

"That sketchy douche."

"I know, right?"

Marci Emerald said, "Let's go, everyone here is so basic."

"That sounds like a great idea."

They left the crowd and made their way to the parking garage. Marci Emerald was having increasing difficulty walking, and Natasha began to worry that she would have to carry her. But they arrived at the car just in time for the Lederhosen Mafia van to pull up. Without much of a struggle, Marci Emerald was pulled inside and off they went.

When they got to Bulb's warehouse, they took Marci Emerald to a small room with a chair and a spotlight above it. They sat the influencer down and tied her legs to the chair. Dave told her he was a photographer, and they were shooting a magazine spread for Kink perfume.

Marci Emerald asked, "Is that why you're tying me up?"

Natasha replied, "Yes, it's going to be sexy."

"Why am I wearing the same clothes and when are you going to do my makeup?"

Zoe produced a makeup kit, pretended to brush and powder the captive, closed the kit and left. Marci remained compliant.

"Where's the camera?"

Bulb arranged the cameras in place and ordered everyone to begin. Raymond stepped to Bulb's right with large cue cards. "Here are your lines," said Bulb.

Marci Emerald was confused, "I thought this was a photo shoot?"

"It is, but we're doing some video for TikTok, Instagram, etc.," Bulb answered, "You know, to get some buzz."

"Oh, right. I'm down. Let's do this."

"Okay, can you see the script from there?" Bulb asked.

"When I'm a bad girl, I wear Kink." She looked at Bulb. "Am I emphasizing the word bad or kink?"

"Bad, definitely bad."

The influencer giggled, "Riiiiight. I'm bad."

"Okay, do it again."

"When I'm a *bad* girl, I wear Kink."

"Great, now read the next card," Bulb directed.

Raymond held up the next card and Marci Emerald read aloud, "When I'm padding my resume, I wear Kink." She looked at Bulb again, "Is this a typo? That doesn't sound sexy."

"No, it's very sexy. Trust me."

"Okay, if you say so."

Bulb insisted, "Read the next line, please."

"When I'm letting someone take the SAT for me, I wear Kink."

She paused for a moment. "Hey, what the hell? That's not funny. You're not going to use that?" She started to get nervous. She looked around the room, but only Bulb and Raymond were clearly visible in the state she was in. "Hey where is Natasha? My agent or mom is usually at these things. Where is everybody?"

"Nobody is here." Bulb held up a riding crop and gave Marci a cold glare. "Let's continue. Read the next one."

Marci read it to herself. "No, I won't read that."

"You will do as you're told, Marci Emerald. We are about to make avant-garde protest art. Read Marci Emerald, read."

Suddenly, a background was rolled behind her. Marci Emerald turned to see the logo of the Lederhosen Mafia. Behind her, masked members of the group danced in authentic costumes as a traditional Bavarian folk song played through a wireless speaker.

The influencer refused to speak. Zoe handed Bulb her dog. Bulb held a gun to Hermes' head. The gun was fake, but Marci Emerald didn't know it. "Read or he dies."

Marci continued. "To all my followers. You are sheep. You are worthless. You disgust me. I have grown tired of your constant praise and worship. The Lederhosen Mafia offers you purpose. They offer you meaning. Put down the shackles of commercialism and celebrity culture. Embrace the chaos of the Lederhosen Mafia. They will not be stopped. Join us or die."

Bulb considered asking her to do it again. But since this went out on Facebook Live, there didn't seem to be much of a point. The damage was done, now they just needed to sit back and bask in the glory of their triumph.

Marci Emerald asked Bulb, “Did that really just happen or am I dreaming?”

Natasha joined them again, “You’re dreaming. Here, drink this.” They gave her another spiked Glühwein, and she was completely out in minutes. In hindsight, they wished they had waited because now they had to carry her.

The rest of the team left in the van while Natasha drove separately. Back at the Christkindlmarkt, the Lederhosen Mafia members woke Marci Emerald up and let her out on the sidewalk.

Natasha pulled up, screeched her tires for effect and attention, then yelled out, "There you are! You had me worried sick. You drank five Glühweins and went to the bathroom and never came back. Let's get you home."

Satisfied she had convinced the handful of witnesses, Natasha took Marci home and put her to bed. The next morning, everyone was in for a shock.

Bulb and the rest of the group were not experts in audio. So, the Lederhosen Mafia had no idea how the music and the spoken word performance would mix on the final product. When the video went out, all people could hear was the music. A few random words were audible, but Marci Emerald was so impaired that you couldn't even accurately read her lips. The world was left to wonder about her rant and were not so sure about her affiliation with this Lederhosen Mafia.

Marci Emerald's German Performance Art (as the video came to be known) got attention for the Lederhosen Mafia, but not in a good way. In the end, they were viewed as a performance art troupe and not terrorists. Marci Emerald's publicist spun it as "painkiller abuse and that she was getting the help she needed in a private rehab center."

In the end, nobody's brand was enhanced by the incident. They would both have to take things to another level.

WHEN THE NEWS of the avant-garde performance hit the alternative message boards, all sorts of oddballs lined up to join the Lederhosen Mafia. Bulb took a dim view of this. Inside, the anarchist was torn. Bulb craved attention. But now people wanted to be like Bulb. And Bulb was singular. At least that's what Bulb told Bulb's self.

Dave was basking in the attention, however. He saw this as validation for his years of being ostracized. Now he wanted to set up a membership site and upgrade their costumes. There was so much to do.

But first, he needed breakfast. He threw off the covers, got out of bed and immediately stumbled over a seafoam green guitar with two strings and a cracked fret board. It hadn't been played in months. He cursed, gained his balance and stomped up the stairs to the main floor kitchen. His mom had long since left for work, but two room-temperature blueberry muffins were waiting at the kitchen table.

He grabbed the muffins, a half-gallon jug of milk, and a paper towel to use as a napkin. Satisfied with his foraging, he stomped back down the stairs to the basement to eat his breakfast and work on Lederhosen-Mafia.com.

MEANWHILE, in an extended stay hotel just west of downtown Carmel, Reggie Klapper turned off his TV in disgust. Speaking out loud to no one in the room, he said, "Give me an NFL lineman with a DUI any day. I can't stand these entitled brats."

Reggie had been in the publicity game for years. But he had to admit the influencer era was wearing him down. He had dealt with spoiled starlets and divas, sure. But they were a different breed. The influencers were technology smart and humanity ignorant. They had a surface-level opinion about everything but a depth of knowledge about nothing.

Reggie was determined to see this crisis through and then fire the Russo family. He had spent the better part of four months living in a hotel trying to put out Russo family fires since the college entrance scandal broke. He stared down at his bare feet in the carpet and wished his toes were in the sand. He missed his home in L.A. He missed his girlfriend, although he was pretty sure she was cheating on him. He missed his kids, but not his ex-wife. He was 100 percent certain she *had* been cheating on him.

He stood, walked to the bathroom, and looked at himself in the mirror. In his mid-forties, his curly black hair had been invaded by grey to an alarming degree during the time he had been in Indiana. *Time to wrap this up and go home*, he thought. But how? How could he spin Marci's public image into something salvageable and then gracefully exit the contract with the Russos?

The Bavarian folk song from the video on every news channel was playing in his head. He cursed, then brushed his teeth. *I know this song is going to be in my head all week. Taunting me. It will be the soundtrack other publicity pros use to mock me at the next convention. I'll be a meme!* He cursed again.

And just as he was about to step into the shower, he had an epiphany. The music. The Lederhosen Mafia. Marci Emerald.

"I don't have to be a meme!" he shouted.

LATER THAT AFTERNOON, a reluctant Bulb entered the Monon Coffee Corner. The Lederhosen Mafia leader loved the smell of coffee, but only drank Chai lattes. After ordering, Bulb approached the only other customer in the place.

Reggie had taken a booth in the back and rose to his feet as Bulb approached. "I'm Reggie," he stuck out his hand.

"I'm Bulb."

"Thank you for meeting me, Bulb. Have a seat." He motioned towards the booth and sat. Although most people are a little unnerved by the presence and intensity of Bulb, Reggie was unfazed. He'd seen everything in this business. He didn't care what you were about, just how the meeting was going to further his agenda.

And today's agenda was kidnapping. It had occurred to him back at the hotel he could turn this whole thing in his favor and get Marci all the goodwill and fan sympathy back. He would have the Lederhosen Mafia kidnap her for real! Well, not for real in the sense of keeping her against her will. More of a disappearing from social media for five days, hiding her in a hotel with the lowest number of stars he could get her to agree to stay in (four) and paying the Lederhosen Mafia to play along.

But first, he had to convince Bulb. "I'm really happy you came. As I said on the phone, I think we can help each other out."

"I'm not sure how that's possible, considering the

bad publicity we gave your client," said Bulb. "But I'm listening."

"From my perspective, there is no such thing as *bad* publicity. If things go bad, mommy and daddy still pay me to spin them right. The only threat to my job is indifference. When the public no longer cares, I'm unemployed."

"You're greedy and cynical. And you're in danger of boring me. Get to the good part."

"That video you filmed with her didn't really move the needle. Sure, it got some views, and the news media is talking about it. Those things are good. But our focus groups have indicated that it doesn't make them like Marci Emerald any more or less. They're indifferent." He sat back and looked at Bulb. "And I'm guessing you're the sort of person who doesn't like indifference."

"You've already done focus groups?"

"This industry moves at the speed of now."

"But people are coming out of the woodwork to join us. I'd say it's just you that has the problem."

"That might be true to some extent. But I see you as someone who is destined for something big. And you've got a long way to go if you want to be a household name like Antifa or BLM."

Bulb sat quietly for a moment and considered Reggie's assessment. "So, what are you proposing?

"I want to hire you to kidnap Marci Emerald. Really kidnap her. Well, sort of."

"This is entrapment. I'm out of here." Bulb started to get up.

"No, wait. I don't want you to break the law, I just want you to record some ransom videos for her while I hide her away. Make the public think she is in trouble so they will forget about the school scandal. After five days or so, we have her pop up in a corn field with torn clothes and looking fashionably haggard and claim she escaped."

"We would still get arrested!"

"No, no," said Reggie. "You and I will make a joint statement claiming it was a rogue group acting on its own but claiming to be members of the Lederhosen Mafia. Marci Emerald claims she can't identify any of her kidnappers. We never actually give you any ransom. Everyone's in the clear."

"I'm not sure how this helps us."

"You get to do all kinds of interviews telling people about how you were vilified in the press, misunderstood, and what you're really about. I'll even help facilitate the TV interviews."

"And what else?"

"Cash. Up front. And more after. You get money to expand or buy more costumes or whatever." Reggie continued, "Speaking of costumes, why are you dressed in black?"

Bulb sized him up. "I'm Bulb. This is how Bulb presents."

"Right. Well, I'm sure you could use more black

apparel," Reggie was going full high-pressure salesman on Bulb. "Or whatever else you're into."

"I'm not into material possessions."

"And that's a lesson we all need to hear," he patronized Bulb. "Maybe you can use the money to expand your platform."

"I want to purchase a fully-functioning trebuchet."

"Is that the weird sex swing people are into these days?"

Bulb glared at him, disgusted by his ignorance. "It is a medieval weapon of war. It is a catapult of sorts. I will use it to fling art and feces upon the masses."

"Art and feces, huh? Do you need a special permit for something like that? Never mind. You know what, forget I asked. How much will it take for you to purchase your Trebu-whatchamacallit?"

"Trebuchet. Twenty-five thousand dollars ought to do it."

"Twenty-five? How big is this thing?"

"Two stories tall."

Although he had acted surprised by the amount, inside Reggie felt this was a bargain. The line item might stick out when he handed in his expense bill to the Russos, but in terms of bringing public sentiment back in Marci's favor, the cost was worth it. Hell, some companies paid more just to have a reality star tweet something.

4

EPISODE IX: EVERYONE IS A GENIUS AT SOMETHING

Two weeks after Bulb and Reggie forged an alliance, they executed the plan. At 2:00 a.m. on a Monday, they arrived at Marci Emerald's home in a black paneled van. Her parents were still denying any wrongdoing from the Mediterranean. Reggie went to the front door and rang the bell. Bulb went around back, put on black leather gloves, and smashed the sliding glass door with a black metal pipe.

More annoyed than startled, Marci Emerald hiccupped and asked, "What are you doing?"

Bulb replied, "It's time. Why aren't you ready?"

The influencer was lying on the couch in a bralette and running shorts. She was binge watching *The Real Housewives of Orange County* and eating hummus with her fingers. "What time is it?"

Bulb grabbed the remote and turned off the TV.

“Hey, I was watching that.”

"Reggie's been ringing the doorbell. Why didn't you get up and let him in?”

"Is it Monday?”

"Yes, it's Monday! Get off your ass, get dressed, and get your stuff.”

"You can't talk to me like that."

Bulb raised the pipe and glared at Marci Emerald. The influencer was both terrified and aroused. Nobody had ever dared challenge her before. Without any more protest, she licked her fingers, rose from the couch, placed the hummus on the coffee table, and adjusted her bralette. Bulb continued to hold the pipe.

Marci Emerald was perplexed and intrigued. Nobody had ever NOT had a reaction to her making chest adjustments. Bulb didn't even blink. The influencer hadn't been this confused since a late-night talk show host asked her to find Hong Kong on a map. She compliantly walked out of the room and towards the foyer.

Bulb instructed, "You get packed. I'll let Reggie in.”

Marci Emerald did as she was told but kept glancing back at Bulb as she made her way up the stairs.

Reggie was surprised when Bulb answered the door. "What the hell is going on," he shout-whispered.

"The debutante isn't ready.”

"What do you mean?"

"When I crashed through the window, she was

watching TV on the couch. She's neither dressed, nor packed."

"This is starting off well," Reggie replied.

"It will be fine, I threatened her with this," Bulb raised the pipe to Reggie, "and she seems to be getting with the program."

"Well, don't hit her. We need her to stay on board with this scheme."

Reggie and Bulb set about staging the home to look like a break-in and struggle. Ten minutes later, Marci Emerald finally descended from the second floor. Marci was wearing black shoes, black leggings, and a black long-sleeved shirt. It was unclear if Bulb took notice. She was also managing three suitcases, one with clothes sticking out. She pushed two of them down the stairs and they crashed to the bottom. "Can I get a little help here," she shouted.

Reggie jumped up and met her at the bottom of the stairs. "You are only going to be in hiding for three to five days tops. You don't need three suitcases."

"I've never been to Wawasee. How am I supposed to pack for a place I've never been to? I have to be ready for all climates."

"Wawasee is in Indiana! You're not even leaving the state."

"Oh," she replied and thought for a moment. "Well in that case, grab the small bag and leave the others."

"We can't leave them here at the foot of the stairs. It will look suspicious. Take them back to your room."

"Help me."

Reggie rolled his eyes. Marci Emerald looked from him to Bulb and back. "Maybe ..." She didn't know how to identify Bulb. "Umm, maybe your friend there could help?"

Bulb raised the pipe again.

"Maybe not," Marci Emerald said, answering her own question. Reggie helped her take the bags back upstairs. When they arrived in her bedroom, the influencer began tossing the contents of her luggage all over the room. When they were empty, she put the bags in the closet.

"You're not going to put any of it away?"

Marci Emerald looked around the room, "Nope. This looks more normal."

He accompanied her back downstairs and with no further complications, they left for northern Indiana.

Reggie Klapper had rented a posh Airbnb on Lake Wawasee to stash Marci for the kidnapping after convincing her it was more photogenic. He decided it was cheaper than having to pay off hotel employees to keep quiet as well. This was done using the shell company Felsham Holdings LLC, a catchall for activities he didn't want traced back to him or his clients. The lake is near Syracuse, Indiana, a little over two hours north of Carmel. Marci was mostly compliant until Bulb and Reggie left. She seemed disappointed that the two would not be sticking around and that the newly formed Kosciusko County

Chapter of the Lederhosen Mafia would be watching over her.

After dropping Bulb off, Reggie went home, showered, and tried to make himself look like a man who hadn't been up all night. He drove to Marci Emerald's home around 11:00 a.m. He attached his phone to a mini tripod and set it on the coffee table, next to the hummus. Then he recorded his reaction to reading the "ransom note" from the Lederhosen Mafia.

"My name is Reggie and I work for Marci Emerald and her family. I have terrible news to share. She has been kidnapped. I was told I couldn't talk to the police, but I could share it on Instagram. The Lederhosen Mafia has claimed responsibility. I've set up a GoFundMe page to help with the ransom. As you know, cruel people have tried to cancel Marci Emerald and she's lost many sponsors. She needs your help. Please give whatever you can."

He uploaded it with the hashtags: #FreeMarciEmerald, #JusticeForMarciEmerald, #LivingHerBestLife and #Sophistlete

Within minutes, a video was posted on Marci Emerald's Instagram account of the influencer tied to a chair, wearing a purple tie-dye bra top and leggings from Sophistlete, and listing the demands of her kidnappers.

"I will die in this cute ensemble from Sophistlete, on sale this week through Sunday, if my kidnappers don't receive $1 million, 12 dozen soft pretzels, and six cases of ... what's this word? She spoke to someone off camera.

A man's voice said, "Glühwein."

"What?"

The off-camera voice hissed, "It's pronounced Glue Vine!"

"That sounds disgusting."

"Back to the script, please."

"And six cases of Glue Vine. Details for delivery to come. They are serious."

The video ended there. By 11:30, it was trending. By noon, it was on CNN. But even though cable news and the world of Instagram were transfixed, the law enforcement community wasn't so sure. Top people at the FBI in Washington, D.C., decided they would let the Indiana office deal with it, if it turned out to be the hoax it appeared to be. Indiana's FBI office, after getting the call from Washington, wanted nothing to do with it and called the Carmel chief of police. The Carmel chief of police decided he didn't much care to be embarrassed by it either, and sent the New Guy, a.k.a. Officer David Lupinski.

Officer Lupinski arrived at Marci Emerald's home just after 1 p.m. The sales-y nature of the ransom video, along with the bizarre video from the Christkindlmarkt stunt, caused him to doubt whether an abduction actually had taken place.

As he approached the house, a gaggle of teenage girls blocked the driveway. They were holding signs that said, "Free Marci Emerald," "Justice for Marci Emerald," along with one sign depicting the influencer in chains (a photoshopped image) with the phrase "Soft no matter how hard life gets." It was an ad for Sophistlete, the athleisure brand that Marci Emerald previously endorsed. The person holding the sign made sure it appeared in the background of the Instagram photos the other girls were taking.

Lupinski was roundly booed as he made his way to the front door. How did they know she had been kidnapped? And how had they had time to organize? He smelled a rat.

He rang the doorbell and Reggie Klapper answered the door. "Can I help you?"

"I'm here about the kidnapping."

"Oh, right, right," Reggie said, as if he suddenly remembered the very thing that had been driving his day.

"Please follow me. I've been working from here since I found out. Want to see the ransom note?"

Lupinski asked, "Did you get it in the mail or at your office?"

"No, it was here when I arrived this morning to meet with Marci Emerald." He pointed to the sliding glass door, "Along with that."

Lupinski was incredulous, "This is a crime scene. Why didn't you call us first before going on Instagram?"

"Do you know who Marci Emerald is?"

Lupinski didn't care for the condescension, but said, "Enlighten me."

"She is an influencer. A celebrity. A social media

icon. She must continue to influence, or the kidnappers win."

Officer Lupinski longed to return to the Detroit police force in that moment. "Get out."

"What?"

"This is an active crime scene," the officer replied. "There may still be some uncontaminated evidence," he paused and glared at Reggie, "but I don't have much hope."

"Can I at least get my stuff?"

"We'll bring it out to you. For now, wait in the driveway with Marci Emerald's fan club. By the way, how did they get here so fast?"

"Instagram, Snapchat, you know. Influence."

Lupinski glared at Reggie. "You know, faking a kidnapping is a crime."

"I'm offended by the accusation."

"I'm offended by how stupid you think the rest of the world is."

"For the most part, they are."

Lupinski didn't have a response. The world was pretty stupid.

He walked Reggie to the front door, opened it and said, "Wait in the driveway or in your car. But don't leave until I give you the okay. After the crime scene unit gets here to do their thing, I'll want to interview you."

"Whatever you say, Officer."

By 4 p.m., the police had finished processing the scene, but the crowd was bigger and there were TV crews. The GoFundMe was up to $89,000 and Sophistlete was sold out of the tie-dye bra top and leggings combo Marci wore in the Airbnb video. The reinstatement clause in Marci Emerald's contract with the brand was activated. Despite cutting ties with her over the college admittance scandal, the old contract stated that if she ever posted an image or video that managed to sell out an underperforming product line, her contract would be instantly reinstated. The brand never thought a canceled influencer could pull that off.

Marci Emerald, despite her pitiful grasp of geography, knew a fashion dud when she saw it. And she knew that no matter how ugly, if she wore the dud in a well-choreographed crisis post, it would sell like crazy. And she knew she could invoke the reinstatement clause. Everyone is a genius at something.

Five days later, when the GoFundMe got to $500K, Reggie instructed the Lederhosen Mafia of Kosciusko County to drive Marci Emerald three hours south to Franklin County and release her in a wheat field. The influencer did a great job of selling her ignorance of where and who had held her captive.

As promised, Reggie did a joint press conference with Bulb to say that no members of the legit Lederhosen Mafia were involved but Bulb stressed their influence was powerful and all-encompassing and must be respected. Reggie also announced that the GoFundMe dollars raised would go to a charity that taught body positive messages to millennials with progeria.

The Carmel police were unable to prove the kidnapping was fake. But Lupinski vowed to keep an eye on Reggie, Marci Emerald, and the Lederhosen Mafia. And just west of downtown Carmel, Bulb rented a three-story warehouse, the tallest in the office park district. Soon after, large shipments of wood and a telephone pole arrived.

5

EPISODE X: ART & FECES

The roundabout at Third Street and Carmel Drive was complete. But as soon as it was re-opened to traffic, scaffolding was erected in the center and covered with tarps. Whatever was going up inside it, the city was keeping it a secret. And that secret was big, as the scaffolding kept getting higher and higher. The new roundabout and sculpture inside were the result of the secret Widemon-Filmore Treaty. As promised, Stanley had dropped out of the race in the final week and Cynthia got her statue.

The land occupying the northeast quadrant of the roundabout contained an office park that time had passed by. While the other three quadrants were shiny and new, this one looked dilapidated by comparison. Mayor Teddy Wiggins had put pressure on the owner to spruce it up, even threatening to take the property via eminent domain, but the landlord had kept Teddy at bay.

Only twenty percent of the office/warehouse space was occupied, and the owner lived three states away. His property manager had lots of excuses for the low occupancy and his boss usually believed him. In fact, the manager was growing weed in eight thousand square feet of warehouse space towards the back of the property and had no incentive to get nosy tenants in the empty offices near the front.

Jerry Padgett, the property manager, also was a sympathizer to the Lederhosen Mafia. And when the group approached him about using the part of the warehouse not claimed by his weed empire, he agreed. He never asked why they needed the tallest, widest warehouse space in the complex. Jerry should have known something was amiss, but he wasn't well-versed on medieval warfare and assumed that they were creating something obscene to embarrass the mayor. Thus, a two-story trebuchet came to be constructed within a block and a half of the roundabout. Striking distance.

During the weeks and months of construction, Bulb was illuminated by the progress. The FBI seemed to have forgotten about the kidnapping and the Lederhosen Mafia appeared to be coalescing under Bulb's leadership. They even stopped caring that Bulb never wore the costume. Day and night like demented Christmas elves, clad in traditional German costumes, the mafia crafted the trebuchet under the instructions of their black-clad leader.

Despite Bulb's typically stark aesthetic and attention to historical detail, Bulb did allow the mafia one luxury: carving traditional scenes from everyday German life into the rolling base of the trebuchet. It effectively made the base of the weapon look like a parade float.

In addition to the construction of the trebuchet, Bulb was busy executing the other facets of the plan. Bulb had the team order four hundred pounds of manure. Initially, this irritated Jerry until he realized that the smell would negate the odor of burning pot, which his own workers had begun consuming too regularly, cutting into both profits and productivity.

Bulb and Co. also managed to secure every kitsch piece of art from central Indiana thrift stores that the Lederhosen Mafia could lay hands on. For weeks, as soon as the Salvation Army or Goodwill put a cheesy painting or craft on the shelves, the Lederhosen Mafia would buy it up. And when you consider the missions of those two organizations, spite managed to help a lot of people in need that month.

WILLY LOOKED at Matt and said, "I'm bored."

"Me too," Tony replied.

"There's nothing to do," Matt agreed. He sat down

the controller for the Xbox One and looked around the basement. The four boys were camped out at Willy's place since there was no school on Labor Day. "Might as well be in school."

Tony threw a half-eaten bagel at Matt, which hit him in the forehead and landed in his Mountain Dew. "Take that back."

Willy laughed and ignored the buzzing on his phone, announcing an incoming text. Matt and Tony scuffled for a few minutes, finally knocking the Xbox off the coffee table. The TV screen went blank. This new development ended the scuffling and the basement entered Panic Mode: Level We Broke It. "We Broke It" is a level of alarm found in children who have destroyed something they truly love (Xbox) or something mom and dad truly love (a crystal vase, for example).

A flurry of activity commenced, which included the unplugging and re-plugging of wires, powering down, powering up, etc. Fortunately, the Xbox shook off its minor concussion and returned to normal functioning. The boys collapsed back onto the Dorito-dusted couch and breathed a collective sigh of relief.

Devon returned from the bathroom, having missed all the commotion. "What were you all yelling about?"

It would be minutes before Willy would check his phone. When he did, he couldn't believe his eyes. From an unknown number, the text read:

Today is the day. 2:00 p.m.at Carmel Drive & Third Street. Watch from outside the roundabout.

"Guys, I think we have something to do."

Matt asked, "What? Is your mom texting you to ask us to clean the garage or something?"

Tony sat up, "I'm out of here."

"No, no wait. Read this." He showed them the text.

Devon asked, "Who is that from?"

"I don't know," Willy replied.

Tony remembered, "Hey, remember that Bulb dude, chick, whatever?"

"Yeah," Matt answered.

"They said they were going to text Willy?"

"Yeah," Willy answered.

Tony replied, "When *IT* was going to happen."

Willy's eyes got wide. "It's happening!"

Matt shouted, "It's happening!"

The four boys scrambled out of the basement and got their bikes. Each texted another boy in the neighborhood to meet them at the roundabout at 2 p.m.

When the big day came, the Lederhosen Mafia had Zoe go undercover (meaning she wore civilian clothes instead of her lederhosen) to live-stream the festivities. This way, they could know the exact moment to fire. Bulb ordered the team to roll the trebuchet out to the parking lot. There were lines painted on the blacktop to help them position the weapon up for the perfect shot. A couple of test firings had been done in the middle of the night a few days earlier using weighted glow sticks.

Over at the roundabout, the mayor and other public figures gathered along with the good citizens of Carmel. The previous afternoon, Mayor Teddy went inside the tarp covering the structure to view the statue. After the Tomb of the Unknown Roadie incident the previous year, he wasn't pulling the tarp off anything unless he knew what was underneath.

The scaffolding had been scaled back to give a view of the statue, while still holding the tarp so it couldn't be seen. The workers had fashioned a ceremonial rope that Mayor Teddy could pull at the ceremony to reveal the statue. As he surveyed the statue and the landscaping around it, Teddy asked the director of public works, "Anything out of order? Are we good to proceed tomorrow?"

"Everything looks fine," the director replied. "The only odd thing was we found glow sticks scattered around the ground."

"Glow sticks?

"Yeah, we think kids must have snuck inside the tarp after dark. We can't see any graffiti or damage, so I wouldn't worry about it."

Teddy should have worried about it.

~

THE BOYS ROLLED up just in time for the start of the ceremony. They parked their bikes and Matt started to cross the road to the center of the roundabout. Willy grabbed his arm. “No, remember. The text said stay outside the roundabout."

"Right. I forgot.”

The boys sat down in the grass next to the road and waited for the fun to begin.

WHEN THE CROWD had assembled and 2 p.m. came, Mayor Teddy made some opening remarks and turned the mic over to Cynthia Widemon. Pleased as punch that her day had finally arrived, even if she wasn't Mrs. Mayor, the former councilman's wife was in her glory. She was dressed in a flowing white robe, identical to the one the crowd was about to see on the statue of Diana. Her speech rambled for fifteen minutes. When she was finished, the crowd wondered if what was inside could ever match the hype they had just endured.

Finally, the public works employees gave the signal and Mayor Teddy pulled down the tarp that covered Diana. She was brilliant and beautiful, forty-two feet (base included) of glimmering white marble. There were gasps as she was unveiled. Striking in her flowing robes and crown. A statement of fierce feminism.

"Diana," said Mayor Teddy. "Marvel in her power. Her purpose. And her ...”

A member of the audience jumped up, pointed over the mayor's shoulder, and cut him off, "Look out!"

A shriek rang out and the first row of guests scrambled for cover. Teddy looked back and up to see what they were looking at. That was a mistake.

He saw the dark ball approaching in the sky. It hit Diana in the chest, splattering manure and secondhand paintings all around her. Shrapnel fell in a 20-foot radius of her base, covering the mayor.

For several minutes, the dignitaries and members of the public surveyed the debris. The contents were beyond their comprehension. Art and feces. How had this just fallen from the sky? It took the mayor a while to overcome his shock and stop staring at the brown splatter on Diana's midsection.

New screams brought him back to the moment as someone shouted, "Incoming!"

The second ball of poop hit Diana just above the knees. The lower trajectory and impact caused a much wider area of collateral damage. Most of the guests had debris on their hair or clothing.

The police chief checked for serious injuries among the people who could possibly fire him, then set about to determine where the attack had originated. As he scanned the sky, he saw the third and final projectile. This one looked different, more fully formed. The projectile gleamed in the sun. It was the head of Mayor Teddy Wiggins.

Witnesses say it was a one in a million shot—something that could never be duplicated. The arc of this projectile was much higher than the first two and came down at less of an angle. Somehow, the open hollow end came down first, on top of the Diana statue.

When everyone felt it was safe to look up, they saw the marble body of Diana, covered in feces, topped by the bronze head of Mayor Teddy Wiggins. A collection of middle school boys rolled in the grass adjacent to the roundabout and laughed uncontrollably. Cynthia Widemon cried and furiously tried to get the poo stains out of her robe, which was neither flowing nor white any longer. Mayor Teddy screamed at the police chief to make an arrest.

Over at the warehouse, the Lederhosen Mafia laughed as they scrambled to make their getaways. Using Zoe's livestream as a guide, they had positioned the three volleys perfectly. And the final shot was more than they could have hoped for. This would be talked about and analyzed for years to come.

The last two members to leave were Bulb and Raymond. The latter poured gasoline around the base of the trebuchet. "Seems like such a waste," he lamented.

Bulb replied, "It has to happen. Great working with you."

He shook Bulb's hand. "Hope we can do it again sometime."

"Maybe someday." Something about Bulb's tone told Raymond this was goodbye for a long while, not just today.

Raymond lit a match and tossed it on the trebuchet. "Take care of yourself," he said over his shoulder as he walked to his truck.

Wailing sirens seemed to be getting closer. The leader of the Lederhosen Mafia walked over to a convertible VW Beetle, turned back, and took one last look at the warehouse as smoke rose into the September sky. Then, Bulb reached into the back seat, and pulled out a red DoorDash hoody and hat. Bulb put them on, jumped into the driver's seat and started the car. The sirens were close now. But as the police drove into the office/industrial complex, they paid no attention as a Volkswagen drove in the opposite direction with the view of a flaming trebuchet in the rearview mirror. Bulb had finally emerged from the ground.

NEVER MISS A BLOG POST

Sign up for my newsletter and get *72 Hours in Savannah* for FREE.

START READING

TALES FROM A ROUNDABOUT

VOLUME THREE

EPISODE 11: GUARD GOATS

Two middle school aged boys hid behind bushes and waited for the back door of Cobblestone Shoppes to open. Right on time, Jacob Saunders stepped out, propped the door with a cinder block and sat down on the sidewalk. He looked both ways and lit up a joint. He then looked at a bush across the parking lot and nodded. The recent college dropout leaned back against the wall and closed his eyes and soon drifted off to sleep.

Tony and Matt crept silently from behind the bushes, crossed the pavement of the access road behind the shops and slipped into the Cobblestone Shoppes' back door. There were two entries into the back of the retail center—a double door and an overhead one for deliveries. Both opened into a wide hallway with employee only access doors to the businesses inside.

Two doors in the hall were slightly opened. "I think it's the one on the right," said Matt.

"Are you sure? From what I remember of the front of the shopping center, it's the one on the left."

"I can't believe these doors only have numbers on them. Why don't they have the store names?"

"I don't know, but let's guess and get moving. Jacob said we only have five minutes."

“He’s not going to know if we’ve been in for five minutes or five hours.”

They both looked at the stoned salesclerk. Matt replied, “You’re probably right.”

Two weeks prior, the boys caught Jacob smoking weed during his break from his Game Den shift. In exchange for their silence, he promised them he would give them unlimited scratch--off tickets to Game Den’s latest prize giveaway. They quickly agreed as they were on a quest to secure the greatest treasure known to gamers: The GameBox Gold.

The GameBox Gold was aptly named–a 24-karat gold-plated gaming system. Supersoft Games had created the limited-edition console and was giving it away via scratch-off tickets found wherever video games are sold. The boys of Lakewood Estates wanted the GameBox Gold more than anything in the world. And they couldn’t believe their luck in having something on a young man who could deliver lots of opportunities to win one.

Jacob tipped them off when the scratch-off tickets arrived. Then he asked them to pick one of his shifts (Tuesday and Thursday afternoons) when he typically was alone. The plan was to lock the front door, put a sign up he was on break, then look the other way as the boys helped themselves to the scratch-offs. Plausible deniability was Jacob's weed-riddled logic.

"Okay, let's go left," said Matt.

Tony pushed the door further open and said, "You guessed right. Let's go." The boys rushed inside the back room of the game store.

"You check for extra tickets back here," said Matt. "I'll get the ones behind the counter."

Tony went into the manager's office and opened doors and boxes looking for tickets. Matt opened the employees-only door to the showroom floor and ran behind the counter. The boys had been inside the store numerous times, plus Jacob had shared where the tickets were kept. Just as Matt picked up the tickets under the counter, a pounding on the front door made him jump. It was an exasperated mom with two kids in tow. He ducked down and scurried back the way he came.

Just as he joined Tony, his accomplice found the rest of the tickets.

Tony held up a box with 100-count stacks of scratch-offs wrapped in cellophane. There were seven stacks inside. He slipped off his backpack and both boys put their tickets inside. They left the store and were about to go outside when Tony's curiosity got the best of him.

He whispered, "Did you hear that?"

"What?"

"Some kind of animal sound," Tony answered.

"So what? We gotta go."

"It will just take a second." He turned and stepped toward the open door on the right. The hallway smelled like a barnyard.

"What are you doing? You're going to get us caught."

"He's stoned out of his mind. I can hear him snoring. We're not going to get caught."

Before Matt could answer, Tony pushed the door open. This back room was laid out differently than the game store. There were several closed doors on either side of a long hallway. At the end, a tapestry hung from the ceiling and served as a divider from storefront to the back rooms. The boys could hear music and low-level chanting coming from the front. The hallway smelled of hay and patchouli. The first door on their right had a sign that said, "Do Not Open."

Tony turned the knob slowly, curious by what sounded like animals behind the door. As he did, a black nose poked out at knee level to the boy. The nose was followed by brown fur and eyes. It was a little goat. Overcome by the cuteness, Tony pushed the door wide open.

Nineteen goats were lined up on the opposite wall eating out of a long trough. In unison, they turned to see the two boys admiring their fellow captive. They belonged to Lydia Forrester and Nathaniel Schwump, the owners of Yoga Yurt. Nathaniel bought them so they could offer goat yoga classes. However, Lydia and Nathaniel lived in an apartment above the retail shops and didn't have a good place to keep twenty goats. Nathaniel said he was working on it. Lydia was running out of patience.

Noting the door was wide open, the goats decided to make an escape attempt. At once, they broke for the door. Seeing the stampede approaching, and realizing he had no way of stopping them, Matt came to his senses. "Shit! Run!"

Jacob Saunders woke up to see two boys and twenty goats running out the back door of Cobblestone Shoppes. He giggled and resolved to tip his dealer the next time he saw him. He closed his eyes and thought of little goats until Lydia shouted at him.

"Dammit! Did you leave the door open and let my goats loose?"

Jacob looked up at her. "No, the little goats were chasing some little dudes."

"What?" She smelled the weed. "Are you stoned?"

He giggled.

"Give me that," she said.

He switched the joint to his left hand and held it up and away from her. "No, this is mine."

"Give it! Or I'll tell your boss you get high on your breaks."

"Okay," he sulked. Jacob handed her the joint and she immediately took a hit and gave it back.

"I needed that," she said. "You better open up your store. Some lady keeps banging on the window."

"Are you going after your goats?"

She looked back at the building. "No, I'll get Nathaniel to do it."

Jacob giggled again.

"Is that funny?"

"Nathaniel kind of looks like a goat."

Lydia seized the joint without asking. She took a long hit, thought for a moment and said, "Yeah, he kinda does." She handed the joint back and returned to Yoga Yurt.

Meanwhile, Willy and Devon were waiting for Matt and Tony to arrive with the tickets. They were holding getaway bikes for their friends at the bottom of a long hill that descended to the parking lot of an apartment complex behind the shopping center.

Willy asked, "What's taking so long? You don't think they got caught, do you?"

Before Devon could answer, Willy shouted, "Look!"

At the top of the hill above them, their two friends emerged from the bushes. Along with them came twenty little goats.

"Look at that! Are they running from the goats or with them?"

"I can't tell," said Willy. "But we better get out of here."

They got on their bikes and watched over their shoulders for their two friends. Matt and Tony made it to the bottom of the hill and jumped on their waiting bikes. The goats kept running.

"Did they have guard goats?" asked Willy.

"No," Matt. "But the store next door did. They don't anymore."

Mayor Teddy Wiggins walked out of the Carmel city offices and across the front lawn to the Carmel City Gazebo. It was unseasonably warm for October and despite the red, orange, and yellow leaves everywhere, Teddy felt like it was spring. Why shouldn't it be, he thought? Isn't spring the time when love is in the air? And love was abundant in the air Teddy was breathing. Well, if not love, then lust that may soon turn into love.

Teddy was on the rebound. The former Mrs. Wiggins left him in a fragile state. She was the heir to the Hoosier Red Tomato fortune and the source of his campaign war chest when he first ran for mayor. But marriage, like tomatoes, can wither on the vine if not tended to. And neither Teddy nor Sheila Wiggins had tended to this marriage for quite some time.

Sheila left Teddy for Diego Sanchez, an alpaca rancher from Peru. In fact, Diego was THE alpaca rancher of Peru, having nearly cornered the market. And since they were in vogue in the United States, he had made a fortune selling alpacas to American farmers and hipsters who wanted to live a more rustic life. He was in the process of opening a Midwest alpaca ranch near Sheridan, Indiana, northwest of Carmel.

Sheila was not so fond of the rustic life and didn't venture near the alpacas after her first tour of Diego's Peruvian estate resulted in some unpleasant spitting—by the alpacas, not Sheila. These creatures are quite well known for their spitting. They spit for all sorts of reasons, including fear and anger. Pregnant females also spit at males when the male wants to get it on—a trait Sheila said she had thought of when she carried Teddy's children.

When Diego first took Sheila to meet the alpacas at his ranch in Lima, he was telling her all sorts of fascinating things about them. He had just finished telling her about their habit of spitting when their food source is threatened, when a particularly devious alpaca spit on Diego's new girlfriend. Sheila didn't care for the inference as she had recently lost twenty-five pounds and wouldn't dare eat whatever Diego's crew fed the alpacas. She daintily wiped the mess from her shirt and moved on with the tour.

Then Diego told her that female alpacas tend to go to the restroom in groups and that's probably why women do it, too. "It is evolutionary, I believe."

Under normal circumstances, Sheila would have

been offended by the chauvinistic nature of his statement as well as the scientifically incorrect idea that humans and alpacas may have shared some common evolutionary tree. But Diego had the sexiest Spanish accent, and everything that came out of his mouth made her swoon. So, she dismissed his nonsense with a giggle and put a playful hand on Diego's arm.

That's when she learned that alpacas would spit when feeling jealous. At least that's what Sheila decided. One of the creatures let fly with a gob of spit, grass, and intestinal bile that smelled like a moldy gym sock, which landed on her hand resting on Diego's arm. Sheila screamed and then dry heaved. Thankfully, she had skipped two meals in a row so she could fit into the jeans she was wearing for her new beau.

At this point, Diego strategically whisked her away to the house, far away from jealous animals and spit. He learned the hard way that keeping Sheila showered in the luxuries the alpacas provided was a better strategy than her having to shower after encountering them. No more tours of the farm.

Teddy had not been so lucky in the post-marriage years. Oh, there had been plenty of women. Power and money have been known to make women overlook a litany of issues that a man might present. And being mayor of Suburb Magazine's "Best Place to Live in America" bought Teddy a lot of overlooking. However, Teddy didn't have the staying power with these women that he imagined he might have, and he had been in a funk.

But now there was renewed hope. Gladys Snell was the senior accountant at the public works department and technically not a subordinate. So, it was completely within the bounds of HR rules that he could indeed ask her out, date her and even make out on the back stairs of the public works building as it was the only place that didn't have a camera.

Teddy and Gladys had managed to last an entire three weeks, so the mayor decided to take things to a new level. Today was the day that Teddy was going to ask Gladys on a trip to Spain. This would be their first extended getaway as a couple.

Teddy walked to the bottom steps of the gazebo. She was standing several steps up from the bottom, on the side not visible from the front of City Hall. Gladys was fifty-three—six years younger than Teddy—with curly auburn hair and a curvy figure.

Gladys wore a grey power suit and heels, taking her 5' height up a few inches. Teddy liked that he was taller than her even when she wore heels. Sheila had always looked down on him when she wore pumps. Which, Teddy lamented, was more frequent at the end of their marriage. Gladys also wore more makeup than Sheila, and Teddy liked that as well.

He climbed a few steps to her level, and they embraced. "You said you had a question for me?" she asked, referring to his earlier phone call that had set up this tryst.

"Gladys, my dear, would you like to accompany me on a trip to Spain? My treat. Private jet and the best hotel."

"Oh, Theodore. Do you mean it?"

"Yes dear. Two weeks from now," he said. "If you can manage it. We'll spend four days in Barcelona and another three in Mallorca."

"What will we do while we're there?"

"I've got us tickets to an opera and a dinner cruise on the Mediterranean."

"All this for me?"

"Yes, my dear."

"Let's do it," she replied.

"Oh, one thing though. If anyone asks, you're going to an international conference on municipal water safety."

"I thought this was a romantic getaway?"

"It is, but this way we can expense it to the city," he said. "It's legitimate business."

She gave him a naughty grin. "You mean you want to give me the business."

Teddy replied, "You're terrible. I like it."

Gladys switched from fantasy to reality. "But seriously, you're not spending your own money. You're billing it to the city. I don't know how I feel about that."

He put his hands on her butt. "I think you feel pretty good about it."

“Could we get in trouble?”

“Of course not. This is what you do when you're in government. You take trips. You charge them to the city. Everybody does it. Besides, there is a conference there. We go to the check-in, register, get the conference program and if God forbid somebody ever questions it, we download the recording of the sessions, and nobody is the wiser."

"Well okay, but it doesn't sound as sexy as when I thought you were spending all that money on me.”

“I am spending it on you,” he said. “It's just not technically my money.”

She scrunched up her nose a little while thinking it over. "Okay, Teddy, I'll go to Spain with you."

Teddy should have been as concerned as Gladys, but the horny mayor thought he was invincible. And horny and invincible are a dangerous combination.

PETER COMMON DIDN'T LIKE his neighbors. He didn't like Mrs. Simpkins, who routinely argued with her children in the front yard. He didn't like the Banks family whose St. Bernard consistently pooped on his lawn. He most certainly didn't like any of the people who lived on the left side of the cul-de-sac.

Lakewood Estates had an annex. The Heffelmeir family farm was the last holdout to sell to the developers and became a late add-on to the housing subdivision when it was being built in the early '80s. As such, it didn't connect to the rest of the neighborhood and there was only one way in and one way out.

When you enter the annex, there was a cul-de-sac on the left and another on the right of the tree-lined main road into the neighborhood. Over the years, people who would describe themselves as Democrats bought homes in the left cul-de-sac and Republicans settled on the right. Down the middle lane were a mix of both.

It was an electoral oddity that was studied by the Political Science Department at Indiana University and various mathematics professors from Rose-Hulman Institute of Technology. They found the mathematical probability of such a distribution of political leanings astronomical and suspected it to be the work of the realtor who originally sold the homes. The political science department sent grad students to the neighborhood each year to check on the status.

One year a Libertarian moved in, causing quite a stir. He bought the house where the two cul-de-sacs branched out from the main road. He was friendly but odd and many in the neighborhood thought he was a hermit. His house was the least well kept, but since the HOA had stopped collecting dues in 1992 and nobody had a clue what the bylaws were, neighbors were at a loss to know who could enforce them, or who to complain to if someone broke them. So mostly, they just complained to each other.

Peter Common most definitely didn’t like the Libertarian. One day while riding his bike, he noticed a strange creature in the back of the Libertarian's property. Peter nearly ran into the mailbox trying to reconcile what his brain was telling him his eyes had seen.

Although he missed the mailbox, Peter lost control of the bike and wrecked. He got up, dusted himself off, and marched up the driveway of the Libertarian's home. The pavement ran straight back to a chain link fence. The garage and house were to the left. The creature didn't move, despite the aggressively advancing neighbor. Peter stopped just short of the fence. The alpaca stared at Peter. He stared back. A voice came out of nowhere.

"What do you want?"

Peter looked around. Seeing nobody he looked back at the creature. "What did you say?"

"What do you want?"

He blinked and looked at the creature again. "I must have hit my head in the fall. I didn't even see your lips move."

"What are you on about?"

"You can talk?"

"Of course, I can talk," said the voice. "Now, what do you want?"

"I want to know what you are?"

"I'm a man, same as you."

Peter looked at himself, then back at the creature. "Same as me?"

"Yeah, same as you. Now what do you want?"

Peter felt a trickle of blood run down the side of his face. He wiped it, looked at the blood on his fingers and realized he had taken a harder spill than he imagined. "I think I want to lie down. I don't feel so good."

"All right then, piss off."

Peter Common walked down the driveway, picked up his bike and walked it home. Upon arrival, he took a double shot of scotch and went to bed. When he woke up, he called Big Bob Moore of Big Bob's Tires, the one neighbor he did speak to and told him about the talking creature.

"The Libertarian has a talking llama with a British accent. I saw it, that is, heard it with my own eyes. Ears. My own ears."

"You've been had," said Bob.

"What do you mean?"

"The Libertarian has an alpaca, not a llama."

"A what?"

"An alpaca," said Bob. "And it's illegal. Or it should be. He also has one of those camera systems with a speaker. You weren't talking to the alpaca; you were talking to the Libertarian."

"I'll kill him."

"The Libertarian or the alpaca?"

"Both."

"You should think about that before you do anything. I've got to get back to work. How's your tread looking? It's been a while since you got tires on that Lincoln."

"I don't need tires, Bob. I need that Libertarian to move out. It's unnatural voting third party. What the hell's wrong with people?"

"I don't know, Peter. I don't know."

From that point forward, Peter Common was the sworn enemy of the Libertarian. There was a constant back and forth of childish behavior and bad blood. One night Peter took it too far and tried to poison the alpaca. He was unsuccessful, but Gary—the alpaca was named Gary— had explosive diarrhea for a week.

In response, the Libertarian built a pen within the backyard fence that kept the alpaca from view. He also spread the word that the animal had indeed been murdered. Finally, he bought a decoy alpaca from a taxidermist in Kokomo. He paid extra for the stuffed animal to be rigged with red LED lights behind the eyes. On nights when Peter would ride his bike at dusk, the Libertarian would place the stuffed alpaca by the corner of the house and turn on his demon eye lights. The first time he saw it, Peter wet himself but managed to keep from wrecking his bike. Then on subsequent Halloweens, the Libertarian paid neighborhood teenagers to place the decoy outside Peter's home with eyes ablaze. The stuffed Ghost of Gary haunted Peter's dreams every October.

One rainy Halloween, Peter vowed to shoot at the

demon alpaca and emptied both barrels of a shotgun through his own front window. The teenagers who placed the decoy were unscathed, but decided they weren't getting paid enough to keep the tradition going and the demon alpaca wasn't seen in the neighborhood again for quite some time. Meanwhile, the real Gary was living his best life inside the secret pen in the Libertarian's back yard.

EPISODE 12: PETTY CRIMES

Tommy Malone didn't come from a bad family. His mother was an interior designer and his father worked for a pharmaceutical company. There was nothing about his upbringing that anyone on the outside could point to and say, "that's where it went wrong." But it did go wrong. Monumentally so.

Tommy was kicked out of Carmel High School with one semester to go in his senior year for dealing weed. Normally, the police look the other way for most low-level drug crimes, as the legal hassle from the well-heeled lawyers retained by Carmel parents simply wasn't worth it. The official policy was Confiscate and Castigate. Then send the kid home, usually in a car that costs more than the officers themselves make in a year.

But Tommy didn't make it easy for the cops or school administrators (who were hesitant to kick anyone out) to look the other way. That's because

Tommy *wanted* to get caught. On the 10th of February, just four days before Valentine's Day, the young man with brown curly hair wearing army fatigues pushed a wheelbarrow to the main student entrance to the school.

Inside were pink cellophane packages of weed and Hershey's Kisses, tied with red velvet ribbon. He began selling them for $3 each, or four for $10. He managed to sell half of his inventory before being arrested.

Tommy hated school and knew this was his only shot to get out. He tried tanking his grades, but his parents either arranged the teachers to allow him more time to retake tests and turn in homework, or they threatened the school with a lawsuit.

He once tried to assault a teacher between classes. But the logistics of a school with 5,000 kids in the hallways prevented the attack. When that many kids have to get to their next class in a short time, they move like salmon. He was strong, but skinny, weighing only 135 pounds. Each time he saw a teacher to take a swing at, the flow of kids moved him along before he could throw a punch. He managed to push a fellow student instead. But that kid promptly beat him up.

He decided selling weed at the main entrance was his best shot. And it worked. Too well in fact, since he went from school to incarceration.

In the juvenile detention center, he met Sean. Sean didn't have the advantages that Tommy had. His father was currently serving fifteen years for check fraud and armed robbery. His mother worked at Dollar General and sold meth to make ends meet. So, nobody could have faulted Sean for winding up like he did.

They struck up a friendship based on the consumption of weed and general misbehavior. One day, they were getting high at Sean's house and decided to rob some homes in Carmel.

Sean took a hit off the bong, leaned back on the couch, and pushed his long blond hair out of his eyes. He had an athletic build and looked like a Southern California surfer, displaced to the Midwest. "I need you to help me rob a house."

Tommy sang, "I wanna be adored ..."

"Turn down the music."

"I wanna, I wanna, I wanna be adored."

"Yeah, you and every chick on Instagram. The Stone Roses were ahead of their time but turn it down."

Tommy reluctantly complied, turning down the music via his phone that was connected via Bluetooth to a giant orange Bose speaker.

"What?"

"I said I need you to help me rob a house."

Tommy giggled, "Right. We going to steal some Doritos? You're all out."

"No, I'm serious. I want to rob a house. I need some fast cash. There's a new *Call of Duty* dropping next week and I'm almost out of weed."

"You're kidding, right?"

"No, I'm not. Besides, I need you to help because I'm not good at it."

"Not good at it. You mean you've done it before?"

"Sure, lots of times. It's just that sometimes I get high and forget why I'm there. I'm afraid I'm going to get caught. So, if you help me, I can go in straight and get high after."

"You want me to help you steal stuff and keep you from getting high while you're doing it? Is that what you're asking me?"

"Yes."

Very high and very hungry, Tommy replied, "Okay, I'm in."

Thus was born the most bizarre and inept crime duo in Carmel law enforcement history. They first broke into Sean's next-door neighbor's home and stole his Doritos–a crime so petty, nobody even noticed.

Because Sean had watched the dog the last time the neighbors were away, he knew that the camera on the back side of the house didn't work. He also knew that his mom had an emergency key to the neighbor's home. So, it wasn't really a break-in, more of an unauthorized visit. But they did steal the chips and a bowl of guacamole with a suspect expiration date. Tommy had the runs most of the next day but assumed it was from the case of cheap beer they also stole from the neighbor's garage fridge.

Next, they robbed a home in nearby Westfield. Sean's dealer, Rico, worked at the call center of the local fiber internet provider. He had worked his way up from sales to call-center quality control. Rico was the guy who listened in on calls, and told customer service reps what they did wrong, often chastising them for *not* upsetting the customer. His co-workers hated him.

By having access to the recordings, he knew when the customers, who agreed to their two-year unbreakable contract, would and would not be home for their installation. And since the company also offered home security services, he knew which ones indicated that they currently were without the safety net of 24-hour monitored security (plus noxious gas protection for only $129 per month).

Confident with the information they had on the homeowners, and agreeing to cut Rico in, Sean and Tommy broke into a four-bedroom ranch with a basement. Inside they found laptops, phones, and credit cards. The TVs they coveted but left in place, knowing they couldn't carry them out quickly and discreetly.

As it was their first break-in together, Tommy started to realize there were items not worth taking. The credit cards left a trail and stores have security cameras. A phone, if active, would be traceable by apps like Find My Phone, and old phones weren't worth much. Still, if they stole enough items, *Call of Duty* would be theirs. It never occurred to Tommy that he could simply buy his friend a copy of the game. There was too much bong resin clouding his judgement, despite the faith Sean had in him to be clear-minded during the burglaries.

So, during subsequent break-ins, they stole collectibles and dog crates. For the latter, they found a secondhand store in Tipton that paid cash, no questions asked. Then the snag came, as it usually does to such criminals. The weed house.

Sean hadn't paid enough attention to Rico's internet company recording for this particular home. Had he done so, he would have realized the homeowner lived in Florida and was renting the home to three IUPUI students. Those "students" were actually operating a meth lab upstairs and a hydroponic weed farm in the basement.

The guys broke in, got high and passed out. It was the best weed they had ever had. When the "students" came home, Sean and Tommy woke up and emptied their pockets to buy as much as they could. This being all their *Call of Duty* money, they needed a few big scores to get back on track. That's when they decided to hit Lakewood Estates.

Sean was a lousy student, lousy worker, and lousy driver. He excelled at few things that society might see as productive, but truly was gifted in getting into a house unseen. He knew how to avoid cameras, knew how to avoid being spotted by neighbors and such. But after the weed house, he was always stoned on the job.

And when he got high on this new weed, he took things from homes that no sane criminal would ever take. From the Robinsons, he took two laptops and all the spatulas. From the McKenzies, he took an antique pistol and a diaper bin filled with dirty diapers. From the Mendozas, he took jewelry and all the couch cushions. But the Baker house was the weirdest of all. He was so high, he forgot to take anything at all. Instead, he built a couch fort in the living room, put Mrs. Baker's makeup on her daughter's guinea pigs, and sponge painted a small powder room with some leftover interior acrylic he found in the garage. Upon discovering the break-in, Mrs. Baker insisted they move back to Boston as soon as was earthly possible.

Officer Lupinsky, who responded to the robbery call, had never seen a guinea pig with blue eye shadow and red lipstick. But then again, he had only been in Carmel for a short while. And Carmel was supposed to be crime free, so he wondered what it all meant. The crime was odd, and the people were odd (at least in his eyes), but there were fewer bullets flying around indiscriminately than in Detroit. He could live with odd, he told himself.

THE LAKEWOOD ESTATES break-ins didn't go so well for Tommy and Sean. The weed was too good and clouded their judgement. After one break-in, they woke up in the back of their van. Tommy was lying on the pillows from the robbery victim's bedroom while Sean was wearing the owner's bathrobe. They searched the van but found nothing of value to sell.

The next robbery didn't go much better. Again, they woke up in the van, with no memory of the actual heist. This time Sean was wearing rain boots, a kilt, and a sweater vest. Tommy was covered in silly string. They managed to steal some jewelry they could sell, but the take was low compared to the risks they were taking. Yet, they were undeterred.

House three yielded $2,000 in cash, and some electronics. But later at home when Sean went to use the restroom, he found the inside of his underwear coated in peanut butter. He was too afraid and embarrassed to ask Tommy how it might have happened.

A few days after the peanut butter incident, Sean and Tommy got a table at the outdoor party deck at Aztec Hillbilly Brewing Company. It was a great place to watch people, or more specifically female people. The bar was part of a redeveloped area south of the arts district called Midtown. It sat right next to the Monon Trail where a steady stream of bikers, joggers, and walkers walked past the day-drinking underachievers.

Tommy watched two women in their twenties go by in matching Sophislete brand leggings. "Do you think if we made enough from robbing houses, I could buy the kind of car that would impress a girl like that?"

"Why don't you just steal a car that would impress a girl like that?"

"Hmm. Don't you think that would be conspicuous

to steal a car in Carmel and then show up on a date with it?"

"Steal the car in Zionsville. Take the girl out in Carmel," Sean replied.

Tommy considered his friend's logic and killed the last gulp of his cream ale. "That could work." Their server arrived with two more beers. Tommy asked her, "I'm doing an informal survey. Can you answer a few questions?"

Inside her head, she thought, here comes a cheesy pick-up line and resisted the urge to roll her eyes. Playing along for the tip, she smiled and said, "Sure, but make it quick, I've got a lot of tables."

"Absolutely. I just need a quick yes or no for each of the following vehicles. Would you go out with a guy who drove a PT Cruiser?"

"No."

"White work van?"

She took a step back, "Creepy. No. Emphatically NO!"

"Black Mercedes convertible?"

She stepped closer again. "Yeah."

"Audi SUV?"

"Yes."

"Bentley?"

"What color?"

"Black."

She played with her hair. "Is that what you drive?"

"Not exactly."

“What do you drive, exactly?

“The white work van,” he replied.

“I gotta go.”

Tommy whispered to Sean as she walked away, “Did you see how she reacted when I mentioned a Bentley?”

Sean did see. "I want to start robbing houses on the west side of Carmel," he said.

"Why?"

Sean took a drink of his IPA. "Bigger houses. Bigger pay days."

"But we don't know that side of town like we know the east side,” Tommy replied. “We might get caught."

"I think it's worth the risk."

"But those houses are really expensive. And that means they have better security."

"Better security? You mean better than the kind that Rico’s employer sells?"

"Exactly. Way better. Hell, I bet some of them even have their own armed guards."

"No way."

"Yes way. I know of one that has a heliport,” said Tommy. “A place that has a helicopter is bound to have maids and servants *and* security."

"Okay, so we don't hit armed guard houses. But we have to mix it up a bit. We've robbed too many houses in the same general area. They’re going to be expecting us."

"Fine, but I want to do one more in the Lakewood Estates neighborhood. There's an annex."

"An anus?"

At that moment, the server returned with a plate of soft pretzels they had ordered earlier. She looked at both of them suspiciously. Sean noticed dipping sauce on her black Aztec Hillbilly Brewing T-shirt and tried to distract her. "You have mustard on your shirt."

She looked at herself, then took one of their napkins to wipe it off. Then she tied her T-shirt so her midsection was exposed, and the stain wasn't. "Part of the fun of this job. You need anything else?"

Staring at her flat stomach, they shook their heads without answering. "All right then. I will let you get back to the anus," she said.

Tommy shook his head and laughed as she walked away, “An annex, you idiot. It's an extra part of the neighborhood. It just doesn't connect to the rest. One street in, one street out."

Sean protested. "No, I'm not doing one of those. I told you that's dangerous if the cops are coming."

"But we can get to it by parking in the main part of Lakewood Estates and cutting through some woods. The getaway van will be in a completely different street with plenty of ways out."

"I like this idea."

~

WILLY'S HOUSE was the site of the scratch-off party a few days later. In all the boys had swiped 500 tickets for the

GameBox Gold contest. They were convinced one of these tickets was the winner.

Joining Willy were Matt, Tony, and Devon. Each boy sat around the kitchen table with a drink, a bag of chips, and a stack of 125 tickets. The room smelled like last night's lasagna and Doritos. They were just about to start when Matt said, "What are we going to scratch these off with?"

Willy asked, "What do you mean?"

"I'm just using my fingernails," Devon replied.

"That will take forever," said Matt. He turned to Willy. "Get some coins."

Willy seemed confused. "What?"

Tony said, "You know, coins! Real money."

"I don't have any real money," said Willy.

Matt put his hands on his hips, "Bullshit, you said your grandma gave you a hundred bucks for your birthday."

"She Venmoed it to me," Willy protested.

Now Tony seemed confused, "Your grandma uses Venmo?"

"You can't be serious," said Matt. "My grandma doesn't even know how to take a picture on her phone."

"Last week," Devon said rolling his eyes, "my grandpa face-timed me from the toilet."

Willy laughed. "Ha! At least you couldn't smell it."

"Of course I could. He was in our house. I could smell it and hear it."

Matt laughed. "Gross!"

Devon changed the subject back to grandmas. “No way your grandma Venmoed you money, Willy.”

"She's only seventeen years older than my mom,” he replied. “She's not as old as your grandmas." The boys pondered the math for a few moments.

"Anyway, you don't get coins for a birthday,” said Willy. “What is this, 1940?"

"Yeah, you get paper money for special occasions,” Matt agreed.

“And then you give it to your parents, and they put it in your Venmo."

Devon asked, "Yeah, they transfer money from their account to your Venmo in the amount of your gifts. But then what do *they* do with it? Do they deposit the cash or keep it?"

“*Your* parents buy meth with it,” said Tony. Devon punched him on the shoulder. He pretended it didn’t hurt. "I don't know, put it in the bank?"

Devon asked, "What if they don't?"

Willy started getting nervous, "What do you mean?"

"What if they stash it somewhere?" Devon continued.

Matt asked, "Like where?"

Tony answered, "In a safe or in a drawer somewhere."

Everyone looked at Willy. "How much did you say you got last Christmas?"

"Five hundred bucks.”

Devon replied, “Your grandma gave you $500?”

"No, *she* gave me $100."

Matt asked, "So, where did the rest of the money come from?"

"Sometimes my mom's boyfriends give me money too. All cash. It was a good year. My mom had a lot of boyfriends."

Devon pressed, "Did you spend it?"

"No, I gave all the cash to my mom, and she transferred the amount to my Venmo and Apple Pay," Willy answered. "Then I spent it."

Matt, knowing where Devon's mind was headed, got excited. "She might not have deposited it. It could still be here in the house."

"Exactly!" said Devon.

"No, guys. I know she put it in the bank."

"Did she," asked Matt. "Or did she tell you that?"

Tony tried to help Willy, "Guys, it's not our money, even if it was here."

Devon ignored him. "Come on, let's go look for it."

Willy protested, "Guys, no! We're supposed to be looking for coins, not cash."

Devon, the tallest and fastest, went first, dropping his bag of chips on the floor. Tony was reluctant but followed anyway. "Where do women hide money?"

Bringing up the rear, Matt answered, "My sister said in her bra."

Tony and Devon turned back at Matt, then looked at each other. All three boys' eyes got wide. Then they sprinted up the stairs.

"Guys, you're not looking in my mom's bras for cash." Willy's voice echoed in the empty kitchen. By the time the smallest boy in the group got upstairs, it looked like a tornado had ripped through his mother's bedroom. There were bras on the floor, bras on the bed, even one on the ceiling fan.

Willy asked, "How did that get up there?"

"That was there when we got here," Devon lied.

"Nuh, uh! Who did it?"

"True story," said Matt. All the boys nodded their heads in agreement.

Devon flicked a bra, and it landed on Tony's head. He tossed it at Matt and inspected his black wavy hair with his hands for any disturbance. "We've been through all the bras. No money," Devon said. "Where else would she hide money?"

Tony held up a sexy corset. "There's a whole other drawer filled with lingerie. Are you sure they hide them in bras?"

"Pretty sure," said Matt. "But go through that drawer anyway."

Willy desperately tried to rein them back in. "Guys, what good is cash going to do us? We need coins for the scratch-offs."

He had lost them. He gave up, went downstairs, and started heating up Hot Pockets while he waited for his friends to finish searching his mom's clothes for secret cash. As he suspected, the smell of the Hot Pockets brought them downstairs.

"Did you put everything away?"

Matt answered, "More or less." They had crammed everything back into the drawers, except for the bra on the ceiling fan.

"Any money?"

Tony answered, "No, it must all be in the bra she's wearing." The boys nodded in agreement.

"Damn, why didn't we think of that? Of course, she's not going to keep Willy's money in the house," Devon said. "She's got it between her..."

"Hey, that's my mom!"

The timer went off on the oven, ending the potential argument. Everyone forgot about bras, and money, and the reason they were there in the first place. After finishing the Hot Pockets, they finally returned to the tickets. Willy remembered his family had a junk drawer that had all kinds of random things in it. He used to get quarters for the gumball machine at the Mexican restaurant from it. Sure enough, Willy found three quarters and two dimes in the junk drawer in the mudroom. Armed with the coins, the boys commenced scratching.

The first four or five were exciting. Numbers ten through twenty still filled them with anticipation. Twenty through thirty found them still hopeful but tiring. By the fiftieth scratch-off, each boy was growing tired of the experience. By seventy-five, they were angry. On it went with no success. The last fifty gave them hand cramps.

Five hundred tickets scratched. Not one was a winner. How could this be? They left the spent tickets, scratch-off shrapnel, and dirty dishes in the kitchen and sulked their way to the basement.

Matt exclaimed, "We wasted a whole day on that!"

"We could have been arrested," said Tony. "And for what?"

"Not arrested. Jacob gave them to us. We didn't technically steal them," Devon replied.

"And what about the goats?" Tony asked. "Do you think they're okay?"

Willy kicked an abused coffee table. "Who cares about the goats? Some other kid is going to get the GameBox Gold!"

"How can we play with this piece of crap, knowing that somebody out there has the GameBox Gold?" Without thinking, Devon picked up the gaming console and threw it against the wall.

The four boys were filled with horror. Not only did they not have the winning ticket, but Willy's GameBox lay in pieces.

Matt grabbed Devon by the shoulders. "What the hell were you thinking?"

Willy couldn't form words.

Tony tried to calm Willy down. "It's okay. I've got a gift card for Game Den. We'll get Willy a used one, but Devon, you're paying me back." Devon nodded, knowing he had really screwed up. Tony continued, "Come on, let's ride to the game store!"

EPISODE 13: TEDDY GOES TO FLORIDA

The International Conference on Municipal Water Safety did not take place in Barcelona as Mayor Wiggins had anticipated. The day after Teddy invited Gladys to go with him, the CEO of the association, who also was a mayor in a small town in Spain, was indicted for accepting bribes from the host city. It also didn't help that he was arrested while playing backgammon in the nude with his personal assistant. A member of the police leaked a picture of the arrest to the local newspaper that in turn shared it with the AP with the naughty bits blocked out. The CEO's wife felt that nude board games went way beyond the assistant's job description and filed for divorce. She also granted a tell-all interview to a European tabloid that exposed all manner of her husband's shenanigans.

As the scandal widened, the date, length, and even the location of the event changed multiple times (each less exotic than the last), until the conference landed in St. Petersburg, Florida. With each change in location, the event became an even harder sell to Gladys. Teddy was persistent, however, and he convinced her that the "Continental Bay Front Hotel & Conference Center was a beautiful, upscale location only a few minutes' walk from the world-famous Dali Museum," a phrase he took right from the hotel's website.

In fact, the Continental was an aging shell of its former glory. And right next door, a fifty-story condo unit was going up. Much of the sidewalk and even the valet parking area were covered with scaffolding to protect guests from any falling construction debris. This less-than-romantic look was reflected by Gladys' first impression upon arriving.

"We're staying here?"

"Darling," Teddy replied. "It's just a little construction." He looked through the car windows at the fencing that surrounded the building. "I had no idea when I booked the trip. It's not like they're going to put pictures of the scaffolding on their website."

She crossed her arms and pouted. "You're the mayor of an important American city. You could have made inquiries."

"Once we get inside, I'm sure it won't be so bad."

Gladys glared at him. "This was supposed to be Barcelona."

"How is that my fault?"

Gladys didn't answer. Instead, she glared at Teddy

as he opened his door and handed his keys to the valet. Once inside, things looked more hopeful. The lobby was clean and bright. A beverage dispenser, filled with ice water and orange slices, was available for thirsty travelers. Teddy and Gladys sighed in relief. Then their Zen moment was interrupted by a woman wearing a white tennis outfit seated at a bench facing the front door. She was arguing on the phone with an airline. "What do you mean my luggage is in Orlando?"

To their left was the front desk. Beyond that the elevators and a glass wall that gave guests a view of the pool and workout room. Straight ahead was a large restaurant and concierge kiosk. Teddy and Gladys noticed a woman and her husband standing in the lobby discussing directions to a restaurant. He was in a T-shirt, shorts, and tennis shoes. She was in a summer dress with a high leg slit and strappy heels. Teddy looked at them and then down at his camp shirt and slacks. He felt overdressed. Gladys looked at her own shirt and jeans. She felt underdressed.

On a bench facing the check-in desk were two young people dressed all in black. One male, one female. The female's face couldn't be seen because she was looking down at her phone. When she looked up as Gladys passed, her face still couldn't be seen through her hair. Teddy's girlfriend shuddered and wondered what she had gotten herself into.

When they checked in, Gladys was incensed that there wasn't a VIP line for her and Teddy. Only one person was working behind the counter, Adam, a recent college grad who looked like he was seventeen. He was checking in a young woman whom he discovered went to his high school. Flirting ensued.

"You're Adam Dunn, right?"

He looked down, then smiled at her. "You read my name tag."

"No, I went to high school with you. I'm Regina Monroe. You were a year older, so you had no idea I existed."

"That's not true. I just didn't own enough black to hang out with you and your friends."

She started to get insulted. "Are you making fun of me?"

"No, it was a joke. I was into that scene too, but my parents were strict. I was jealous of you."

"I was jealous of you."

Gladys cleared her throat.

Regina gave her a "back off" look. She turned back to Adam, "I can't believe you work here. That's so cool."

Adam asked, "What are you in town for?"

"We're here for the Cult concert tomorrow night."

Gladys tsked and rolled her eyes. Regina shot her another glaring look.

"I wish I was going to that show. I love the Cult."

As the young woman's body seemed to relax while talking to Adam, her bag began to make clinking noises. Gladys knew there was liquor in the bag and prayed that this woman wouldn't be in the room next to her. This feeling only increased when Regina pointed to the two Goths at the bench to indicate they were staying with her. Teddy, on the other hand, heard the clinking bottles and wondered if the hotel bar was open yet.

"These are my friends from Carmel, Indiana," Regina said. "Raven and Bram, this is Adam. Adam, this is Raven and Bram." Adam waved.

Bram nodded, flipping his jet black bangs up and down. Raven waved, but didn't take her eyes off Teddy, who seemed familiar. Teddy couldn't tell if she was looking at him, with all that hair. But he avoided eye contact with everyone just in case.

If Teddy was worried about being recognized, his companion surely wasn't. Gladys stepped up closer to the counter to the right of Regina and tapped her nails on the Formica. "Look, can you have the reunion later? I need to get to my room."

"What is your deal lady?"

Adam sensed these two were about to explode on each other and went into bomb diffusion mode.

"Regina here is your room key. Let's catch up later." Turning to Gladys, Ma'am I can help you now. What name is your reservation under?"

Regina held back for the sake of Adam. But she had a huge crush on him in high school and all those feelings had come back the moment she entered the lobby and saw him behind the counter. This time she would have him. And no impatient old lady was going to get in her way. As she walked away, she muttered under her breath, "entitled bitch."

Without missing a beat, Gladys responded under breath, "pagan hag."

Oh, it's on, thought Regina to herself. *I'll get her before the weekend is over.*

After that, check-in went smoothly and Teddy escorted Gladys to the fourth floor. Gladys was relieved to see no sign of the Goths when she got off the elevator and walked down the hall.

Once inside their room, Teddy tried to get romantic, but Gladys rebuffed him. "Not yet. I need a pee and a drink."

"Should I order room service?"

"No, let's go down to the bar," she replied.

Teddy winced, believing the presence of liquor only steps away from the bed increased his odds exponentially. But drinks are drinks. And drinks could lighten the mood and make her forget the less-than-ideal surroundings. And that could get him right back up to the room for his social agenda.

"To the bar it is. I'll let you use the restroom first."

Gladys took her toiletry bag into the restroom and closed the door. Teddy started unpacking the suits he would wear at the conference. When she emerged from the bathroom, Gladys said, "That toilet is a little weak. It flushed but didn't seem to have much power."

Teddy, wanting to show off his handyman skills, said, "I'll give it a look while I'm in there." He shut the door and suddenly felt compelled by his colon to have a more significant moment in the bathroom than he intended. When he was done, the toilet wouldn't flush.

The mayor panicked. He pulled off the tank lid. Fiddling with the mechanisms, he looked around for a plunger and cursed mightily under his breath. After ten minutes, he heard, "Are you all right in there?"

The mayor emerged defeated. "We have to move."

"What?"

"We can't stay in a room with a broken toilet. We're going back down and asking for another room."

Gladys started to push her way in. "Nonsense, maybe I can fix it."

"No, no." He held up his hands. "Don't go in there."

"I need my toiletry bag."

"I'll get it." He turned and reached for the bag. Gladys pushed inside. "Oh Theodore! That's awful."

She left him alone in the bathroom and sat on the bed. Gladys said nothing as Teddy repacked his suitcase and they returned to the lobby. Adam greeted them warmly. "Is everything okay?"

"We're going to need another room. The toilet doesn't work in room 412."

"My apologies. Let me see what I can find." Adam upgraded them to a suite on the 13th floor.

This softened Gladys' stance on the state of her romantic getaway, but it wouldn't be until later in the evening that she succumbed to Teddy's advances. And even that didn't go as planned. As they were leaving for dinner, they were spotted by the Goths, who were staying in the suite across from them. Regina decided to get some payback for interrupting her chat with Adam and called him.

"Front desk, this is Adam. How may I help you?"

"It's me, Regina. I wanted to know if you could help me pull a prank."

"What do you have in mind?"

Regina told him what she had in mind.

"Are you crazy? You could get me fired."

Regina told Adam what depraved thing she had in mind for him if he helped.

Adam was speechless.

"Adam, are you still there?"

"Yeah, I was just trying to figure out if that was physically possible."

"Trust me, it is. I did it with the drummer for the Psychedelic Furs and he's taller than you."

Adam was silent again.

"Still with me, Adam?"

"Yeah, I don't know. I need this job."

"Oh, and I'm 100 percent sure I can get an extra ticket to the Cult tomorrow night."

"And you'll still do the thing with the ..." He looked up and there were new guests at check-in. "Right, Ms. Monroe. I'll send someone up with the key right away." Click. "Are you checking in?"

While Teddy and Gladys were away, the Goths hid a Bluetooth speaker in their room. Once they returned, the Goths waited for them to have enough time to get in bed and start fooling around. That's when the unlucky lovers got introduced to the guitar intro to *Love Removal Machine* by the Cult. The mood was killed immediately and the two frantically tried to find the source of the music. Regina selected *Spiritwalker* next. By the time the song finished, the neighbors on either side were pounding on the walls and calling the front desk.

Teddy eventually found the speaker but couldn't figure out how to turn it off. Regina skipped the song to *Lil' Devil.*

"Turn it off, Teddy."

"I can't! I've hit every button."

"Who listens to this filth. Throw it out the window."

"I can't. I might hit someone down at the pool."

"Teddy, this vacation is about over."

"Right. Out the window." He slid the patio door open and threw it out (just as Regina skipped to the song *Rain*), being careful not to watch it drop and risk being spotted.

Below, an unrelated group of Goths in for the concert (who only visit the pool at night) heard the ruckus and looked up. A blue JBL speaker playing *Rain* landed safely in the boxwoods next to the pool. They cheered and sang along, "Here comes the rain ..."

Back on the 13th floor, Teddy was trying to console Gladys. “I bet it was that goth whore.”

The aforementioned goth whore had her door cracked across the hall so she could hear the meltdown more clearly. She and her friends laughed as Gladys tore into Teddy, the hotel, The Cult, and the goths.

"That guy looked like our mayor," said Raven.

"Nah, I think the mayor is taller," Bram replied.

"You're probably right."

Regina said, "Quiet, she's yelling again." Regina realized that Gladys was screaming at Adam and felt bad about it.

However, she sent her two traveling companions down to the pool and had Adam come to her room. There she made good on her obscene promise to Adam, and he wasn't even the least bit upset about neglecting the front desk and being fired the next day.

When the conference was over, Teddy and Gladys left St. Petersburg and drove to Longboat Key for an additional four days of sun, sand, and sex. Unfortunately, for Teddy, there was much more of the first two and less of the third than he would have liked.

On day one, Teddy had planned for an afternoon romp after lunch. They had spent the morning on the beach and had made their way to Starfish Grill to try their world-famous blackened grouper sandwich. While there, they were recognized by two different families from Carmel. One of the wives asked for a selfie with the mayor and her family. He reluctantly agreed and they took the picture with Starfish Grill in the background. The other Carmel wife had been in an eighteen-month long Instagram competition with the first woman. She had her family selfie taken with the pier and the pelicans in the background.

For the rest of lunch, the two women monitored their Instagram feeds for likes on their own and the other's photos. As one pulled ahead in coveted affirmations from people she didn't even like, she looked up and smirked at the other. Meanwhile, Teddy hoped that they wouldn't take any pictures of his traveling companion, so he had plausible deniability. The stress didn't go to his head. It took a southernly route and impaired amorous pursuits for the rest of the afternoon. He rallied that evening and they went to sleep satisfied.

On day two, their afternoon love fest was about to start when the family from hell arrived at the pool below their balcony. Two moms, already intoxicated, carried cocktails down to the beach while leaving their four kids to run amok at the pool. The oldest boy walked right up to the pool rules sign and shouted, "Let's break ALL of these rules."

Say what you want about today's youth, these kids were thorough and detailed in their breaking of the rules. And they did it like a punk rock concert with decibels at jet engine levels. They ran, they dove, they brought food and drink into the pool. They didn't just bring glass onto the pool deck; they threw juice glasses from their mom's balcony. One boy covered himself in sand, then dove in without showering. Every rule. Gleefully broken. Teddy and Gladys decided to forego their lovemaking and go for a walk.

Day three was more of the same with the kids, but the evenings were quieter, and they were able to have some fun. However, things got dicey on checkout day. On the way to the airport, their flight got canceled. Unable to find a suitable alternative that day, they got a hotel room at the airport and a next-day flight. They started drinking in one of the Tampa Airport bars. Drinking led to the munchies and Gladys spied a Starbucks not far from the bar.

"I want a lemon loaf."

"A what?"

"A lemon loaf from Starbucks. Pay our tab and let's go get one."

Teddy should have suggested the chicken wings or hummus. Any of the appetizers at the bar would have saved him from what happened next. Gladys dragged the half-drunk mayor to Starbucks and five minutes later they emerged with two lemon loaves. Another five minutes and they were up in their room.

Their curtains were completely open. A driving rain had started, and visibility was only at about a hundred yards. Normally, you could see the tram from terminal to terminal, the runway, and the stadium where the Tampa Bay Buccaneers played football.

One thing Teddy loved about Gladys was she tended to get horny after booze and/or dessert. So, he wasn't entirely shocked when she got a wicked idea. "Take off all your clothes."

Teddy liked where this was going and complied. "Okay. Now what?"

"Get on the bed." Teddy obeyed and watched as Gladys unwrapped herself and the lemon loaf. "Open wide."

Teddy's eyes widened as she crawled onto the bed with him, broke off a piece of lemon loaf and rubbed the icing on his chest. Then she handfed him what remained. Neither one realized the rain had stopped the moment she undressed, and the sun had burst through the clouds.

Visible now, but unnoticed by the lovebirds, was the tram from Terminal Three. On board, a Peruvian alpaca rancher with a camera shot pictures in rapid succession. When he was done, he looked at his female traveling companion and said, "Sheila, I think I just captured two people having sex in the hotel."

Sheila shook her head in disgust. "With the windows open? What kind of depraved people would do that at an airport hotel? Nobody I know, that's for sure."

But she did know somebody that depraved. And it would be far more disgusting than she imagined.

~

In the lead-up to the primary election, Peter

Common called the campaign offices of the Republican party where he had considerable pull. He believed he had a way to hit the Libertarian right where it hurts.

"Hamilton County Republican Party, Sherrie Grandstaff speaking."

"Who's in charge of signs this year?" Peter asked without saying hello.

"I can schedule a sign delivery for you. Which candidate were you wanting to support?"

"All of them."

"Why that's very generous of you. Who am I speaking to?"

"Peter Common. I want them delivered tomorrow. Can you handle that?"

"Why yes Mr. Common. And I'll let Mayor Wiggins know you called. Would you like these at your home, business, or both."

Peter gave her the address of the Libertarian. "Remember, tomorrow."

Mrs. Simpkins, whom Peter despised but this week had been more than useful, tipped him off that the Libertarian was in the hospital for a heart procedure and returning home in a few days. Common wanted him to return home to see all the political signs. Maybe it would give him a heart attack, he thought. Common knew that Libertarians don't believe in publicly-funded primaries. They believe the parties should pick the candidates via their own member-funded conventions.

When the Libertarian returned home, he didn't

have a heart attack. But he knew who had filled his lawn with political signs. And he immediately went to work devising a plan to get him back.

To enact his revenge, he hired a local twenty-something to generate photoshopped images of Peter Common and his wife in compromising positions in public around Carmel. It might have worked had he not hired a perpetually-high young man who robbed houses.

They met at Starbucks. "I've got a job for you," The Libertarian said to Sean.

The Libertarian, being pro-marijuana legalization, didn't mind that Sean partook. But since he reeked of weed as they sat down, he wondered if the young man was smoking so much that he might be incapable of carrying out the mission. The Libertarian was right to be concerned. Just before the meeting, Sean had partaken of a few edibles (in the form of brownies) and smoked on the way for good measure.

"My sources tell me you're good with social media, hacking, and Photoshop."

"Yeah, I'm not bad."

"Are you currently employed in tech or graphic design?"

"No, me and my buddy rob houses." The Libertarian gave him a startled look. Sean paused. "I mean I'm currently in the used home goods market." He giggled.

"Never mind. Doesn't matter. What I need is

someone to Photoshop some pictures of a guy having sex with his wife in public and to post them on social media. If you can put it on either of their Facebook accounts, that's even better."

"Why do you want to do that?"

"Revenge, why else? Can you handle it? And can you make it look realistic?"

"Yeah, yeah. I can do it." Sean asked, "How much are you offering?"

"Will $500 cover it?"

Sean was expecting $50, so this was beyond his wildest dreams. *I can stop robbing houses to pay for Call of Duty,* he thought. "Sure, dude, that will cover it."

The Libertarian took out a file and gave it to Sean. Inside were photos of the Commons, their social media profiles, and their address. "Anything else you need?"

"No, that will do it. Just to recap, you want pictures of this guy's wife having sex with you in public. Then post them all over the internet."

"No. Pictures of *him* and his wife. Not me."

"But how does him having sex with his own wife give you revenge?"

"Because the pictures will be of them having sex in public! This will make the people of Carmel think he's some kind of pervert."

Sean asked, "What does this guy do for a living? I don't want to prank a cop or a judge. Somebody who could make my life hell."

"Don't worry, he's not in law enforcement. He sells halftime and timeout entertainment supplies."

"He sells what?"

"You ever go to a Pacers game and see the cheerleaders shooting T-shirts out of a gun?"

"Yeah."

"He sells those."

"The T-shirts?"

"No, the gun."

“Oh. Okay. I guess I can do it." He thought for a moment. "It might make him a star, though. You know people have sex in public all the time and put it on TikTok?"

"What's TikTok?"

"It's a video app. I thought since you knew about Photoshop and Facebook, you would know about TikTok."

"I have a life."

"Yeah, right. You're paying me to make fake dirty pictures." The Libertarian started to turn red, and Sean sensed his $500 evaporating. "But I'm sure you've got a good reason, so let's do this.”

The Libertarian eyed him quietly for an awkward moment. “How soon can you pull this off?”

“I can do it in the next couple of days.”

“Great. I’ll Venmo you the money as soon as I see the images online.”

Sean thought, *He knows about Venmo. But not TikTok. Weird.*

~

FIFTEEN MINUTES LATER, the Lakewood boys arrived at Cobblestone Shops. As they passed the yoga store next to Game Den, they noticed a sign that said, "Goat yoga classes temporarily cancelled."

When they walked into Game Den, the store manager held up his hands. “Oh, no. All of you, out.”

Tony asked, “But why?”

The twenty-something store manager brushed greasy black hair out of his eyes and pointed behind the counter, “Look at the poster.”

And there it was: Tony and Matt’s faces screen-captured from the store video surveillance. “Banned for life” in all caps was below their pictures. “And their friends, too.”

"I'm not going to call the cops, or even press charges for what happened the other day. Jacob confessed to letting you in to get the GameBox Gold tickets,” said the manager. “But none of you can come in here ever again."

They left the store dejected.

Willy asked, "What do we do now?"

Matt thought about the question. "Maybe we take this as a lesson?"

Tony replied, "You sound like my dad."

"Yeah, but this time the dad voice in my brain is right," said Matt. "We deserve this."

Devon asked, "So, now what do we do?"

They sat on the curb and watched cars come and go. Nobody spoke for a good ten minutes. Finally, Matt broke the silence. "Anybody still have a wiffle ball bat?"

"I think I do," said Tony.

Matt asked, "Any bases?"

Tony said, "There are some my sister uses for softball practice."

"Let's go play wiffle ball at Willy's," said Matt.

Devon protested, "Wiffle ball? Outside?"

Willy responded, "What else are we going to do?"

"Uh, play GameBox at Tony's," Devon answered. "It's only Willy's console that got destroyed."

Willy reminded him, "Yeah, by you!"

Matt said, "It doesn't seem right. If Willy can't play at his house, none of us should. It serves us right."

Devon answered, "Okay, I'll play wiffle ball if you stop sounding like every dad in the neighborhood."

"Deal."

Tony asked, "Should we invite more guys?"

Devon asked, "Why?"

"There's only four of us," said Tony. "It's no fun playing two on two."

"Okay, we'll get the wiffle ball stuff and the bases," Matt said. "You two go round up more people."

And for the first time in many years, a wiffle ball game

was organized in Lakewood Estates. Moms and dads did doubletakes on their way home from work. Nostalgic parents even stopped to see a few innings. A retired baseball coach watched with tears in his eyes. And nearly every dinner in the neighborhood was served late that night.

A WEEK LATER, Sean was getting high with Tommy and planning their next break-in when he got a series of angry texts. *When am I going to see those pictures?*

It was the Libertarian, looking for his revenge.

Tommy asked, "Why is your phone blowing up?"

"Ah, some guy is paying me to Photoshop someone having sex and then post it to social media."

"Screw him. Let's load the bong again."

"He says he's not paying me until I do it."

"Paying you? How much?"

"Five hundred dollars," Sean replied.

"What? Get your laptop out and get to hacking. We could stop robbing houses!"

"That's what I thought when I took the job," Sean said.

"Then why haven't you done it yet?"

"I don't know. It's been a busy last few days. Robbing stuff. Getting high. I've got a lot on my plate."

"But if we had $500, we wouldn't have anything on our plates. Except getting high and playing *Call of Duty*."

"Okay, don't be a nag."

Sean got out his laptop and started working on the photos. "Except something's not right about this. The guy said he wanted revenge. But he wanted me to Photoshop these two married people having sex in public. Wouldn't the guy he wanted revenge on be angrier if the photos were of another guy?"

"Makes sense to me."

"So why wouldn't he want me to Photoshop himself having sex with her?"

"That makes more sense. Were you high when you met him?"

"Of course," Sean replied.

"Well, there you go. I bet you got it all confused because of the weed. I bet he wanted you to Photoshop him having sex with the other guy's wife."

Sean took another hit. "You're right. Let's find pictures of that guy instead."

THE LIBERTARIAN SAW the notification alert on his phone and punched in his four-digit password. A text from Sean read, *I've done the job. Venmo me the money.*

He replied, *Send me the link to the social media posts.*

Sean answered, *Here you go.*

A series of links appeared in the Libertarian's feed.

The first was to a post on Carmel Social Media's Facebook page. The headline read, The Nasty Sites of

Carmel. It featured Margie Common, naked but strategically covered by her partner while engaged in randy activities in various roundabouts, in the Arts District, the City Hall Gazebo, and on the steps of the Palladium. In each photo, only the back of her partner's head was visible. Except for the Palladium shot. In it, a topless Margie was being embraced from behind by the Libertarian as his right arm covered her breasts to the extent necessary to comply with Facebook's terms of service.

Sean thought he had created a masterpiece. The Libertarian realized he might get shot before the day was over.

Where is my money? texted Sean.

You idiot. You put me in the picture, not her husband.

I thought you wanted revenge, Sean replied.

I thought you wanted to get paid.

Hey, I can take the pics down just as easy as I put them up. No revenge for you.

The Libertarian replied, *There are already 37 comments. I don't think you can put that genie back in the bottle.* At that moment, the Libertarian's front window exploded. *In fact, I'm sure of it.*

He ducked down and started to dial the police. Then he realized he would have to admit to a crime when they asked why he thought his window had been shot out. He hung up and waited. A second shot blew a hole in his portrait of Ayn Rand, whom many believed he resembled when he went too long between haircuts. The comparisons often embarrassed him, but he was too much a fan of her books and politics to get rid of the painting. In this case, it was the first time the mistaken identity had worked in his favor.

After thirty minutes or so, nobody had kicked in the door and no other shots had been taken. He set about cleaning up the glass and considering his next move.

Meanwhile at the Common house, Peter prepared to confront his wife. Initially, he had planned to shoot her after he shot the Libertarian. But after blasting the Libertarian's front window and killing watercolor Ayn Rand, he realized he was out of shotgun shells. He came home to reload, and the box of ammo was empty. It was also then that he realized his wife wasn't even home.

In Midtown Carmel, a male server at the Fork and Ale poured champagne for Margie Common and her friends, who were there to celebrate the anniversary of Cindy Braverman's divorce from the HVAC king of central Indiana, Douglas Braverman. Cindy was getting 20K a month in alimony and living in the Braverman family home with six bedrooms, eight bathrooms, three kids, two cocker spaniels, and a new nanny who looked like Carla from "Cheers." The previous nanny was the current Mrs. Braverman.

Margie's neighbors, Mary Mills and Tonya Douglass joined them. Both were blond and on their second marriages. And both lived in the left cul-de-sac that drove Mr. Common nuts.

The champagne gave way to martinis and the ladies started taking pictures of their drinks, their appetizers, the restaurant's light fixtures, and each other. After posting several "Living our Best Life" photos on Instagram, one of them got bored and took a look at Facebook.

Tonya suddenly gasped and showed Cindy her phone, "Hey, Margie, did you know your picture is on Carmel Social Media."

"Nice try," Margie replied.

Cindy did her best to train her vaguely unfocused eyes on the screen to be sure of what she thought she saw. "No, seriously, and you're having sex all over town."

Margie Common grabbed Tonya's phone. "No, God no."

Mary tried to console her. "Don't worry, it's not with your husband. See." She held up the picture of her on the steps of the Palladium. "You go girl. Who's he?"

"Oh, no! That's the neighbor my husband hates."

"The Libertarian? No way!" Tonya grabbed the phone. "It is!"

"Not bad looking," Cindy said. "You could do better, but hey, not judging."

"Well, I'm pissed you didn't tell any of us you were getting some on the side." Mary dug the olive out of her dirty martini. "I want some on the side."

"I'm not getting anything on the side," Margie insisted. "These are fakes."

Tonya was skeptical, "They look real to me."

Margie said, "I'm asking the moderator to take these down."

Cindy gulped the remainder of her French martini and set it down hard, nearly breaking the glass and drawing the attention of the last table of customers not already watching them. She eyed a table full of accountants who were supposed to be at a training seminar. "They're all bastards." Then their server returned, and she cupped his butt cheek. "Except Ryan, here. He's one of the good ones."

He corrected her but didn't remove her hand. "Chris. My name is Chris."

Cindy asked, "Why didn't Ryan say goodbye?"

He ignored her confusion. "Are you ready for the check?"

Cindy pointed to herself with her free hand. "I would like another drink."

Chris looked at the others, hoping they would cut her off, so he didn't have to do it himself. "Ladies?"

Tonya said, "I'm ready to go if you are?"

Mary was still focused on Margie's predicament. "What do you think Peter is going to say?"

Margie thought for a moment, then said, "Cindy's right. Let's have another drink."

EPISODE 14: WHENEVER YOU SEE MY UVULA

Nicholas Kennedy beamed with pride as Mayor Teddy Wiggins cut the red ribbon signifying the re-opening of the roundabout at 116th Street and Gray Road. It had been closed for eight weeks while a concrete and steel nature scene was assembled inside the circle. It was commissioned by the Carmel City Council and Nicholas was heavily involved in the process. It included pine trees, deer, squirrels, rabbits, hawks, and a majestic eagle with a fish in its talons. All the things that might have been seen on this very spot before the people and the day spas and the coffee shops came.

The art was created by Splatter, a visual artist who works in a variety of mediums. His Chex Mix furniture exhibition at the Cleveland Museum drew admirers from around the world and was destined for a premiere in New York City. Unfortunately, it didn't survive the

Shaker Heights School District's annual fourth grade field trip to the Cleveland Museum. After hearing the news, Splatter was inconsolable for nearly six months.

Then Nicholas Kennedy called. He offered Splatter the opportunity to create something on a large scale. Something with permanence. Something that would be admired by a sophisticated art-loving city, not eaten by fourth-graders with juice box stains on their shirts. The artist jumped at the chance to create a visual statement that would be worshiped by thousands of motorists every day.

The process took nearly six months to complete, with most of the pieces finished in Splatter's undisclosed warehouse location near Chicago and then assembled in Carmel. The roundabout was closed for six weeks while it was repaved, the sidewalks widened and paved with brick, and the forest scene set in place. Blue solar-powered lights were placed all around to give the scene a moonlit glow at night.

All was peaceful and relaxing, except perhaps for the fish caught in the talons of the eagle. However, the bird was suspended 25 feet in the air, so it's hard to say with any degree of certainty what the mood of the fish was. Kennedy's mood was off the charts, however. He had won the day. He even made a presentation after he was introduced by the mayor himself. Splatter was not there for the opening but did say a few words via Facebook Live. Attendees were asked to pull out their phones and watch the eccentric artist's remarks.

Splatter finds openings tedious. So, he livestreams his acceptance of the attendees' awe and admiration from a hot yoga salon in Evanston, Illinois.

For Nicholas, this was his first real win since *the incident*. Nearly a year before, Nicholas had auditioned for "American Idol." He lost. Then he did something drastic. He dropped out of Indiana University Law School, taking the money he would have spent on tuition and using it for plastic surgery. Unbeknownst to his parents (who paid the tuition), he had his uvula reconstructed.

When Nicholas was seven, his best friend Tommy Harcourt dared him to place a small rodent in his mouth. Since four other boys from the neighborhood were watching, Nicholas accepted the challenge. Not having any say in the dare, the mouse felt no obligation to play along and immediately tried to chew his way out of the predicament by tearing into young Nick's uvula. He quickly realized what a mistake this dare had been and attempted to set the mouse free. The rodent took most of the uvula with him upon exiting.

For Cecilia Kennedy, this was the last in a string of embarrassments her husband and child had caused her, and she demanded that they move from Boston to "somewhere civilized in the Midwest if there is such a place." There was no point in living in Boston if you're not a real Kennedy, she had told her husband. And by real Kennedy, she meant related to the family that routinely has airports and federal buildings named after them. Her husband had lured her in a Beantown bar by implying he was related to those Kennedys. Instead, his parents were heirs to the Kennedy Foot Powder fortune. So, they were wealthy, just not revered. Cecilia needed to be revered.

The family moved to Carmel, Indiana, and though Cecilia never claimed to be one of the airport Kennedys, she never bothered to correct anyone who mistook her for one, either. And since there was good money in the foot powder business, nobody suspected a thing.

Young Nicholas thrived in Carmel. His mouth healed and he began to excel in school and lacrosse. But his dream was to be a singer. After hearing their son practice for weeks to try out for the school musical, the Kennedys wanted their son to be a lawyer. When the day came to audition, Nicholas didn't get the part. When it was time to try out for the next musical, Nicholas didn't get the part. When it came time to try out for the Young Greyhound Voices of Tomorrow, Nicholas didn't get the part.

Each time he tried, he failed. And each time he failed, his parents lied and said it's not you, it's your missing uvula. They thought telling him he had no discernible musical talent would be bad parenting. So, they blamed the uvula, thinking their son would accept this limitation and give up. He didn't. Even in college and law school, he continued to audition and not get chosen. So, after his "American Idol" failure (and the subsequent five million views of his audition on

YouTube by people making fun of him) he dropped out of school and got his uvula rebuilt.

It was at this point that his parents had to sit him down and explain that his uvula wasn't the problem. It was his lack of pitch. His inability to read music. His inability to mimic music. His inability to form sounds that any creature with ears would consider music. Nicholas didn't take it well. Screaming at the top of his lungs, with the success of his recovery from uvula reconstruction surgery hanging in the balance, he told them in no uncertain terms what lousy parents they had been.

"Had you told me sooner, I would have kept playing lacrosse," he yelled.

"You really should whisper," Cecilia said. "That thing in the back of your mouth might fall out. And since your father and I have apparently paid $30,000 to put it there, we would like it to stay put."

This enraged Nicholas even further. "Whenever you see my uvula, I want you to remember the lies you've been telling me my whole life." He let that hang out there for a moment, then asked, "What else did you lie to me about?"

"I have no idea what you mean," she answered.

"Is the airport in New York really named after dad's cousin?"

Cecilia looked at her husband, who said nothing. She responded, "There most certainly is an airport named after your father's cousin."

"Really?"

"Well of course," she hesitated.

"Mom! Really? Tell me the truth."

"It's just not the one in New York, darling."

"Where is it?"

"Rochester."

"Rochester, New York?"

"Rochester, Indiana," Cecilia answered.

Her husband looked at them both. "Lots of foot powder business in that part of the state."

Exasperated by this revelation, Nicholas left his parents' home and spent weeks considering his future. In the end, he chose to go back to law school and dedicate himself to becoming a patron of the arts. Since his own art (music) had made him a laughingstock, he would become respected again by bringing the best young artists of all types to Carmel.

And today, his vision had become reality. He had brought Splatter's genius to Carmel. And Splatter had delivered a striking work of art. But as the crowd started to disperse, he noticed something missing. The original plan had called for an eighteen-inch high, twenty-four-inch-deep limestone ring to border the inner curb of the roundabout. This was to prevent a car from accidentally driving into the center and destroying any of the animal sculptures.

He pulled Mayor Teddy aside, "Your honor, I just have one question. I was so blown away by the magnificence of this scene that I completely forgot the limestone ring around the center. What happened to it?”

Wiggins looked both ways to make sure the press and anyone else he didn't want to hear were out of range. "We ran out of money."

"You ran out of money? How could that happen? I went over those budget numbers again and again."

"Look, Nicholas. We really appreciate your help on this, but you're a volunteer. You don't understand the workings of city government." Teddy paused, distracted by a couple of small goats that had arrived in the roundabout. "There are overruns and unforeseen circumstances and requisitions and whatnot."

"Mayor, I know how to read a budget. I'm an attorney ..."

"Not yet, you still haven't finished school and passed the bar." Teddy waved to get the attention of the chief of police and pointed to the goats. The chief shrugged, as if to say, "What do you want me to do about it."

Teddy glared and nodded at the goats again. The chief got Officer Lupinsky's attention and nodded at the goats. Officer Lupinsky looked around and realized he didn't have anyone to nod at.

Nicholas continued, "I'm almost an attorney. I'm not stupid. What happened to the ring money?"

Teddy looked around again to make sure nobody was listening. "We had to use it on another roundabout."

"Which one?"

"I can't say."

Nicholas studied him for a moment and then his eyes got wide. "Last month when someone drove through the roundabout on Main Street and didn't stop, a source told the *Indy Star* that the car had a municipal license plate." His voice got louder. "Is that where the money went?"

"Keep it down!" The mayor looked around to make sure no one heard. "Things happen, Nicholas. Good things and bad things." He paused and gestured toward the sculptures all around them. "And if you want good things to keep happening to you, let this go. We'll find some money next year to build the ring."

"Let's hope no city vehicles find their way into this roundabout in the meantime," Nicholas answered.

That pissed Teddy off, but he knew the young man was right. And he knew he needed his silence for the time being. And since Cecilia Kennedy was a major campaign donor, he would indulge Nicholas for now.

It was a busy day at the Carmel Police Department. The day before, the mayor had announced that the vice president of the United States was coming to the city to make a speech on car safety. What better place than the city that had reduced traffic accidents by 84% by installing over 100 roundabouts? The mayor was beaming with pride. The police were buzzing with activity. Preparations were being made and strategies being lined out. So, the least senior officer was given the job of responding to Wanda Baker's 911 call about a break-in at her home in West Clay, a neighborhood on the west side of Carmel.

When he arrived at their home, he found Mrs. Baker crying on the front step. Mr. Baker was trying to console her. A young girl wearing princess wings rolled by his car on skates before he could exit. She was carrying a small animal with white fur (maybe a rabbit or a guinea pig, he thought, which had pink and blue streaks on its side.

"Good morning, I'm Officer Lupinsky."

"Thank God you're finally here," Mrs. Baker wailed.

"Has anyone been hurt?"

"My daughter, for starters. She's been traumatized."

Lupinsky looked at the girl on roller skates. She was singing to her pet. "Her?"

"Yes, her. Her animals have been violated."

Now Lupinsky was concerned. "Violated. You mean the burglar physically harmed them in some way?"

Her husband intervened. "I'm Ted Baker. My wife means that the intruder put makeup on our daughter's three guinea pigs. We don't believe they were harmed in any other way."

"Oh, good."

Mrs. Baker said, "What?"

"I don't mean it's good that they have makeup on, just good that they weren't violated in any other way."

The Bakers stared at the backtracking policeman. He asked, "Are you sure the house is clear now?"

"Yes, I walked through the house after we discovered there was a break-in," Ted Baker said.

"Okay, not a good idea. Next time call us in case the perpetrators are still in your home."

"I had my gun. I would have shot them if they were."

Not liking where this was headed, Lupinsky pressed on. "Why don't we start at the beginning? What time and how did you discover the break-in?"

"We got home at 9:30 this morning. We were in Boston all weekend for a family celebration. My parents' 50th wedding anniversary."

"Oh, congratulations."

"Thank you."

Mrs. Baker rolled her eyes at the exchange of pleasantries. "Oh, for heaven's sake. We're never getting to 50 if we don't go back to Boston. I hate it here in Indiana." She looked at Lupinsky. "You probably love it."

"I just moved here myself, ma'am."

"And where are you from," Ted asked.

"Detroit," he responded. Looking at the glare from Mrs. Baker, he brought them back on task. "Now, what did the thieves take?"

"Nothing we can tell so far."

"Nothing? They just broke in and put makeup on

your pets? By the way, who was watching your pets while you were gone?"

"Another girl in the neighborhood. She was dropping by to feed and water them. Her mother got our mail. They said everything was normal at 6 p.m. on Sunday night. So, it happened between then and 9:30 this morning."

"Okay, I'll need to get their names and information in a minute."

"To answer your other question, that's not all they did. But I think it's best if you come inside and see for yourself."

Lupinsky followed the homeowner inside. It was elegantly decorated, not the barnyard chic that had dominated interior design lately, but more of a classical east coast style. However, that elegance had been greatly disturbed in the living room. Cushions and pillows from every room in the home had been assembled into a giant structure that reached the ceiling. It was reinforced by stacked dining room chairs and covered by a sheet.

"What do you make of that?" Baker asked.

"It's a couch fort. The most elaborate one I've ever seen."

"Couch fort? I thought it was some sort of hippy commune thing. Or a Stonehenge replica."

"No, that's a couch fort."

"If you say so. Who were they trying to keep out?

"Good question. Anything else?"

"Yes, follow me."

Off the hallway that led between the kitchen and living room was a powder room. Baker opened the door. It smelled like fresh paint. "Here you go."

"I don't follow."

"He or they painted it."

"What?"

Mrs. Baker had caught up to them. "You don't think we do that do you? Sponge paint went out five years ago!"

Mr. Baker continued, "He found an old can of paint in our garage and painted this bathroom."

Lupinsky took notes. "I'll get someone over here to get prints. Anything else?"

"Yes, let me show you my daughter's room."

He followed Mr. and Mrs. Baker down the hall and up the stairs. They took him to their daughter's room. There were two guinea pigs in a large cage. Both were wearing raspberry colored lipstick and blue eyeshadow.

"Why would someone do this?"

"I don't know. Maybe the better question is how? How do you keep a guinea pig still long enough to apply eyeshadow?" He was afraid to ask the next question. "Anything else in this room disturbed?"

"Not that we can tell," she said. "Is this some kind of pervert? Are they trying to send a message to us about our daughter? Is she safe?"

"I don't think this has anything to do with your

daughter. But I understand your concern. I'll see if we can have a regular patrol out this way for a while."

Officer Lupinsky asked, "Any idea who might have done this? Any neighborhood kids who have pranked you before? Problem with a neighbor?"

Ted replied, "I bet it was Newgarden."

"He a local kid?"

"Former neighbor."

"And has he trespassed on your property before?"

"Yes, but not for a while. But we had big problems with him a few years ago."

A few years ago ...

Ted Baker heard a loud and determined knock on his front door, just as he was about to sit down to read the *Indianapolis Star* newspaper. He had worked all morning—mowing the yard, trimming the weeds, and watering the new trees he had planted along the sides of his backyard. He was tired, irritable, and not pleased with the interruption to his quiet afternoon at home. His wife and daughter were visiting his mother-in-law two hours away, which in Ted's mind was the best place for her to be.

He swung open his door to find his neighbor, Terrance Newgarden III, standing on his porch, holding a dog-eared document.

"How are you this afternoon, Mr. Newgarden?"

"Newgarden the third, if you please."

"Certainly. How can I help you?

"You can start by tearing town those trees."

"What?"

"Particularly, the ones that border my fence, AND the ones along your back fence."

"Why? They're Spartan Juniper trees? There won't be any branches going over the fence and into your yard."

"I take umbrage at your tone, sir. And at your trees."

"Umbrage?"

"Umbrage."

"And why do you take umbrage?"

"Because they will eventually obstruct my view of the neighborhood." He shook the document in Ted's face. "And it's against the covenants."

"It is not. I went to the HOA before I planted them."

Newgarden vigorously leafed through the HOA covenants. Unable to find the rule he wanted, he looked back at Baker. "They're wrong. That rule is in here somewhere and I'll find it. And then those trees are coming down."

Ted replied, "It's been nice talking with you, but I've got better things to do with my afternoon. Come back when you've had more umbrage."

Terrance Newgarden III had never had a door slammed in his face before, let alone faced someone who had the guts to tell him off in such sarcastic manner. He really took umbrage at that.

After complaining to the HOA and his attorney,

writing a strongly-worded letter to the editor of the *Carmel Bugle,* and making numerous visits to the Baker front porch to express his feelings of umbrage, Terrance decided to take matters into his own hands. On Halloween night, as the Bakers were having dinner and entertaining trick-or-treaters, they heard what sounded like a whoosh of wind and saw a fireball light up the backyard. Running to the back door, Ted and his wife saw a man running toward the Newgarden house. He was on fire. It seems Terrance was going to burn the trees down and blame it on kids pulling a Halloween prank. Instead, he set himself on fire.

"So, you believe this man might have been the one to break into your home?" asked Lupinsky.

"Yes, we heard he's out of rehab and living on his own."

"Next door?"

"Oh, no. He was wrong about the tree rule. But there is an HOA clause where if you commit a felony against another homeowner or their property, the association can force you to sell your home."

"Huh, who would have guessed?"

"It's a comprehensive HOA agreement," Baker said.

Officer Lupinsky said, "Mind if I take one more look around?"

"Be my guest."

He walked back into the living room and considered

the couch fort. Then he peeked in on little Laura as she debated her mother on whether the makeup had to come off the guinea pigs. Finally, he inspected the newly-painted powder room.

He rejoined Ted on the back deck. "Mr. Baker, I'll look into the Newgarden fellow..."

"Newgarden the third. If you don't call him that, he will remind you."

"Newgarden the third. Right. Anyway, I don't believe this has anything to do with him, but I will cross the T's and dot the I's."

"Why don't you believe it's him?"

"It's too childish. Now granted, setting your trees on fire wasn't the most adult solution to his grievances, but it was about him. This," he looked back at the house, "this looks like the work of a teenager. Or a juvenile-minded young adult. This is something a stoner would do. Somebody on a weird acid trip."

"Are you sure?"

"I've been wrong before, but this sure looks like somebody on psychedelic drugs to me. I've seen these HOA grievance types. Your ex-neighbor would have sent a message. Made a point." He looked back at the house again. "There's no point to this."

~

Peter woke up with the empty shotgun still in his lap. He was sitting in the same chair from the night before. Next to him was an empty fifth of Jim Beam. He stood up and set the gun against the wall. His back ached. His head was pounding, and he was sick to his stomach.

He went into the kitchen and poured some water, drank it down fast, and realized he had seen something out of the corner of his eye when he came into the room. It was one of those moments where your brain shouts to you that you saw an anomaly a good minute after you actually saw it. He stepped back from the sink and turned his head to face the hallway that led to the garage.

The door from the hallway was open. Beyond that, he could see daylight coming through a door from the garage to the backyard. His view of the backyard was blocked from the large piece of machinery he vaguely remembered setting up the night before, but he was certain he could see a leg on the ground. His trap had worked. He stepped around the 150-shot T-shirt cannon he had loaded with baseballs the night before. Lying just outside the door from the backyard to the garage was Margie Common.

Peter knew from the color of her skin and lips that she was dead. Despite that, he checked her pulse, confirming she was the new ex-Mrs. Common. Margie had come home drunk and rang the doorbell, unable to successfully put her keys in the front door. When that failed to rouse her husband, she went to the backyard to enter via the small garage door that was never locked. Upon opening the door, she was met with a barrage of 150 baseballs that hit her in less than fifteen seconds. The machine had been ordered by the University of Nebraska for the upcoming season and Peter was going to deliver it personally.

Nobody would believe he hadn't killed his wife on purpose. The sex photos were on the web, and he had shot out his neighbor's window and his Ayn Rand painting. The same neighbor with whom she was having sex in the pictures. Not that he hadn't previously planned on killing her, her mother, and the Libertarian. In fact, he had mapped out the whole thing in the office he had above the garage. His plan was to do it in winter, but things were now in motion. He had to act fast.

Peter looked around for something with which to wrap the body. Then an idea popped into his head. He quickly ran to their living room and pulled up an area rug his wife had always lied about. She had bought it during the Memorial Day sale from At Home, but always bragged to their friends that it came from Milan. He wrapped the body in the rug and loaded it in his vehicle. He then drove her to Founders Park and dragged her body down the path to the protected wetlands. He knew it was risky to stash her in a public space, but he also knew the ecology of the wetlands meant she likely never would be found.

Along the path he ran into a small goat that refused

to get out of the way. Angrily he kicked the animal, and it ran away with a whimper. Peter dug a hole in the marshy grass and placed her body in it. It was so dark when he left that he didn't notice the twenty goats lined up along the path waiting for him to leave.

After he started his car, the herd followed a goat with a slight limp to where Margie Common was buried. They dug her up and dragged the rug back onto the path to be discovered the next morning.

Jodi Werner liked to walk in Founders Park every morning at 9 a.m. It's how she cleared her head after getting the kids off to school. She was a stay-at-home mom currently, with no real desire to rejoin the workforce. She used to work as an office administrator at a dentist's office. Then her boss got handsy. She spurned his advances. He got persistent. Then Jodi got the idea to record him and take the video to a prominent attorney in town.

Her boss was now in a difficult position. He was wealthy in his own right, but his father-in-law owned the practice—part of a chain of twenty dental offices. Divorce meant he would no longer be employed and not inherit (via his wife) the lucrative business. So, he managed to find seven figures to keep Jodi quiet. The hush money and the alimony her husband paid meant that Jodi didn't have to work again in her life.

But that didn't mean she didn't have stress and today was no different. Her son poured cereal and milk down the front of his clothes and had to change. Her daughter had a meltdown when the smallest droplet of milk that can be seen by the naked eye landed on her princess shoes. The princess shoes were "ruined," and this was the darkest day in her seven years on this planet.

Jodi suggested wearing her other princess shoes and her daughter looked at her as if she had just defecated in the kitchen. Which the family dog then did, having been ignored all morning.

So, Jodi was really in need of her usual de-stressing trip to the park. As it turns out, the scene at breakfast would prove to be the calmer part of her day.

As she wound along the path, she noticed something odd. What looked to be a herd of miniature goats blocked her progress. One sat atop what looked to be a rolled-up area rug. The rest congregated on either side of it. As she approached, the goats started to disperse until the only one left was the one sitting on top the rug.

The goat stared at Jodi.

She stared at the goat. Then she stepped back and looked at the entire picture. Based on the uneven shape, there must be something inside the rug, she thought.

She looked back at the goat. He nodded at her, jumped off the rug, and started up the path.

Jodi watched him and kneeled at the end of the roll to see if she could peer inside. She took out her phone and turned on the flashlight. Before looking, she looked at the goat. It nodded once more, then walked along the path until she couldn't see it anymore. She looked inside the rug, and she could see hair, matted with blood. Jodi screamed.

When Officer Lupinsky arrived at Founders Park, a small crowd was gathered in the parking lot. He approached them and a Carmel Clay Parks & Recreation employee broke away and said, "I'm Larry from the parks department." He pointed to a brunette woman dressed in workout clothes. "She found the body on one of the trails."

"Okay, can you ask her to come with us?"

Lupinsky made a few notes. Larry returned. "This is Jodi Werner. She found the body about ten minutes ago."

"Hi Jodi, I'm Officer Lupinsky. Can you tell me what happened?"

"I was walking along the trail, and I came upon this heard of pygmy goats."

"Pygmy goats?"

Larry corrected her, "Miniature goats is the PC term. Pygmy is culturally insensitive. It's triggering to the goats."

Lupinsky looked around. He didn't see any goats. "I didn't realize goats are that sensitive. What do they have to do with the body?"

"They were on the body," said Jodi.

"Please tell me they weren't eating it?" Jodi became nauseous and started to retch but fought it off. Lupinsky apologized. "I'm so sorry, I realize how awful that sounded."

"No, it's okay. The goats were congregated around a rug. The body is rolled up inside."

"Oh, that's better, I suppose. Were you alone on the trail?"

"Yes. Aside from the goats."

"Did you see anything else unusual or any people acting strange when you arrived at the park or on the trail?"

"No. Again, aside from the goats."

Lupinsky looked at Larry. "Are there normally goats in the park?"

"There aren't 'normally' goats anywhere in Carmel. Do you think they have something to do with the murder?"

Lupinsky shook his head. This was going to be a long day, he thought. "No, I don't."

"I do," said Jodi.

"Why do you think so?"

"They wanted me to find that body. One goat wouldn't leave until I looked inside the rug."

Larry, "You should question them."

"Question the goats?"

"Well on second thought, you are police and they're likely to be traumatized by your presence. I should probably do it."

Lupinsky saw an opportunity to get rid of the insulting and obviously crazy park employee. "You know, that's a good idea. You round them up and see what you can get out of them. In the meantime, Jodi, could you show me to the body?"

Larry marched off in the opposite direction while Jodi led him to the body. Sure enough, there was the rug from At Home and inside was the corpse.

"Are you going to unwrap the body? I don't think I can watch."

"No, I'm calling in detectives and a crime scene unit. I'm just going to secure the scene until they arrive."

She looked nauseous again. "Good. Do you have more questions?"

"Did you go beyond this spot or back to the parking lot after you discovered the body?"

"Back to the parking lot."

"Okay, if you can wait there, I'll speak with you again once the detectives arrive. They will have more questions. Okay?"

"That's fine."

Jodi looked around at the park. “I came here to lower my stress. It didn’t happen.”

Lupinsky thought about his brief time in Carmel. “I feel the same way.”

Larry returned and interrupted before Jodi could respond. "The goats are in the back of the park, near a creek. They're pretty shaken. I think the police presence is unsettling to them."

Lupinsky replied, "Well, you can tell them to relax. I've decided not to retain them as witnesses today."

"They'll be so relieved."

Just for fun, he added, "Although they probably shouldn't leave town. Neither should you."

Larry scoffed. "Fascist." He stomped off in the direction from which he came.

"Another happy customer," Lupinsky said.

"I don't think he's ever been happy," said Jodi.

"You're probably right.”

EPISODE 15: THE GRATITUDE OF GOATS

Two days later, Tommy and Sean met at Sean's place. Tommy asked Sean, "Are you stoned?"

"Nope."

"Are you sure? We need to focus on this one. I've got a feeling about this one."

"I promise, I'm clear as a bell."

Tommy didn't believe him but started up the van and drove toward Lakewood Estates. In fact, Sean was clear as a bell. Or as clear as someone who smoked the volume of weed he consumed regularly could possibly be. And that meant he wasn't at all prepared for what he would see at the Common home.

On the east side of Carmel, the neighborhood backed up to a creek, a small woods, and a quarry behind that. It had the advantage of eliminating the possibility of development on that side of Lakewood Estates, but it also meant that various forms of wildlife often drifted into the neighborhood. Just the night before, when Sean and Tommy drove through the neighborhood to scope it out, they noticed a pack of pygmy goats running between two of the houses.

On this day, they drove to the back of the main part of Lakewood Estates, parked the van at the end of street that bordered the woods, and found the trail that connected to the annex.

When they exited the trail, there were houses on either side they could approach from the rear. The archcriminals kept to the backyards while moving down the street to a place they had identified the afternoon before. It was the only home without a security monitoring sign or visible cameras.

They knew from some basic internet searching that the homeowner worked in Westfield, another suburb about 20 minutes away. He usually arrived home around 5 p.m. They learned from Facebook that his wife was in Florida. Feeling certain they had plenty of time, and nobody watching, they broke a window on a back door. Inside the house, they went to work. Sean kept telling himself, "I'm not going to get high. I'm not going to get high."

During a sweep of the first floor, Tommy noticed a package leaning against the small window by the front door. He glanced outside and didn't see anyone. Confident no eyes were upon him; he opened the door and grabbed the box. It was from Supersoft Games. And it was the size of a GameBox.

"Score! There's a GameBox on the front porch that's brand new."

Sean asked, "Wouldn't it be crazy if it was the GameBox Gold everyone has been looking for?"

"Yeah, I heard the winning ticket was from Carmel."

"Well, we're taking it and we'll find out when we get home," Sean said. He brought the box inside and then went upstairs to look for more things to steal. "I won't get high," he whispered to himself.

He went into a bonus room that had been built over the garage. It was painted blue with a white ceiling. On the opposite side of the room from where he entered was another door. Normally this would excite him. The criminal instinct would tell him this is where something valuable is hidden. But he approached it with dread this time. "It must be the weed withdrawal," he thought. "I will not get high."

On the doorframe was a padlock, hanging from a hook. The owner had forgotten to lock the door and it was open a few inches. Sean pulled it open the rest of the way and found a light switch. He turned it on and took in the scene. He dropped to his knees and said, "I've got to get high."

On the main floor of the house, Tommy found an office with a small home safe. The keys were still in it. He opened it and found a stash of rare coins, jewelry, and vintage baseball cards from the 1920s. This was the jackpot he had been waiting for. Maybe he could buy a

Bentley. He thought of the server at Aztec Hillbilly Brewing Company as he emptied the safe.

After loading everything of value into his backpack, he set it next to the GameBox and went to find Sean. He called out in a whisper shout, “Sean, are you done up there?”

No response. He walked to the top of the steps, “Sean? Are you done?”

Still no response. “You better not be in here getting high.”

He found the bonus room and saw Sean sitting on the floor staring into the room beyond. He could see the smoke coming from Sean’s joint.

“What the hell? I'm doing all the work and you’re up here torching up?”

“It’s my third,” Sean confessed. “And I had a few acid tabs.”

“What? Why? You know how important today is.”

Tommy crossed the bonus room and Sean warned him, “If you see this, you’re going to get high, too.”

“Bullshit. Man, can’t you do anything right?” He stepped up behind Sean and looked into the room. He tried to speak, but all that came out was a chirp. He fell to his knees.

"Do you see this?"

"Yeah, I see it."

"We'll never unsee it."

“I know. Give me a hit.” Sean passed it over.

On the wall opposite the door were four very realistic—but fake—heads. One was an alpaca. One was a man (the Libertarian from down the street). And two were women (Peter Common's mother-in-law and his wife). Each had fake blood dripping from the neck. Painted in fake blood on the wall was the phrase "Life Goals."

"Should we alert the police?"

Tommy replied, "Nah, I think we should get the hell out of here."

"Yeah, that's a good idea."

Suddenly, they heard sirens and squealing tires. "They're onto us!"

Both men ran down the stairs. Sean grabbed the GameBox and Tommy took the backpack. They ran out the back door just as Peter Common crashed his car into the garage door. As the two burglars ran through the backyards of the Lakewood Estates Annex, all eyes of the neighbors who were home and heard the sirens were on the front yard of the Common home.

The police apprehended Peter Common, and upon opening his trunk found his mother-in-law, still alive. Neither Sean nor Tommy had a clue that the police weren't there for them.

Tommy and Sean got separated during the getaway. Tommy guessed that if the police knew about the break-in, they probably also knew about the van. So, he took a path that ran toward the quarry and the road that the trucks took in and out. He hoped he could hide there or find a way out and come back later for the van.

Meanwhile, Sean's acid hits were kicking in. Not long after they got separated, he tripped and fell, dropping the GameBox. Everything was fuzzy in his eyes. Mud and rock and leaves were hard to distinguish. His stomach growled. Or was his stomach outside his body? He couldn't be sure. But the sound didn't come from within. Down on all fours, he looked up and saw the eyes. They looked like kaleidoscopes and made him giggle. The kaleidoscope eyes belonged to a dog that was staring at him. "Nice doggy," was all he could get out. The doggy stared back. Sean reached out for the animal that had begun to growl, hoping to show he wasn't a threat. As he did, he realized now there were three doggies. Or was it the drugs?

"Nice doggy. Come here and let me scratch your belly."

He stumbled toward the doggy. The coyotes lunged toward Sean.

THE BOYS of Lakewood Estates heard the commotion and rode their bikes down from Devon's house. They had been reading online about how the winner of the GameBox Gold was a middle-aged man from Carmel, Indiana. The article showed a picture of a guy who looked like a grumpy neighbor they had. So, the sirens were a nice distraction.

Tony circled around the moms who had gathered to compile the gossip.

“I always knew he was a psycho,” said one.

“You know his wife hasn’t been seen in a week,” said another.

“I better change before Channel 8 gets here to do the story,” said a third.

Tony rode back over to where the other boys were waiting. “I heard that guy killed his wife and buried her in the quarry. Let’s go look!”

"That can't be right. I heard they found a body in the park," said Matt.

"Then he buried somebody else in the quarry," said Tony. "Let's check it out."

“No way, I’m not going in there,” said Willy. “There’s snakes and coyotes.”

“I’m going to look,” said Tony. “What else do we have to do?”

The rest of the boys watched as Peter was shoved into the back of the police car. “Could be some bodies in his house or backyard,” said Matt. “I’m waiting here to see if they bring any out.”

“Me too,” said Devon.

“Me three,” said Willy.

“Fine, I’ll look myself.” Tony ran off to explore.

. . .

Tony was alone but confident as he approached the woods. About forty yards down the path, he came upon a box. He turned it over and saw that it was addressed to Peter Common, now surrounded by police. It was from Supersoft, and it was the size of a GameBox. He squealed for joy and picked up the box, hugging it to himself.

His squeals caused a disturbance in the woods. A coyote approached from the direction he had been walking toward. He heard more rustling behind him. He was too terrified to turn around. The coyote in front of him was scary enough. And it had blood around its lips. The creature growled at him. No, not at him, Tony thought. Beyond him. Then he heard animal sounds. Not like the growl of the coyote. Less aggressive, but scary just the same because he knew it wasn't just one animal. The boy slowly turned his upper torso and neck. His legs were frozen in fear.

Behind him stood twenty pygmy goats. Bleating and baring teeth at the coyote. They advanced and the coyote weighed his options. He could take any of them individually, but a human and twenty goats might be a challenge. He growled, snorted, and turned tail.

The goats surrounded Tony, their liberator from the hell of yoga classes. He let out a sigh and bent to one knee to pet the goats. The closest nuzzled around him. He thanked the goats and they continued on their way. Then he stood and walked out of the woods, carrying the GameBox Gold. Tony was about to become a legend in Lakewood Estates.

OFFICER LUPINSKY TURNED his squad car right into Lakewood Estates just as two goats walked aimlessly into the road. He stopped and waited for them to cross, then looked around to see a place the goats may have come from or were going toward. Nothing seemed logical about goats in this neighborhood. But he recently had visited a crime scene that included a guinea pig with lipstick and eyeshadow, so he was prepared for anything.

He was called to the neighborhood to check out a suspicious van. Homeowner Dale Gordon met him as Lupinsky pulled up the address on his note from dispatch. Gordon was middle-aged, plump in the mid-section, and had a receding hair line. He seemed jumpy.

"I called it in, officer."

"Yeah, what seems to be the problem?"

"That van, it's been here for three days." He pointed to the white Chevy creeper van.

"Three days, huh? And you're just reporting it now?"

"I thought the driver was watching the house." He looked around nervously.

"And that didn't scare you until today? Why is that?"

"My wife thinks I'm cheating on her. I thought the

van was a private investigator watching to see if I had anybody over while my wife was out of town."

"Why does your wife think you're cheating on you?"

"She found some of my client's underwear in the back of my car."

"I can see where that might raise suspicion," Officer Lupinsky replied.

"I told her it was our seventeen-year-old son's." Lupinsky gave him an odd look. "I mean his girlfriend's underwear. I don't think she believed me."

"And now you think your wife has a private investigator looking into your every move."

"Well, I did. And since I am not doing anything wrong while she's away, I thought I was saving myself a messy divorce by just parading around like normal while this scumbag took pictures of me."

"And now?"

"And now I think maybe she hired somebody to kill me and he's watching me from that van."

Lupinsky shook his head and cursed Hollywood like all policemen do from time to time when confronted by the typical American brain that has been marinated in too much television.

"If the guy in the van was a hitman, he would be quite possibly the worst one who ever lived," the officer responded. "A *real* hitman wouldn't be camped visibly in front of your house for three days. You would never see a *real* hitman coming."

At first, the homeowner stared at Lupinsky with his

mouth open. Then a very dim light went on inside Dale's mind. “I suppose you're right. It's just my mind is all wrong. It's her fault." He thought for a moment, then smiled. "I guess the good news is that I'm in the clear."

"The clear for what?"

"For getting a divorce."

Lupinsky couldn't resist. "So, the underwear in the car was just a misunderstanding?"

"Oh, no. Her sister and I really were in the back of my car. I just mean my wife doesn't suspect anything."

Lupinsky looked at his watch. It wasn’t even 9a.m. and he had already reached the point in the day when he lost respect for humanity. Normally, that came after lunch. "Why don't you wait inside your house? I'm going to have a look at the van."

He circled around the vehicle and called in the license plate number. He tried the front doors; both were locked. Lupinsky pulled out his flashlight and pointed it inside. Then he walked around to the back and tried the lock on the rear door. It opened.

In disorganized piles inside the van were stolen items from the recent Carmel robberies. A rare-to-impossible event was about to occur: a home break-in case would be solved. He was sure there would be evidence inside of who committed these crimes. And he wondered what caused the thieves (the police were sure it was more than one) to abandon the van. Were the morons responsible as dangerous as the homeowner they had arrested just a few days before?

He called it in and waited for the detectives and forensic team to come and do their bit.

Interviews with the neighbors produced nothing. The few people who saw the van didn't remember the driver or when it arrived. Most just wanted to complain about something they felt the cops should be doing, including but not limited to stopping Pete Haniford from burning his leaves, making kids pull their pants up, and shooting the coyotes that had been prowling in increasing numbers around the perimeter of the neighborhood.

Lupinsky was exhausted by the end of the day and slumped into the front seat of his car, ready to go home. He sat there for a moment, pondering the recent events of the last few weeks. Before he could start the ignition, he noticed movement to his left in the direction of the woods. He turned to see a coyote walk from the woods and into the street. It was sniffing the ground, like Lupinsky's dog did when he walked him around his own neighborhood. It was that same way his dog behaved if another dog had been walked ahead of him.

The officer assumed the coyote was tracking another animal. Curiously, it walked right up to the spot where the back of the van had been the past three days. The coyote looked each way, licked its lips, then turned and walked slowly back into the woods.

~

DIEGO SANCHEZ LOOKED at the pictures he had taken on his recent vacation to Siesta Key, Florida. There were pictures of dolphins playing, pelicans fishing, and turtle nests on the beach. There were happy pictures of his new soulmate as they did a sunset dinner cruise, beach walks, and cocktails by the pool. And there were revolting pictures of two middle-aged out-of-shape Midwesterners feeding each other cake while naked.

Normally, it wasn't like Diego to be a voyeur. And he wasn't sure why he had his camera out and his lens pointed toward the hotel while on the airport tram. But fate must have been guiding him. Because as he studied the pictures, he realized the face of the man looked mighty familiar. It had to be a coincidence. He decided it couldn't be the guy they resembled, but just for a laugh, he sent them to his girlfriend anyway.

"Have a look at these pictures I accidentally captured," he wrote. "Remember, I said they looked like they were having sex? They were doing more than that. And the guy looks like your ex!"

Sheila got the message on her phone and opened the picture. She was having a late lunch at Cake Castle with her friend, Cecilia Kennedy. She put down the phone and motioned for the waiter. "I'll have the cake of the day." He started to leave. "And the cake of tomorrow if you've chosen that."

"We have. It will be the same as the cake of today."

"Then why not call it the cake of the week?"

He nodded toward a table of skinny women celebrating a bachelorette party next to Sheila and Cecilia and said, "You can't eat cake more than once a week and keep a figure like that. So, we never get the same customers in the same week. We can get away with it."

"Fair enough," she replied. "Bring me the cake of the day on a plate and the cake of tomorrow in a to-go box."

Cecilia asked, "Oh no honey. Are you depressed?"

"No, I'm celebrating."

"Celebrating what?"

"That I can finally get my ex to give up the vacation home near Colorado Springs."

Cecilia was confused. "What? I thought that was the only property you let him have in the divorce."

"It was. But now I'm taking that too. And the best part is, I won't even have to fight him for it."

"I don't believe it. No way Teddy hands that over."

"There is a way. And he will." The server returned with her white chocolate raspberry truffle deluxe cake of the day. She took a bite and savored it for a moment. "Better than sex. Speaking of which, Diego just texted me pictures of my ex having sex in a Tampa hotel room with a Carmel city employee."

"You are kidding. How long have you had Diego spying on him?"

"That's the thing. We weren't. Diego just happened to be shooting pictures on the tram at the Tampa airport. He had no idea that Teddy was there."

"Can I see?"

Sheila handed over her phone. "Sick little perv is having her rub icing on his chest."

"Gross." She paused as the waiter stopped to refill their coffees. "How can you eat cake after seeing that? "

"Because I'm going to ask for the house in Colorado in exchange for deleting these."

Cecilia's mind started racing. "How did you know it's a Carmel employee?"

"Oh, I still have friends at city hall. They told me these two have been making googly eyes at each other for months."

"Are you sure it's him? This picture is a little fuzzy."

"See the scar under his left kneecap?"

"Oh, yeah."

"The bike incident."

Sheila shook her head.

Several years back, Teddy had been riding his bike on the Monon Trail in the summer all the way up in Westfield during the NFL mini-camp. The Colts cheerleaders were practicing there too, and this resulted in Teddy taking his eyes off the path. The resulting crash into a tree left Teddy with injuries that required surgery and lots of apology gifts to his soon-to-be ex-wife.

"So, when are you going to hit him with it?"

"No time like the present." She sent a text with the pictures and the simple message, "Call me."

Sheila took a bite of her cake, a sip of coffee, and then held up three fingers. "In three, two, one." Her phone rang.

"Good afternoon, Theodore."

Teddy asked, "How did you get those pictures?"

"It doesn't matter."

"It sure as hell does, you succubus. How low can you get? Spying on me?"

"She's a city employee, Teddy. Not a good look for you."

"How much?"

"The house in Colorado."

"Are you out of your mind?"

"Too much, Theodore? Okay, I need to go now. I've got to call the *Indy Star.*"

"All right. But this is low, even for you. Where the hell am I supposed to go on vacation? You got everything else."

"Why not back to Tampa? You seemed to be having a great time there. By the way, I'm so glad you decided to explore the whole food while making love thing *after* we split up."

"Delete those damn pictures."

"Oh, and one more thing."

"What?"

"I want alpacas to be legal as pets in Carmel."

"What? Why the hell would you want that?"

"Just do it."

"How do I know you will delete all the copies?"

"You don't. Goodbye Teddy." She hung up.

Cecilia asked, "Alpacas?"

"Long story. I hate the things, but Diego might move in soon."

"Will you really delete them?"

"Of course. They're disgusting, and after I get the house in Colorado, there is nothing that man has that I could possibly want." She laughed, "I've already taken it all."

***

As soon as Cecilia got home, she texted Teddy. Within two minutes, he called back. She thought she was alone, so she put it on speaker phone. "How many people did that witch show those pictures to?"

"Just me. I want something too."

"You're on thin ice, Cecilia."

"So are you."

"I want the Hamilton County Executive Airport named after our family."

"I can't do that."

"You can and you will. Or else those pictures go public."

"Do you have copies too?"

She lied. "Of course. Sheila and I are old friends. She leans on me when you hurt her."

"Oh brother. No, Cecilia. I can't do it because that airport isn't in Carmel! It's in Westfield." He wanted to call her several names at this point but thought better of it.

"Then name something after us that *is* in Carmel. A building or a park."

"We have a park coming online in 2024 as part of one of the redevelopment projects. I can name that after you."

"Done."

"And you'll destroy the pictures?

"Say no more."

Teddy thought his day couldn't get any worse. His administrative assistant called, and he answered. "Nicholas Kennedy on line one."

"Take a message," he yelled.

"He said if you say, 'take a message,' to ask you what flavor of cake you recommend at the Tampa airport. He said you would know what that meant because I sure as hell don't."

"That little shit! Put him through."

His admin transferred the call.

"Hello, mayor."

"You little weasel! What do you want?"

"I was listening in when my mom called you."

"That witch!"

"She didn't know. I was in the other room."

"I don't give a damn. One blackmail request per family is my limit. You got your park named after your family. I'm done."

"You're done when I say so. I want my ring, and three more roundabout art projects."

"Before today, I was going to give you more projects to oversee. Now, I don't know why I should give you any, you ungrateful little twerp!"

"You know why. Because you may have the *Carmel Bugle* in your pocket, but the *Indy Star* would love to run this story."

"All right, I'll find the money for your ring."

"And three projects."

"One more project."

"Two."

"Done. Now delete those damn pictures." He slammed down the office phone so hard his admin assistant, Ms. Fitzsimmons, jumped in the other room. Teddy thought about his counterpart in Spain, persecuted for how he chose to play backgammon in the nude. And now he was being blackmailed for how he chose to have an afternoon snack in the nude. "Love is love, damnit," he said out loud. "And we politicians shouldn't be persecuted for who and how we love. I wonder if the LGBTQ crowd would be open to adding a 'P'?"

Ms. Fitzsimmons, who heard all of this because she recently began recording Teddy out of sheer boredom, decided that this would be a great day for her to begin her tell-all memoirs.

TALES FROM A ROUNDABOUT

VOLUME FOUR

EPISODE 16: MEET THE MELVINS

Tears streamed down Joe Melvin's cheeks as he revved the engine of his Ford pick-up truck. The transmission was in neutral as he rhythmically pushed the gas pedal and considered his lot in life. It was past 11 p.m. on a Wednesday and the only illumination in Joe's world came from his headlights and the dashboard. Dolly Parton was singing about losing her man on the country oldies station. With his left hand he tapped somewhere close to the beat on the steering wheel while his right hand turned up the volume.

Between his legs was a bottle of Jack Daniels. He attempted a swig, and nothing came out. He peered inside and cursed, "Not you too, Jack." He threw the bottle to his right, intending to send it out the window. But it wasn't rolled down, so the window shattered, leaving broken glass on the threadbare seat and the ground outside the truck.

Joe Melvin turned Dolly up even louder. As he did, the DJ cut off the end of the song to tell listeners, "You're listening to the Heartbreak Hour on WKTY, Country Hits. A solid hour of break-up songs and countryfied blues. Don't forget to tune in tomorrow and you could win tickets to see Keith Urban."

Joe answered the DJ, "There ain't gonna be a tomorrow, dammit! Why'd you cut off Dolly?" He paused, then shouted, "Cain't anything go right today? Huh, universe? Whaddya got to say for yourself?"

The radio went quiet, and Joe thought maybe the universe was going to answer him. But the silence was only a few seconds of dead air the producer forgot to cut from the forthcoming commercial. When the pause ended, the universe—or the voiceover—said, "Do you suffer from ED?"

Melvin turned the radio off and said, "The hell with it. Let's get this over with."

He revved the engine again and watched for any car lights in his rearview mirror. He and his truck were sitting on a small gravel drive leading into a quarry off of 106th Street, in southwest Carmel, Indiana. When Joe had arrived, the access road was blocked by a metal chain tied to two concrete posts to keep people out after hours. Joe tried to cut the chain, but his bolt cutters were old and rusty, and they broke when he gave them a squeeze. He had cursed at the chain, the bolt cutters, and Pete's Hardware for selling him defective tools twenty-five years prior. Then he got back in his truck, backed it up, and drove through the chain.

Since then, he had listened to exactly forty-seven minutes' worth of the Heartbreak Hour and drank all his liquor. It was time. With nothing more to live for and nothing more to stop him, he dropped his transmission into drive, pressed the gas pedal to the floor, and drove his truck towards the quarry. But just twenty feet shy of the gaping man-made hole in the earth, it ran out of gas. The engine sputtered to a halt, and the truck came to a stop at the edge of the quarry.

Joe Melvin got out and cursed the truck, the quarry, the moon, and his life. He kicked the truck. Then he reached in, put it in neutral, and moved to the back to push the truck over the edge. Joe had a large belly, but his 48-year-old frame was solid, and he managed to get the truck over the edge. As it sailed down, he remembered he was meant to be inside. He jumped and yelled, "Dammit, wait for me!" With eyes closed and the air rushing by him as he plummeted into the quarry, Joe smiled for the last time in his life and the first time in weeks.

~

Officer Lupinsky stood on the edge of the precipice with several of his Carmel, Indiana, police colleagues, a couple of curious guys from the fire department, and the office manager of the quarry. A crane was slowly lifting what used to be a Ford truck to the top of the giant pit. A fire had erupted when it pancaked at the bottom, but the license plate was still discernible as well as a bumper sticker that said, "Majestic as Fu," the last two letters having been destroyed by the fire.

A quick check of the plate returned the name Joe Melvin of Sheridan, Indiana, and Lupinsky drew the short straw for notifying the family. The body had been found several feet away from the burning wreck.

Sheridan is northwest of Carmel, Indiana, and it took Officer Lupinsky about thirty minutes to get there. When he arrived, he discovered a manufactured home that wasn't in much better shape than the truck that had been brought out of the quarry. The front door was open, and a screen door rested against the house a few feet away. Some of the windows were boarded up while others were open with no blinds. As Lupinsky walked up the gravel driveway, a raccoon tumbled out of an overturned trash can. It looked at the uniformed officer briefly, then waddled confidently on its way.

Lupinsky reached the front door and looked in. On a dingy couch with cigarette burns, a basset hound was watching TV. The dog turned towards the officer, gave a perfunctory bark, then went back to *Jersey Shore*. Lupinsky called out, "Hello. Anybody home?"

Geraldine Melvin appeared from the kitchen. She wore a tight tank top with no bra, and cut-off denim shorts. On one foot was an ankle boot, the kind people with injuries wear. On the other was a cowboy boot. "What the hell do you want?"

"Are you Geraldine Melvin?"

"Who wants to know?"

"I'm Officer Lupinsky of the Carmel Police Department."

"Carmel? What's the Carmel police want with me?"

"Maybe you should sit down." He nodded towards the couch.

"Can't. Dog's watching *Jersey Shore*."

Lupinsky looked at the dog and back at her. "How about the kitchen?"

"I'm not talking to the Carmel cops." She turned toward the kitchen behind her and shouted, "Mama, I ain't gotta talk to the Carmel cops, do I?"

Mama shouted back from the kitchen, "Hell no. You tell him if we got any business with the police, it's gonna be local boys. Not some uppity Carmel cop."

Lupinsky shook his head. "Ma'am, this is about your husband."

"He only deals with Sheridan police too." Geraldine paused. "Not that he's a snitch or nothin' 'cause he ain't."

"Mrs. Melvin, your husband is dead."

"You mean dead, dead? Or as in, he's dead if he don't cooperate with the Carmel police?"

"Dead, dead."

"Since when?"

At this point two boys aged 11 and 9 entered the

room. Both were carrying baked sweet potatoes in each hand. Lupinsky was still standing in the doorway.

"Since last night. Are you sure you don't want to talk somewhere?" He looked at the boys and back at her. "Maybe spare them the details."

Geraldine answered, speaking to the boys but looking Officer Lupinsky in the eyes. "Boys, this is the Carmel police. He's come to tell us Daddy's dead."

Neither boy cried or hugged their mom or said a word. They just threw their sweet potatoes at Officer Lupinsky and returned to the kitchen. Two sailed past him, one hit him in the chest and the other hit the door frame. Lupinsky stepped back off the steps and into the grass in case they were going to reload.

Geraldine moved closer to the doorway.

Lupinsky continued, "It appears he may have committed suicide. Was he depressed about anything?"

"Can't say that I know. He was a private man. But he did leave a letter in his office."

"His office?"

"Yeah, come in, I'll show you."

Lupinsky came back to the doorway and looked over her shoulder for any sign of the boys. "Is it safe?"

"Oh, sure. I'm guessing she's feeding them pie now. They'll be occupied for a bit."

"I just don't want to get hit again."

"Well, if you do, you take it up with their grandma. I warned Mama they don't like sweet potatoes."

Lupinsky followed her to a bedroom with a couch, a

small desk, and a computer. An envelope and a letter lay on the keyboard. "Geraldine" was written on the front of the envelope.

Dear Geraldine,

I no longer want to live. I've always suspected them boys ain't mine. And I don't luv you no more. So, this is goodbye.

PS: Your mom is an evil witch, and I would say it to her face if I wasn't leaving this world for good. And you can tell her that. I don't care.

"When did you discover this?"

"Four days ago."

"And you didn't think to call anybody or go looking for him?"

"No."

"I take it you weren't close?"

"Not so much lately."

"You think that's why he might have been depressed?"

She shrugged her shoulders.

"And that part about the boys not being his?"

"He's right. I sleep around." She gave him a mischievous grin and twirled a lock of her long brown hair.

Lupinsky couldn't believe the level of indifference coming from Geraldine Melvin. "Well, I've done my duty here. I'm going to leave you some paperwork, explaining how things work from here. There is also a number for our department." A sweet potato exploded on the wall next to him. He instinctively drew his gun. The boys ran back to the kitchen. Geraldine bit her lower lip, stepped closer and stuck out her chest. "Say, you're pretty handy with that gun," she said as she pawed at his shoulder.

The officer holstered his weapon and stepped out of reach of Geraldine. "I've got to go. Call if you have any questions."

"Oh, I'll call all right."

Lupinsky made it out without being molested by Geraldine or pummeled by the boys. The widow smiled as she read over the paperwork and moved to sit on the couch. The dog growled and she let him finish *Jersey Shore* without further distractions.

"SHEILA and I have decided to get married and move to Florida." Carmel Mayor Teddy Wiggins scanned the faces in the room to read their reactions. Silence. Everyone stared back at him for a moment with blank faces. Then Big Jim Davis started laughing. Little Jim did too. Big Jim was a tall, skinny man in his seventies. Little Jim was his short and round fifty-three-year-old son. They looked nothing alike, but their laughs were the same.

Larry Fitzgerald of Fitzgerald and Sons Concrete stood up using a cane, took two steps, and stood beside Teddy at the front of the conference room. He slapped

Teddy on the back and said, "Dammit Teddy, if you don't get funnier every year you're in office."

Bob Lawrence from Timeless Construction laughed and said, "You almost had us there, Teddy. Now, let's get back to business. I've got a scramble at Carmel Hills Country Club at 11:00." Bob was the youngest man in the room, having recently turned fifty. He was a health nut and could have passed for forty with slicked-back black hair and a year-round tan.

The mayor replied, "I'm not kidding."

Larry laughed and slapped Teddy's back harder. In fact, he laughed so hard he swallowed an ice cube he had been sucking on since he had drained his whisky when the meeting had been called to order. Big Jim nearly choked too. Not on ice. He was the first person to realize that Teddy was serious.

"I proposed last night." Teddy cleared his throat and waited to see if any more choking would erupt. "We're getting married in December and moving to Clearwater in January."

"Clearwater? Who the hell moves to Clearwater?" asked Bob Lawrence. "Is she a Scientologist?"

"Not that I know of ...," Teddy trailed off. "Come to think of it, we never discussed religion. This has all been very fast."

"Which means you won't be doing it. You're going to take some time to think this over and not make any hasty decisions," ordered Big Jim.

Little Jim added, "Besides, the primaries have

already happened. How the hell are we going to get a puppet?" Big Jim shot him a look. "I mean a candidate to take your place?"

"I've thought of that," Teddy answered. "It's not too late to get an independent on the ballot and tell everyone he's a Republican."

Larry slapped Teddy on the back again. This time it wasn't because he thought Teddy was funny. "You little twit. Even in a hardcore Republican stronghold like Carmel, we can't get people to pull the lever for an independent. They're lazy and stupid."

"Yeah, how do you think we kept you in all these years," Little Jim added.

Larry continued. "You have to run. Four more years, Wiggins. I need four more years and so does everyone in this room." He looked around and everyone nodded. "Your Scientologist will have to wait."

"I never said she was a Scientologist."

"You're moving to Clearwater," said Bob. "Either she is, or her family is."

"That's ridiculous," Teddy replied.

Larry stood up, "Not as ridiculous as you leaving us hanging without time to get a candidate in place."

"No, this can work. I'll throw my endorsement behind anybody you choose. I'll work my tail off for you guys between now and November. And once you have your new hand-picked mayor, I can ride off into the sunset."

Big Jim threatened, "If this doesn't work, you'll ride off on a pole. Tarred and feathered at that."

Teddy gulped. "Now, now. No need to be like that. We've all had a lot of years together. And I've helped you all make a lot of money during that time. Can't you be happy for me?" He looked around the room again. Nobody was happy, least of all *for him*.

The men sitting in the Carmel City Hall conference room with Teddy represented the four largest construction companies headquartered in Carmel. Each had generously donated to Teddy's campaign war chest over the years as well as to certain members of City Council. In return, they had received an unending supply of projects, sweetheart land deals, and preferential tax abatements. Teddy was the face of progress and transformation. The men around the table were the ones who actually pulled the strings.

But Teddy was finished with running America's finest city. He was ready for warm weather, sandy beaches and a second chance at love with his fiancée Sheila. He didn't give a damn about the men in the room anymore. They couldn't provide him with the things she could, and now he valued those things more than the money and power that came with being a mayor. He couldn't believe he was actually thinking these thoughts. But love has a way of disrupting a man's thinking. Scientists say it has something to do with blood flow.

~

TEDDY'S second meeting that day was with the conservative members of the City Council. Currently, that group consisted of six (out of eight) council members. The other two being a Democrat and a Libertarian who had won on a technicality. Everyone was suspicious of the latter.

The outgoing mayor's mission was two-fold. First, he wanted to let them know about his decision to retire so that the most ambitious members could begin to jockey for his job. Secondly, he wanted to suggest he be honored with a farewell float at the upcoming Fourth of July parade, which had grown to legendary status in the state. Residents begin staking out their spots nearly two weeks early, roping off sections of sidewalk and putting out their chairs. *The citizens believed that being able to count on everyone's leaving untouched the scattering of chairs, blankets, umbrellas, etc. along public sidewalks proved that Carmel was still 'The safest little city in America' but it's possible that the belief, like the scattered place markers, was a load of crap.*

They gathered in the same conference room as the morning meeting. In attendance were long-time councilman George Fillmore, newcomer Nathan Hearn, Marcia Gladstone-Davis (wife of Big Jim Davis), Cindy Fiztgerald-Welch (sister of Larry Fitzgerald), Natalie Gladstone-Lawrence (sister-in-law of Bob Lawrence, sister of Marcia Gladstone), and Larisa Wiggins (niece of Mayor Teddy). The City Council was more inbred than European monarchy.

"Everyone, I would like to start the meeting by letting you know that I will not be seeking reelection." Once again, Teddy scanned the room. This time, there was no coughing or laughing. Each one was calculating their next power move. He could see the wheels turning in their heads.

Marcia Gladstone-Davis spoke first. "Did you piss off Big Jim?"

Teddy replied, “No, this is my decision.”

“Oh, have you told Big Jim?” Marcia asked.

"Yes, I've spoken with the various high-impact donors to the party." This was the euphemism they all used for the Big Four construction companies.

Marcia continued, "I bet he was pissed."

"He wasn't pleased," Teddy replied. "But we've agreed that the best course of action is to get an independent candidate on the ballot and then we all throw our support there."

Larisa saw an opportunity, "Can't we just run another Wiggins and capitalize on the name recognition? It happened in Indianapolis." She was right of course. The Democrats had a long-time Congressman retire and simply ran his grandson in his place. Half the electorate didn't even know the difference. Even less knew he had been fired from the Sheriff's Department for sleeping on the job. Now he sleeps in Washington.

"No way you're moving to the front of the line,"

Natalie Gladstone-Lawrence objected. "I don't care if you're his niece. You're only thirty-three and have been on this council for what? Five minutes? No way we're putting her name forward." She looked at each member in the room, daring them to defy her.

"Now, let's not get into any debates on who it's going to be today. There's plenty of time for that," Teddy said.

Natalie cut him off. "Don't think we're going to tolerate any nepotism. We know where *your* bodies are buried."

That caught Teddy off guard, but he recovered. "I've promised not to intervene and support whomever the party decides. It will be up to you in this room and the party committee of course."

"Don't be ridiculous. It will be up to the Big Four," said Marcia.

Natalie replied, "Never say that out loud." She looked around the room.

Teddy said, "Nobody's taking the minutes. This is an informal meeting. Off the record."

"Fine," Natalie said.

"My second bit of business is more of a request. I would like you to introduce a motion in the next City Council meeting to approve funds for a going-away float to celebrate my accomplishments these past twenty years."

"Are you serious?" asked Cindy.

George Fillmore spoke for the first time, "Smart

move. You could use it to introduce your successor as well."

"No, that person can have their own float. This one is about me."

"I suppose you've earned it," said Marcia. Teddy was surprised. "I'll introduce the motion," she continued.

"I'll second," said George. "Consider it done, Teddy."

"By the way," Marcia said. "Where are you going when you retire?"

"Clearwater."

"Clearwater?" asked Natalie. "Twenty years and I had no idea you were a Scientologist."

EPISODE 17: THE WILL

Officer Lupinsky arrived at work early on a Tuesday with coffee and a fresh donut. He normally passed on donuts, due to the stereotype, but Johnny's was having a special promotion, and these were too good to pass up. So, he was in a good mood and hoped to get some paperwork done before everyone else arrived. But the mood didn't last long. As he walked in the door, he was informed by his boss that he would be heading to Madison, Indiana, with a U.S. marshal to transfer an inmate.

"Can't someone else do this today?"

His boss nodded to a gentleman approaching Lupinsky's desk. "Nope. Here comes the marshal. I'll let you two get acquainted." He walked away without even introducing them.

He stood up, "I'm David Lupinsky."

"Hi, I'm Carl Perkins," he said as he offered his hand to shake. "No relation to the musician."

Lupinsky shook his hand and noticed that the marshal was wearing cowboy boots. Blue suede cowboy boots to be exact. *He may not be related*, Lupinsky thought, *but he's obviously a big fan. This isn't going to go well.*

His fears were justified. For the entirety of the two-hour drive, Carl the marshal played Carl the musician on the car stereo via Bluetooth from his iPhone.

Carl Perkins the marshal was as old as Lupinsky imagined the singer might be (if he were still alive). In fact, Perkins the marshal was only fifty-seven years old. Smoking heavily from his early twenties had aged him quickly. His wife had passed three years before and his only son lived in Portland, Oregon. The son owned a vegan smoothie shop and free-range gourd farm. He didn't visit Indiana all that often. Carl the marshal was a creature of habit. He wore the same brown suit every day (he owned three that looked identical), sported the same crew cut from his time in the navy, and kept plugging away at the only job he had known for thirty-two years.

Lupinsky learned from the marshal the purpose of their trip was to pick up a prisoner in Madison and deliver him to Carmel for the reading of a will. Normally, this wouldn't be done, but the will stipulated that Rusty Stubbs be at the reading in person. And since the attorney handling the probate of the estate was a close personal friend and golf partner of Circuit Judge Donavon Tate III, red tape parted like the Red Sea.

Lupinsky disliked the assignment, but as he was still the "new guy," he got stuck doing the pick-up with the marshal. On the opposite end of the spectrum, Perkins was the "old guy" whom the U.S. Marshals Service gave low-risk busy work to keep him out of their hair. The ride down was uneventful. Superficial chit-chat punctuated the breaks between Carl Perkins the musician's songs.

When they arrived, Carl Perkins the marshal asked Lupinky, "You don't like Carl Perkins all that much, do ya?"

"What? I like him just fine."

"I noticed you didn't sing along much."

Lupinsky stammered, "I'm more of a Rolling Stones guy, I guess. I don't know many of the words."

Perkins glared at him for an awkward moment that seemed to never end. Finally, he cracked a smile and slapped Lupinsky on the shoulder, "I'm just messing with you. I won't make you listen on the way back. Besides, the prisoner and the countryside will provide a better soundtrack."

Lupinsky thought that was an odd statement, but nearly two years in Carmel had caused him to question what *was* odd anymore.

RUSTY STUBBS EMERGED from a long hallway flanked by two Jefferson County Sheriff's deputies. The prisoner stopped on command and muttered to himself while rocking back and forth. He had black greasy hair that hadn't seen a shower in at least a week. He had already been allowed to change into civilian clothes from his prison-issued ensemble. Now he was wearing a concert T-shirt from a death metal band neither Carl nor Lupinsky recognized: Banshees of Fate. The Banshees were either an all-female band or five men in drag. Lupinsky couldn't tell, but he was certain that all five were giving the world the middle finger.

Rusty had on torn jeans, construction boots, and as he was being uncuffed, he was allowed to put on a heavily worn leather jacket.

Carl asked, "My notes say he's to be cuffed for the ride. Why are you uncuffing him?"

"My notes say you take him in your own cuffs. Mine stay in Madison," answered the deputy.

Carl nodded without a word and cuffed the prisoner. Lupinsky signed the necessary paperwork, and the two men led Rusty Scrubbs outside.

"Your file says you're a dirtbag, but not a violent one. So, behave yourself, and this will be a pleasant drive to Carmel," Carl instructed Rusty.

"We gonna stop at MacDonald's?" he asked emphasizing the extra "a" he added to the name.

"No, we're not stopping anywhere," Carl the marshal added.

"Well, shit. I was wantin' me some MacDonald's. Oh, well, once I'm rich, I'll get all the MacDonald's I want."

"Rich?" asked Lupinsky. "What makes you think you're going to be rich?"

"I'm going to a will readin' right? Some ol' buzzard I never even met done left me some money."

Carl responded, "You realize once the will reading is over, you're going back to jail."

"Nah, I don't think so. Once I get my money, I'll hire one of them good lawyers. Get me off like that," he held up his cuffed hands and snapped his fingers.

The two officers looked at each other and shook their heads. Carl smiled and said, "We're going to take the scenic route home."

"You don't have to do that on my account," said Lupinsky.

"They told me you were relatively new to Indiana. No, I think you would benefit from seeing more of the Hoosier state. Besides," he looked back at their prisoner, "I don't think he's going to mind."

Rusty rocked and muttered in the back seat. Lupinsky asked, "How much longer will it take going the scenic route?"

"Thirty to forty minutes longer. It will be worth it. You don't have anywhere you need to be right?"

"I suppose not."

Carl pulled away from the Jefferson Sheriff's Office and made his way to Highway 421. A few miles north of the town, they reached the south end of Big Oak Nature preserve. Lupinsky was struck by the beauty of the trees but puzzled by the security fencing around the perimeter.

RUSTY PRESSED his face against the window of the car to look at a hawk. It flew off and Rusty caught a glimpse of a deer. Then a couple more. Finally, a large five-point buck was in his sights. He remembered hunting deer with his dad as a teenager. He leaned over a bit to raise his cuffed hands as high as he could. Armed with an imaginary rifle, he aimed and pulled an imaginary trigger just as the buck took a step forward. His imaginary shot blew the deer into a million pieces. For real.

RUSTY SCREAMED and jumped to the opposite side of the back seat. Carl cracked a slight grin but pretended to ignore him. It also occurred to him that they hadn't put a seat belt on the prisoner, and he considered stopping for a moment so Rusty wouldn't hurt himself. Then he thought, *It will be more fun if I don't.*

Lupinsky asked, "What the hell was that?"

"You're from Detroit. You've never been around a tweaker before? His brain's fried."

"No, not him. I thought I heard an explosion." Lupinsky scanned both sides of the road, even grabbing the rearview mirror, irritating Carl. All he could spot was a completely different set of deer than the ones Rusty had witnessed.

"I didn't hear anything," Carl lied.

Lupinsky looked back towards the deer. Something spooked them and they ran west away from the road. One of them blew up, causing Lupinsky to shout, "That, that," he pointed. "What the hell is going on?"

Rusty screamed louder, while sliding off the backseat and onto the floor.

Carl laughed. "That? Oh, this used to be a proving ground. Old army base that dates back to World War II. They closed it down and turned it into a nature preserve. Still test anti-aircraft guns there, I believe. Anyway, they haven't found all the land mines that were scattered about the place." He looked back to where the deer had been. "I'd say the local wildlife is helping them out in that regard."

"You mean this is normal?" asked Lupinsky.

Rusty started to confess his sins to an imaginary priest. "Bless me father, for I have sinned."

"Normal for this neck of the woods, yeah," Carl replied.

Lupinsky continued, "You drove this way just to spook me with the exploding deer, didn't you?"

"Yep."

Rusty continued, "I stole a car, a guitar, an amp, and some of my stepsister's clothes. But I only wore them that one time, I swear."

Lupinsky looked back at Rusty. "And what about him? I think you've scared him straight."

"I doubt he will remember it tomorrow," said Carl.

"I don't know. A thing like that sticks with you for a long time. Seeing a deer explode."

Rusty continued his confession, "And I took that bag of BBQ potato chips from the convenience store. But they was stale, so that shouldn't count."

Lupinsky shook his head, "I don't think I can take two hours of him confessing his sins. You got a forest with non-exploding wildlife you can drive him through?"

"No, but there's a good local donut shop up the road a ways. Everybody feels better after a donut."

A quarter mile later, they saw a coyote chasing a rabbit. The rabbit darted left, and before the coyote could change direction, it exploded. Lupinsky grabbed the dashboard. Rusty, who had sat back up, screamed and got back on the floor. Carl Perkins the marshal pressed play on his iPhone and turned up the volume on "Matchbox" by Carl Perkins the musician.

~

Clarissa Montgomery checked herself in the mirror. *Am I wearing too much makeup or not enough?* she wondered. *How much does one wear to the reading of a will?* She faced the same level of indecision when choosing her dress earlier. But now she was out of time, and she had to drive from her home in Avon to Carmel, some forty minutes away.

Both places were suburbs of Indianapolis, but that's where the similarities ended. Avon was a blue-collar community, often derided for its endless strip malls and two Super Walmarts about five miles apart. Carmel had the second-highest per capita income in the state and was known for endless roundabouts and homes the size of Walmarts. At least, that's how Clarissa perceived it. Like many people in the Indianapolis metro area, Carmel was the place they loved to hate. Most of them rarely, if ever, had been there, so their strongly held perceptions often were inaccurate.

The will was being read at the Carmel Sheraton Arms Hotel. Clarissa nervously hid in the back, still wondering why she was there. She let her eyes roam around the mid-size banquet room of the hotel. It was newly remodeled and looked considerably more luxurious than the Holiday Inn conference room where she and her Mary Kay friends met twice a month in Avon. A woman in her late sixties, who stopped trusting her husband in her thirties, got breast enhancements in her forties, and lip injections in her fifties, turned to scowl at Clarissa.

An older man in overalls was sitting next to Clarissa. She made a few glances in his direction trying to size him up but without coming across as rude. He looked as out of place as she felt. He wore overalls that were clean but tattered. His salt and pepper hair showed clear signs of hat head—the John Deere cap currently in his lap. A woman sat next to him in a floral print dress that had seen better days. Clarissa assumed she was his wife. Her hair was greying and pulled back in a ponytail. She wore no makeup, and her appearance reminded Clarissa of the Pentecostal women who lived at the end of her block.

Sitting next to her was a younger man in his thirties. He wore a black AC/DC T-shirt, black jeans, and red Converse Chuck Taylors. His eyes darted around the room, and he seemed very nervous.

She continued to take in the scene around her. The curtains were open, letting in bright sunlight that was almost blinding. The room was divided with fifty chairs on either side of an aisle in the middle. At the front was a podium with a microphone and two chairs. In the row in front of her, a blond woman looked familiar. She reminded Clarissa of an actress whose name she couldn't place.

~

D.L. HALIBURTON DIED DOING what he loved most: having sex. Unfortunately, he wasn't having sex with his wife at the time, so the *Carmel Bugle* reported he died in his sleep. Even in death, the paper was afraid to cross him. His romantic partner at the time of his passing was Mrs. Haliburton's yoga instructor. She fired the yoga instructor and took up Pilates.

In many ways, Catherine Haliburton had been ready to be rid of her philandering husband, and her yoga instructor, for that matter. So, she wasn't too distraught about her husband's passing. She had loved him when they first met, but thirty years and at least that many of his affairs later, she had grown tired of the man. His vast wealth would ease his passing. The only thing that worried her was the number of people filing into the room where the will was about to be read and if she was going to have to share any of her late husband's estate with any of them. She eyed a middle-aged woman with brown hair and a simple blue dress who slipped self-consciously to the back row of the room. Catherine Haliburton gave her a nasty glare, assuming she was one of D.L.'s many one-night stands or temporary flings.

SUDDENLY, there was a commotion as two men escorted a man in handcuffs into the room. "Why can't we get MacDonald's first?" said the man in handcuffs.

"There's no time," said Officer Lupinsky. "You should have eaten the lunch we had for you at the station."

Rusty Scrubbs, the man in handcuffs replied, "That was a baloney sandwich. Ain't no rich guy eatin' no baloney sandwich."

"You're not a rich guy," said Lupinsky.

"Well, I will be, soon as this will readin' gets done. Then you'll have to treat me with respect. Buy me MacDonald's and such when I ask. It's different for rich prisoners. I seen it on an episode of *Cops*."

Carl Perkins, the marshal, asked Lupinsky, "You want me to hit him over the head, so he sleeps through this?"

Lupinsky considered the offer. "Yes. I mean no. Yes, I would love to have you shut him up, but there are too many witnesses with their iPhones out right now recording this."

Perkins scanned the room and counted eight phones documenting the arrival of one Rusty Scrubbs, possibly rich convict. "I believe you're right." He pulled Scrubbs close and whispered in his ear. "Now, you're going to be quiet until your name is called or I'm going to drive you back to that place where the deer explode and leave you there. Got it?"

Rusty Stubbs nodded his head emphatically and didn't speak. As much as he loved fireworks and movies with lots of mindless explosions, he had no desire to see any more wildlife blow up. The officers led him to a row and sat on either side of him. Rusty trembled slightly. Carl Perkins the marshal noticed and grinned ear to ear.

~

After watching the arrival of Rusty, Catherine Haliburton grabbed Stanley Davis, the family attorney, by the shoulder, "This is turning into a damn circus. Can we get this started?"

He looked over the room and replied, "I believe everyone is here, so yes, we can."

"I still don't understand why we had to do this here."

"We had no choice," he replied. "Our office doesn't have a meeting room large enough to hold all of the interested parties."

She looked at the cross-section of humanity behind her. "What interested parties?" She pointed at herself, "*I'm* his wife. Was his wife." She pointed to three disinterested twenty-somethings in the first row. "There are our children," she paused and waived at three additional teenagers in the second row, "and yes, the illegitimate kids he fathered. Who the hell are the rest of these people?"

"They've all been named in the will, Mrs. Haliburton. And they all are required to be here."

She turned back and looked at all the people. Her kids turned to look who they were going to be sharing the inheritance with, and this caused the illegitimate kids to turn and look too.

She turned back to Stanley. "This is your fault. Whose side are you on?"

"Your husband's, Mrs. Haliburton. These were his wishes."

"He's dead. You're supposed to be on my side now."

"You know I'm legally bound to execute your husband's will faithfully. Now, please. Can we begin?"

"I'm going to contest the hell out of this will," she said. "You know that, don't you?"

"Mrs. Haliburton, you haven't even heard it yet. How can you be so sure?"

"How many people are named in this will?"

"Seventy-five."

"That's how I can be so sure," she answered.

D.L. HALIBURTON HAD GROWN to resent a variety of people in his final years—not the least of whom was his wife. Some of this was his cantankerous self and some may have been due to cognitive decline, although there was no proof of it. Family lawyer Stanley Davis had suspected as much when D.L. wanted to amend his will and had his client examined to cover himself in case the family challenged the amended document. They would anyway, but at least he would have proof of a sound mind.

Of course, the changes D.L. wanted for the will

would make anyone think he was crazy. Stanley wondered if he was spiteful or just loved a good joke. Indeed, many of the people in the room were women or the children of women he had had dalliances with over the years. But some were random strangers. D.L. wanted to irritate his wife and mess with the heads of total strangers. So, one day he picked out fifty random people from the state of Indiana. He took their names from stories he found online, yearbooks he had an assistant pick up at a garage sale, and even an old phone book.

With list in hand, he picked fifty random possessions of varying value and willed the items to them. D.L. told Stanley none of the fifty people knew him or knew why they were chosen. In addition, D.L. didn't separate them from relatives, kids, and acquaintances who were named in the will. The will was written in such a way that several random people were named before the first relative. His wife wasn't named until number 46, and the kids were in the low sixties.

In all it made for an entertaining reading of the will. The event began with Miles Sjogren from Goshen, Indiana. "To Miles Sjogren, I leave the marble statue of David that stands in the lobby of our downtown office."

There was much rumbling through the room as many recalled a picture of Mrs. Haliburton at the New Year's Eve ball in 2011 with her hand on David's naked bum. She was holding an empty bottle of champagne and the director of media relations for Haliburton and

Associates was holding *her* bum. He spent a good deal of 2012 looking for a new job.

Next came Sue Talbot of Rushville, Indiana. "To Sue Talbot, I leave Seasons Two and Five of my. *M*A*S*H* DVDs."

"Enough, this is madness," Mrs. Haliburton interjected. "It's clear my husband was mentally unfit when this will was written."

Stanley replied, "According to the doctor I had examine him, he was fine." He paused, "Mentally, anyway. This may be unorthodox, but it's legal and it reflects his final wishes. So, we must continue."

"I'm suing you."

"I'm sure you will," Stanley answered.

"What? How dare you take that tone with me?"

"If I have a tone, it's because you're interrupting. There are a lot of people here for the will and they would like to get on with their day."

"Well, I'm sorry I'm interrupting the reading of *my* husband's will."

She sat down in a huff and Stanley proceeded, "And to Nicolas Webb, I leave the weathervane on the top of my barn."

The couple sitting next to Clarissa looked at each other in wonder. She overheard the wife ask, "Nick, why did he leave you a weathervane?"

"I have no idea. I've never met the man," Nick responded.

Stanley's assistant approached Nick and handed

him an envelope. "Enclosed are instructions on when and where you can retrieve the gift you've been bequeathed."

Nick asked, "Could you tell me, is the weathervane still attached to the barn?"

"It is my understanding that yes, it is indeed still attached."

"So, I'm supposed to take it down myself?"

"Instructions are in the letter."

Nick's wife chimed in, "I'm starting to think that Mrs. Haliburton is right. This guy was nuts."

Nick opened the envelope and skimmed the instructions. He turned to his wife. "I think you're right."

STANLEY CONTINUED, "Next up, to Mandy Pepperhorns, I leave the lifeguard stand at the Carmel Hills Country Club pool, which I personally paid for and can take back at any time I choose. This being the time I choose."

"Ahh, isn't that sweet," said Mandy.

Alex, her boyfriend and a lawyer himself, squirmed a little. "Why did he leave you that? Did the two of you ever ..."

She glared at him. "No, we never whatever you were about to say. I guess he just saw my act." Mandy was an exotic dancer and performed under the name Mandy Pepperhorns. She looked enough like the lifeguard in the movie *The Sandlot* that she took the persona of the actress. "Maybe he wanted me to start the performance from on top of the lifeguard stand. I hope Sunny will let me incorporate it into the show."

"I thought you were thinking of giving it up?"

"Money doesn't grow on trees. Unless you're planning on putting a ring on this," she held up her left hand, "*and* making me a stay-at-home wife, I gotta earn." Alex didn't respond. "And since that's not going to happen any time soon," she put her hand on his shoulder to console him, "seeing you're going through a divorce right now, let's just keep this light and simple. Okay?"

Alex was in deep smit with Mandy, but he knew she was right. He needed to keep his focus on getting through the divorce and being there for his kids. If Mandy was still there afterwards, so be it.

CLARISSA WAITED another thirty minutes to hear her name. Partly because of the number of bequests and partly because Mrs. Haliburton kept protesting. Stanley announced, "And to Clarissa Montgomery, I leave my Audi SUV."

In an instant everything got cloudy. She thought she heard a woman shout, "That motherf..." but she couldn't be sure. Clarissa's car had been on its last leg. And with one kid in college and one about to graduate, she had been struggling to make ends meet as it was. Her ex-husband hadn't paid alimony in years, and she wasn't quite sure where he even was. So, for all the random gifts that D.L. left, this one had the most impact. Clarissa wept.

Stanley's assistant handed her an envelope, and she could barely form words. This was the win Clarissa had been praying for since last year.

CATHERINE HALIBURTON WAS NEXT. She got all the houses (Carmel, Miami, and Greece), his shares in the business, and roughly $40 million in cash and securities. She was relieved. Up until now, she had worried one of these random people in the room with her would get all or most of it. *She sent her assistant to the hotel bar to get her a vodka and tonic. "Make it a double. And bring two."*

OFFICER LUPINSKY SMELLED her before he saw her. It was a combination of cigarettes and cheap perfume. Before he could turn around, he heard Geraldine Melvin say, "Officer, when you get done with him, you wanna put those cuffs on me?"

She stood at the end of the row, holding a lit cigarette, dressed in a black tube top dress and stripper heels. Gone was the ankle boot she had on when he first met her. "You gonna let me in?" she asked Carl Perkins the marshal. He leaned back and let her squeeze past him. Rusty tried to grab her butt, but Carl slapped his hands. Lupinsky leaned back to let her in, and she nudged her butt closer to him anyway. She sat close and didn't even try to keep her voice down.

"Hi darlin'. You been thinking about me, 'cause I haven't stopped thinking about you since you was over at my place."

Lupinsky nervously looked at Carl Perkins the marshal. "I was just there to notify her about her husband's passing." He looked at Geraldine. "What are you doing here?"

She pawed at his epaulets. "I came here for the will. Didn't know my cute officer was going to be here too." She took gum out of her mouth and stuck it under her seat. Then she held up her cigarette. "Need a fix? I'll share."

Lupinsky turned red and was horrified to see that the entire row in front of him had turned around to hear his reply. "No, I don't want a fix, and you can't smoke in here. Put that out."

She shrugged and dropped it on the carpet, squishing it out with her shoe. "Mama and the boys made me late. Did they already call my name?"

"No, they didn't call you yet," Lupinsky replied.

She put her hand on his thigh. "If I win a million, you want to help me pick out a new trailer home?"

He moved her hand off his leg. "No, and what do

you mean by win? This isn't the lottery. It's the reading of a will."

"Will, lottery, it's all the same."

"Did you know the deceased?"

"No, but I think my husband did. They told me something was left to him, and I could come in his place."

At that moment they heard Stanley say, "And to Joe Melvin, I leave one million dollars, my parade float, the contents of my storage unit, and my undying love."

"His undying love?" asked Geraldine.

"His storage unit? What storage unit?" asked Mrs. Haliburton.

"His parade float?" asked Mayor Teddy Wiggins, who was now standing at the back of the room.

Stanley replied, "I see this particular section of the will has raised a lot of questions, but we need to keep moving. I'll address those after we've concluded the reading it through to the end."

RUSTY STUBBS WAS STARTING to get antsy. He twitched and squirmed, but kept his mouth shut, remembering Carl Perkins' threat. Finally, it was his turn. Stanley called out, "To Rusty Stubbs, I leave our river view estate on the Ohio River in Harrison County."

Rusty jumped up and before Carl Perkins the marshal could stop him, he leapt into the aisle and started dancing a jig, whooping and hollering like he was at some country hoedown. Catherine Haliburton, who by now was drinking vodka and tonics like water, nearly choked on an ice cube laughing. It was the one bequest in this bizarre series of events that she could get behind.

The Harrison County Estate, as it was called, was no estate. Yes, it was technically along the Ohio River, and it was a plot of land the length of a football field, but only eight feet wide. It stretched between two mansions that were part of the Haliburton family's property for nearly a century. At some point, D.L.'s grandfather had pissed off his own grandfather and had his inheritance cut down to that sliver of land. It was assumed he would accept the family humiliation and sell his plot to one of his siblings. But he didn't. He kept it for spite and there has been nothing on the land but an outhouse and a small dock for ninety years. Now, it would be occupied by this Rusty character. *At least D.L. got one right*, Mrs. Haliburton thought.

Stanley's assistant came to deliver the instructions. She saw the handcuffs and hesitated. Carl Perkins the marshal said, "You can give that to me. I'll give it to him when he quits dancing." She nodded and handed it over.

When he finally settled down, Rusty said to Lupinsky, "See I told you I's gonna be rich. You can take me to the rich people jail now. After we go to Mack Donald's, of course."

"Of course," Lupinsky replied. He looked at Perkins and rolled his eyes. "Ain't that right."

Perkins smiled. "Makes sense to me. Let's all go to 'Mack Donald's.' You buying, Mr. Rich Guy?"

As the men tried to slip out of the room, Geraldine grabbed Lupinsky's arm. "Will I see you again? I could use some help blowing that million dollars."

"I doubt it, Mrs. Melvin."

"Call me Geraldine."

“I doubt it, Geraldine.”

“Ah, come on honey,” she leaned in closer. “I got a wild imagination.”

"Goodbye, Geraldine."

As they slipped out, Stanley's assistant motioned for her to follow him. He walked over to the mayor and told them both, "When this is over there will be a quick meeting with the two of you and Mrs. Haliburton regarding the will."

Mayor Teddy asked, "What for?"

"You've been named in the will too, Mayor Wiggins. But for both you and Mrs. Melvin, to get your share, you have to agree to Mr. Haliburton's terms."

Teddy pressed, "What terms? What is this about?"

"I can’t get into it now, but it involves a parade."

Geraldine asked, "He wants us to throw him a parade?"

"No, it’s related to the Carmel Fourth of July parade."

Mayor Teddy, Mrs. Melvin, and Mrs. Haliburton were ushered into a smaller room with a conference table and eight chairs.

"Please have a seat," said Stanley.

"What is this all about?" asked Mrs. Haliburton

Stanley didn't address her but spoke directly to George Melvin's wife. "Mrs. Melvin, you receive $1 million as the next of kin to your husband George. You also receive a parade float, and the contents of Mr. Haliburton's storage unit located at 1900 East 146th Street. The rent has been paid through the end of the year, so you will have plenty of time to empty it or continue using it as you wish."

Mrs. Melvin screamed, stood up and kissed the attorney on the forehead, leaving a bright red lipstick mark. Mrs. Haliburton shook her head and said, "Great! Another one of his whores."

"I was NOT one of your husband's whores."

"She wasn't, Mrs. Haliburton," Stanley said. And with some small smirk of satisfaction he added, "Her husband was."

The two wives said in unison, "What?"

"Let me continue with the mayor and maybe that will clear it up," said Stanley. "Mrs. Melvin gets the parade float, but it must honor George and D.L. Haliburton by displaying the art they made together in the next Carmel Fourth of July parade. Teddy, you will receive $400,000 if you agree to D.L.'s terms."

Mrs. Haliburton interrupted, "What art?"

Teddy said, "What terms?"

To Mrs. Haliburton, Stanley replied, "When they were both alive, they would meet secretly and create sculptures in their own unique way."

Geraldine asked, "And what way was that?"

"They welded naked together except for the protective apron and helmet." Then he turned to Teddy. "Mr. Mayor, for you to receive this money, you must agree to the contents of the storage shed being displayed on a float during the parade."

"And what are the contents of the storage shed?" Teddy asked.

Mrs. Melvin echoed, "Yes, just what the hell is in there?"

"Inside the shed are the sculptures that George and Haliburton created together out of steel."

"I don't believe it," Geraldine interjected. "My husband never sculpted a thing in his life."

"On the contrary. He and George would meet in the aforementioned storage unit, disrobe, put on protective helmets and aprons, and weld metal sculptures of people and animals. Their creative relationship went on, as far as I can tell, about three years."

Mrs. Haliburton said, "That sick bastard."

Mrs. Melvin asked, "Your husband or mine?"

"Both." She took a shot of vodka from a flask. "I'm not going to allow this to happen. I'm not having my husband's homoerotic art on display for the whole town to see."

"Actually, there's nothing erotic about the art," said Stanley. "The figures are abstract for the most part and not engaged in any sexual behavior."

"Well, the art might not be erotic, but the manner in which it was created certainly was," said Mrs. Haliburton.

"How did they keep from burning their ..." Mrs. Melvin trailed off.

Teddy was seeing dollar signs. "Sounds okay by me. I agree to the terms."

"Teddy, I thought you were on my side," said Mrs. Haliburton.

He pleaded with outstretched arms. "Mrs. Haliburton, this is what your husband wanted."

"What about what I want?"

"And to get my money I have to agree too?" asked Geraldine.

"Yes, that's correct, Mrs. Melvin."

"For a million dollars, you can roll those sculptures through the streets of Carmel, and I'll do a naughty dance on 'em if you like," she said. "Did they make any poles?"

Stanley blushed. "That won't be necessary, but I appreciate your cooperation and enthusiasm."

"I'm suing to keep this from happening."

"I anticipated you would, Mrs. Haliburton," said Stanley.

She turned to the mayor, "You know, Teddy, I'm not contributing to your next campaign."

Since he hadn't made the news of his retirement public yet, he said, "I'm sorry you feel that way, Mrs. Haliburton

EPISODE 18: TRENDY BOOZE

Doug Murphy paced back and forth in the reception area of the Aztec Hillbilly Brewery headquarters in Carmel, Indiana. It was only a month until the Fourth of July, and Doug was the city employee in charge of corporate sponsorships for both the parade and the Carmelfest event that accompanied it. Carl Bernard had called him for an urgent meeting that morning. Bernard was the vice president of marketing at Aztec Hillbilly and the man who had committed $100,000 worth of sponsorship to the mayor's favorite event. Murphy was worried they were about to pull their commitment. After the Bud Light fiasco, beer companies were reevaluating all their partnerships, no matter how safe they might seem.

Doug started to take off his jacket, but realized his armpits were soaked with nervous sweat and pulled it back on to hide his stains and embarrassment. He continued to mutter to himself about the counterarguments he intended to use. "We're as American as apple pie. It's a Fourth of July parade. Who's going to boycott you for that? Think of the children. How can we afford rides if there's not a beer sponsor for the Tilt-a-Whirl?"

Regina Simpson tapped her feet and hoped her boss would hurry up. Doug's muttering under his breath made her nervous. *This guy is about to come unhinged*, she thought. *And the frat boys running this brewery don't pay me enough to take a bullet from a nut job.* She dug pepper spray out of her purse and kept an eye on Doug.

A light blinked on her phone. "Mr. Bernard will see you now," she practically shouted. She stood up, adjusted the Dashiki slipcover on her office chair, and motioned for him to walk in front of her. No way she was going to turn her back on the guy who had just talked to himself for 15 minutes in her lobby. This was her lobby. Her place of Zen. No muttering white boy was going to mess that up.

At the last second, she stepped in front of Doug and opened the door to Mr. Bernard's office. “You can go in." She shut the door behind him and returned to her desk. She replaced the pepper spray and dug out some weed edibles that she drove to Michigan to buy every other month. Regina took a deep breath and decided it was all Mr. Bernard's problem now.

"Douglas, have a seat. Welcome." Carl Bernard

motioned to a set of leather chairs in front of his oversized cherry desk. "Thanks for seeing me on short notice."

"Oh, no problem. Unless there is a problem?" Doug was sweating and already losing his composure.

"Do you want a drink? Some water or a beer? I think we can make that happen." Bernard laughed and indicated the window behind his desk that overlooked the production floor of the brewery below.

"No, I'm fine." He wasn't fine.

"Let me get to the point." Bernard frowned and that made Doug sweat even more. "I know that lots of banners and whatnot have been printed for the parade. Lots of marketing already done." He paused for moment and then leaned forward. "But we want to make a change."

There it was. The news Doug had been worried about since he got the call from Bernard's assistant the previous afternoon. The news that had kept him up all night. He forgot all the objections he practiced and went right to begging.

"Oh, Mr. Bernard. Please don't do this to us now. I don't have time to secure another sponsor."

"Another sponsor? What the hell are you talking about?"

"You said make a change."

"In products! Did you think we were dropping the event?" He laughed, and Doug felt embarrassed. "No, we just don't want our beer brand to be the sponsor." He got up and walked over to a small fridge next to a fully restored coin-operated deer hunting game. The graphics on the side of the game showed a deer in the crosshairs of a hunting rifle. Doug thought the deer looked like him.

Bernard pulled out a white can and tossed it to Doug. He ducked instead of catching it. The can skidded off the desk and onto the floor.

Bernard shook his head. "Doug, relax for heaven's sake." He grabbed another can from the fridge and walked it over to him. Bernard pointed to the labeling. "What do you think of that?"

Doug looked it over. It was white with a metallic grey silhouette of a person holding a can and a cell phone.

"We want to know how quickly we can change all the banners, signage, and social media marketing to Trendy Booze. It's the newest lifestyle brand in the Aztec Hillbilly family of products. We're still in, we just want to promote this product instead."

Doug's initial panic had started to subside. "You mean this stuff is actually called Trendy Booze?"

"Yes."

"You're kidding me. When you first handed it to me, I thought that was a placeholder."

"No, that's the name."

Doug looked from the can to Bernard. His initial fear of being dropped by the sponsor had given way to disbelief. "Did you come up with this yourselves or did you pay some outside firm for this? Because if you did, you got ripped off."

"What do you mean? Our in-house people came up with this campaign and it's brilliant. Today's young people want you to get right to the point. They don't want to sort through a bunch of options on the shelf. Sure, we could go the craft beer route and come up with all sorts of names like Rail Splitter Lager and Dragon's Breath IPA. But this is about social proof and influencer marketing and all that shit."

"Huh? Can you repeat that in English?"

"We put a silhouette of pretty people with a can in one hand and a cell phone held up in a selfie pose in the other and we sell the hell out of it to teens and twenty-somethings."

"Teens? It's alcohol."

Bernard replied, "Oh, don't be naive. You didn't get drunk when you were in high school?"

"Well, yeah, but ..."

"No buts. Any booze manufacturer that tells you they aren't considering the vast underage drinking market is full of shit."

"Okay, but what's in it?"

"Does it matter what's in it?" He answered himself. "No, of course not. What matters is which influencers we get to swallow it on TikTok."

~

Over at Marci Emerald's condo

"They want me to swallow *what* on TikTok?"

"Trendy Booze," said her agent.

Marci looked at her phone. "Oh, I'm not getting good reception here. I thought you said something X-rated at first."

Her agent dropped his Red Bull on his desk when he considered what she might have thought he said. "Shit!"

"What?"

"Nothing, I just made a mess." The agent, Ray Daniels, grabbed a box of Kleenex from a drawer and tried to keep the spill away from his laptop. "Um, just so we're clear in case I'm approached, and as your agent, I need to know these things, what if someone *does* want you to do something X-rated?"

“Look, you little sleaze ball, I'm not doing it. I considered Only Fans when the university thing went down. But now that I'm back with Sophislete and have my own line, I'm not that desperate. Besides, the new reality show contract has a clause. You should know that."

"Right, I just wanted to know where you stand on the variety of offers we get, so I can act on your behalf."

"No, you just want to know if you're ever going to see me naked, you little perv."

Her agent said nothing, both confirming Marci's

suspicions and making her wonder what she actually paid this guy for anyway.

Marci was tired of waiting. "So back to this booze thing. How much are they offering?"

"They will pay every time you drink it on TikTok. $25K for around the house. $40K to be seen in public with a can in your hand. And $75K if you'll post Instagram and TikTok scenes of you hosting a pool party and serving it to your guests."

"What's it taste like?"

"I haven't tasted it," Daniels lied. It tasted like bull piss. "But if you hate it, you wash it down with whatever you want when the cameras aren't rolling."

Marci considered the offer while she watched traffic going by from her fourth story condominium window. She had come a long way since her fall from grace as an influencer a year and half ago. She had been caught up in the university admissions scandal where wealthy families paid money under the table to have their kids admitted to schools where they didn't qualify for entry. Some of the parents had been convicted and sent to jail. The ones with better lawyers paid hefty fines. The ones with the best lawyers like Marci's were suddenly dual citizens and living in Europe.

Since that time, Marci had been kidnapped by a fringe group of activists called the Lederhosen Mafia. This made her a sympathetic character again in the eyes of the fickle public, and she had even managed to get an endorsement deal with Sophislete (the athleisure brand for women who lean more towards leisure than athletics).

And in just a few weeks, Marci would start filming her new reality show on the Home Network. The premise for the show was that she would be rehabbing a house in the trendy Irvington neighborhood in Indianapolis. In reality, she would be filmed at a Victorian house in Carmel, Indiana, while a separate crew would be rehabbing an identical house, built by the same builder, in Irvington. This was the only way that Marci Emerald would agree to do it, and since this was reality TV, none of it was real.

But there was no guarantee the show would be a hit. She knew she had to take good offers while she was still marketable.

"Marci, are you still there?"

"Tell them $125K for the party and they're catering the food too," she replied.

"Consider it done," her agent said.

DOUG MURPHY REPORTED BACK to Mayor Teddy after his meeting with Aztec Hillbilly. "I've got great news!"

"Out with it," Teddy chugged the last of a Starbucks coffee and checked his loosened tie to see if he had dripped on it. "I've had a bad morning, and I could use some good news."

"It went better than I expected, Mr. Mayor. There's a little hiccup, but I think it's going to work out in our favor."

"Hiccup?" asked Teddy. "Doug, you know I don't like hiccups."

"In your favor, sir."

"In my favor? Since when has a hiccup ever been in anyone's favor? When was the last time you hiccuped at dinner, looked at your wife and said, 'that was fortuitous?'"

"Sir, please let me explain." Teddy leaned back and crossed his arms but stayed silent. "Mr. Mayor, they would like to change their sponsorship from their beer to their new lifestyle drink called Trendy Booze."

"But we've already printed ..." he shouted.

"And they will cover the cost to reprint and expedite new signs, etc. And for the trouble, I've asked them to foot the bill for your float as well."

Teddy grinned. "Outstanding, Doug. That is outstanding." He thought for a moment. "Let's keep that money for my float thing between us, Doug."

"Sir?"

"Maybe the taxpayers don't need to know about that arrangement is all I'm saying. Now, any other good news?"

"Yes, they have secured Marci Emerald, the influencer, to ride on their float to promote Trendy Booze. This will be the float in front of yours."

“Right in front of me. Is that a good idea? Will she get more attention than me?”

“No sir, this is great. It means all eyes will be on the parade when the two of you roll by.”

"Well done, Dougie, my boy. Well done." He stood up, came around his desk, and shook Doug's hand. "And I'll be putting in a good word for you with my chosen successor." He paused, realizing he hadn't meant to say that last part out loud. "Of course, I mean my elected successor. It's the voters who get to choose."

"Of course, sir," Doug replied.

"Of course," the mayor emphasized. "Looking forward to your next update."

THE LOBBY of the Elysian Hotel in downtown Carmel, Indiana was buzzing. It was filming day for Marci Emerald’s organic social media posts for Trendy Booze, which meant nothing would be organic about the short videos they were about to shoot. Each one was planned, orchestrated, and staged. There was a lighting team, a make-up team, a wardrobe person, and wrangler for Marci’s new golden-chihuahua-doodle named Taco Belle. The person who sold her the dog said it was one of a kind. It had the body of a chihuahua but the curly hair and long legs of the popular golden doodles. The dog was extremely self-conscious and needed constant reassurance. Hence the dog wrangler to keep it occupied while Marci was filming.

A middle-aged man wearing a black V-neck T-shirt, black velvet blazer, black jeans, no socks, and black velvet loafers entered the lobby. He looked around like he was waiting for applause. Marci's agent, Ray Daniels, stood up.

"You must be Ray," said Carl. He paused to leer at the influencer, "And this must be the social media darling I've heard so much about."

"Marci, I would like you to meet Mr. Bernard of the Aztec Hillbilly company," said her agent.

Carl Bernard clasped her hand in both of his and leaned into her personal space. "I'm thrilled to finally meet you, Ms. Emerald."

She batted her eyes and put her free hand on top of his. "Call me Marci," she said. Marci knew how to schmooze and flirt with the money men of the various companies she endorsed.

Bernard looked around for the Aztec Hillbilly marketing team and on cue they rushed up to serve. "Get Ms. Emerald and Ray here a Trendy Booze."

"Of course, sir," said a staff member in a Trendy Booze T-shirt. He popped the tabs on two cans and handed them over. Then he grabbed a third and gave it to Bernard.

Marci held up her can and said, "Cheers." After taking a drink, she wrinkled her face and said, "Dear God, that tastes like bull piss."

A horrified Ray glanced at Bernard for a reaction. He shrugged it off and took a drink from his can.

Ray said, "Now, I know it's not that bad. Let's all have a drink." He took a sip from his own can and quickly thought of a lie. "Not bad, sort of an earthy tone I'm catching there."

Carl Bernard got a call on his cell phone. The ringtone was "I'm Too Sexy." He looked at Marci and said, "Too sexy, am I right?" He winked, and she gagged a little in her mouth. Her agent noticed but wasn't sure if it was the smarmy comment or the Trendy Booze.

He took one more sip as Bernard walked away. At first, he tried to swallow, then let some of it dribble out of his mouth. Then it was too much, and he spit it on the floor. "Nope, that's bull piss. 100 percent."

"I'm not drinking this, Marci said.

"We've already cashed the check." He glanced back at Bernard, who was distracted with his call. "Give me that." He took her can and walked over to a tree in a giant brass pot. Checking once more to see that Bernard wasn't looking, he poured both his and Marci's drinks out and handed her back the can. "You can pretend to drink it the rest of the day. I'll find some herbal tea for you to pour in there."

"I'm off herbal tea. I'm on tri-hydrogenated root water with hemp whip."

"I'm not even going to ask what the hell that is. But I do need to know where to get it."

"Don't worry, Dina has it," she nodded her head

towards the dog wrangler. "She keeps it in the backpack with Taco Belle's anxiety meds."

"Taco Bell, you brought lunch?"

"No, Taco Belle. My new dog." She pointed to the wrangler and her bizarre pet.

Ray looked at the dog and shuddered. "What breed is that thing?"

"It's a golden chihuahua doodle. The only one in Carmel."

"No offense but it looks like a Far Side comic come to life."

Marci asked, "Far Side, what's that?"

"Never mind," said Ray. "He's done with his phone call."

Bernard approached the influencer and her agent. "I'm sorry, we've got a distribution problem down at our brewery in Florida. A couple of the guys were running a cock fighting ring after hours and we got raided. I won't be able to stick around and watch you looking pretty and swallowing my stuff." He gave her another wink.

Her agent said, "No problem at all. We will miss your input, but rest assured the team here has it all in hand. We'll make sure everyone knows how much Marci enjoys Trendy Booze." On cue, he and Marci held up their empty cans and pretended to drink.

~

Back in the mayor's office, Teddy was sharing his thoughts on his final parade as mayor. "Doug, I've been thinking about my float. I want it to start with a model of the sleepy little town that Carmel was when I took office. In the middle, a model of Carmel as it is today, and then a futuristic model of what Carmel could look like in the future. The past, present, and future of our city. And right in the middle of it, I'll be sitting on my throne ..." He coughed and changed his mind. "Or whatever chair you feel is appropriate for such an occasion."

"Yes, sir, we can make that happen. I'll get some artists on it right away," said Doug. "That is unless you would like to choose the artist?"

"Not sure I can take a risk on that Splatter guy again," he muttered under his breath. "Use Premier Parades," he said to Doug.

Premier Parades was on the south side of Indianapolis. The company builds floats and supplies parade float parts and materials for organizations throughout the country. Anyone who's watched the Tournament of Roses Parade, Macy's Thanksgiving Day Parade, or even Disney's Christmas Parade, has seen Premier's work.

"Do want to see a mock-up first or for it to be a surprise?"

"I trust you but not that much. Yes, I want to see a mock-up before you pull the trigger on this. Understood?"

"Yes sir, I understand."

"Good. Now if you will excuse me, I've got other matters to attend to."

This is going to be the best Fourth of July parade yet, Teddy thought.

~

ON THE OTHER side of town, Marci spit out a mouthful of Trendy Booze. "This is going to be the worst Fourth of July ever."

"It's not that bad, is it?" asked Ray. "I thought this Cherry flavor was better than the original."

"Okay, so it's cherry-flavored bull piss," said Marci. "It's still bull piss."

"How can you even know that?" he asked.

She gave him a *you're-about-to-die* look. "Just make sure all the cans I have to drink that day are filled with my root water."

He wrote it on his iPhone. "Root water."

Marci added, "Hydrogenated root water with hemp whip."

"And if they are out of this hemp whip?"

"The hemp whip isn't in it," she replied. "It's what they do to it."

"I'm not following you."

"The bottles are whipped with ropes made out of hemp to symbolize the decolonization of the beverage industry and to center water in an equitable space before it is consumed by people of privilege."

He looked at her, dumbfounded by the words that had just come out of her mouth. "Why can't you just drink bottled water like the rest of us?"

"Like some peasant colonizer? Do you even know what I'm about?"

"I'll order the hydrogenated root water ..."

"With hemp whip."

"With hemp whip. Anything else?"

"Can you pick up a bag of vegan dog treats for Taco Belle?"

"She's vegan?"

"Of course."

"Of course," he replied. Ray left to run the errands and wondered how his life had turned out this way. He'd entered college wanting to become an environmental attorney. Suing companies that polluted the environment. By the time he left, he had an offer from a firm that represented athletes and celebrities—an offer he grabbed without a moment's regard to his former idealism. Marci Emerald had him wondering if it was too late to change his life.

MATT, Tony, Devon, and Willy had been riding their bikes around town with no particular agenda. They were still banned from GameStop for the scratch-off ticket heist and nobody they knew with a pool was home. They had made their way downtown and were riding on Third Street. When they turned the corner on Maple, they discovered the roads and sidewalks were temporarily blocked. A film crew was shooting exterior shots on an old Victorian house. It was one of the few that had survived the downtown Carmel house holocaust of the past fifteen years. Timeless Homes had been buying small, *older homes with unique, almost irreplaceable elements of charm and nostalgia* as fast as possible. Then they would level them and build behemoth homes that started at three quarters of a million dollars and up.

Matt recognized what was happening. "Hey, this must be where Marci Emerald is filming her show. I saw it on TikTok."

Tony replied, "Do you think she's here now?"

Before anyone could reply, Marci exited a small trailer and made her way to the sidewalk that ran in front of the house. The boys watched the camera crew get in position and a man and a woman giving her instructions. The man had red hair and was an inch shorter than Marci. The woman was dressed in a black shirt and black pants, despite the summer heat.

Devon declared, "I'm going to get on TV."

Willy, the shortest of the boys, pushed forward to get a better view. Then he looked up at Devon and asked, "How?"

The boys surveyed the cordons which had a couple

of staff members attending them. Two were about ten feet apart, one covering the sidewalk and one covering the street.

Devon said, "You guys ride up to the guy covering the street, I'll turn around like I'm going to go home. Act like you're going to try to go around him and see if you can draw the guy over who is covering the sidewalk. As soon as he gets distracted, I'll ride through the yard around the barrier and onto the sidewalk behind Marci. Hopefully, I time it so the camera is rolling."

Matt answered, "You know they will just film it again without you, right? You won't get in the show."

"Yeah, I know that. But maybe they will have a blooper DVD one day, and the shot of me riding behind her while the director cusses and says 'cut' will be on it."

The boys all nodded their heads as they had watched many blooper videos over the years. Matt, Willy and Tony confirmed they were in and rode off to cause the distraction. Devon rode away and hid himself and his bike behind a tree. As soon as the sidewalk guard moved to help his colleague with the other three boys, Devon took off with his phone camera rolling so he could capture the fun.

"TODAY, we're back at this beautiful home in the Irvington neighborhood of Indianapolis and we will be ripping out walls to make way for our open concept design. What do you think we will find in its 140-year-old walls?"

Marci Emerald delivered the lines flawlessly, but the director yelled, "Cut! A kid on a bike rode behind you while we were recording." Bruce Willow, a forty-year-old short man with fiery red hair, shouted, "How did that kid get past the cordon?"

Marci and Bruce watched as various members of the crew tried to corral Devon. He eluded their attempts while filming it all with his phone. Trina Parker, the film school intern dressed in black, had an idea. "You know, the kid makes it seem more organic. Like a real neighborhood. Maybe we shoot it again but have him riding without his phone held up and filming?"

Bruce whipped his head around, ready to put this lowly intern in her place. *How dare she suggest something to me,* he thought. *For heaven's sake, I've directed an episode of "Ellen."* Bruce had been dining on that one moment for the past fifteen years. In fact, he filled in on that episode due to the normal director being hospitalized with an emergency appendectomy. Bruce was fired afterwards as Ellen thought the final edit included too many shots looking up at her chin. Rumor has it that the comedian is notoriously self-conscious about her chin. Since then, Bruce had mostly done Geico commercials and the occasional Home Network pilot. None of the pilots had been picked up until Marci's home renovation show.

But Trina had heard the "I directed an Ellen" speech

enough times in the last few months to know how to manage Bruce. So, before he was able to spew expletives at her for suggesting something to him, she stoked his ego. "Adding the kid and other occasional neighbors might be your best idea yet. What sets you apart from directors of all the other home improvement shows."

Bruce stood a little straighter and exhaled slowly. "Yes, that could set me apart." He looked at the crew trying to catch the kid with no success. "Everyone, I've had a great idea." Trina turned her head and rolled her eyes. "We're going in a new direction." Devon had circled back towards the director in his attempts to elude the crew. "Kid, you want to be in this show for real?" he called out to him.

Devon hesitated. "Is this a trick?"

"No, it's not. I want you to ride behind her again while she's doing her lines. This time though, without using your phone to film it."

"Just me or can my friends ride with me?"

Bruce looked at Trina. Trina mouthed, “How many?”

“Three more,” he responded.

Trina nodded her head and said, "Yes we'll take them." She quickly added, "The more kids, the smarter your idea will look."

Bruce turned back to Devon, "Sure, your friends can be in it too."

THE BOYS PLAYED their parts in Marci's TV show and were allowed to share a heavily edited version of Devon's video on TikTok. Parents were called, releases were signed, and all the T's and I's were crossed and dotted. Except for one. In both the boys' video and the show's own social media, they made it a point to insist the boys were neighbors. What they forgot was that two of them were wearing Carmel Greyhounds T-shirts. However, the show is supposed to take place in Irvington, a neighborhood of Indianapolis. And the local high school is Irvington Prep. And if someone in that school district was wearing a Carmel T-shirt, they likely wouldn't survive the day. Social media users spotted that immediately. Suspicions grew. Conspiracy theories took off like wildfires. The show producers tried to explain it away as a deep fake hack. They released a second video with the boys in different T-shirts. Most people forgot by the time the next popular meme went viral. But not the members of the Lederhosen Mafia.

THE NEXT DAY, Marci Emerald scanned the parking lot for people who might recognize her. The coast was clear, so she quickly got out of her Lexus SUV and scurried for the door that led to the apartments above the

Cobblestone Shoppes shopping center. She was dressed head to toe in Sophislete activewear and she held her Jet City coffee cup so the logo was visible to the camera crew that was following her.

Cobblestone Shoppes was a mixed-use development with retail and restaurants at street level, and three stories of offices and apartments above. This type of building had become popular in Carmel, and they were popping up like mushrooms throughout the city. It was also Marci Emerald's new "home."

As part of her comeback from social media cancelation, her manager and publicist decided that she needed to look like less of a nepo baby. Part of that rebrand meant not living in her parents' mansion in the Village of West Clay and living "on her own" in an apartment in Carmel. Of course, she didn't *actually* live there, they just filmed all the at-home scenes for her new Home Network reality show at the apartment. For her, going to the apartment was going to work.

Her team had rented an office on the second floor and a one-bedroom apartment on the third floor. Through the magic of television, they made the audience think the office was a second bedroom in the apartment.

Marci took the stairs to the second floor, then the team stopped filming so she could walk the corridor to the office and preserve the illusion. She opened the second-floor door, and a miniature goat ran past her and down the stairs. Marci turned to the producer and said, "You see why I don't want to live here?"

She continued into the hall and the crew followed. There were twelve offices, six on each side of the hall. Marci's was second from the end on the right. It had a view of the street on the opposite side of the building from where she entered.

The office door next to hers had a sign that said JWEB. A man wearing a baseball cap emerged, saw the camera crew, and stepped back inside. The crew thought they smelled breakfast cooking. As he slammed the door behind him, Marci thought she heard him say, "They're onto us."

Once inside, the team resumed filming Marci. She made a phone call to a contractor who was being filmed by a second crew. He proceeded to share several "unexpected" complications that were going to cost more money. Marci argued for a workaround. He said he would see what he could do. It was all scripted, just like all the other home renovation shows. The complications added drama and drama added viewers and viewers sold advertising and advertising sold cheaply made goods at Target, the exclusive home to the Marci Emerald line of furnishings for Gen Z "It Girls" called *Marci's Home*. And this year, Target and Home Network were co-sponsoring a float in the Fourth of July parade that would feature Marci Emerald.

When she hung up and the cameras turned off, she

said, "What the hell do you think is going on next door?"

Going On Next Door...

Holden, a new recruit to the Lederhosen Mafia, was certain they had been spotted by Marci's team. "She's on to us, I know it."

Zoe answered, "Relax. She's not on to us. For all they know, JWEB still rents this space."

Dave asked, "What does JWEB mean again?"

Thaddeus used tongs to hold up a slice of bacon and explained, "Jews Who Eat Bacon."

"And why is Thaddeus making bacon?" asked Dave. "He's a vegetarian."

"Because it's bacon," Thaddeus replied. "And don't tell Lydia I've lapsed." Lydia was Thaddeus' life partner. Together they owned a goat yoga studio that was currently short on goats.

For the past week, the Lederhosen Mafia had been spying on Marci Emerald and her reality show crew from the office next door. Lydia had recognized Marci in the hall one day and tipped off the Mafia. She also told them that JWEB, the Jews Who Eat Bacon, were shutting down their secret club but still had two months on their lease. Zoe agreed to sublet for the two months on the condition that they left their JWEB sign on the door.

They left the sign and the bacon that Thaddeus was preparing.

Lederhosen Mafia had been bored for months. Their former leader, Bulb, had ridden off into the sunset after their last big prank: using a medieval trebuchet to fling art and feces onto a statue being unveiled to the public. Since then, they had lacked purpose and direction. They had almost disbanded. But as fate would have it, one of their members lived right across the street from the house where Marci was filming scenes for her fake rehab show. All of the neighbors had been paid $10,000 for the inconvenience and to not disclose the show's secret. But Dave lived with his parents and didn't sign the agreement.

Now their old nemesis, Marci Emerald, had given the Lederhosen Mafia their mojo back.

Zoe Rose, who had ascended to the leadership role in the group, despite being the youngest member, looked around the room. Eleven people had shown up and were crammed in the conference room of the small office suite. To open it up a bit, the members of JWEB had taken down a wall between a small breakroom/kitchenette and the conference room. Six vegetarian members of the Mafia were pinned against the far wall, horrified by Thaddeus and the bacon. The other five had empty plates and were salivating. Nobody was wearing lederhosen.

Zoe began, "Thank you all for coming." She pointed to the wall between their space and Marci's office. "Last year, we made fools of ourselves trying to take down Marci Emerald. This summer, we're going to have the last laugh."

Dave asked, "We're not going to kidnap her again, are we? We're lucky we're not in jail."

"No, we're not going to kidnap her, Dave. We're going to embarrass her publicly."

"Where?" asked Natasha.

"At the Fourth of July Parade, of course."

There was a buzz throughout the room. In part because of Zoe's words and partly because the bacon was ready and being distributed to the carnivores. Zoe fought the distraction of the delicious smell and her stomach growled. Apparently, her digestive system was unaware of her moral objection to eating meat.

"We have a source at Aztec Hillbilly Brewing that told us she's going to be on their Trendy Booze float," Zoe continued. "We're going to harass and heckle her, then cause a disruption."

"Are we going to build another trebuchet?" one of the members asked.

"No, we aren't," Zoe continued. "Have you ever been to a sporting event and seen those T-shirt cannons?"

A few people nodded their heads. She continued, "Well, I have an idea."

Holden interrupted, "Don't you think it's risky to be meeting right next door? Spying on her, sure. But having all of us together only a few feet away is crazy."

"Why are you so paranoid?" asked Thaddeus. "Have

a gummy." He tossed a bag of THC gummies towards Holden. Multiple hands grabbed for the bag, but Dave intercepted it first. He took one and passed it to his right.

"I don't need a gummy," Holden said. "I need to know why we are here."

Zoe explained. "Normally she's not here at this time of day, so yes, this was a risk. But we'll start doing these meetings at night because we know she doesn't stay here. Besides, being right next door is the best place to spy on her."

Everyone seemed satisfied with the explanation except Holden. "I don't know. This place is too out there for me. Besides the risk of getting caught, I saw a goat earlier in the hall."

~

Earlier in the ***Hall***

Lydia chased the runaway goat down the hall outside her fourth-floor apartment. She had arrived home with groceries and was opening the front door when the little guy pushed his nose through and off he went. She dropped a bag of vegetables and hummus, and a tomato rolled the opposite direction of the chase. Someone had propped open the door at the end of the hall that led to the stairwell, and the goat was already to the third floor when she looked down the steps. She chased it to the second floor, the nimble little creature widening his lead as he went.

The door was propped on the second floor, too, and the goat entered the hall and ran to the opposite end. Lydia looked inside just in time to see the door open, and the goat ran past the people entering from the far end. Rather than pursue him down the hall, she continued down the stairs, sprinted the distance to the other stairwell and met the goat at the door. She sat down, picked up the goat and caught her breath. She looked him in the eye and said, "Maybe the universe is trying to tell me to stop teaching goat yoga."

The goat bleated, but to Lydia it sounded like, "You think?"

She began a conversation with the goat. "But I can't back out now. We have a float in the Fourth of July parade that's already been built. It has goats on it."

The goat bleated.

"They're fake goats, of course." The goat looked at her skeptically. "I don't have the money to redo it and change the signage."

The goat bleated again.

"I know but we need the exposure. This could really turn things around for us."

The goat started chewing on her sleeve. Lydia didn't notice. She was staring into the future, four weeks to be exact. "The Fourth of July parade is going to change our lives."

EPISODE 19: PARADE PREPARATIONS

Stanley Davis requested that a police officer be present at the opening of the storage unit. Mostly because Mrs. Haliburton insisted on being there with her new lawyer, who was helping her challenge the will. They wanted to inventory the contents before a hearing could take place.

Due to Geraldine Melvin's flirtatious behavior at the reading of the will, Officer Lupinsky hoped he wouldn't be the one to draw the assignment. He did. So, on June 22, just twelve days before the parade, the unlikely group gathered at the 141st Street Super Storage and mostly shouted at each other.

Mrs. Haliburton spoke to her attorney but nodded at Geraldine Melvin. "I'm going to see to it that this whore gets none of my late husband's money."

"First of all, I ain't no whore," Geraldine replied.

"And I wasn't seeing your late husband. My late husband was. So maybe *they* were the whores?"

"Well, if you're not a whore, why are you wearing five-inch heels, a mini-skirt, and a see-through blouse at 10 a.m. on a Tuesday?"

Geraldine looked herself up and down and tried to pull her skirt down a little. "I'll have you know I'm wearing this to show respect to our men in law enforcement." She looked at Officer Lupinsky and smiled.

He coughed and turned away. Mrs. Haliburton rolled her eyes and conferred not-so-quietly with her attorney. Geraldine circled around Officer Lupinsky. "Don't be shy, honey, I can see you're blushing a little."

"I was just coughing because of the pollen. That time of year for me."

"Right, baby." She ran her index finger across his badge and winked. "Whatever you say."

Lupinsky tried to recover. "Shouldn't this thing be starting by now?"

Stanley called for everyone's attention. "I have the key and we're ready to begin. We have four guys from Mallory Movers here to bring everything out so we can inventory it, and then put it back in until the legal issues are resolved. Per the judge's ruling, I will hold onto the key, and nothing will be permanently removed until after the hearing. Are you all ready to begin?"

As much as Stanley hated Mrs. Haliburton, these were billable hours, and he wasn't stuck in his office or a courtroom. So, he had a spring in his step and a smile on his face. He felt like he was in an episode of the TV show *Storage Wars.*

As the participants followed Stanley to the storage unit, Geraldine tried to hold Officer Lupinsky's hand. He brushed her off. "You say 'no' now," she told him. "But there's going to be a lonely night soon when you're going to be thinking about me."

"I really can't get involved."

"Why? Is there a Mrs. Officer Lupinsky? I don't mind."

"Well, *she* might."

"So, there is a Mrs. Lupinsky."

"There is. Well, there was." He hesitated. "It's complicated."

Geraldine grabbed his arm and made him stop. "Honey, look at these legs." He tried to look away. "Look." He looked. "Now, keep looking all the way up." He looked all the way up, unavoidably pausing here and there. "There ain't nothin' complicated about this." She winked again.

Stanley opened the storage unit and stood back. Mrs. Haliburton started to barge right in, but he stopped her. "Please Catherine, let the movers bring the contents out item by item, and your attorney and I will keep separate running inventories."

Thus started a long process that took about two hours. Not that there was that much stuff, but they had to keep Mrs. Haliburton and Mrs. Melvin from hitting each other. When the movers were done, they counted forty sculptures of varying sizes that were crafted by the two men. The only thing that didn't survive the day was a mirror that hung above a work bench in the unit. Taped to it was a picture of the two men, wearing welding aprons and nothing else. Mrs. Haliburton hit the picture with an umbrella and shattered the mirror. Both attorneys agreed to leave the mirror and the picture off the inventory as neither Mrs. Haliburton nor Mrs. Melvin seemed to be interested in the remains.

Lupinsky considered keeping the damaged photo as evidence in the event Mrs. Haliburton murdered Mrs. Melvin—a growing possibility as the day wore on. But Mrs. Melvin grabbed his butt as he leaned over to pick it up. The surprised officer yelped and straightened up immediately, forgetting the photo. Lupinsky turned and faced the not-so-grieving widow. "Mrs. Melvin, I can't get involved with you while I'm here on official business."

"I understand." She saluted him and then gave a little wiggle. "So, when this is over, and you're off duty, maybe you can come over and unofficially give me the business."

Mrs. Haliburton shouted, "Whore!"

"Stay out of this." And once again the officer and the attorneys had to separate the two women. This time they weren't quick enough.

~

Mrs. Melvin was ushered into a conference room by the jail guard. Waiting for her were Stanley and her own court-appointed attorney. They had been discussing the assault charges she was facing because she had wrestled Mrs. Haliburton's umbrella from her and hit her over the head with it. The blow didn't cause any serious damage, but everyone in attendance at the storage unit inventory discovered that Mrs. Halliburton wore a wig. She had Geraldine arrested, but then decided it was better to drop the charges and have her attorney pay everyone to sign a non-disclosure agreement so her hair hat would remain a secret.

Stanley spoke for both attorneys, "Mrs. Melvin, I have great news."

"You do?"

"Yes, both of your cases have been settled. The judge sided with us and will allow the will to be executed without further interruption from Mrs. Haliburton."

Geraldine asked, "And the assault?"

"Mrs. Haliburton dropped the charges. You will just need to sign a paper agreeing to never mention that you've seen her without her hair."

She laughed. "Her head was sort of purple and squishy, wasn't it."

"I don't know," Stanley replied and straightened his tie. Lying always made him straighten his tie. "For the record, I have never seen it."

"But you were right there," Geraldine protested. "She practically fell in your lap."

"As I said," he replied, fixing the tie again. "For the record I have never seen Mrs. Haliburton's scalp, nor do I believe that she wears a wig."

"You're kidding me, right?"

"As your attorneys?" Stanley and her court lawyer said in unison. Each turned to the other and waited to continue.

"Okay, as my attorney? Attorneys?" she looked back and forth at them.

Stanley continued, "You're getting out of jail without anything on your record, and she's not going to fight you on the will anymore. For a get out of jail free card and a million dollars of her late husband's money, I would pretend I never saw the purple squishy thing for the rest of my life."

It only took a split second for her to consider. "The old lady has a full head of gray hair," Geraldine replied. "Pretty as a sunset and all natural."

"That's better," said the court attorney, suddenly feeling he needed to say something to justify his presence in the room. "You'll be processed and out of here in an hour or so. Maybe sooner."

"So, I'm gonna get my money?" she asked.

"Yes, you are," Stanley replied. "And the sculptures can ride on the float."

"Do I have to keep those after the parade? I noticed they was mostly goats and unicorns."

"You can do whatever you want with them."

"I was thinking of donating them to some charity or something," she said.

"That's well within your rights," Stanley said.

"Well, I don't want to look at 'em myself. Especially knowing how they was made. Can you believe that? Two grown men welding naked?"

"It certainly is unusual."

"And to think you know a person, sharing a trailer and whatnot with them. Oh, well, I guess you never know."

"I suppose not," said Stanley. "Any other questions before I go?"

"Oh, one last thing," said Geraldine. "Any chance you can give me that Officer Lupinsky's personal cell number? He's kinda cute."

"You'll have to ask him."

"I did," she said. "He's playin' hard to get."

ON THE MORNING of June 20, twenty-two alarm clocks went off at precisely 4 a.m. at the Serenity Senior Living Center in Carmel. William Ketring forgot why he had set his alarm and commenced to beating it with his cane until it was in pieces. He could still hear ringing (from the other alarms on his floor) and vowed to get his hearing aid batteries replaced.

The other twenty-one residents who had set their

alarm clocks began to assemble in the hallway in various states of dress. The Russell sisters, Gracie and Sylvia, wore winter coats. Eighty-four-year-old Abner Jacobs entered the hallway naked, but he did have a plastic grocery bag tied to his walker. Inside the bag were rolls of duct tape and police caution tape. Gracie Russell blushed ever so slightly, but Sylvia was unfazed. She had seen Abner naked before.

Gracie called out, "Are you all ready?"

"Is it time for breakfast?" one of the seniors asked.

"No, it's not time for breakfast. We're going to reserve our spots, remember?"

"Oh, yeah," someone shouted.

"So, let's stop talking and get to reserving," shouted Abner.

Gracie asked, "Are you going out like that?"

"There's no time to waste. Besides, I'm not ashamed of my equipment." He lifted one leg and posed. "Most of you have seen it anyway."

Gracie couldn't bring herself to look at his eighty-three-year-old equipment, so she looked away and announced, "All right everyone, let's go."

Nearly everyone followed Gracie. Bobbie Newman forgot what they were doing and turned right when the rest of the group turned left. They made for the lobby. She headed towards the cafeteria. The five seniors behind her followed her lead all the way. In the dark cafeteria, they settled into their usual chairs and waited for someone to set the tables. It would be two hours before they were discovered.

Meanwhile, nobody seemed to notice the attrition in the ranks as the remaining seniors made their way out into the parking lot, walked south for a block and a half and onto Carmel Drive. Here they took the caution tape that Abner had provided and began to wrap it around two trees, one near the street and one near the edge of the sidewalk. From there, they stretched the tape twenty feet to another tree and a yellow gas line pole. Thus, they made a rectangle between the sidewalk and street in yellow caution tape, held up by duct tape.

And with this singular act of conquest, a section of prime parade route became theirs. Myra Franks, the strongest and most mobile of the group, began barking out instructions. "Unfold these chairs I brought." Members of the group lined up in front of Myra's wagon and she handed each a chair.

"Abner, your bare ass better not touch one of my chairs. I expect you to be fully dressed when the parade takes place."

"I know, I know. Carmel Police already told me I couldn't come to the parade naked last year. Or maybe that was a few years ago. Anyway, I'll throw on a Speedo or something."

Myra replied, "Sweet fancy Moses, nobody wants to see that either. Don't you have any pants?"

"None that I care to wear. Make you a deal. I'll wear my robe."

"No deal. It's likely to be 85 degrees out on the Fourth of July. You'll be out of that robe before the Carmel High School marching band has played a note."

He thought about arguing further but decided against it. Myra was the only woman in the senior home he couldn't shock, intimidate, or outwit. She had worked her entire adult life in a warehouse, beginning on the loading dock, moving up to foreman and finishing as shipping manager. Myra was tougher than most of the men at the company. She had to be, as usually she was the only woman at the warehouse (save for a revolving door of receptionists the company hired).

"All right, fine. I'll wear pants. But I won't wear underwear." He walked away with his chair and placed it on the grass between the road and the sidewalk. To test Myra, he started to sit.

"Abner, don't even think about it." Myra had eyes in the back of her head.

With all the chairs emptied from Myra's wagon, their mission was complete. Some of them hugged each other, the emotion of the moment getting to them. Nobody hugged Abner, although Sylvia may have gotten precariously close to his equipment during the scramble for the chairs.

Of the sixteen seniors who made it out to the parade route, all but one made it back to the Serenity Senior Living Center straight away. Abner decided it was a fine day and wondered how long he could wonder around town naked until a cop or good Samaritan guided him back to the senior home.

THAT SAME EVENING, Jeanie Norwood crept silently into the bedroom of her closest friend, Sarah Jones. Sarah's husband was out of town and Jeanie knew how to disable the alarm from countless times taking care of the cat when the Jones family vacationed in the Dominican Republic. It made Jeanie feel superior knowing that Sarah was still planning to go to the DR next spring. The Norwoods would be vacationing in Saint Croix this year, thank you very much, assuming her husband's year-end bonus was in the same ballpark as last year, Of course, Sarah might not be taking a vacation at all, given what Jeanie planned to do next.

The high school social studies teacher stood over a sleeping Sarah and wondered who her euchre partner would be next week when the Motivated Moms of Carmel School Kids got together at Monon Coffee. Maybe Hillary Weems. Hillary's older daughter was a middle school cheerleader and that could open doors when the time came for her own daughter to move from elementary school next year.

Yes, Hillary it is, she thought. *I'll float the idea on Facebook tonight. Or maybe after Sarah is arrested. Mustn't seem too eager. That might call attention to me. Well, let's get on with it.* She placed a pillow over Sarah's head, not to smother her but to keep Sarah from identifying her if the needle woke her up. With a swift maneuver, she stuck the needle in Sarah's arm and held the pillow while she thrashed momentarily. The sedative worked quickly. And soon, Sarah was dead to the world.

Dead is what she deserved, Jeanie thought, *but this was much more delicious.* She was tired of keeping up with the Sarahs in this town. She was ready to become the Alpha Female in her circle. With a second needle, Jeanie loaded Sarah's arm with enough heroin to fail the drug test that all the employees of The Greyhound Clinic were going to have to take tomorrow morning.

The failed drug test and the heroin Jeanie had left in Sarah's office that afternoon would be enough to get her fired, arrested, and safely out of the Motivated Moms of Carmel School Kids. Jeanie was certain that such shame would keep Sarah from showing her face at the July Fourth parade. But just to be sure, Jeanie had taken Sarah's chairs and replaced them with her own. This was, after all, the Carmel, Indiana, Fourth of July parade.

Sarah slept soundly while Jeanie continued to justify why she was here. *She deserves to die*, she reasoned. *She took my spot. My spot! Sarah Jones knows my family has always staked out the twelve feet of prime real estate in front of Fraction Bank for the parade. Six years we've had that spot,* she raged. *And that was after working our way up from four horrible years in front of Taco Bell.*

Jeanie still hadn't forgiven her husband for the chalupa incident. *What kind of jackass gives a toddler half a chalupa?*

Her husband had missed the Indiana Pacers float featuring the Pacemates (the only float he had really wanted to see) as he was changing a chalupa-filled diaper (it came out as it came in) in the Taco Bell bathroom. This incident became a source of tension in the Norwood marriage that routinely bubbled to the surface over the years.

And yet with all this history —all of which Sarah was privy to—she had callously set her family's camping chairs in the very spot Jeanie and her family had claimed for the past six years. It was a prime spot. To the left was Councilwoman Cecilia Davis's family, and to the right was the granddaughter of Town and Country Real Estate mogul, Vincent Van Dorn.

Jeanie would not relinquish this spot for some upstart wife of a probate attorney who had her eyes on an invitation to the Van Dorn family Labor Day Gala. Jeanie always got her invite at the Fourth of July parade. Hand delivered, in a linen envelope. Sarah would not be intercepting Jeanie's linen envelope. Her friend was always jealous of Jeanie's invite. And since Sarah was younger, prettier, and had a more handsome husband (though less accomplished), Jeanie always feared she might be replaced by Sarah in the social pecking order.

Convinced that she had successfully sabotaged Sarah's status, Jeanie slipped out of the bedroom and downstairs. She had to cross through the kitchen to get to the garage and let herself out. A full moon illuminated the kitchen through a giant bay window in Sarah's breakfast nook. Jeanie caught sight of a linen envelope. It was opened so she slid out the card and turned on her phone to read the message. Sarah already had her invite to the Van Dorn Labor Day Gala.

Jeanie cursed, then fueled by rage, tore the invitation like tissue. Realizing she had created evidence she had been there; she picked up the pieces and stuffed them in her pocket. Of course, she forgot to take the pack of needles she had set down to read the note. And a piece or two of the invitation were missed on the kitchen floor. She opened the door that led to the garage, reset the alarm, and left. Jeanie's rage had made her careless. Her foolproof plan was already starting to unravel. Even worse, Sarah was going into convulsions upstairs.

"HEY, have you guys ever seen the movie *Animal House*?" asked Tony.

The Lakewood boys were camped out at Matt's house. School was out for the summer; it was raining for the third straight day, and they were getting bored.

Matt kicked Devon's foot off the coffee table. Not because his foot was on the furniture. The basement furniture was trashed from the boys' numerous sleep-overs. This was out of boredom. "No, what's it about?"

Tony replied, "College."

Willy asked, "College? Why would you want to watch that?"

"Because there's girls and drinking," said Tony.

"Matt's sister goes to parties all the time here," Willy replied. "You don't have to wait until college for that."

"Yeah, but this movie is about how they used to do it in the old days. It's pretty funny."

Willy said, "Doesn't sound funny."

"Trust me, it is. But the reason I thought of it is they had this homecoming parade, and the frat guys trashed it."

Matt asked, "So?"

"So, I was thinking it would be funny if we came up with a way to prank the Carmel Fourth of July parade."

Devon, who had not said a word in over an hour, sat up straight. "What do you have in mind?"

"Well, in the movie they worked all night to turn a car into a tank, basically. Then they hid it under a cake."

"They hid a tank in a cake? That must have been some huge cake," said Matt.

"Not a real cake. A parade float that looked like a cake. Then when the moment was right, the tank car came out of the cake and caused all sorts of mayhem."

Devon asked, "And you think we can pull that off? None of us can drive."

"I know, but I thought we could come up with something."

Devon wasn't giving up. "Can anybody enter the parade?"

"I think so," said Willy.

"Somebody check the rules," Devon ordered. "Do you have any ideas?"

Tony replied, "We could do a golf cart in a cake."

Devon wasn't impressed. "A golf cart? How much mayhem can you commit in a golf cart?"

"Hey, I'm just throwing out ideas."

Willy asked, "Why do you guys want to commit mayhem anyway?"

Tony and Devon replied, "Cause we're bored."

“And it’s fun to say mayhem,“ Devon added.

Everyone seemed to see the logic in that and went back to scheming.

Then Devon looked at Matt, "Hey, you haven't said much, and I just remembered your dad had a float in the parade last year."

Matt became uneasy. "No, guys, you can't hijack my dad's float."

Tony ignored the protest. "What's the theme this year?"

"They're honoring the anniversary of one of the Carmel public parks. It's supposed to look like a life-guard watching over swimmers in the pool. He wants my sister to be the lifeguard, but she said she doesn't want to be on display in her swimsuit. My mom offered to do it, but he said she was too old. He's been sleeping in the living room for the past week."

"Wait a minute!" Devon stood up, knocking over a stack of Mountain Dew cans. "I've got it. The greatest idea ever! Tell your dad you found the lifeguard."

"What are you talking about?"

"Mandy. Mandy Pepperhorns."

Willy's eyes got as big as saucers. "Mandy Pepperhorns?"

"That's right," said Devon. "We convince Mandy to be the lifeguard, do a little show on the parade route and we will be legends!"

"The parade committee would never approve that," said Matt.

"What do you mean? They already have approved a lifeguard," said Devon. "They just don't know she's going to perform. Am I right?"

Matt said, "Technically he's right. The float is already approved. But my dad will never go for it."

"Dude! All you have to do is show him a picture and he'll go for it. We just won't tell him she's going to perform."

Willy asked, "And how are we going to get her to do it?"

"We pay her!" said Devon. "Just find out how much she gets paid to do her show at the Neon Boudoir and offer her the same money to do it live on the parade route."

"Seriously? I bet it's a lot of money." said Willy.

"Between the four of us, we could come up with it," said Devon. "But, I have an even better idea for how to get most of the money."

Willy thought about the last time he saw Mandy Pepperhorns and smiled. "This could work."

"No, it couldn't," said Matt. "You guys are crazy."

"But just think if it did," said Tony.

The boys sat in silence for five minutes, thinking about Mandy Pepperhorns dancing from atop a lifeguard chair in the streets in Carmel.

"I'm in," said Willy.

"Me too," said Devon.

Tony answered, "Yeah, let's do this."

"My dad will never go for this," Matt protested.

Devon asked, "Do you still have a picture of Mandy as your screensaver?"

"Yeah," Matt replied.

"Give me your phone," said Devon

"No," he held it away, but Tony grabbed it and tossed it to Devon.

"What's your code?"

"I'm not telling you my ..." Devon, the largest of the boys, put him in a headlock. "Okay, okay! 3435." He let go and Matt rubbed the back of his neck and glared at Tony starting the whole thing.

Devon texted Matt's dad a picture of Mandy in her one-piece red swimsuit. Along with the picture he wrote, *She's a friend of Devon's and she's willing to be the lifeguard for the Fourth of July parade. 200 bucks?"*

He clicked send, tossed Matt his phone back, and they all waited. He was guessing on the amount but figured they could pool their money and make up the difference if needed. Less than twenty seconds later, they got a reply from Matt's dad. *Tell her I'll pay her $300 if she puts on an extra big smile and waves to the tent in front of the wine store.*

Matt texted his dad back since Devon had returned his phone. *Why there?*

His dad replied, *The Motivated Moms of Carmel School Kids love the Parks Department.* Clearly things were still frosty in the Moller house, but Matt didn't get the sarcasm.

"MANDY, YOU'VE GOT A PHONE CALL."

"Who is it, Lou?" Mandy asked the manager of the Neon Boudoir, the club where she worked. Lou held the door to the dressing room open but averted his eyes. He always did this, even though these same women were about to go out and perform in various stages of undress for the paying customers.

"Didn't say. Just said he wanted to hire you for an appearance. Line two."

She picked up the phone, "This is Mandy."

A voice of a young boy asked, "How much do you charge for an hour?"

"Hey, look kid, I ain't a prostitute. I'm hanging up."

"Wait, wait, I didn't mean it like that. I, I mean, we want to hire you to be in a parade?"

"A parade?"

"Yeah, a Fourth of July parade. The float is for the Parks Department, and it will look like a pool with a lifeguard stand. We want you to be the lifeguard."

"And you want me to do my act? Unless this parade is taking place in San Francisco or New Orleans, I can't do my act in public. I'll get arrested."

"Not your full act. Just dance some and smile and wave. It's an hour or so of your time and we'll pay you $300."

"I usually get much more than that for in-person work."

"But this will be easy, and you won't have to take off your clothes." He paused and she could have sworn she heard giggles in the background. "Unless you want to, but that's entirely up to you." More giggling.

"You sound like a kid. You aren't playing me, are you? You don't sound old enough to have seen my act."

"I haven't seen it. But you come highly recommended. I'm an intern. I may sound young but I'm in college." The rest of the boys rolled on the couch and snorted with laughter.

Mandy replied, "I don't know. Recommended by who?"

"Alex Thompson," said Devon. Tony blushed. He

didn't think the rest of the guys knew his dad was dating Mandy.

"Hmm, he didn't mention a parade to me."

"Please? It would be the best float in the entire Carmel parade with you up there."

"Did you say Carmel?"

"Yes."

"You are asking me to dance on a parade float on the Fourth of July in Carmel, Indiana?"

"Yes."

Matt whispered to Tony, "We're going to be a legends."

Mandy put her hand over the phone and whispered to her fellow dancers, "I'm going to be a legend." Then she said to Devon, "I'll do it."

Devon grinned and turned to the other boys. "She'll do it."

EPISODE 20: THE PARADE

When the residents of the Serenity Senior Living Center returned to their reserved spot on the morning of the Fourth, they found squatters. The seniors' caution tape had been cut down and a tent was set up where many of their chairs had been. To their credit, the squatters had stacked those chairs neatly against a tree. Next to the tent were four bikes.

William Ketring and the rest of the seniors stepped back while Sylvia and Gracie Russell began to beat on the side of the tent with their canes. Groans and shouts followed and even a few curse words.

"Get out of that tent, you foulmouthed hooligans," said Sylvia.

"I didn't storm Omaha Beach to have my parade spot stolen by a bunch of hippies," yelled William.

Abner Jacobs, who had been missing from the

senior home for hours, staggered forward. “You weren’t at Omaha Beach,” he reminded William.

“I wasn’t?”

“No, you weren't part of D-Day in World War II, you were a payroll clerk at Fort Harrison during Vietnam. You never left the country during the war. Hell, you never left Indiana.”

“Well, at least I wore a uniform. You’re not even wearing pants.”

This was true. Abner was naked, save for a large American flag draped over his shoulders. Both men turned back to the tent to see the Lakewood boys emerging. “What are you kids doing camping here? Do your parents know? What makes you think you can steal our spot?"

The questions were coming fast and furious from the seniors and the boys couldn’t keep up. Finally, Gracie whistled, and everyone was silent.

“Now. Tell us why you’re here,” Gracie demanded.

Devon said, “We camped out all night so we could have a front row view of the boob...”

Tony cut him off, “Of the bougie floats.”

“Bougie?” asked Sylvia.

William turned up his hearing aid. “Bougie? Is this a pride parade? I thought it was Fourth of July.”

“Bougie doesn’t mean gay,” said Abner, who stepped between Gracie and Sylvia, giving the boys a full view of his nakedness. “It means rich or pretentious.”

"How do you know what bougie means?" asked Sylvia.

He posed for effect, "I get around."

The boys giggled at the naked man.

William said, "Whatever it means, you boys have to go. This is our spot."

Matt pleaded, "Can't we squeeze in here and watch with you? We won't take up much space."

"And we'll run and get you drinks and stuff," Devon added. "The parade doesn't start for hours."

The seniors contemplated this offer and decided having a few willing and able-bodied boys to bring them water and other necessities wasn't such a bad idea. The ladies were somewhat suspicious of their motivation, but the men were all too happy to be waited on. And the Lakewood boys didn't mind having something to do while they waited for Mandy's show.

They had camped in this spot the night before because it was strategically across from the place where Matt's mom would be watching the parade. They knew that this was where Matt's dad had instructed Mandy to give an extra wave. It was also where all the parade floats would stop and perform because ...

... ACROSS THE STREET from the seniors, city workers were placing bunting around a set of reserved bleachers where various dignitaries were to sit for the parade. Normally, this would be set up closer to city hall along the parade route, but a sidewalk replacement was underway, and the location was moved at the last minute. It seems the sidewalk work had been vandalized in the days leading up to the parade. Video caught four kids on bikes, but not their faces. The new location was a prime spot, as special floats, marching bands, and other performers would pause there. Next to the VIP bleachers was the wine store parking lot and of course the Motivated Moms of Carmel School Kids. As the city workers finished the bunting, three men in black trench coats, dark sunglasses, and green Tyrolean hats approached.

TRUE TO THE attorney Stanley Davis's word, the float with the late Messrs Haliburton's and Melvin's sculptures was tasteful. It had a banner with the name of the two artists across the top and matching banners down the side that said "In memory of" with a picture of the two artists from the chest up. It was the same as the photo that Mrs. Haliburton destroyed on the day of the storage unit inventory.

Despite the lurid nature in which they were created, none of the sculptures were erotic or distasteful in any way. There were metal sculptures of a pig, a llama, and an alpaca. The alpaca gave Teddy pause, but Stanley said it must be included. Oddly enough, there was a collection of small goats, twelve in all, that were elevated above the rest of the sculptures. It seemed they were watching over the rest of the animals, and in some strange way the attendees themselves. Odder still was one sculpture that looked like Marci Emerald's unique dog, Taco Belle.

Stanley the attorney asked Mrs. Melvin if she would like to ride on the float, but she said she wanted to watch with "all the other rich people, seein' now that I'm rich." She left her boys at home with their grandma. They weren't disappointed as they had a full day planned of fireworks and throwing sweet potatoes at other kids in the trailer park.

Mrs. Melvin managed to find a spot on the parade route where nobody ever had dared put a chair. Between the Motivated Moms of Carmel School Kids' staked-out spot and the employees of Carmel Wine Factory, there was exactly 17 inches of grass right on the curb. It had been an unwritten rule that nobody put a chair between those two groups. But Geraldine saw the spot and put her chair down. Her outfit—a red bikini top and white cutoff jean shorts, with a blue belt—got completely opposite reactions from the two sides.

The ladies of the Motivated Moms of Carmel School Kids told her she couldn't put her seat there. The men of the Carmel Wine Factory told her she was welcome and asked if she wanted something to drink.

The female employees of Carmel Wine rolled their eyes but said nothing as they were used to this sort of behavior from their male colleagues. When the Motivated Moms protested louder, the Carmel Wine men reminded them that the ladies in their group were drinking free all day. They begrudgingly allowed the newcomer to stay. But Geraldine was now a millionaire, and she felt she belonged on the parade route as much as anybody. So, she tuned out the Carmel Moms and flirted with the Carmel Wine men.

Down the street, the parade was about to begin. The boys were just back from their final errand for the seniors, and they settled in for the show. They also had charged all their phones in the senior home's lobby so they could get plenty of pictures and video. Behind them stood more men in black trench coats, dark sunglasses, and Tyrolean hats. They made the boys uneasy at first, but thoughts of Mandy made them forget this odd group of parade attendees.

Willy asked, "Do you think we'll get full nudity?"

"Of course not, you idiot. This is a parade. She'll just dance all sexy and keep her clothes on," Tony answered. "She's not going to risk getting arrested."

Matt was starting to have doubts. "My mom is going to kill my dad for this. Then he's going to kill me."

"Legends, you guys. We're going to be legends," said Devon. "Don't lose focus. Carnage is small price to pay for becoming legends."

Suddenly they heard the sounds of clapping and cheering. Band music filled the air. A drum major led the high school band. And behind that, floats stretched as far as they could see.

THE BOYS GOT EXCITED when they saw the Trendy Booze float coming with Marci Emerald aboard. They knew that behind her would be the mayor, and behind him would be the Parks Department float featuring Mandy Pepperhorns.

The Trendy Booze float was built to look like the Welcome to Carmel sign in the Midtown district of Carmel. Marci was supposed to alternate between taking selfies and waving to the crowd. Surrounding her was an army of pretend influencers taking selfies and handing out samples to anyone who could pass for drinking age.

Unfortunately, Marci Emerald wasn't prepared for the heckling she got at the instigation of the Lederhosen Mafia. All along the parade route they had members planted holding up signs accusing her of hosting a fake home renovation show. She started to drink her root water nervously and ran out only a block and a half into the parade. Then she turned to the cooler full of actual Trendy Booze, trying desperately to wave and smile while drinking the lukewarm cherry colored bull piss. By the time she got to the VIP platform and bleachers, where she was scheduled to make a statement, she was drunk and nauseous. It was time for her to do her little shout-out to Trendy Booze and her HGTV show. But alas, the Indiana heat was too much.

"I would like to thank my sponsor, Trendy Booze, for their amazing support of Carmel and this year's Fourth of July parade." So far, so good. She delivered her line flawlessly. Then, just like they rehearsed, she held up the can and said, "To Carmel and Trendy Booze! Have a happy and safe Independence Day. Cheers!" And then she drank another hit of Trendy Booze. It was all her system could take, and she launched cherry-colored vomit all over the faux influencers pretending to take selfies at street level.

Marci's dog, Taco Belle, decided this was all too much and leapt from the float. Hours later she was found on the Haliburton float next to the golden-chihuahua-doodle sculpture.

Screams ensued. In the opposite direction, a goat ran down the parade route. William Ketring nudged fellow senior citizen Abner Jacobs, giggled, and said, "Would you look at that!"

That nudge launched the 84-year-old Serenity Nursing Home resident out onto the street, still without pants. The police couldn't stop Jacobs because they were about to make an arrest across the street ...

... WHERE GERALDINE MELVIN lit up when Officer Lupinsky arrived. When he pulled out his handcuffs she nearly swooned and said, "Now that's what I'm talking about."

"I'm not here for you," he replied.

She looked at the Motivated Moms and said, "Don't tell me you got your eyes on one of these bitches?"

"Who are you calling a bitch?" asked Jeanie Norwood.

Officer Lupinski asked, "Are you Jeanie Norwood?"

"Yes, I am," replied the teacher.

"I'm afraid you're under arrest for the murder of Sarah Jones."

"What?" She looked around at the rest of the Motivated Moms of Carmel School Kids. "Murder? Did one of you put an exotic dancer in a cop costume up to this prank?"

The ladies looked to the officer for explanation. "We have evidence that you drugged her in order to get her spot at the parade."

"Get her spot? She tried to take *my* spot." Jeanie turned and tried to explain to the group. "The nerve of that woman. Putting her chairs in my spot. Some things you just don't do in polite society."

"Polite society?" asked Lupinsky. "Do you hear yourself? It's just a parade spot. The Carmel Fourth of July parade is not worth killing over." More than a few people coughed and avoided the eyes of the officer. The Motivated Moms turned away, shunning Jeanie as Officer Lupinsky cuffed her. "But the parade isn't over," Jeanie pleaded. "And I was only trying to make her a little bit sick."

As Officer Lupinski started to leave with his prisoner, Geraldine asked, "Who do I have to kill to get cuffed by you, officer?" She nodded towards the Motivated Moms and said, "I'm happy to take out any one of them."

They both looked down as a small goat ran between them. He continued, "Don't even joke about that," he replied.

"Ah, come on," she said. "You look like you could use a few laughs."

He shook his head and surrendered a little grin as he walked away. "You could arrest me at your place," she offered.

He stopped and turned around. "Why my place?" he was curious.

"It's probably safer at yours," she replied. "Mama made sweet potatoes agin'."

Officer Lupinsky laughed and winked at Geraldine Melvin. As he left, while considering Geraldine's offer, he spotted three people dressed in black trench coats, dark sunglasses, and Tyrolean hats. *Man, this town is weird*, he thought.

Mayor Teddy's float arrived at the VIP bleacher location. He could see the commotion coming from whatever was happening on the float in front of him. People were screaming. An influencer vomited in the distance. To his left a woman was being arrested. Three goats ran in the opposite direction from which his float was headed. His big moment was coming off the rails.

"No, this can't be happening," he muttered. Then he shouted, "Someone find out what's going on." One of his aides ran up ahead to assess the situation. The float in front wasn't moving. As Teddy craned his neck to see what was happening, a naked 84-year-old man jogged by and waved. Teddy waved back, but not with his usual politician's smile. This was more of an incredulous look and an understanding that the parade of recognition he so desperately wanted was going to be remembered for chaos in the streets. There would be no moment of adulation for him. The crowd was moving away from the street. People were covering their eyes.

While the police were distracted, the Lederhosen Mafia struck. They threw off their trench coats to reveal their lederhosen and commenced with the chaos. With the T-shirt gun, they fired cans of Trendy Booze at the model of the city on Teddy's float. Their barrage obliterated future Carmel first, then past Carmel. Other members, armed with super soakers filled with New Cherry flavored Trendy Booze, sprayed the mayor and the model of current Carmel. The scene looked as if the mayor had been shot and bled all over the miniature city. As if on cue, a large sign on the float lit up with sparklers around each letter. It was the slogan his aides begged him not to use, but he wouldn't budge. It read, "Teddy Wiggins: He gave his blood for this city." At this precise moment, a freelance photographer took the picture that would later appear in full color on the front page of the *Indianapolis Star*.

BUT THE FUN wasn't over. The Parks Department float came to a stop in front of the wine store. Mandy gave Matt's mom a wave just as she took a sip of chardonnay. She spit the drink all over Mrs. Haliburton, who still hadn't quite recovered from the vomiting influencers. In her frenzied panic to wipe herself off, Mrs. Haliburton's wig came off again.

The Motivated Moms were still processing the arrest of one of their own, and now they were watching a woman dancing on a lifeguard stand in a red one-piece swimsuit. Mandy saved her best performance for this group, an abbreviated version of her act. With no pole to use after her dismount from the lifeguard stand, she had to improvise. And with all the kids present, she kept it mostly PG. Mostly. At the end she gave mouth to mouth to a fellow stripper who she had convinced to come with her and be her "drowning victim." Vice Principal Margot Felton-Douglass nearly fainted. Councilman George Fillmore grabbed harder and harder on his wife's leg until it turned purple.

Seeing her husband getting turned on by the performance was too much, so Mrs. Fillmore dumped a bucket of popcorn on his head. The incoming mayoral candidates would spend much of the next day fielding questions, assuring donors that their prospective administrations would not condone such behavior and blaming Teddy for the debacle.

Abner, still naked and now evading some newly arrived officers, eventually doubled back to Mandy's float and his nudity gave her the gumption to flash one breast quickly before the floats started moving again. She also caught a glimpse of the boys as she danced around and paused briefly, knowing instantly they had been behind it. She tilted her sunglasses down just for a moment and gave them a wink. Then the float started moving again.

Across the street in the bleachers, the deputy mayor turned to his assistant and said, "Fire the Park Department's chief tomorrow."

But Matt's dad had dirt on the deputy mayor, so they both agreed later to fire Sid in accounting.

When Mandy finished and her float moved on, the Lakewood boys walked silently toward a patch of grass and each lay down, staring at the sky. As far as they were concerned, the parade was over. And it was the best one they had ever seen. They agreed to never watch another one, as none could beat a vomiting influencer, a bloody mayor, and what Mandy would later claim was a wardrobe malfunction.

Behind Mandy and the Park Department's spectacle was Lydia's goat yoga float. After all the chaos, spectators were treated to one last amazing scene. One by one, all the goats that had disappeared from Lydia's studio months ago, came down the street and leapt onto her float. Lydia knocked down the cardboard goats she had put on the float to make room for the returning real ones. Fans cheered and Lydia cried with joy while the real goats chewed on the cardboard ones. After the parade, she was booked solid for a year.

On Monday morning, Sid Pearce, a 63-year-old accountant from Sheridan, Indiana, drove into work at the Carmel accounting office. He had worked there for thirty years and had seen many things, some good, some bad. Some legal, some not. He occasionally discovered irregularities but could always be convinced they were "perfectly normal and legal. Especially legal."

Sid was the perfect patsy. Old, near retirement. Never asked questions. At least no follow-up questions.

On his way to work, Sid did what he always did on Monday. Stopped at the gas station on Rangeline Road and bought a lottery ticket. He paid for his gas, a Peanut Butter Snickers and the Powerball quick pick and finished his trek to work. Once he got settled in at his desk, he listened to his voicemail. Three different people told him to be in the conference room at 9:00.

At 8:53, he made his way to the mysterious meeting, topping off his coffee and stopping to check his tie for debris from his breakfast and his nose for debris of another kind. When he got into the room, there were three department heads and the mayor. They seemed to be arguing.

"What's all the shouting about?" asked Sid.

The city HR director interrupted, "Maybe this argument shouldn't be happening in front of," and she nodded towards Sid.

"Right, right," said Teddy. "Why not take Sid to your office? We'll stay here and settle this."

Sid followed the HR director into her office.

She began, "I'm sorry, we're letting you go."

"What? Why?"

"Because a stripper showed her breasts at the Fourth of July parade."

"But I wasn't even there."

"But you allowed it to happen."

"I'm an accountant, I don't have anything to do with the parade."

"You were part of the steering committee and approved the float."

"I've never been part of any committee."

She replied, "That's not what it says in your resignation letter."

"What resignation letter? I haven't resigned."

"The one you wrote after we fired you." She handed him a typed letter. "Please sign here."

He skimmed the letter. "It says here I was acting alone and knew it would happen. I don't know anything about this. Besides, why would I write a resignation letter after you fired me?"

"You know, when the mayor came to me with this idea, I said the same thing. But he said it would look better if you tried to explain yourself via a letter."

"So, this is the mayor's idea, that I take the blame for something that I had nothing to do with."

"Not just his idea. He and the rest of the department heads in the conference room decided they're not going down for this. But you're almost at retirement age. And we're offering a generous severance package."

"But I didn't do anything. Why are they blaming this on me?"

She sighed and said, "Because you're expendable."

"Expendable? And what if I sue the city for age discrimination?"

She put her hand on his, "Sid, do you really want to do that? I'm sure there's a misuse of funds somewhere they can throw at you. You can roll the dice and see if you spend the next ten years in prison. Or you can take early retirement and a generous severance package."

He yanked his hand back. "Early retirement? You people are ruthless as hell! I'm suing."

"Don't sue, Sid."

"I'm suing ..." Sid didn't finish that thought. Instead, he fell to the floor as he went into cardiac arrest.

***

He woke up on Wednesday, his wife and son at his side.

"Dad, do you remember what happened?" asked Sid's son Adam.

"Yes, they blamed some stripper on me and were going to fire me."

"Yeah, dad. They fired you and you had a heart attack."

"I didn't do it. We're going to fight it."

A nurse intervened. "No stress right now. He's got to remain calm."

His wife changed the subject. "Honey, you had a lottery ticket in your pocket. Big jackpot," she waved it at him. "Let's see if we won a buck or two. Adam, call up the number on your doohickey."

Adam Googled the lottery numbers for the Monday drawing. He read them out slowly and Mrs. Pearce nearly had a heart attack herself. The ticket dropped to the floor and Adam picked it up. He checked the numbers, and they had won the $100 million jackpot. They all screamed, and the nurse had to settle them down again.

Adam asked, "Dad, what are you going to do with all that money?"

"We're going to move to Carmel," he said. "And I'm running for mayor."

NEVER MISS A BLOG POST

Sign up for my newsletter and get *72 Hours in Savannah* for FREE.

START READING

ALSO BY JEFF STANGER

Quick Mystery Novels

The Fungo Society

Tangled In The Web

Quick Mystery Short Stories

72 Hours in Savannah

Sexy Shoes

Keep Your Eye On The Money

Other Novels

Trolley Dodgers

Kansaska

Best of the Blog Series

Common Side Effects

I Bought a Chore

The Cottage Cheese Incident

Tales From the Vaccination Line

www.ingramcontent.com/pod-product-compliance
Lightning Source LLC
Chambersburg PA
CBHW051539030726
47592CB00001B/52

* 9 7 8 1 9 3 9 5 7 9 0 3 4 *